SNAPSHOT

GEORGE WALLACE

DON KEITH

SEVERN RIVER PUBLISHING

ALSO BY THE AUTHORS

The Hunter Killer Series

Final Bearing

Dangerous Grounds

Cuban Deep

Fast Attack

Arabian Storm

Warshot

Silent Running

Snapshot

Southern Cross

Also by George Wallace

Operation Golden Dawn

Never miss a new release! Sign up to receive exclusive updates from authors
Wallace and Keith

severnriverbooks.com/series/the-hunter-killer

PROLOGUE

The Sea of Okhotsk—bounded by the Kuril Islands and Hokkaido, the northernmost Japanese Home Island, but mostly by jutting peninsulas and Asian shorelines long claimed by Russia—is a strange and curious place. More than anything, it is unforgiving. Its murky, ice-mottled waters can morph from a glass-smooth calm into a raging maelstrom before a sailor can even contemplate seeking shelter in a safe harbor. The land surrounding the sea is equally mysterious, empty, and forbidding. Except for some dilapidated seaports that ship out the production from a few hardscrabble mines and oil fields, the lonely coniferous snow forests of the taiga are populated mostly by Siberian tigers and wolves. Half a planet and seven time zones away from Moscow, the bosom of Mother Russia, well east of even the vast nothingness of Siberia, this pool of rimy seawater and desolate shore is mostly a forgotten land.

On the mainland, almost equidistant from the deep ice of the Arctic Ocean and the East Siberian Sea to the north and the Sea of Okhotsk to the south, the long-forgotten encampment of Vesenny 69 sullies the snowy landscape. There, where the sub-arctic taiga melds into the Arctic tundra, the rude assembly of log-and-mud huts sits, seemingly abandoned. They appear to have finally surrendered to decades of deep, crushing, packed snow and neglect.

Vesenny 69 has historical significance, though. It was the last of the Union of Soviet Socialist Republics' infamous gulags. But Vesenny 69 was different. It was a camp that did not officially exist. Nothing about it appeared in the Ministry of Internal Affairs' official records. It simply was not there. This secret camp had been reserved for the Soviet Union's most hardened and dangerous political dissidents and enemies. Ones who still had some value—grueling, soul-breaking labor—to offer to the advancement of the proletariat and the state, yet who were best kept hidden away to protect the people from their dangerous ideas concerning such arcane, decadent fantasies as democracy and capitalism and the rights of free men and women.

Isolated in the roadless, trackless wilderness, the only way to reach the gulag—or to leave it—was a wintertime trek of over two hundred miles down a nameless, frozen-over stream, all the way to the first road out at the little outpost of Chersky on the Kolyma River in Siberia. At one time, two hundred or so inmates at the gulag labored at mining the meager veins of gold that spider-webbed out beneath the permafrost. It was a slow go, but the trickle of bright, sparkling minerals helped fund the oppressive costs of the government. Or the lavish vacation homes of the political leaders and favored oligarchs of the USSR.

The isolation and brutal conditions left the prisoners with no illusions. The only way they could ever leave this awful place would be in a crude pine box buried below the permafrost. The only civilizing consolation was that the Vesenny 69 camp had a few women dissidents among its men prisoners. Even under such impossible conditions, a few romances developed and thrived.

Then, deep in the winter, in December of 1991, during a night when the camp thermometer registered −45 degrees C, the first child of the gulag was born.

Apparently unrelated, a few days afterward, there was another momentous event. Without explanation, the guards and their commanders all walked away, disappearing downstream, swallowed up by heavy snow and fog.

This left the dazed but now free prisoners—including the newly arrived infant boy with the especially strong cry—totally to their own devices. In the beginning, their only goal was survival. But over the ensuing years, that would change. Mightily change.

Ψ

Ivan Dostervesky throttled back on the snowmobile as it crested a low rise. Gazing out into the snow-blown distance, he smiled. Nothing seemed to have changed here at all. The thick trees of the taiga formed the same seemingly impenetrable wasteland that he remembered so well. No signs of another human being for as far as he could see in any direction. Employing a pair of powerful binoculars retrieved from his pack, he peered off to the northwest, the direction he had been headed before he paused. There he could just see the merest hint of smoke rising from the remnants of Vesenny 69.

Good. It was a reassuring sight. Some of the others were already gathering there, getting ready. Still, as the oldest among them and the designated leader of the Children of the Gulag, Dostervesky would have preferred being the first to arrive for the reunion. The first to begin building the fire, literally and figuratively. But the unexpected blizzard— even the state meteorologists of Mother Russia had become hopelessly corrupt and lazy—had delayed his leaving Chuvanskoye. Then the deep, wet snow had bogged down the snowmobile so much that the short two-hundred-kilometer run had required that he camp in the wilderness for two nights, trying to find sleep despite the distant a cappella serenades from the wolves.

Dostervesky restowed the binoculars. Then he checked his Saiga Sporting SA 7.62mm rifle safely stowed and ready in its scabbard at his side. Likewise, his SR-1M Vektor 9mm automatic pistol, tightly strapped in its shoulder holster. The last few kilometers were the most hazardous. The Children of the Gulag were well and truly family, but survival depended on being overly careful, whether with the wild animals of the forest or the much more dangerous ones who walked upright and sported opposable thumbs.

For certain, after the discussions and decisions of this day, life was going to get very dangerous indeed. But if by some miracle of hope and determination they were able to accomplish their goals, he and the other Children would soon redraw the political maps of planet Earth.

1

The bitter wind swept down across the bare tundra and forested taiga with a vengeance. Nothing diminished its strength or blocked its way as it left the shoreline behind and roared out across the frozen Sea of Okhotsk, only miles and miles of driven snow and thick ice. The landscape was just as it had been for eons. But this was already, after only its first month, one of the coldest winters in this barren land's history. Every living creature had disappeared earlier than usual, seeking the deepest, warmest shelter that it could find to hibernate. Nothing moved except the driven snow and wind-tossed limbs of the conifers.

Beneath a meter of solid ice, Jim Ward squinted as he peered at his control panel and carefully piloted his miniature submarine toward a rendezvous scheduled to take place hundreds of miles inside hostile Russian waters. Silent electric motors pushed the small black hull through the pitch-black sea, but the only way for him to tell they were moving was the read-outs on the panels in front of him. The wan winter sun was up there, he knew. And there was a modicum of daylight yet. But that old orb was nowhere near bright or direct enough this time of the year to send its rays penetrating through the thick ice on the sea surface overhead. And even if a few stubborn rays did find their way through, there was nothing to see down there, anyway. Maybe the odd pelagic fish out in search of lunch.

Ward's submarine, oddly dubbed by the US Navy a "Dry Combat Submersible" or "DCS," was so quiet that the fish were in danger of inadvertently bumping into its hard steel skin. It was large enough to transport a pilot and a navigator along with up to eight combat-ready SEALs. However, DCS Hull 4 was mostly empty on this trip. The only ones aboard were SEAL Commander Ward and his copilot/navigator, SEAL Lieutenant Junior-Grade Willy Duncan. The forward passenger compartment and the lock-in/lock-out compartment were both empty. Ward and Duncan were in the cramped command section located in the DCS's aft-most chamber. That was where they controlled the fourteen-ton sub.

"About time for the next waypoint," Ward called across to his copilot. For the past three days, the pair had ridden the DCS over two hundred miles, mostly while it was under control of its autopilot system. They had lifted off the back of the submarine USS *George Mason* while in the Sea of Okhotsk's deep central basin, well to the south of their current position. Finally, they were nearing their destination at the far northern end of that mysterious body of ice water. And well within territorial waters where their incursion could be considered an act of war by the Russians should they be detected. Ward well knew that, considering the state of relations between Russia and the United States these days, fire and brimstone would certainly be a possibility should they be noticed.

Regardless, it was now time to make final maneuvers to get them to the point for the secret rendezvous that brought them and their vessel way up here. A meet-up that would absolutely expose them and their submersible to possible detection. Ward could only hope whatever it was that required a person-to-person meet-up in this inhospitable place would be worth the effort. And the risks.

Willy Duncan hunched over the navigation display panel.

"Just a second, boss," the young SEAL responded. "Taking a fix on the TERCOM sonar now." He swiped his fingers across a couple of pop-up commands on the touchscreen. Then he sat back, stretching as he watched the big flat panel relating the results as the sonar computer did its job. The screen display slowly built an image as the covert navigation sonar painted a picture of the bottom of the sea stretching out ahead of the DCS. At the same time, the computer matched what sonar was showing to the bottom contour map stored in the device's memory chips.

A light blip on the screen that signified the DCS's position suddenly shifted slightly, a couple of yards to the right to correct their actual position, and then it automatically updated the inertial navigation system.

"Dead on course," Duncan reported. "Time to come right to course zero-five-five. Yam Island rendezvous point is ten miles ahead on that bearing."

Ward punched the new route they would follow into the autopilot and could feel the change as the DCS smoothly swung around and steadied up, now aiming to the northeast.

"Probably as good a time as any for us to come up and see if our passengers are ready for pickup," Ward said. "Willy, what does the ice on the ceiling look like?"

Duncan shifted the TERCOM sonar beams so that they were now looking upward.

"Solid ice returns for as far as it can see," he announced. "Maybe we can find open water closer inshore. The meteorological weenies seemed to think that there are some hot springs near Yam Island and they should prevent ice formation."

"Yeah," Ward grunted. "That's why we picked it for the rendezvous. Hope those eggheads are right. This little tub won't be very good at punching through thick ice, and I'd rather not announce our arrival by blasting a hole through it. But if we have to...they made sure we knew to do whatever it took to make this little conclave happen."

It took the pair another couple of hours, but they finally located one of the promised hot springs. And as predicted, there was a small patch of open water only a few hundred yards off the high, rocky beach that edged Matykil Island, the largest bit of land in the Yam Island group.

Ward carefully raised the sensor mast until its video camera just peeked above the water's surface. The large-screen flat panel in front of Ward showed a dark, gray, cloud-covered sky merging into a gunmetal sea. The steep rock cliffs of Matykil Island filled one whole quadrant of the view. The rest was flat, open, empty sea ice. And nothing else.

"Okay," Ward said, considering the bleak landscape. "Willy, see if our friends are ready for their Uber pickup."

Duncan hit a button on the radio, setting loose a burst of super-high-frequency digital data. It was the agreed-upon signal to set up the rendezvous.

Then they waited. And waited. After two hours with no reply, Ward lowered the mast and let the DCS settle down easily to the sea bottom.

"All right, then. Let's get some dinner and then hit the rack," Ward said. "The plan is for us to wait twenty-four hours here. Then we try again. If no luck on the second attempt, we turn our happy asses around and head home and chalk this one up as a fun sightseeing cruise into the lovely Sea of O."

"Without even checking out the local nightlife?"

"Not unless you consider listening to me snore to be nightlife, Willy."

Ψ

Ivan Dostervesky was beside himself with frustration. Finally, after all the preparation and anticipation, it was time for the Children of the Gulag to emerge from the shadows, spread their wings, and claim their rightful place in the realm of mankind. Years of carefully planned and precise maneuvers all to set their little group of freedom-seeking dissidents into a position in which they would declare themselves to be a free and independent nation. To get ready to finally throw off the heavy yoke of Mother Russia.

All this, only to be stymied by a faulty snowmobile carburetor.

"Boris, how much longer?" he irritably questioned his companion.

Boris Paserivich was one of the senior Children of the Gulag and Dostervesky's lieutenant. "About the same as I reported to you five minutes ago, Ivan. But maybe five minutes closer to resolution." He bled some more gas out of the carburetor on the obstinate snowmobile's engine. "Until I get the water out of the fuel lines, it will continue to freeze up and block the feed and we are going to sit here and get on each other's nerves. If you want to walk, the rendezvous point is only fifteen miles due east."

Boris pointed off in the direction that was directly opposite from the setting sun.

Dostervesky shook his head and watched as Boris leaned over again to continue to fiddle with the carburetor. Both men knew it was fortunate that they had not yet reached the open ice when the snowmobile decided to stop running. With some punishing pushing and shoving, they had managed to get the beast into the sheltering lee of a rock face. Their tent gave Boris a reasonably warm place to work—at least warm enough that he was able to remove his gloves.

Dostervesky looked at his watch. They had missed the first rendezvous window by a half hour. The next one was only twenty-four hours away. If he should miss that, the whole delicate process of convincing the Americans and then setting up a meeting would have to start again from the beginning. How could he explain to the admiral who oversaw US Naval Intelligence that his grand and historically ambitious plan had been sidetracked by bits of ice forming in the gas line of a snowmobile engine? Even if the admiral still took him seriously and was still willing to allow the get-together, to reschedule, many precious weeks would be lost.

With delay came a loss of resolve. Loss of resolve could result in diminishment of the will to believe. And the will to believe was essential if they were to successfully accomplish what they intended.

Ivan Dostervesky grabbed his cross-country skis and his backpack from where they were strapped to the back of the snowmobile. Boris did not bother to look up.

He buckled on the skis, checked his GPS receiver, and turned to Paserivich.

"If you somehow get this beast fixed in the next six hours, head out onto the ice and find me. If you cannot find me, go back to Magadan and tell the others that I am meeting with the Americans. Unless you hear otherwise, everything will still progress according to the schedule on which we have agreed. The biggest thing right now is to get the mining team up to Vesenny. We will need all the gold we can get pretty quickly if these negotiations pan out. Understood?"

Boris started to say something, to assure Dostervesky he would fix the machine shortly and catch up to him out there on the frozen sea.

But Ivan was already out the tent flap and gone. He skied haltingly down the rocky beach and then found a zigzag path around mounded-up ice on the sea surface, headed more or less east.

2

It was midnight when the blizzard struck. However, in the land of near sunless winter, midnight was just a position for the hands on a clock and nothing more. A winter cyclone blew relatively warmer, moisture-laden air from the Sea of Japan up to and over the mostly ice-covered Sea of Okhotsk. There it collided with a fast-moving Siberian cold front tumbling southward out of the Arctic like an express train. When the wet, warmer air met the frigid wind of the front, it instantly dropped its temperature, causing the warmer air to lose its moisture in the form of vast quantities of thick snow. There was total white-out within minutes.

Ivan Dostervesky was almost halfway across the frozen surface of the sea on his hike to Matykil Island. He was making very good time when the blizzard hit. Instantly his vision dropped from being able to see the far-off horizon all the way down to not being able to see his own gloved hands if he stretched out his arms. Born and raised in the Arctic, he instinctively knew that his survival hinged on finding shelter. He would have to get out of the wind and snow. And quickly. But he was in the open, out on the sea ice that stretched off in all directions. Where could he possibly find any place to get out of the wind and blinding snow?

His only chance would be to build some kind of snow cave, maybe within the protection of one of the ice pressure ridges that heaved up four or five meters high all around him. As he slogged the last seven miles or so since leaving Boris Paserivich, the balky snowmobile, and the shore, he had cursed the ridges popping up to obstruct his path. He had to ski far out of his way to get around them, as if picking his way through a maze, yet still try to maintain his course due east. But now, one of those damnable hillocks might just save his life.

Skirting a particularly tall and steep pressure ridge, Dostervesky found just what he needed. A snowdrift, already piling up before the driving wind. Working quickly, he dug a trench in the snow, carefully tamping the walls to make them as solid as possible. There was only enough accumulated snow to build the walls about a meter high. Working quickly, he laid his skis and ski poles across the top like rafters and then spread out his little tent over the supports to form a roof. Not much insulation, but at least it would protect him from the wind as the snow rapidly built up while the storm blasted through.

It would have to suffice. There was nothing more he could do to make the shelter any better. He would die if he did not get out of the wind before frostbite or hypothermia set in. He crawled through the tiny entrance, shoved his pack in behind him to cover the opening and keep the wind and snow out, and huddled in his crude snow cave.

Now to sit and wait out the storm. And hope it did not last days, as they sometimes did this time of year. But while he waited, he could build resolve for trying to complete the remaining distance to within range to confirm the meeting point, even if he had to leave the shelter and brave the blizzard to do so. The men waiting for him would not tarry, and he could not blame them. They would be in real danger.

Sitting there in the cold darkness, he also had time to think.

Dostervesky's mind drifted back to Vesenny and to the very earliest days of the Children of the Gulag. Life had gotten even more difficult for a while when the Russians suddenly left. His parents had told him of the hardships they all faced. Some of the same, as always. Weather, scarce food, vast distances to travel if they decided to leave. Some different challenges and even more difficult to overcome without the opportunity to prepare for them. Providing their own necessities, medical care, and more. They relied on their wits and survived as best they could. Or at least a majority of them did. Some did not. Anger and resolve mostly got them through. That and the determination to raise the Children and to instill in them the idea and plans for the eventual breakaway to true freedom.

From his earliest days, Dostervesky had accepted the idea that the guards had been Russians and the Russians were the enemy, the oppressors. His own people were always the People of the Gulag, the parents of the Children, separate and apart from the Russians. It had been the Russians who had imprisoned the People merely because of their opinions and their courage to express them. Or for their refusal to worship the state as a god. The Russians and the People were no longer fellow countrymen, brothers, kinsmen. Then, on that fateful day, the Russians simply fled, abandoning parents and children, casting them aside like so much worthless trash. Their former guards naturally assumed the prisoners would not survive.

But when they did, the ideas began to flourish, even as they eked out a bare existence on the edge of the forest. As their numbers had slowly grown through procreation, the parents honed and shared with the Children the potential to create their own sovereign nation, one where thoughts and freedom could thrive and gulags would be no more. Not to ever be forgotten, of course, but their one-time existence and what they stood for providing a constant source of their strength.

Over the years, they made contact with others who had also managed to survive in similar gulags after they too had been abruptly abandoned. The Children of the Gulag were not surprised to learn there were others like them spread across what the outside world called the Russian Far East. Or that some of them had independently contemplated a similar future. Not to try to escape to another nation. To building their own, right there, in the only home the Children had ever known.

The Children began calling the region *nash dom*, or "our home." Slowly the dream of *Nash Dom* truly becoming Our Home, free from the Russians or anyone else, grew and spread. The Russians had abandoned them in this land. It was surely their destiny to claim it as their own, putting their own mark on it from its inception.

It had all been nothing more than a dream until the eventful day, almost two decades before, when they discovered that the unimpressive gold vein that the Russians had exploited at Vesenny 69—one their captors were convinced had been mostly mined out—actually contained far more gold than anyone could ever have imagined. And once discovered, it was relatively easy to dig it out. Under the guidance of Dostervesky and others among the Children, the gold was secretly mined and then cautiously smuggled out to hungry markets around Asia. Smuggled out in ways so as not to spook the market or give anyone any idea of where it was coming from. As gold prices soared, the cash from the sale of the mineral was carefully hidden in banks and investment institutions around the globe, relying on trusted friends and relatives who had long since abandoned Mother Russia. Most of the money was saved, but some was used to purchase modern technology, defensive weapons, the required machinery to continue to pull the gold from the frozen ground, and the day-to-day needs of the Children and the older people who were left.

Children from other gulags had also discovered in their area deposits of lithium, iridium, and ruthenium—and other obscure but precious commodities—each of which suddenly had value on the world market and could fund their cause.

Dostervesky and the Children finally had the assets to make their dream of *Nash Dom* come true. But now, they needed help. Help from someone who had an ax to grind with Russia. The timing finally seemed right. Russia was clearly preoccupied with spreading influence and annexing territory to the west and south, primarily east of the Urals, from Ukraine and Turkey to Syria and Iran. No one seemed to care what was happening in the Far East, other than Vladivostok, where the Russian Navy's Pacific Fleet was headquartered.

But who? The Americans? The Chinese? The Japanese? Korean, North or South? Dostervesky did not really care. He would try them all. The USA was the first on his list but only because he now had a contact high within that country's navy. A contact whose name was provided by someone inside China who had somehow, impossibly, heard about the cause of the Children and reached out. And for some reason supported them and their dream and trusted Dostervesky to keep that support and help completely confidential.

Dostervesky shook himself from his reverie. The wind had abruptly fallen silent. The blizzard had blown by even more quickly than he had hoped. That happened sometimes, too. Or it could also be only a short lull. Either way, he knew it was his only chance. He pulled his backpack away from the entrance and started to crawl out. But the snow had piled even deeper than he had expected, covering the opening. Heavy, wet snow. He was effectively buried.

He glanced at his watch. There was only an hour to the last rendezvous time, and he still needed to cover ten kilometers. It would take some tough skiing if he had any chance of making it.

With a frustrated groan, Dostervesky began to dig furiously, desperately, using both hands.

Ψ

Jim Ward slowly lifted the DCS from its resting spot on the muddy bottom. It was time to come up and make one last attempt to contact his passenger. If no one replied, then they would head back to the *George Mason* empty-handed. He was already dreading the conversation he would have to have with his father, Admiral Jon Ward, Director of Naval Intelligence. Telling him that the carefully planned and very risky mission he had assigned them had been a bust, a waste of time and taxpayers' dollars and the bit of fiction the admiral had concocted to steal his son away from his usual SEAL duties.

"Excellent training opportunity, though," his dad might tell him, but only if he were in an especially good mood.

It was odd that Ward was thinking of his dad just when Willy Duncan spoke up, saying, "At least you got your chance to be a submarine skipper, like your dad."

"What? Oh, you mean driving this mop bucket?" Ward grinned as he began the procedure to wake up the remainder of the DCS systems and prepare to bring it back to the surface. "To his credit, he never tried to talk me into going into the 'sewer pipe service.' You know why he picked submarines?"

"Can't for the life of me figure why anybody in his right mind would," Duncan answered.

"He wanted a command where he could know the first name of every man in his crew, where they were from, and whether or not he could depend on him when the feces hit the bladed air-moving device," Ward told him. "Reckon the captain of an aircraft carrier can do that?"

"See, that's something else you got, there, Skipper."

"What's that?"

"You know my name, you know I'm from Mobile, Alabama, and you know I got you covered when it all goes to hell. And I'm your entire crew, right?"

Ward grinned and winked. At the same time, he repeated the maneuvers to bring the DCS back to the small patch of open water and to raise the sensor mast. Once again, they looked out on a world of all whites and grays and the stark, black-rock island.

"Willy, send the wake-up call," Ward directed. "Let's hope he's got his ears on this time."

"What makes you think our passenger is a 'he'?" Duncan shot back. "I'm dreaming that 'she' is a beautiful, blond Russian doll with legs that just don't stop."

"You been sniffin' something again," Ward said with a chuckle. "Sorry to shoot down your *Love Boat* dream. We both know odds are we're picking up some old Russian guy that stinks of vodka and borscht."

"What in hell is borscht, anyway. Doesn't sound like..." Duncan stopped, listened, and suddenly held up a hand. "Got a reply signal. Weak. Best bearing to the west. Shifting to voice comms."

Ward nodded. Duncan spoke Russian into the microphone.

"Nasha poxitsiya v dom kilometre k zapadu ot pozitsii."

Our position is one kilometer west of point.

Now, whoever they were meeting—beautiful blond lady or fat, old Russian dude—would know that the boat was a full kilometer west of the agreed-upon rendezvous point. If that was an issue, too bad. Nobody gave the US Navy the opportunity to decide where those hot springs were located.

The reply in Russian came quickly and with a hint of excitement. *"VA v odnom kilometre k zapadu ot vas. Budet cherez chas."*

I am one kilometer west of you. Will be there in one hour.

Ward glanced up at the digital clock. One hour was a hell of a long time to stick around these parts with their antenna up. Even though all the communications had been quick and in Russian, and despite the fact that Duncan had a passable Russian accent, at least over a radio, Ward well knew that the Russians kept a very close monitor on any electronic emissions anywhere in the Sea of Okhotsk. These had been disputed waters for a long, long time. Voice communications in this ice-covered part of the world would arouse immediate interest, even if it was in the language of the local natives. But they did need to continue listening for other comms from the passenger, just in case he got into trouble.

So, they had to assume that they would probably have visitors pretty quickly. The nearest military airfield was in Petropavlovsk, on the far side of the Kamchatka Peninsula. That was over four hundred miles away. Even if the Russians were eavesdropping and scrambled a fast flier to investigate, the SEALs and their passenger had an hour. But not much more than that.

"Willy, get a dry suit on and get ready to go topside," Ward ordered. "I'm going to surface this tub and snuggle up against the ice edge. Let's see if we can do this transfer without anybody getting wet. And I don't need the weather guy on the nightly news to tell me it might be a little bit nippy topside."

"Probably a tad colder than it gets down on the Redneck Riviera," Duncan said, mimicking a shiver.

"Redneck Riviera?"

"Gulf Shores, Alabama, all the way to Panama City, Florida. World's most beautiful beaches. Miles and miles of sugar-white sand and emerald-green water and tanned beach bunnies. I'll take you there someday, and the only ice we'll have to deal with will be in your margarita."

Forty-five minutes later, Ivan Dostervesky was safely onboard the DCS, they were southbound, and they were reasonably safe beneath the thick ice and recent heavy snowfall.

By the time the Russian Tu-214R reconnaissance jet flew very low overhead, the DCS was already five miles south of the pickup point and Ivan Dostervesky was gratefully enjoying his second cup of hot, black coffee.

3

Brian Edwards stepped out into the control room on the *Virginia*-class nuclear submarine USS *George Mason*. He proudly watched as his team calmly went about their job of driving his boat through these dangerous waters. The Sea of Okhotsk was inside the very heart of the Russian Far East. The entire sea was claimed by Russia as her territorial waters. Any sub found here would be treated as hostile. They would be attacked with no warning and without mercy. Those were the facts. But his team was going about their duties just as they would if they were in far warmer and much friendlier waters.

Back in the Cold War days, American submarines plied these waters carefully but with relative impunity. To the point where the USS *Parche* actually sent divers out to tap Russian underwater communications cables. Then they returned repeatedly to harvest the intelligence garnered via their clever clandestine splice.

Before that, late in World War II, La Perouse Strait at the far southern edge of the sea and just north of the Japanese Home Island of Hokkaido became a useful but dangerous exit for US submarines from the Sea of Japan to the Pacific. Several wrecks of those boats remain on the sea floor as memorials to the ones that did not make it and the boats and their crews that were lost. Or, as the submariners say, "On eternal patrol."

In 1941, before the war, the Kuril Islands, at the southeastern boundary of the Sea of Okhotsk, was where the Imperial Japanese Navy made final preparations and assembled its fleet of aircraft carriers and escorts before heading east. That was because the area was so remote that they were unlikely to be observed before steaming off on a route of almost due south, straight to Pearl Harbor, Hawaii.

But times were certainly different now. Technology had changed by orders of magnitude. Edwards had to deal with the very real possibility that the Russians had seeded the sea floor with bottom sensors that might detect the *George Mason*. They would report back to the Russian base, either in Vladivostok, way to the south, or to Petropavlovsk, over on the far side of the Kamchatka Peninsula. Either way, the first hint they would have that they had been found was when ordnance began raining down on their heads. And that could ruin any submarine skipper's day.

Normally—if ever anything could be considered normal for an American submarine hiding in the Sea of Okhotsk—Edwards and the *George Mason* would have entered the area while either stealthily trailing some Russian submarine or being snugged up close to the coast with an ESM mast up, vacuuming from the radio-frequency spectrum all the electronic intelligence that they could collect. But today was not normal. Their one assignment was to wait patiently in the sea's deepwater basin, right at the edge of the pack ice, and to be ready to pick up Commander Jim Ward whenever the young SEAL brought his DCS and its passengers back from his trip way up north. All they could do in the meantime was make looping, three-knot figure eights at a depth of three hundred feet.

"Morning, Skipper," Lieutenant Bill Wilson greeted Edwards as the senior officer rifled through the displays on the command console. "We've been blessed with a real quiet watch so far. Only sonar contact is Sierra Two-Seven, now bearing two-six-three. He's been pinging away up at the ice edge all night. Sonar classifies him as a Horse Jaw low-frequency active sonar. It's usually carried on *Udaloy*-class destroyers. The only one we know of in use in the Pacific Fleet is the *Admiral Panteleyev*. She was commissioned in 1991. Must be a real rust bucket by now. Range is tracking in excess of fifty miles. The probability of detection is about as close to zero as you can get. If she stays true to her schedule, she should be heading back to Vlad to refuel sometime today."

The old Russian destroyer had been providing the only point of interest in an otherwise boring operation. She seemed to be on a two-days-at-sea, two-days-in-port schedule, doing little more than patrolling aimlessly around the northern reaches of the Sea of O. But at the end of her two-day sea period, she always managed to be way over at the extreme western edge, ready to dash home to Vladivostok.

Wilson continued his report. "Weps reports that all weekly fire-control checks are complete and sat. All systems restored to normal operation."

Edwards nodded. All he said in response to the considerable amount of data was, "Good." Wilson had worked with Edwards long enough to know that was high praise. The skipper continued studying the sonar displays. He was engrossed in the self-noise displays. One of the basics of the submarine service was that remaining hidden, cloaked in silence, was vital to not only the vessel's successful completion of its mission but also to its very survival. These displays would reveal if any stray bit of sound energy might be escaping out into the surrounding water. If so, it could be a very bad thing. And especially out here in the Sea of O.

Edwards nodded his head ever so slightly. Everything looked to be well into the green. So far.

"Engineer is back aft, watching a reactor protection system alignment check and keeping an eye on Jerry Billings," Wilson said, continuing his status report. "It's his first qualified watch as Engineering Officer of the Watch."

Edwards visibly lightened up. This was just like the Eng (sub-speak for the boat's Engineering Officer or Chief Engineer). Lieutenant Commander Jeffrey Otanga had reported aboard and relieved as Engineer just before they cast off lines for this deployment from Pearl Harbor. In reality, Otanga was still learning his job, but that had not stopped him from playing mother hen to everyone in his department. He had even promised Edwards that every man and woman in his section would pass his qual exams and be officially "qualified in submarines" by the time they got back to Pearl. Every man and woman. That was a tall order.

"Anything on comms?" Edwards asked.

"No, sir," Wilson replied. "The A-DSTP buoy is plotting thirty-two miles to the southeast. We received an acoustic health signal half an hour ago, right on schedule, so it's working. No pages, though, so the boss must not have any mail for us."

The Advanced Deep Siren Tactical Paging System—or A-DSTP on the Navy's list of seemingly endless acronyms—allowed a submarine to be in contact with the boss back home and still stay deep and hidden while they were—as submariners liked to say—off doing things that they really weren't doing in places where they really weren't. The system was very simple. When the boat first arrived in-area, they launched an A-DSTP buoy out of the trash disposal unit. While the submarine drove away to do its mission, the buoy floated up until its radio antenna just broke through the surface. At the same time, an acoustic hydrophone dropped down until it reached a preset optimum depth for acoustic comms. When everything was ready, the A-DSTP sent a quick burst message announcing that it was up and ready to go to work. From then on, any time home base wanted to contact the sub, they simply sent a text to the A-DSTP buoy, which promptly sent out a coded acoustic message to the boat. Acoustic range on the buoy was about fifty nautical miles, so the sub had a pretty large area it could play in and still be available for instant call-up. And the buoy's batteries were good for about a week. If the mission took longer, the buoy simply scuttled itself with the last bit of energy provided by the fading batteries, and the sub launched another one.

The whole thing allowed the boat to stay deep with nothing from the sub itself ever piercing the surface. And if some fisherman happened to snag the buoy, there was nothing about it that would reveal what it was or who it belonged to. The best way to stay hidden and stealthy was to never poke a mast up above the surface and into the air. Especially when that air was over waters as hostile as those in the Sea of Okhotsk.

"All in all, sounds pretty boring," Edwards offered. "And mostly I'm in favor of boring."

"Yep," Wilson agreed.

"Let's keep it that way, then. I'm going to the wardroom for a cup of coffee. Have your messenger round up the XO, the COB, and the department heads. It's about time for everybody's favorite, the weekly planning meeting." The XO was the submarine's Executive Officer, second in command. The COB, or "Cob," was Chief of the Boat, the most senior enlisted man aboard.

Bill Wilson started to acknowledge the request, but Edwards had already disappeared out the door.

Ψ

Boris Paserivich carefully edged up to the snowy ridge and peered out over the top and down through the trees. His small troop of miners remained huddled together, behind him and farther down the slope. All except Daniil Semenov, who was slithering up the slope to rest next to Paserivich.

The pair lay there, silently watching the activity taking place in a small clearing a hundred meters down the hill from them.

"You see what I mean, Boris?" Semenov whispered. "I almost stumbled into the middle of them by accident. It's fortunate that I heard their snowmobiles and dived for cover before they came over that ridge over there. That's when I came back to warn you and the others."

Paserivich grunted.

"I guess that water contamination in our gasoline was a bit of good fortune after all. Otherwise, we'd not have been on skis today." He peered at the group with his binoculars, studying them carefully. "Military police," he muttered disgustingly, more to himself than to Semenov. "But what are they doing way out here?" Then, in a slightly louder voice, he asked, "How many do you make out down there?"

Daniil Semenov carefully scanned the men taking a rest in the small valley. In addition to being the Children's top mine supervisor, Semenov was reputed to have the best eyesight of anyone at Vesenny 69.

"I see a dozen. Six snowmobiles. Two troops each. From their general direction, they are heading toward our gulag. But why? Why would they be going there?"

Boris Paserivich kept his binoculars to his eyes as he answered.

"No idea. As far as the Russians are concerned, Vesenny 69 is long since abandoned and reclaimed by the elements. They certainly have no reason to send out a patrol in winter weather unless they suspect something. Absolutely not the *Voennaya politsiya*, either. Their nearest base is way over in Nelemnoye, in the Sakha Republic. That's over six hundred kilometers away. They are here for a reason. Not a good thing for us."

The dreaded *Voennaya politsiya* were the strong arm of the Russian military way out in these far-flung, sparsely populated wilderness areas. They enforced the law—or at least whatever the Russian government decided the law was—with a brutal and heavy hand. They had a well-earned reputation for arresting, trying, and punishing their victims all in one quick operation, then quickly forgetting where the bodies were buried. Figuratively and literally. Out here, thousands of kilometers from anything resembling civilization, there was usually no one to question or complain.

"Is it possible that they captured Ivan Dostervesky after he left you and went on to the…"

Paserivich dropped the binoculars from his eyes and gave Semenov a withering look.

"Not in that blizzard, on the open ice. Even if they had, no amount of torture would have gotten any information of value from him." He took a deep breath. "Besides, they would not have caught him alive. You can be sure of this."

With that, Paserivich slid down the back side of the slope until he was far enough to stand and still be shielded by the hill. Semenov quickly joined him, dusting the snow off his fur coat. They quickly told the other miners what they had seen.

"It appears that they are setting up camp, bedding down for the night," Semenov observed.

"Agreed. They have graciously given us some time, but we must get going," Paserivich told him. "We have a hard night of skiing ahead of us. We must be at Vesenny and execute our defensive plan before the *Voennaya politsiya* can get there on their machines. We must be ready to welcome them properly."

With that, the group skied away, almost silently, promptly disappearing into the darkness of the thick forest.

Ψ

The dim light of dawn was struggling to offer up any useful illumination on the eastern horizon as Boris Paserivich got his little team settled into their long-since-assigned-and-prepared ambush positions. With only himself, Semenov, and a half dozen untrained men armed with a mixture of Saiga 7.62mm semiautomatic or Baikal 9.3mm bolt-action hunting rifles, Paserivich recognized that they would be at a disadvantage against their visitors in any kind of standing fight. If they did not take out most of the *Voennaya politsiya* with their first fusillade, they would be gold miners fighting with deer rifles against well-trained soldiers using automatic weapons as well as explosives they were able to employ with deadly effectiveness if allowed the opportunity.

Paserivich had been one of the few to lobby for an arsenal of more powerful defensive weapons and a dedicated, trained force of men in case someone caught wind of their existence and intentions. Especially now that they had the wherewithal to afford such firepower. Most felt they were too far from Moscow or anywhere else for anyone to notice. Not until they eventually declared independence. Then, with world opinion bought and paid for through the media, and with most countries on their side, they would peacefully secede. And it would be too late then for the distracted government in far-off Moscow to do anything.

From the looks of that patrol, quiet, peaceful secession was probably not going to happen unless they took care of this "problem" completely and with no witnesses. This day, simple surprise would be their strongest advantage.

Paserivich also knew that he had one other major edge over the attackers. His men were all Children of the Gulag. They had been raised hunting for game since they were capable of holding, aiming, and firing a rifle. They were all expert shots. Their existence had depended on using these very rifles to put meat on the table. He and his small cadre of defenders had been given enough advance notice that they were able to choose the best of several potential ambush locations. And they had planned and practiced for just such a scenario for years.

He spread his team out in a line atop a low ridge. The *Voennaya politsiya* would necessarily have to make their way down a short, steep, barren slope and then cross a frozen-over stream for any practical approach to the dilapidated buildings of the gulag. Especially if they were still two-to-a-vehicle on the snowmobiles. They would know soon enough by the noise of the motors if they were. And even if they approached on foot, giving up the advantage of speed on the vehicles, this was still the only practical approach.

Even if the force somehow made it past the ambush, the others inside the compound were waiting, equally lacking in real firepower but armed with the same well-practiced marksmanship and dedication to defending the dream. That included the children of the Children.

Hoping it would not come down to that last stand, Paserivich moved quickly from hide hole to hide hole, repeating the same instructions for each man. "Do not begin shooting until I fire the first round. Aim only at your designated target. Make the first shot count. And the second one, too. Then move. Do not remain here in this hole hoping for a third shot. We want to minimize the chance of their radioing that they have been ambushed."

Each man nodded grimly. They had heard this same litany in so many drills. Now, though, it was about to be for real.

Paserivich had just dropped into his own hole—long since hollowed out and made ready amid the undergrowth—when he heard the unmistakable high-pitched whine of the approaching snowmobiles. That confirmed for him that the approaching men still did not necessarily anticipate an ambush. Or even resistance. And that they were thankfully following the route for which he and his men had prepared.

Seconds later, the first machine burst into view over the ridge, coming at top speed, going airborne for a few meters before dropping into the snow and accelerating down the slope. Five more just like it leaped over the crest of the hill in rapid succession.

Paserivich put the cross hairs of his gunsight on the lead driver's head, followed him for a few seconds, and then squeezed the trigger. The man's skull exploded. Before the passenger could even realize what had happened, Paserivich had shifted his sights to that man's chest. The 7.62mm round struck home, tearing through his torso before exiting near his spine. He was dead before he knew anything had happened. The snowmobile skewed hard and tipped over onto its side, where it continued to whine and spin around madly, kicking up a cloud of snow and frozen earth. The dead driver's hand was jammed against the throttle, keeping it fully open.

Only then was Paserivich aware of the other gunfire from all around him. And he could see that the others had done their jobs well. Only a couple of the passengers had survived the first two salvos. They both hid behind their respective machines and fired wildly at the ridgeline with their AK-12 automatic rifles on full auto. Using thick brush for cover, Paserivich scooted down and along the slope to a position where he could get a better angle on one of the shooters. He was aware that Daniil Semenov was doing the same thing farther up the way.

The brush offered no protection from the random bullets. Paserivich slid behind a small willow. Still not much cover, but the best available. Then both attackers popped up from behind their snowmobiles to again spray fire at the ridgeline in hopes of hitting something. To maybe buy time so they could grab a radio and call for help.

Paserivich and Semenov were ready. Simultaneously, they both unleashed rounds. They saw the military policemen pitch backward, as if jerked by unseen cords, already bleeding dark red into the snow.

Just as quickly as it had started, the fight was over. The whole thing took less than two minutes from the first shot.

Paserivich cautiously stood and then approached the killing field. He quickly checked to be sure that all of the *Voennaya politsiya* were, in fact, dead. As he rolled the last one over and felt for a pulse at the man's throat, Daniil Semenov walked up.

"We lost one man," Semenov sadly reported. "Nikolai Popov evidently tried to get a third shot off. He caught a round that penetrated his hide hole. And we have one wounded. Kirill Sidorov will walk with a limp for a while, but he will be all right."

Boris Paserivich studied the carnage for another moment.

"It could have been far worse," he finally acknowledged. "We will miss Nikolai. He was with us from the beginning. We will have to inform his wife and children, then we will bury him in the mine, in the place of honor." He waved toward the *Voennaya politsiya* bodies and their gear. "Now we need to quickly take care of this garbage. They had no opportunity to report they were in trouble, but they will be missed when they do not check in. They need to be far away if they are ever found." He thought for a moment. "Drag them and their machines beneath the brush and trees for the moment. See that the snow does not look disturbed from the air. The Omolon River is two hundred kilometers west. When it is dark, we will convene a work party and get everything moved over there and dropped through the ice. Chances are our unfortunate visitors here will never be found. Their loss will be just another mystery of the Far East. And even if they ever are found, it will be far away from here or any of the other allied gulags."

Semenov looked at his leader with concern. "Boris, you know there is something else we must consider, right?"

"Yes. I know. Why would the *Voennaya politsiya* ever have a reason to come here after all these years?" He watched the men already busily hiding the evidence of the ambush. Then he glanced back, in the direction of Vesenny 69. "I fear we have a spy among us."

"Yes."

"But we must not lose sight of one more thing," Paserivich said, his voice solemn.

"What is that, Boris?"

"The first shots of the new revolution have just been fired. And the first patriot has died for the cause."

4

"Officer-of-the-Deck," ST1 Josh Hannon called out. "New contact Sierra Three-Five and Sierra Three-Six. We got a three-five-hertz tonal on the thin-line. Best bearings three-zero-one and two-three-nine."

The control room in the *George Mason* had been quiet as the watch team carried out the normal midwatch routine. The boat was cruising on lazy, random courses, waiting for Jim Ward and Willy Duncan, with their passenger and the DCS, to return for the planned rendezvous. However, just because they were killing time did not mean that they were not alert and on their toes. The Sea of Okhotsk was no place for a US submarine to let down its guard. Not for a second. The sonar team, including Josh Hannon, was currently using all of their sophisticated, highly sensitive sensors to probe the waters around the *George Mason*. They wanted to make sure that no one snuck up on them and got the drop on the submarine.

The most sensitive sonar sensor in their arsenal was the TB-29X thin-line towed array. It was actually a mile-long string of hydrophones that was being towed at the end of a mile-long tow line, giving the submarine a two-mile tail. Every sonarman in the fleet liked to brag that the TB-29X could detect a whale fart at a thousand miles. Then, in a few seconds, the complex computer algorithms in the BQQ-10 sonar system would spit out the whale's age and gender. Only problem was that because the TB-29X had a conical beamformer, the system actually showed two contacts, one on each side of the array. They were on ambiguous bearings, and there was no easy way to tell on which side of the array the contact was actually held.

LCDR Jim Shupert, the on-watch Officer-of-the-Deck and the boat's Navigator, stepped over to the command console and punched in some buttons. He could then see the same display that Josh Hannon was looking at over on the starboard side of the control room.

He studied the display, then asked, "Hannon, you got a class on him yet?"

"Not yet. With a thirty-five-hertz line, best bet is an Improved *Severodvinsk*-class Russian sub," Hannon replied. "But before we spend much time worrying about this guy's hull number, suggest that we determine bearing ambiguity and bracket his range."

Shupert gave a low whistle. Hannon was right. They needed to see exactly in what direction this guy was, and how far away. Especially if Hannon was also correct about the make and model of the newcomer.

The Improved *Severodvinsk* was the most advanced submarine in the Russian Fleet. For quieting, the real test of capability for a submarine, it was almost on a par with the *George Mason*. However, this boat was nearly twice the size of the *George Mason* and carried a deadly array of weapons. Despite its size, it was a whole lot faster than the *George Mason*, reportedly topping out at almost forty knots. At last report, Navy Intel was saying that the Russians only had three of them, and they were all operating up in the North Fleet. So, what was one of them doing over five thousand miles from where he was supposed to be?

"Nav, suggest you call the captain," Hannon offered. "By the time you've done that, we'll have a leg on this guy and be ready to maneuver. And just in case the skipper asks, bearings are drawing forward, now three-zero-two and two-three-eight. Recommend reversing course to resolve ambiguity and get a second leg."

A submarine relies on passive sonar as its primary sensor. Unlike radar or active sonar, passive sonar does not automatically provide a range to the target. Not course or speed, either. Passive sonar only provides two "truths": target bearing and received frequency. The only way to solve for range, course, and speed is to perform a series of maneuvers called "legs" and then analyze the bearing and received frequency for the target on each leg. Eventually the correct solution will fall out from all of the possible ones. But it takes time. That is why ASW—anti-submarine warfare—is sometimes called "awfully slow warfare."

Shupert picked up the phone and called Brian Edwards in his stateroom. Edwards responded on the second ring, sleep thick in his voice as he answered.

"Captain."

"Captain, Officer-of-the-Deck," Shupert reported. "On course zero-nine-zero, speed four, depth three hundred feet. We have a new TB-29 contact, Sierra Three-Five and Sierra Three-Six, currently bearing three-zero-two and two-three-eight, respectively, both drawing forward."

"Let me guess. Something Russian and submerged."

"Based on a three-five-hertz tonal, tentative classification is Improved *Severodvinsk*. I have a leg on this course, reversing course to two-seven-zero to resolve ambiguity and get a second leg."

Shupert could hear the skipper shuffling around his stateroom, getting dressed as he listened to the sonar report.

"Nav, station the section tracking party," Edwards directed. "Concur on the course change. Get the XO. As soon as you regain contact after the maneuver, man battle stations silently. And check the status of self-noise. Make damn sure that *George Mason* is a hole in the ocean. I'll be out in a few seconds."

Shupert had barely put the phone down when he sensed Edwards was standing beside him. Jackson Biddle, the sub's Executive Officer, stumbled into the control room a few seconds later, short-cropped hair spiking, and rubbing sleep from his eyes. He sent the messenger of the watch for coffee as he entered control.

Edwards and Jackson huddled with Shupert around the sonar display on the command console.

"Skipper, steadying up on course two-seven-zero," Shupert reported. "Array will be stable in fifteen minutes."

"Longest fifteen minutes in show business," Edwards muttered.

Since the TB-29X was essentially a mile-long garden hose stuffed with hydrophones and another mile of tow cable, it took time for it to straighten out and give accurate bearing information after any change in the ship's course. Of course, until it did, they were blind. There was nothing they could do but wait until Hannon told them that the array was again stable.

After what seemed an interminable delay—Biddle was well into his second cup of thick, black coffee—Josh Hannon finally pronounced that the array was stable. They then waited impatiently for either Sierra Three-Five or Three-Six to reappear on the screen.

There was nothing.

As happened all too often, while they were doing what they had to do, the Russian submarine disappeared. Maybe he turned away. Maybe he secured whatever pump was causing the thirty-five-hertz noise that had first grabbed their attention. Nobody could be certain. All they knew was that they had lost track of him. And that could be good or bad.

After searching fruitlessly for another hour, Edwards turned to Jim Shupert.

"Nav, our friend was heading to the east when we lost him. Let's stay real quiet and head over to the west end of our box. Maybe that reduces the chances of our butting into that guy again." Their "box" was the geographical area in which they were supposed to be operating, and it was known only to those who needed to know where they were. Edwards checked his watch. "We still have three hours until rendezvous time. Run a complete self-noise diagnostic, and also make sure all the systems to dock the DCS are checked out. I want to get those SEALs and their hitchhiker aboard as quickly and quietly as possible. Then I want to sneak out of town without anyone knowing we were ever swimming in this pond."

Ψ

Commander Jim Ward eased back on the controls, slowing the DCS to a hover. Four days steaming south under the ice had been a trying experience. Ward was amazed at the endurance the improved DCS was exhibiting. The new aluminum-seawater batteries seemed to have near unlimited power. They had kept the lights on and the screw turning for more than a week now and kept them moving over seven hundred miles beneath the thick ice overhead. Even so, being stuck in this little sewer pipe for that long—and for almost half the time with a Russian who really, really wanted to smoke a cigarette—made Ward even more pleased that this little excursion was almost over.

Or at least he hoped it was. Ideally, the *George Mason* had not been shooed away by some pesky Russians pushing their high-and-mighty sovereignty over these godforsaken waters. The submarine would have no choice. They would necessarily skedaddle, leaving Ward, Duncan, and their yacht to their own devices. And Ward was pretty sure there was not enough battery power left to get them to Hokkaido, Japan, the nearest friendly territory, or through the Kuril chain of islands and out into the vast Pacific Ocean.

"Willy, you sure the nav system has us at the rendezvous coordinates?" Ward asked his copilot, even though he knew the answer already.

Ivan Dostervesky sat quietly behind the pair and watched wide-eyed as they maneuvered the miniature submarine. The man was not at all familiar with such technology.

"Yep, sure as I can be," the young SEAL answered. "Inertial system says we are right where X marks the spot."

"Okay, then I wonder where our ride is?" Ward replied. "Sonar is not showing anything. Nada. Zilch. Naught."

"Is something wrong?" the Russian asked, frowning. "Have we missed the location of the meeting?"

"No time to panic," Ward offered. "Our sub could be real close and we'd not know it."

Dostervesky nodded, but the worried frown only intensified.

"Let me try the homing signal another time," Duncan said. He swiped across the touchscreen and hit the button to send out the weak acoustic homing signal. No need for the Russians to hear it in Vladivostok. Then all three men stared hard at the acoustic comms screen, almost as if willing a reply to pop up.

Then, as if in answer to their prayers, the coded rendezvous message suddenly appeared. They breathed sighs of relief, practically in unison. Then they laughed nervously. The tension was broken.

"*George Mason* is four hundred yards dead ahead," Duncan said as he monitored the homing beacon. "Boy, is that bitch quiet! Nothing on sonar.

We would have blundered right past her without that beacon. Or bumped heads."

"Get on acoustic comms and tell them we are coming in," Ward ordered, but Duncan was already sending the message.

"They are ready for us to dock. *Mason* hovering at zero speed. They do report a two-knot crosscurrent from the port side. You may have to remember how to parallel park, Skipper."

Duncan read the text message as it appeared on the screen.

"Piece of cake," Ward said.

"Cake?" Dostervesky was frowning again.

Ward carefully steered the little sub until it was hovering directly over the mating surface atop *George Mason*. He gingerly adjusted the thrusters while watching the closed-circuit TV that showed him a murky view of the mating ring. At the same time, he allowed for the crosscurrent as he felt it try to shove the DCS off its intended track. The current made the already delicate maneuver that much more difficult. The slightest miscalculation or too strong a correction and the miniature sub could go tumbling down the side of the much larger *George Mason*. Not only could that possibly cause damage to both vessels, but the noise would sound like a ringing church bell to anybody listening to sonar within miles of their position.

When he was precisely in position, Ward deliberately lowered the DCS until he felt the latches grasp the mating ring, firmly attaching the two boats together.

It took only a couple of minutes to open the hatches, and then the three climbed down the ladder into the *George Mason*. Icy seawater dripped down their collars as they descended.

Ivan Dostervesky was still wide-eyed, but he no longer carried a frown on his face. He had replaced it with a broad smile.

5

Avacha Bay lies on the Pacific Ocean side of the Kamchatka Peninsula, three hundred kilometers north of the land mass's southernmost tip. Except for a narrow mouth of water that allows access to the ocean, it is completely surrounded by towering volcanic mountains. The bay's deep waters have historically provided mariners protection from the storm-flung northern Pacific.

Vitus Bering first brought the Russian culture to this wild land, founding the village of Petropavlovsk there in the 1740s. But the Soviets really brought attention of some quarters to this forgotten part of the world when they built a large submarine base and shipyard across the bay in Vilyuchinsk in the 1950s. With direct all-year access right out into the Pacific, Vilyuchinsk—or Petropavlovsk-Kamchatsky 50, as it was then known—quickly became the most watched submarine base in the world, watched by intelligence gatherers associated with navies from all compass points. Several generations of American submariners spent countless days and nights watching the fog-shrouded coastline around "Petr," waiting for the Russian boats to come out and play and get themselves and their tactics observed and documented.

Even with the fall of the Soviet Union and the near demise of the Russian Navy, Petr remained the linchpin in Russia's far eastern defense system. The submarine base and the shipyard were both later modernized and greatly expanded. The piers were home to a dozen *Kilo*- and Improved *Kilo*-class diesel boats as well as half a dozen *Akula*-class nuclear attack boats and three SSGNs (submersible ship, guided missile, nuclear). All this activity soon made Vilyuchinsk the largest submarine facility in the Pacific. Added to that, since the Vilyuchinsk-Petropavlovsk area was so isolated, every bit of material needed to support the base and the towns supporting them had to come in by sea. The Mys Mayachnyy light at the mouth of the bay greeted an endless stream of ships that came and went from the busy harbor each day and at all hours.

The sun had just disappeared behind the mountains when the Improved *Severodvinsk*-class submarine *Yakutsk* surfaced a couple of kilometers off the channel entrance. As the dark shadows deepened, it melded in nicely with all the shipping vessels and the usual swarm of fishing boats.

Captain First Rank Ivgany Yurtotov donned his heavy, fur-lined parka and thick Arctic mittens before he climbed the long ladder up to his submarine's bridge. A week in the Sea of Okhotsk, exercising with the old destroyer *Admiral Panteleyev*, had been good training for his crew, but the ancient vessel had been anything but a challenging pretend adversary. Yurtotov shook his head. He could not imagine taking one of those ships up against one of the new American *Virginia*-class submarines. And especially if the Americans were shooting back.

He affectionately touched the cold steel hull of the *Yakutsk*. His submarine. Here was a ship that he would gladly and confidently take anywhere. His boat was the fastest, quietest, and most deadly submarine in the world. That was not merely his opinion. The rest of the world's military powers would, for the most part, agree.

Finally, Ivgany Yurtotov emerged into the cold, clear night. This long climb up the ladder had become more and more difficult for him lately, and he was almost always winded when he reached the bridge. But he would not complain.

Besides, once on the bridge, the chill air and view of his surroundings helped him catch his breath and forget about the burn in his thighs. The sea around him was alive with the lights of dozens of steamers and fishing boats. The sky overhead was lit up by seemingly a million stars defying an inky sky. The mountains lined up directly ahead of them, forming a dark, looming mass with only a few pinpricks of light—defensive installations of various types—breaking their blackness.

Yurtotov grunted. He was still getting acclimated to his new home after years of sailing in the Northern Fleet. However, the stark beauty and haunting isolation of this place certainly held an attraction.

"Captain, control room." The submarine captain jumped at the sudden noise of the loudspeaker. It had disturbed his quite pleasant reverie. "Harbor control has cleared us to enter port. We are to tie up on the west side of Pier Four at the Vilkovo base. They want to know if you require a pilot for entering port."

Yurtotov snorted. This was the locals' way of indicating that he was not yet accepted. Their strong hint that he was probably not competent to drive the *Yakutsk* through Avacha Bay's confined and congested waters. Well, it was time they learned different.

"Control room, inform harbor control that we do not need a pilot. Also tell them that we do not desire any tugboat assistance when we come alongside."

Yurtotov smiled. It was an opportunity to give these provincial yokels a lesson in ship handling, topped off with a seminar on the finer points of line handling.

Yurtotov calmly watched as his crew steered smoothly past Mys Mayachnyy light to starboard. Then Mys Stanitskogo to port. He then had to skirt an outbound deep-draft tanker before rounding the headland and steering to the west-northwest.

The Vilkovo submarine base was positioned on the back side of a point of land that jutted out into Avacha Bay and looked very much like the head and long neck of a sea turtle. Some other local mariners felt it more resembled a certain part of the male anatomy and had bestowed that name on the feature. But to get around it, Yurtotov would have to steer the *Yakutsk* through a fishing fleet heading out for a night's work as he brought his boat home. Of course, every fishing boat seemed to feel the need to draw closer to get a better look at the monster submarine. Yurtotov was required to either blast the ship's horn or yell continually on the bridge-to-bridge radio, commanding the fishing boats to stand clear.

When the Mys Kazak light was thankfully off his starboard beam, Yurtotov came to due west and then south to round the sea turtle's head and enter the Bukhta Krasheninnikova. Pier Four was the fourth pier from the west end of the waterfront.

Yurtotov brought the boat around until it was parallel to Pier Four and then used the ship's single screw to ease the vessel ahead. A mild wind was blowing down from the northwest, and he deftly took advantage of that bit of energy to nudge the boat closer to the pier as it inched forward. One final quick hit of an astern bell to stop the boat and he was home, safely, smoothly, impressively.

Yurtotov smiled as a couple of his linesmen jumped across to the pier and dropped their lines over the bollards. The evening's ship-handling lesson was complete. Yurtotov was only mildly disappointed that more observers had not been present to see and spread the word about the extraordinary seamanship skills of the submarine's crew and its highly experienced commanding officer.

Yurtotov had no idea that his ship handling was being closely observed from across the waters in the fishing hamlet of Vilyuchinsk. The observer had no opinion on the captain's skill or how deftly the crewmembers handled the big ropes. He carefully stored his high-power binoculars before he sent a coded text message that the *Yakutsk* was back in port.

Ψ

Luda Egorov stared out through the patches of frost on the window. The familiar vista never lost its hypnotic attraction for her. From her perch high up in the *Vladivostok News* building, she could easily look down on the Russian Navy's Far East Headquarters or, on an unusual clear day, see the horizon far out to sea. But she was most interested—and especially on this day—in the naval facilities, in its piers and buildings lined up along the north side of Golden Horn Bay. And the impressive cluster of structures beyond the Zolotoy Bridge where the naval shipyard's drydocks and construction ways filled much of the remainder of the harbor's edge.

Out her office window, she had been witness to the changes down there over the years. Once bustling, most of the piers were now lined with gray-hulled warships that only moved up and down with the tide, never out of the harbor. They were streaked with rust and stank of decay and rot. Few of those once useful ships were able to get underway, even if needed. Those among them that could still go to sea depended on their stricken sister ships for repair parts that were stripped from them as needed. Once all those had been scavenged, the donor vessels disappeared overnight, never to return. Egorov knew they were now either in the breakers, in salvage yards in India, or fifty miles out, on the bottom of the Sea of Japan, providing reefs for fish alongside the hulks of sunken World War II vessels.

As she sipped her tea and pretended to be editing a story coming together on her computer monitor, Luda Egorov still watched with considerable interest what little activity there was down there. The old destroyer —Egorov knew it had been operating out of Vlad for almost thirty years— the *Admiral Panteleyev*, slowly backed away from the pier and eased out into the open channel. Nothing noteworthy there unless put into context with other information Egorov had just learned and was so anxious to share.

The *Vladivostok News* building's location at the corner of Svetlanskaya and Ulitsa Aluetskaya Streets, as well as Egorov's corner office with the wide windows, also offered a superb view out over the blue waters of the Amurskiy Zaliv. The broad bay separated Vladivostok as well as the rest of the Muravyov-Amursky Peninsula from the mainland of the Russian state of Far East Asia. The bay seemed to always be dotted with hundreds of fishing boats. They were always in motion, too, either heading out into the rich fishing grounds of the Sea of Japan or returning, heavily laden with the fruits of the sea and their labor. In among those boats, huge container ships and car carriers eased their way into and out of the city's bustling terminal facilities. Egorov remembered reading somewhere that over a quarter of a million cars a year entered Russia through these terminals just from Japan alone. It helped now that the head of the harbor was kept ice-free year-round by the thermal discharge from the power plants' cooling towers.

A giant LNG (liquefied natural gas) tanker, lying low in the water with its burden of volatile fuel, slowly made its way down the Amurskiy Zaliv, heading out to the open sea. The Russian-flagged ship was the final link in a distribution system that connected power-hungry customers all around the Pacific Rim to the massive Kovykta and Chayanda gas fields of central

Siberia. That included a four-thousand-kilometer-long pipeline leading to a brand-new liquefaction plant and terminal just on the northern outskirts of Vladivostok.

Egorov often wondered why so many nations were willing to make a deal with the devil, just for the privilege of being able to buy its fossil fuel at ridiculously high prices. But, as she well knew, whoever had control of the oil spigots held sway over much of the world.

However, Egorov's thoughts and rapt attention were not centered on Russia's decaying surface navy nor the bustling sea trade arrayed before her. As the regional editor for the largest news media organization in the Russian Far East, she had spent the last twenty years carefully and delicately shaping the reported news to fit the narrative. That had allowed her to successfully maintain her job, her observation position, and a decent salary.

But it also gave her the opportunity to perform another far more crucial responsibility.

Luda Egorov, the rather frumpy-looking, late-middle-aged news maven had a very closely held secret, one of which no one else in this city had an inkling. Not her chief editor, who had never had a reason to question her journalistic abilities. Or loyalties. Not the paper's executive director, a man she rarely saw anymore now that he neared retirement. Not even her late husband of twenty-two years who had succumbed to pneumonia a few years before.

None suspected Luda Egorov was one of the Children of the Gulag. Even if they had, most of her contemporaries would have not known much about the Children. And maybe only slightly more about the gulags. That was simply a subject best left untouched and not discussed in modern Russia.

Egorov's *dedushka* (grandfather) had been a senior geologist for the hated Dalstroy, the Far North Construction Trust. That was the organization that ran the mines in the Russian Far East. They were also responsible for the construction of the roads, railroads, and port facilities that serviced and supported them. To maintain a sufficient labor force to build and operate these facilities in such an extremely harsh and remote wilderness, Dalstroy oversaw more than a thousand gulags across Far Eastern Russia and made certain they were occupied with adequate slave labor to get the job done.

Egorov had only faint early-childhood memories of her *dedushka*'s office and their fine house in the rude settlement of Magadan up on the Sea of Okhotsk. She and her parents lived with her grandparents while her father attended Far Eastern Polytechnical Institute in Vlad, studying geology with the assignment beginning with his entry into primary school to follow his father in the field, whether he wanted to or not.

But her grandfather had gotten tangled up in Russia's complex and dangerous post-Khrushchev political machinations. The entire family was quickly and quietly relegated to the gulags.

From the gulags to the top floor of the *Vladivostok News* building had been a very long, arduous, and dangerous road for Luda Egorov. The dangerous part was mostly because she was secretly serving as the Children's chief spy in Russia's most important far-eastern city, literally keeping a close eye on the Russian Navy. And patiently developing sources throughout the military establishment there.

And on this day, she had some vital information that she needed to relay to Ivan Dostervesky, as quickly but as securely as she could. She had just returned to her office after having lunch with Ilya Kozlov, the man who had served as governor of Russia's Far East Federal District since the seat of the district had been moved to Vladivostok in 2018. Kozlov just happened to have been a close friend of her departed husband. Ilya was rather fond of vodka, and as usual, he was plastered during their lunch before the main course was served. And also as usual, the governor was anxious to share his concerns with the woman he had been attempting to bed for years.

Today, Kozlov had been most vocal about what he saw as the unrealistic demands that Moscow was making on him way out here in the Far East. They seemed to think that every important decision revolved around central Eurasian Russia and that he was nothing more than a source of supply for everything they needed to solve their problems farther west. His was becoming a skeleton picked clean by the vultures at the Kremlin. The unexpected difficulties in the liberation of the Ukraine and now the new Islamic insurgency that had broken out along the Kazak border held all of the Kremlin's attention.

Ilya's voice had devolved into such a drunken slur before dessert that he was difficult to understand, but Luda was able to get enough to know that the Politburo had ordered him to ship all of the Far East Army's armor and heavy equipment from Vladivostok and other installations in the Far East to Omsk, in western Siberia, in an attempt to quickly and brutally put down the Islamic insurgents before most of the world even knew what was going on there. But that was not all. Practically all of his troops were to be sent as well. All the planes in the air force had already flown away, some to Omsk, some to support the Black Sea Fleet at Sevastopol. By the end of the month, the Far East District would be stripped bare of troops, with barely enough to maintain a rudimentary police force.

Another vodka and Ilya Kozlov had passed out, falling face first into the crumbs of his honey cake. Luda Egorov was certain from past experience that when he finally came around and sobered some, he would have no recollection of this conversation or the secrets he had spilled. She had never used his drunken revelations in her day job. But such indiscretions had been invaluable to the plans of the Children of the Gulag.

His rants did much to explain the unexpected troop movements that many of her sources were reporting. It was vital that she passed the information to Dostervesky, but he was traveling to meet the Americans. She had already decided that she would not share the intelligence with Boris Paserivich. For some reason, and she was not at all sure why, her well-honed instincts were telling her that not everything up there at Vesenny and with Dostervesky's number two man was what it seemed.

Patience was a virtue that had helped make Luda Egorov so valuable to her cause. And had also kept her alive. She would not abandon caution at this crucial point. She would wait until she could speak with Ivan Dostervesky about what she had learned and why she felt it was so crucial to the timing of their plan.

She was certain he would now agree that it was time to fire the starter's pistol.

6

Rear Admiral (lower half) Joe Glass paced the pier anxiously, working off the usual nervous energy but also looking for a particular spot. The stars on his uniform were pretty much brand-new. The name tag proclaiming him as Commander – Submarine Group Seven was even newer. The change of command had taken place only the previous week. He was still trying to find his way around the labyrinth that was Naval Base Yokosuka. And what better way to learn his way around than to walk around the sprawling base?

The 568-acre naval facility had originally been laid out for Imperial Japan by a French engineer way back in the 1860s. It had served as the Imperial Japanese Naval Arsenal right up to the end of World War II. Yokosuka then became what was now the US's largest and most capable overseas naval installation. And it served as home base for the mighty Seventh Fleet. But with everything being stuffed on a little finger of land jutting out into Tokyo Bay, it was difficult to miss the fact that the central part of the base was dominated by a huge rock that towered over everything. Buildings were necessarily stuck in every random corner of the base, so pedestrian navigation could be quite difficult. The only thing that Joe Glass knew for sure was that the piers—and the specific one he was looking for—were down at the water's edge.

He did not want to be late. Today, an old friend and battle buddy was bringing her spanking new *Virginia*-class submarine into port for her very first West Pac port call as skipper. Glass was determined to meet her at the pier and make her welcome. But first he had to find Berth Eight. So far, that effort had left him walking around in circles. He was quite aware that he had gone past the Navy Fleet Exchange building for the fourth time.

Glass suddenly spied a familiar black shape floating out there in the outer harbor. He glanced at his watch. Well, Henrietta Foster and the *Gato* were on time, but that was not surprising. If he hurried, now that he had some idea which direction he should be walking, Glass figured he could arrive at the pier just as the lines were coming across. And he could stand there looking as if he had been waiting for a long time.

A cold, drizzly rain began to fall as Joe Glass waited for the traffic light that would allow him to legally cross Howard Street. The usual heavy base traffic on this main artery would not stop for a jaywalker, even if he did sport stars on his collar. Then, when the light finally changed, he charged down Forrestal Street at a brisk pace. As expected, he saw the sign for Berth Eight just as the big black submarine was coming alongside.

Henrietta Foster stood tall on top of the submarine's sail as she watched her team secure the boat to the berth while calmly conveying instructions to the tug that was nudging USS *Gato* up against the foam-filled Yokohama fenders tied along the berth. He knew she was also sending instructions down to her team of line handlers that were deftly tying and securing the submarine to the pier.

Totally professional. But Glass expected nothing less from any crew commanded by Henrietta Foster. She had paid her dues all along what had been a challenging career path, beginning with being the daughter of a career Navy enlisted man, not seeing her dad for months at a time while she, her mother, and three siblings packed up and moved from one home port to another. Then being among the first women to be accepted into the submarine service. And one of the first African American women to achieve a command position.

When he could tell everything was under control—as a former submarine captain himself, Glass knew how busy and tense this maneuver could be—he cupped his hands around his mouth and yelled, "Commander Foster, welcome back to West Pac and the pointy end of the spear!"

Foster looked over, spotted him on the pier, and gave a wave when she recognized Joe Glass. "Thank you, Commodore...er...I mean, Admiral," she called back. "Glad to be back out here. *Gato*'s ready to kick butt."

"Don't doubt it," he responded. "And I may just have some assignments that will give you the chance to prove it."

Both watched as a pier crane swung the brow across and settled it over the gap between the pier and *Gato*'s broad deck.

"Admiral," Foster shouted, "why don't you come in out of the rain. It'll take another five minutes to wrap up here, and then I'll meet you in the wardroom for a cup of coffee."

Joe Glass waved his acceptance of the invitation, hopped across the brow, saluted the ensign now flying on the flagstaff at the boat's stern, and asked the topside sentry for permission to come aboard.

"XO, is that you?"

Glass looked across the deck to the line-handling team that was wrapping up squaring away topside. An older, burly man was moving toward him with a huge smile across his face. He snapped a sharp salute and said, "You don't recognize me, do you?"

Glass looked at the man closely. "Seaman Cortez?" he said questioningly. The man looked vaguely familiar, maybe like someone's older brother.

"Yes, sir," the sailor answered. "Only now it's Master Chief Cortez. Would you believe I'm COB here now? This boat is a world different than the old *Spadefish*, but sailors are always the same."

Glass chuckled as he remembered the gangly kid who was one of *Spadefish*'s best planesmen, when he was not in trouble for some prank or the other. "You got that right, COB. Congratulations on being senior babysitter on *Gato*."

As the two were discussing old times, the duty officer popped his head through the hatch.

The young officer saluted and said, "Admiral, welcome aboard the *Gato*. I'm Lieutenant Miller. The skipper asked me to escort you to the wardroom." He promptly dropped back down the ladder, leaving Glass to follow.

Joe Glass had just sat down at the wardroom table, hot cup of coffee in hand, when Henrietta Foster stepped in, grabbed her own mug, and plopped down in the seat at the head of the table.

"Hen, I can't tell you how great it is to see you with that command pin on," Glass told her, waving toward the gold star pinned just below Foster's name tag. "After all that fun you had on *Boise*, I knew you'd be back with your own boat pretty quick."

Foster had served as executive officer on USS *Boise*, and the sub and her crew had been a part of a truly harrowing showdown involving the Chinese People's Liberation Army Navy. Good had prevailed over evil, but not a hint of the story would ever show up in the *New York Times* or on CNN.

"Thanks, Admiral," Foster said over the rim of her cup, a sly smile on her face. "You have to admit the rain out there today is a little colder than the last time we talked. I do miss the old *Boise*. I told my mom it was like a classic sports car that you really love to drive, even if it's not the newest and flashiest."

"I know exactly what you mean," Glass said with a nod. "But you got to love this one, right off the showroom floor, right?"

"Not just yeah, but hell yeah! The *Gato* is a great boat, and she can do a lot of stuff that we didn't even dream of on the *Boise*. I think I'll keep her. Especially since I just proved I can back her into the garage."

"I'm just glad they're back to giving boats names that sound like submarines again," Glass said with a chuckle. "Guess they were running low on states to name them after. Now, you need to get your crew off on some R&R for a few days. MWR has set up some tours up to Tokyo and a barbeque over at the beach on Recreation Bay. And you should get your khakis off the boat and over to the Sanctuary. We need your crew well rested but ready to go in a hurry. You're underway at the end of the week, and I guarantee you aren't going to get much rest where you're going."

Foster sat up in her chair and gave Glass a long look. She knew him well enough to be aware something serious was in the works. And obviously she and her new boat were going to be a part of it.

"Any hints, boss?"

"Not today," Glass shot back. "Get your XO, Nav, and Ops over to my headquarters bright and early Friday morning, and we'll give you the whole dump." Glass took a quick look at his watch. "I hope we get a chance to catch up at some of the social things. But in the meantime, I need to hustle over to Atsugi and meet Admiral Ward. His flight in from DC is due in an hour."

So, Admiral Jon Ward was a part of whatever was going on. Director of Naval Intelligence. And whatever was about to happen had taken him from his office and brought him all the way to Japan.

Henrietta Foster's antenna was definitely up now. But she also knew Joe Glass had meant what he said. She would find out the details when the time came.

Glass took a final swallow from his cup, sat it on the counter, congratulated Foster again on her command, and headed topside.

Ψ

A bitterly cold wind rushed down out of Manchuria, only to be buffeted upward by the Hamgyong Mountains before slamming directly on top of Pyongyang like a frozen fist. Pellets of snow and ice were hurled down the wide, empty boulevards, harshly peppering anything in their way, before ultimately drifting up against the dull, gray Democratic People's Republic of Korea government buildings. Streetlights garishly illuminated the major thoroughfares and public squares, even though there were practically no cars to be seen there at six p.m. on a Wednesday night. Brilliant lights blazed from the windows of tall but empty office buildings and hotels. However, the service streets were dark, lit only by the full moon overhead when it occasionally broke through the frigid overcast.

A camouflage-green MD 500 helicopter flared out and settled onto a small helipad that had been built up out of the silt and muck dropped over the millennia by the Hapjang River as it flowed into the sluggish Taedong. The pilot expertly balanced his ancient craft against the blowing crosswind as he brought the bird down to land. Almost immediately, the passenger door swung open and a man emerged. Bent into the wind, he crossed the cement pad and slid into the warm interior of a waiting Mercedes limousine. Once the passenger was inside and the door was closed, the limo accelerated down the Hapjang River Road at a high speed. Meanwhile, the helicopter lifted off and disappeared into the snow to the east.

"Ambassador De, I trust your flight was smooth." The voice was that of a second passenger in the limo, in the front passenger seat, his face lit only by the dim lights from the dash. He turned to look at the newcomer in the back seat. "I am Dukkeobi. Minister Ja awaits you at the Kumsusan Guest Palace, exactly as your President Tan Yong requested. The minister asked that I escort you to the meeting you have solicited and which we are more than happy to host."

The man in the back seat was Nian Huhu De, Special Ambassador Plenipotentiary for the People's Republic of China. The North Korean could tell, even in the dim light, that the ambassador was not especially happy.

"The flight was the flight," he said angrily. "But you really must update your in-country air traffic control systems and integrate it with ours. Once we crossed the Yalu, your controller had the audacity to try to reroute our flight because some commercial flight from Japan was claiming priority. That, of course, would never happen with our system."

"Yes, Your Excellency," Dukkeobi acknowledged, trying to placate De. "I will see that the matter comes before the People's Committee on Air Safety." There was no chance that would ever happen. Both men knew it.

The limo turned sharply and then swung through a set of gates manned by a platoon of armed sentries. They all saluted as the black vehicle sped past them and up to a covered white-painted porte cochere with garish gold trim. An immaculately uniformed guard opened the passenger door as a phalanx of guards briskly came to attention, two rows of them in dress uniforms formally arrayed up the broad stairs despite the biting wind and bits of snow. An officer with a sword drawn stood at the foot of the stairs and made a sword salute. The guards snapped to "present arms."

Ambassador De stepped out and headed up the stairs without acknowledging the guards or their salutes. A short, heavyset man dressed in a gray morning coat and matching waistcoat stood at the head of the stairs watching the Chinese ambassador climb his way. As De approached, the man made a sharp bow and said, "Your Excellency, I am Gan Tong Ja, Foreign Minister for the Democratic People's Republic of North Korea. Welcome to my homeland."

De stopped to catch his breath as he listened, then snorted obvious disapproval.

"Where is Minister Jug-Eun? My directions were explicit that I was to speak with him. Only him."

Gan shook his head sadly and pursed his lips.

"I am afraid that Na-Ege Jug-Eun will not be available," the Foreign Minister explained. "He showed disrespect for the Supreme Leader."

De immediately understood. By using Jug-Eun's name alone, without his official title, meant that the minister was out of favor and, almost certainly, no longer among the living. And the simple phrase, "disrespect for the Supreme Leader," meant that the man's demise had likely been by execution for treason. These people really were ruthless.

"So be it," De acknowledged. "Let us go someplace where we can talk privately. Then I have an important message along with a request from President Tan that must be conveyed accurately and completely to the Supreme Leader and his closest advisors."

Minister Ja nodded, signifying he understood the importance of the matter to be discussed. Then he turned and led the ambassador into the Palace's grand reception area—now cold and empty but configured for a large gathering with a thousand tables set for a formal dinner—then across to a cramped office hidden in one corner. He motioned for De to take a seat at a small conference table, then took one for himself on the other side.

"Now, Excellency, please tell me what is so important as to cause a man of your stature to fly to our humble country in the throes of winter?" Ja asked as he poured them each a cup of soju. "I can assure you that anything spoken in this room is most secure. Our security is extreme, but even so, the room was swept for listening devices moments before you arrived."

De politely took the tiniest taste of the potent Korean liquor. Ja grandly knocked his back in true Korean fashion.

"Minister, we have learned that a group of dissidents who call themselves the Children of the Gulag are now in the process of fomenting a rebellion in the Russian Far East," Ambassador De slowly explained, as if communicating with someone of limited intelligence. "They plan to form a breakaway state while our Russian friends are otherwise occupied with their problems in the Ukraine and along the Kazakhstan border. Not to mention all their economic woes after straying so far from the true socialist path."

"And how do you and your nation suggest that we help our Russian brothers in this...?" Minister Ja began.

De raised a hand.

"Please, it is best that you allow me to continue, and it will all be clear in the end. These Children of the Gulag are, of course, seeking outside support for their rebellion and secession. They need arms, money, probably troops. But above all they will need acceptance on the world stage. Enough so Russia will have no other choice but to grant them sovereignty. And, as you know, such acknowledgment from Russia will be necessary for the dissidents to become their own recognized nation. We can expect the Americans to jump in, as is their wont whenever some group or another is crying out for freedom. The Japanese will also join in. They have coveted the Kurils and Sakhalin Island ever since they lost them to Russia at the end of the War of Resistance Against Japanese Aggression."

De took a small sip of the soju. He could tell he had raised the interest of this replacement minister.

"Yes. Please go on, Ambassador."

"President Tan looks upon this as an opportunity. As a chance to sow discord in the North Pacific region at America's expense and probably with some Russian embarrassment. He chooses to leave the impression with the world that the Chinese government will not be involved in this nasty business. He will make noises decrying the separatists and voicing support to our stalwart ally. But he wants our close friends and brothers in the DPRK to secretly provide arms and training to the Children. And to guide them to actions that are sure to cause Russia to respond with violence and America to end up properly chastened. Please understand. No trace of this assistance can be tracked back to the DPRK or to China. And for your nation's assistance in this matter, President Tan is willing to provide access to our sixth-generation fighter aircraft and to double our imports of steel and coal from the DPRK. We can also discuss some substantial increase in foreign aid, too, payable as soon as this ugly affair has run its course."

Ambassador De put down his cup of soju. He was mildly surprised to find that it was empty. Perhaps the bitter cold had left him thirsty. Or maybe the excited look on the face of the man across the table called for a bit of celebration.

"I will be most pleased to tell the Supreme Leader of your desires, Mr. Ambassador."

"Very well. Now, if you would please recall that horrid helicopter, I must promptly return to Beijing. President Tan requests that the Supreme Leader will provide an answer to his modest proposal no later than the end of this week."

7

Air traffic control cleared P-8 Poseidon Flight 853 for a final approach course of one-eight-zero and instructed the pilot to use runway one-eight. Joint US and Japanese Naval Air Facility Atsugi had only one set of parallel runways, and they were built due north and south. Flight 853 swung wide to the west over Mount Fuji and then lined up to make its turn onto final for runway one-eight. As the bird descended, the plane's commander requested ground taxi priority to Atsugi's VIP terminal. It was promptly acknowledged.

The Poseidon flared out and kissed the deck, marking the end of a very long flight nonstop from Whidbey Island in Washington State to the base, located southeast of Tokyo. With the prevailing headwinds, the trip this time had taken just over eleven hours. The dull gray aircraft taxied up to the VIP terminal and came to a halt precisely at the large Atsugi NAF emblem painted on the apron. As the jetway pushed up against the aircraft, the passenger hatch swung open. Admiral Jon Ward stepped out into the late afternoon sunshine, the only passenger to disembark from the aircraft, and took in a deep breath of the fresh, cool air. He had just started walking toward the terminal as Flight 853 turned away from the VIP terminal and taxied down to base operations.

He was barely inside the building when Joe Glass grabbed him in a bear hug.

"Damn, good to see you, Skipper!" Glass said as he stepped back and clapped the senior officer on the back. The two submariners had been friends and shipmates since they served together on the old *Spadefish* many years before, Ward as the commanding officer and Glass as his executive officer.

"Great to see you, too, XO," Ward answered with a broad grin. "Uh-oh... I mean, Admiral. I haven't had a chance to formally congratulate you since you pinned that star on. But you know I take full credit for preparing you."

"As well you should! How long you in town for?" Glass asked as he took Ward's bag from him. "The car's right outside. And I sure hope you don't have dinner plans for tonight. I've already found a place that serves the best curry udon in all of Japan and has a sake selection that just doesn't stop."

Ward smiled but held up a hand.

"Sorry, Joe. This is just a quick layover. The *Ronald Reagan* is sending a COD to pick me up, and it'll be here in half an hour. The Osprey is flying me out to the *Green Bay*. She's supposed to be somewhere just south of the Kurils."

He steered Glass toward an alcove in a corner of the terminal where they could not be overheard.

"Well, maybe next time," Glass told him.

"For sure. And there will be a next time. Okay, couple of things, Joe." Ward looked around, just to be sure. Nobody anywhere near them. "We're getting that DCS off of *George Mason*'s back and bringing it onboard the *Green Bay*. Then we'll return the *George Mason* to you for regular business. That switch should be completed by the time I get out there. It seems that Ivan Dostervesky will only meet with me, and if it weren't for the intermediary who put this guy in touch with me, I would have already told him to pound sand. But at least we'll see what he has to say that's so damned important before we get back in port. It's really hard to be interrupted on a gray hull lost in the broad Pacific."

"You said there were a couple of things, Skipper," Glass prompted.

Ward reached into his carrying case and pulled out a folder from which he extracted a satellite image. He handed it to Glass. "Yeah, this showed up in Petr yesterday."

The image showed a large, black-hulled submarine tied to a pier. There looked to be plenty of activity swirling around it.

"Russian boat," Glass said. "And from all the personnel, I'd say she's readying for underway. That looks like some kind of heavy transport vehicle there at the brow, and those are definitely guards of some kind around it. I'm not sure what cargo they're taking onboard that beast. Maybe groceries, maybe a weapons load."

"You wasted lots of years looking through periscopes, Joe," Ward said with a slight smile. "You would have made one hell of an intel weenie. You're right about the boat. Intel is IDing this as an Improved *Severodvinsk*-class. Best guess by all of us is the *Yakutsk*. That's the only Improved *Severodvinsk* unaccounted for. And they noticed the truck and guards, too. The real question is what is this bad boy doing all the way over here from the Northern Fleet. Something's up. May or may not have anything to do with this command powwow with Dostervesky. But answering tough questions is why God blessed us with submarines. I want you to get Henrietta and the *Gato* parked off Petr just as fast as you can, and let's see if we can find some of the missing pieces to this jigsaw puzzle."

Glass nodded. "Got it. We'll have her underway tomorrow, just as soon as we can load groceries."

Simultaneously, the two officers heard the roar of a pair of massive turboprops and turned to see a CMV-22 Osprey taxiing up to the VIP terminal.

"Joe, looks like my rather noisy ride is here. I'll take you up on that curry udon when I get back."

Ward shook Glass's hand and turned to step out of the alcove. He stopped and looked back.

"Seriously, congratulations, Joe. I'm damn proud of you. But I'm not one bit surprised."

Ψ

It was an especially dark night, made even more so by the heavy cloud cover that curtained out a full moon and the soupy fog that dimmed the pier lights at the Russian submarine base at Petr. Everything was bathed in a hazy gloom.

Even so, the pier was bustling. A working party was topping off the diesel fuel for the Improved *Lada*-class diesel submarine *Yaroslavl* as she sat moored at the end of Pier Sierra Two. At the same time, another working party was efficiently loading the submarine with stores, shuttling them on hand-trucks from a refrigerator truck that was parked at the head of the pier. A third group struggled to remove the shore-power cables that had been supplying the submarine with electricity while she was docked there. The boat's throbbing diesel engines only added to the cacophony of sound while their exhaust merged with the fog.

Senior Lieutenant Matvey Preobrazhensky had just finished the myriad tasks necessary for a successful early-morning underway. He was dead tired and really needed to go lie down for a while. He glanced at his watch as he headed toward his stateroom. Maybe there was time to catch a quick nap. But it was 0300 already, and the new commanding officer, Captain Third Rank Andrei Turgenev, had left instructions that all was to be ready for an 0800 underway.

Preobrazhensky sighed as he ran through a mental checklist. Of course, there was no time for a refreshing nap. Not even a quick one. Not if he wanted to stay in Captain Turgenev's good graces. The captain had taken command of the diesel boat only the week before. This was to be his first underway with this submarine. Now was the time to make points with his commander, not get off to a bad start with him. Turgenev's demanding reputation preceded him. Preobrazhensky was certain that if the underway did not go smoothly, he would very quickly be counting blankets at the Arctic underwater research station on Kotelny Island. The lieutenant shivered at the very thought and, exhausted or not, headed back to the bridge to continue to observe from there.

It continued to be a mundane underway. The crew was doing everything by the book. Preobrazhensky had little to oversee by now but hours to kill. From his high perch, he used his binoculars to scan other activity within view. It was surprising how few boats were here now in this once thriving facility. At the moment, the only lit-up and active submarine he could see besides his own was the newly arrived *Yakutsk*, docked over at Pier Four. He was mildly curious about what that boat was even doing in Petr, but he had long since given up being astounded by the decisions of the Russian Navy.

Just then, a black-painted Ural-4320 heavy-duty six-by-six truck lumbered down the pier. It was speeding much too fast, causing the working parties to scatter out of its way as it growled past them. Then it came to a halt right at the head of the brow. The truck's tailgate swung down, and a dozen combat troops quickly piled out.

The soldiers were in full combat gear and heavily armed. The man who appeared to be their leader wore the stars of a naval captain lieutenant. But he otherwise bore no unit designation. He marched over the brow and up to the topside guard, where he demanded that the officer in charge be summoned immediately. But Preobrazhensky was already on the way.

Four members of the team quickly set up a cordon around the truck and the submarine's brow, roughly shouldering the crewmembers aside. The remaining troops got busy unloading the truck. By the time Senior Lieutenant Preobrazhensky made his way to the brow, the team's gear was stacked on the submarine's deck and the truck was backing away down the pier.

"What is this?" Preobrazhensky asked as he walked up to the towering combat-clad officer. "Who the hell are you, and what do you think you are doing on my submarine?"

The officer looked at him for a long moment with no emotion on his face whatsoever. Then he shoved a wad of official documents at the submarine officer.

"You will have your men take our equipment down to the torpedo room. And be careful. Some of it is quite...delicate." He spread his hands, fingers extended, indicating it was explosive. "You will be taking us to sea with you for a very important mission. Were you not briefed by Submarine Flotilla Headquarters?"

Preobrazhensky shook his head, frowning. "We have heard nothing. Only that we are getting underway for a routine training mission."

The submarine officer was perplexed, but such foul-ups were not unheard of. Best thing, he decided, was to keep this rather aggressive officer happy until Captain Turgenev arrived and could learn more about this important mission. He could then sort it out with headquarters. At this time of night, there would be no one at that big gray building anyway. Not even someone who would answer the phone, let alone figure out this problem.

Still, it was concerning. Who were these people, and why were they so pushy?

The officer snatched back his orders and grunted. "Maybe you have heard of the 101st Combat Swimmers Detachment of the Spetsnaz? You can call me Mark. And, Lieutenant, that is all that you have clearance to know at this point. You are not authorized to say anything about our presence to anyone. Do you understand?"

Preobrazhensky noticed that the officer's hand rested on his holstered pistol.

The Spetsnaz unit was famous and much feared, especially in the Russian Far East. Rumors abounded that their original training camp had been adjacent to a gulag. There they would "recruit gladiators" from among the prisoners for to-the-death combat training. These were not men to be trifled with.

Twenty minutes later, the combat team and their gear were safely ensconced in the *Yaroslavl's* torpedo room while the officer known as Mark stood in the open bridge cockpit atop the submarine's sail. From there, he was able to observe everything that transpired on the pier. No one in the sub's crew questioned anything as the team unpacked their weapons and quietly moved about the ship as if they belonged there. Indeed, they were given as wide a berth as possible in the constricted interior of the submarine. If the captain or Lieutenant Preobrazhensky wanted them to know anything, they would have told them.

Captain Turgenev arrived promptly at 0730. He marched across the brow and was greeted by Senior Lieutenant Preobrazhensky topside.

"Captain, all preparations are complete to get underway," Preobrazhensky told him with a snappy salute. "All stores and fuel are loaded. The batteries are fully charged. Electrical power is on the diesels. And our riders are all onboard."

Turgenev gave Preobrazhensky a questioning look. "What riders? We are not supposed to have any riders for this underway."

"Captain, they arrived early this morning," the Duty Officer tried to explain. "Their orders are very highly classified. Perhaps their officer can explain this to you."

"Very well," Turgenev grunted. Perhaps this was a test of some kind. Or another snafu. They had become aggravatingly common of late. "Where is this officer?"

Preobrazhensky glanced up at the sail. Mark was no longer there.

"He was up there. On the bridge. Perhaps he saw you arrive and is now down in the control room waiting for you to come aboard so he can explain his mission."

Turgenev harrumphed, checking his watch yet again. "Or perhaps this is another classic foul-up from the flotilla. We can sort this out yet. Let us see, and at least if they are not supposed to be on our vessel, we can still get them off-boarded and be underway on time."

The submarine captain dropped down the ladder into the control room. There, he was immediately met by a GSh-18 nine-millimeter pistol. Its snout was leveled at a spot directly between the captain's eyes.

"Good morning, Captain," the man holding the pistol said with surprising warmth. It was the commander of the troops who had come aboard. The one who called himself Mark. "You, your fine submarine, and its crew are now prisoners of the Children of the Gulag. You will do exactly as we say, and you will be treated courteously." The warmth vacated his voice. "But should you cross us, you will die. The choice is entirely yours. Now, shall we get underway? We have much to accomplish together."

Ψ

Jim Ward settled back in the command chair and began the process to bring the DCS back to life. The mini submarine had been sitting like an inert lump on the deck of its much bigger sister sub, the *George Mason*, for the past week, doing little but drawing electrical power from the nuclear submarine. Ward and copilot Willy Duncan spent a day changing out the aluminum alloy anodes on the DCS's aluminum-seawater batteries.

Unlike a more common lead-acid or a lithium-ion battery, the aluminum-seawater type could not simply be recharged after every use. When they were discharged, the available aluminum in the anodes was used up, and they had to be replaced. Fortunately, the geniuses who designed this vessel made certain it was a rather simple procedure to remove the old anodes and bolt in fresh ones. Such an easy one that Duncan did not even bother to ask his commander the usual rhetorical question that began with, "Skipper, did we go through BUD/S and become Navy SEALs so we would have to...?"

After that quick swap, the DCS was fully ready to go again, and the SEALs had nothing to do but eat, work out, and enjoy submarine life. But that relaxing little cruise was about to come to an abrupt end. It was time to ferry their mysterious passenger on to his destination. One that now appeared to be out there on the surface of the storm-swept North Pacific.

Ward finished his scan of the control console. All looked normal. Glancing over at his copilot, he asked, "How are we coming with the check-list, Willy?"

"Ready to energize systems," Duncan replied. "Introducing seawater into the batteries."

He reached over and hit a button on his panel. As seawater flooded into the battery cells, the power display immediately started showing current flowing from the battery stack under their feet. He scrolled through a couple of screens on his auxiliary display until he got to the main electrical distribution command screen.

"On own-ship power. Ready to divorce power from the *GM*," he reported.

Ward grunted. "Now if our passenger would just get his butt safely aboard, we could be on our merry way. You have the latest vectors to the *Green Bay* ARG's MODLOC?"

ARG was "Amphibious Ready Group," and it would be at its MODLOC, or "Miscellaneous Operational Details, Local Operations." The military would never revert to plain language when more complicated terms and cryptic anagrams could be concocted. The ARG was just hanging around at one point in the ocean.

Duncan replied, "The ARG is MODLOC at forty-three-point-six-eight-seven north, one-five-eight-point-seven-one east. That puts her seven miles due east of our location. *George Mason* reports solid sonar contact *Green Bay*. Vectors locked into the nav system and confirmed."

As Duncan was finishing his report, Ivan Dostervesky popped up through the loading hatch.

"Apologies, gentlemen," the Russian said as he dropped into a seat behind the two SEALs. "I was thanking Captain Edwards for his gracious hospitality. Are we ready to go?"

Ward barely nodded as he keyed his microphone. "*George Mason*, this is *Little Boy*. Ready to launch. Confirm launch speed and depth."

"*Little Boy*, *George Mason*, confirm depth two hundred, speed zero. You have permission for launch. Safe journey. It's a tad rough up there."

Ward disconnected the lock mechanism and smoothly lifted the DCS up and away from the motionless submarine. He settled out on a course of almost due east, directly toward the rendezvous point with the *Green Bay*. At three knots they had a journey of a little over two hours ahead of them. Time to sit back and relax with a cup of coffee.

Right on cue, Willy Duncan produced a thermos and poured a hot brew for each of the three of them. Dostervesky pulled a bottle of vodka from his pack and dumped a generous dollop into his cup. The two SEALs politely demurred on his offer of a slug of the stuff.

As Ward steered the DCS toward the group of warships, he gradually brought the little submersible up to one hundred feet. Even at that depth, it was easy to feel the pitch and heaving of the stormy seas. As best he could determine from his sonar displays, the seas were coming from the northwest, probably straight out of Siberia. That would be a brutally cold breeze up there.

Willy Duncan called out, "Have acoustic data link with *Green Bay*. They are at rendezvous location. Reporting seas running five to seven feet out of the northwest, sea state four to five. They are requesting your intentions."

Nice, Ward thought as he ran his hands through his hair. Even those surface navy guys were worried about snatching the DCS out of the water in these conditions. These sea states were right on the hairy edge. A wrong move at the wrong instant could easily spell disaster. The *Green Bay* was an LPD—a "landing platform dock" designed to dock and transport smaller amphibious vessels or carry landing craft and troops for a land assault— that displaced over twenty-five thousand tons. The DCS displaced about twenty-eight tons. It was easy to determine who would win out if they both tried to occupy the same space at the same time. The law of max gross tonnage always prevailed.

The safe thing would be to head back to the *George Mason* and wait out the storm. But his Russian passenger had shared enough with Jim Ward to let him know that some mighty big plans depended on this meeting happening as quickly as possible. And within a very specific timeline. But the Russian still had not shared with young Ward exactly with whom that meeting would be.

"Let's go up and take a look," Ward finally said as he tilted the nose of the little sub up to periscope depth. Then, in his best airline pilot voice, he continued, "Make sure all tray tables are in their upright and locked position and all seat belts are fastened. We may encounter some unexpected turbulence."

The DCS's periscope depth was much shallower than a typical submarine's, only about twenty feet. As a result, the little vessel was much more at the mercy of the waves. And before Ward knew what was happening, he experienced just that.

The surface forces grabbed the submarine and forced it upward. The DCS bobbed on the surface, broached, high if not dry. The storm tossed the little boat all the way up to the wave tops and then dropped it down into the deep valleys. The periscope picture on the display alternately showed leaden, gray skies and greenish-gray seas, interspersed with driving rain, bits of sleet and snow, and frothy sea spray.

Ivan Dostervesky had quickly turned green and was beginning to heave. Jim Ward tossed him a plastic bag.

"Don't you dare barf on my deck, shipmate," he growled. "Use the bag." He turned to Duncan. "Willy, get radio comms with the *Green Bay*. Find out if they have the well deck flooded down and the doors open yet. We can't stay out here long."

"Boss, you sure you want to do this?" Duncan asked, even as he lined up the comms system to talk to the LPD.

"*Little Boy*, this is *Green Bay* landing officer." The voice crackled loudly over the speaker. "We're on course three-one-two to give you as much lee astern as we can. Waves running four feet in the lee. You picked a bad day to pay us a visit. Decision is yours on landing."

The bigger ship had lined up to theoretically give the DCS a patch of relatively calmer waters directly behind her. But not that much calmer.

"*Green Bay*, *Little Boy*, we are coming in," Ward informed the landing officer. "My best speed is five knots. Request you make four knots."

He then used the periscope image to line his boat up on the LPD. He could barely make out the lee, the calmer water that the landing officer promised. But he could easily see the massive ship's stern regularly pitched high overhead until the open stern doors looked like a massive dark maw. Then the ship dropped down until it was almost lost in the waves, much lower in the water than the mini sub.

"Willy, we're only going to get one shot at this," Ward said through clenched teeth as he shoved the steering stiff-stick over to the left to counter the waves that insisted on ramming his bow to starboard. He was using his arms to push with all his might, even though he knew that the hydraulically controlled stiff-stick would not respond any better than if he used his fingertips. "And we don't want to dent the taxpayers' little submersible toy."

"Doing my best, Skipper," Duncan answered. "Bow thrusters are online. I'm using them to help push the bow around."

The pair fought the boat to keep it headed directly toward the LPD's well deck, located at its stern. Gradually they closed the distance until the ship's open stern door filled their entire field of view.

"Willy, tell the landing officer to talk us in and for him to be really chatty," Ward instructed. "When we cross the sill, we're going to lose the relative one-mile-per-hour speed difference. He's going to need to tell us exactly when we cross the sill since it will be out of our range of view. We'll need to back down hard or we'll find ourselves up the ramp parked among the Humvees they're hauling."

The landing officer, stationed on a platform right at the stern door, as requested, began a steady litany of distance and bearings for the DCS as Ward crept up on the rear end of the pitching surface ship. Sweat poured from the SEAL's brow as he concentrated on keeping his boat aimed directly at the center of the door, despite all the natural forces out there that were trying to propel him sideways.

Finally, the landing officer yelled that they were crossing the sill, the back edge of the big water-filled hole in the ship's stern. Ward jammed the throttles full astern just long enough to bring the DCS to a halt in the "swimming pool." He could only hope a wave did not decide to wash them back out, toward the structures on the ship's deck or back into the angry Pacific.

But they had landed in the right spot. Ward had the motors idling as lines captured and pulled the little submarine over against the port wing wall of the landing well. The vessel's stern door was swinging shut as Ward and Dostervesky popped out of the DCS upper hatch. Crewmen helped Ward across to the wing wall and then returned to assist the very shaky— and still green-complexioned—Russian as he made his way.

A junior officer waited to escort Ward and Dostervesky up to the commodore's cabin, leaving Willy Duncan and the landing officer to put the DCS to bed.

Young Jim Ward entered the commodore's mess—the amphibious ready group's commodore's dining area—to quite a surprise. There was his father, seated with the ARG commanding officer, leisurely enjoying a cup of coffee. It was not the first time his dad had shown up to unexpectedly greet his son in some odd spot or the other on the globe. Most of the time, it was official business. The world's trouble spots seemed to attract the attention of both warriors.

The elder Ward jumped up and grabbed his son in a bear hug.

"Damn, it's great to see you!" He pulled away to look him up and down, as if inspecting for damage. Then, jokingly, he added, "After watching that landing, I see why you became a SEAL and not a submarine driver."

Jim Ward looked confused for a second about his father's presence here. Then the light came on.

"So, you are the senior official that is holding this meeting in the middle of a sea blizzard. I should have guessed."

"I keep turning up like a bad penny, I guess," the admiral said. "It's been a good trip so far. I got to spend three minutes with my old XO Joe Glass, and now I get the briefest of hugs from my one and only boy. Who would have thought? Now, who's your friend here?"

The admiral nodded toward the disheveled Russian standing there unsteadily next to the SEAL.

"Dad, let me introduce to you Ivan Dostervesky, representing, as I understand it, a group called the Children of the Gulag. Ivan, this is Admiral Jonathan Ward, Director of Naval Intelligence, United States Navy. I believe, based on recently acquired knowledge, that he is the man you risked life and limb to come out here to meet with."

"Yes. Yes, it is," Dostervesky said, his voice now a bit stronger. "We have much to discuss, sir. And so very much depends on our conversation."

Jon Ward glanced at his son. They might have just had as much of a visit with each other as this trip would allow.

"Thank you, Commander," the elder Ward said to his son. "And thank you and your team for the fine job in completing the mission successfully under, as usual, less than ideal conditions." The admiral turned back to Dostervesky. "Let's head into the flag cabin. We will be more comfortable there and won't be disturbed."

The two men had turned and were walking away when Admiral Ward suddenly stopped and turned back toward his son, who was already leaving the mess.

"Wait a sec, Commander." Jon Ward pulled a small wrapped box from his bag. "Damned if I didn't almost forget. Your momma sent these for you. Your favorite. Russian tea cakes she baked herself."

With a broad grin, the SEAL double-timed back to grab the box. And the admiral took advantage of the situation to again give his boy a big hug.

"Hey, I know you couldn't tell her you would see me, right?"

"I told her with a wink and a smile that I might accidentally bump into you out here somewhere, so just in case..."

"Thanks, Dad. I love you. Tell Mom thanks."

"You be careful out there, son. I love you." They parted, and Jon Ward rejoined the Russian. "And don't worry, Ivan. I have another box of the tea cakes for us. A wise expert on all things military once said, 'No important discussion can be fruitful without proper accompanying sustenance.'"

It took a moment for Dostervesky to translate in his head. "Oh. Sun Tzu? Churchill?"

"No. Another great expert on war and warriors. Ellen Ward. My wife. Jim's mother."

8

Berth Eight, Fleet Activity, Yokosuka, Japan, was alive with hustle and bustle. A steady stream of trucks shuttled from the NAVSUP Fleet Logistics Center warehouses down to the berth where most of the *Gato*'s crew lined up for an old-fashioned stores-loading party. Modern submarining had still found no better way to quickly load and store supplies on a boat. A line of men passed boxes and crates of foodstuffs off the trucks, across the brow from pier to sub, and then down the hatch into the depths of the vessel. There, more men rushed to stow everything in an orderly, well-planned fashion, although the process did not resemble either description. By the time they were done, all of the freeze boxes, chill boxes, and dry storerooms would be packed from deck to overhead. At that point, they would start using "alternate storage locations." The showers would be filled with potatoes while number-ten cans of food would be stacked up and cover the decks. The crew would literally eat their way back down to the decks, but in the meantime, they would be walking on their suppers.

As boxes of green beans and five-gallon cans of ground coffee were man-handled down into the submarine, technicians from the Fleet Repair Activity were completing another crucial chore, working alongside *Gato*'s sonarmen to make absolutely sure that the boat's primary sensor was working at its best. Senior Chief Jim Stumpf sat reared back on his chair, watching as his team huddled with the technicians. They were flipping between screens on their handheld devices as they bounced back and forth between what their IETMs (*Interactive Electronic Tech Manual*) said they should be seeing and what was actually showing up on their BQQ-10 sonar displays. So far, the system was passing perfectly. However, for some reason, they were taking longer than Chief Stumpf knew they should be. Then he remembered back to his time as a young sonarman, back on the *Cheyenne*. In those days, if there was a stores-loading party topside, he would make certain to drag out the testing so as not to have to be a part of the heavy lifting going on up there.

Stumpf smiled as he stood and headed out toward the chiefs' quarters. The sub's CO, Henrietta Foster, stepped into the control room just as he was leaving.

"How's the sonar grooming going?" Foster asked. "You going to be able to button it up for a seventeen-hundred underway?"

Stumpf chuckled and nodded toward his team. "Skipper, I expect they'll be able to button everything up just about the same time the stores load is done. Funny about that interlock, isn't it?"

Foster smiled. She knew exactly what the sonarman was saying. Those sailors preparing the ship for underway could avoid the more strenuous loading of stores if the final steps of their assignments were completed about the same time as that job was accomplished. "Sailors never change. You seen the COB?"

"Topside kicking butt last time I saw him," Senior Chief Stumpf answered. "But I'd bet he's probably in the chief's quarters by now, hiding the last of the pistachios."

Foster knew precisely what he was implying there, too. All down through history, it was rumored that the chiefs had a tendency to hide the best of the "gedunks" (treats) during stores loads for later personal use or crew motivation through judicious distribution at the right time. Of course, no one had ever been able to prove such a thing.

"Well, go find him and tell him to meet me, the XO, Eng, and Nav in the wardroom at thirteen hundred." Foster turned without waiting for acknowledgment and headed in the general direction of her stateroom.

Ψ

The wardroom clock chimed two bells for thirteen hundred as Henrietta Foster stepped into the compartment, poured herself a cup of coffee, and took her place at the head of the table. The Chief of the Boat, Master Chief Jesus Cortez, was right behind her and grabbed a seat at the opposite end of the table. The XO, Lieutenant Commander Eric Householder, was already seated at Foster's right hand. The Navigator, Lieutenant Sharon Woolsey, had a seat on the XO's left. The Weapons Officer, Lieutenant Rick Sanson, sat next to the Nav. No one had ever assigned seats for these onboard meetings in the submarine's wardroom. It was simply the way it always had been on this and most every other boat in the US Navy.

Foster looked around with an irritated expression on her face. She turned to Householder. "Okay, XO, where's the Eng? Did he not get the word on this meeting?"

Householder nodded. "He did. He just called. The nukes are bringing steam into the engine room. M Div repacked the port hundred-and-fifty-pound steam reducer during the shutdown. He wants to make absolutely sure it's holding before he comes forward."

"Okay," Foster grumbled. But she understood. Just another of those less-than-glamorous chores that had to be done and that never got mentioned by the Navy's recruiters on their PowerPoints. "We can brief the transit over to Petr now. But as Senior Watch Officer, he really needs to be here for the mission brief."

But just then, Lieutenant Commander Steve Hanly, the Engineer, burst into the wardroom and plopped down breathlessly in the empty chair to Foster's left. "Sorry, Skipper. We have steam in the engine room. The reducer is holding fine. We should be on ship's power and divorcing from shore power in about half an hour. I wanted to be sure before this meeting."

Foster nodded. "Good. Underway is at seventeen hundred. You and your guys ready to support it?"

Hanly, a Mississippi native, fell into his best Southern drawl. "God willin' and the crick don't rise. Everything's lookin' fine as frog hair so far."

Foster allowed herself a small grin before turning to Woolsey. "Nav, your people ready?"

Sharon Woolsey answered in her usual crisp New England accent. "Yes, ma'am. Courses are all laid in, nav systems up and operating normally. We're ready to go."

"Weps?" Foster asked, turning to Rick Sanson.

"Yes, ma'am. All systems groomed and checked out. We're ready to go."

"COB?"

Jesus Cortez looked up from his coffee cup. "Skipper, stores load is almost wrapped up. Just about everybody has made it back from the recall."

"Just about? Who's missing?"

"We still have two sailors that haven't checked in. Reilly and Gomez headed up to Tokyo and haven't answered either cell phone calls or texts."

A look of concern crossed Foster's face. "Well, I'd say they have about four hours to get back aboard before they miss movement. COB, call the base master-at-arms and see if they can help us find our wayward sheep. Maybe start by checking every brig between here and Tokyo."

"Not those two, Skipper. They're good boys. We'll find them. Probably on a sightseeing bus or something." Master Chief Cortez stepped out of the wardroom to make the call while the Nav started the mission brief.

She projected on the big screen a chart of the Petropavlovsk area on the Pacific Ocean side of the lengthy Kamchatka Peninsula. Everyone noticed that the active volcanoes that ringed the city were marked on the map.

"After we do a thorough ASW sweep of our op area, we will plant our A-DSTP comms buoy here." Woolsey tapped a spot out in deep water about thirty miles southeast of the box labeled "Op Area." "That should give us covert comms coverage for the entire zone. Then we station ourselves in the Avachinskiy Zaliv, right at the harbor mouth, snuggled up close to the twelve-mile limit. Our mission is to wait and watch for that Improved *Severodvinsk*, the *Yakutsk*, to come out and play." A grainy image of a Russian sub tied to a pier popped up on the screen. "This guy is our target. This is the *Yakutsk*. Fourteen thousand tons, four hundred and forty feet long. Intel is giving him a top speed in excess of forty knots and a max operational depth in excess of two thousand feet. He has ten torpedo tubes and can carry thirty-two *Kalibr* missiles in four vertical tubes, pretty much like ours."

Foster held up a hand, interrupting the Nav. "And he is really, really quiet. Not a customer we'd want to treat lightly. When he comes out—and somebody is convinced he will and soon—we'll really need to be on our toes. This guy plays in the big leagues. We need to slip in behind him and follow him to wherever he's going and see what the hell he's doing there. Our mission is to find out why he left the Northern Fleet and suddenly showed up out here. Any questions?"

They all shook their heads, even as they exchanged curious glances. Foster stood and picked up her coffee cup.

"All right, then. Let's get *Gato* out to sea and put our new ride to work. It's time for us to have some fun."

But she had lost her smile by the time she stepped over and refilled her coffee cup.

Ψ

The Spetsnaz officer—still known only as Mark to the crew of the Russian submarine—sat to one side in the *Yaroslavl's* cramped control room. From there, he watched every move while pointedly holding his automatic pistol in his lap. He had not moved from this seat in hours. Nor had he shown any signs of fatigue or inattention. Meanwhile, the Russian crew of the *Kilo*-class submarine did their best to give a wide berth to what they had decided was a terrorist. Members of Mark's own team would periodically approach their vigilant leader, exchange a few whispered comments, and then go off to carry out whatever his orders had been.

Captain Third Rank Andrei Turgenev sat on a similar bench a few feet removed from Mark's perch. The submarine captain was quite sure that Mark and his Spetsnaz pirates meant to dispose of him and his crew just as soon as possible. For now, it appeared that the killers did not have the expertise to drive his submarine, nor were they taking any opportunity to learn how. That meant that for now, his crew was needed and probably safe. But for how long? At some point, they would almost certainly become disposable. And the intruders seemed well armed and trained, surely able to take out the sub's crew.

Mark had kept the boat's captain prisoner on the bench since passing the Mys Mayachnyy light at Petropavlovsk harbor's mouth. Then, with the landmark disappearing on the horizon behind them, dropping below the surface of the Pacific Ocean, Mark ordered the captain to make a series of maneuvers obviously intended to throw off any possible pursuers.

By the time Mark was satisfied that they were well and truly alone, darkness had fallen. The uninhabited rocky coast of the Kamchatka Peninsula loomed darkly only a thousand meters off their starboard side. The surf crashing against the high cliffs made the perfect wall of noise in which to hide an escaping submarine. The roar of the breaking waves blanked out any pursuers' sonar. At the same time, the nearby cliffs made radar searches futile.

Finally, Mark slowly rose to his feet and stretched. He waved his pistol at Turgenev, signaling that he should also stand. He then motioned the captain over to the navigation charts near the middle of the control room. Mark pointed to a spot on the map that depicted the entrance into a deep, narrow fjord that opened away from the sea several miles further down the coast.

"Captain, you will arrive at the mouth of Bukhta Russkaya precisely at midnight. You will stay exactly one kilometer off the coast as you steam from here down to that point. Do you understand my directions, sir?"

Turgenev nodded. The instructions were clear and easy enough. The coast was quite rugged, and remaining only a thousand meters away from the rocky shore would require careful and precise navigation, but they could approach their destination slowly. They had almost five hours before midnight, and the fjord was only ten miles away as the seagull flies. Of course, the many headlands and bays they would necessarily have to shadow would mean that they would end up traveling almost twenty miles.

"And may I ask what you want us to do when we arrive?" Turgenev asked.

"You will receive your directions when the proper time comes," Mark growled. "For now, you will simply follow my orders precisely."

Turgenev was uneasy, both with taking commands from someone not his superior in rank and also having them come from a person he now considered to be a hijacker. He turned to order Senior Lieutenant Matvey Preobrazhensky to make the necessary course and speed changes to arrive at Bukhta Russkaya at midnight. Clearly the hulking Spetsnaz lieutenant—

if indeed he was a Spetsnaz lieutenant—intended to make a rendezvous with someone else inside the isolated and lonely fjord, but what did that mean for Turgenev and his crew? The submarine commander did not like the only conclusions he could possibly draw.

The *Yaroslavl* pitched and yawed as the surging sea tried mightily to drive the submarine into the granite cliffs like another piece of driftwood. Lieutenant Preobrazhensky spent the entire five hours with his eye to the periscope, trying his best to pierce the black night. He sensed more than saw the rocky shore so close to the submarine's starboard side. Only an occasional streak of white indicated where waves pounded land. Sweat poured off his brow and down into his eyes as he constantly ordered speed and course changes to thwart the sea's relentless grip.

The control room's digital clock rolled over midnight just as the *Navigatsiya Stashy Michman*, Quartermaster Master Chief, called out that they had reached the entrance to Bukhta Russkaya. As ordered. The harrowing voyage was over. Maybe.

Mark shoved Turgenev to the periscope so the two of them could confirm where they were. Mark motioned Turgenev to take the first look. Turgenev slowly spun it in a complete circle. Sure enough, the narrow fjord stretched out for about five kilometers of calm black water ahead. Its mouth, though, was no more than a kilometer wide. Steep, treacherous granite cliffs lined both sides of the rectangular box. Assuredly, there were more cliffs blocking the far end, but they were now hidden from view.

Mark nudged Turgenev aside and peered through the scope. He looked long and hard down the center of the Bukhta Russkaya before stepping away. Then he ordered, "Proceed slowly down the exact center of the waterway. Stop when you are one kilometer from the end, and then surface this ship."

It took over an hour to journey down the slim fjord and then to surface the submarine. The water was glassy calm and the winds had dropped to little more than a cold zephyr when Turgenev and Mark reached the bridge and looked out at their surroundings. Tranquil as it was, Turgenev's sea sense told him that there was a storm brewing. He could smell the wind and snow already barreling down on them from out of the Arctic. By sunrise, the seas would be pitching and this narrow sliver of water would be a maelstrom, with the submarine in danger of being dashed against the granite walls.

Then both men saw a light flash three times from the dark beach. Mark produced a flashlight and answered the signal.

"Now, Captain, order your crew to open the deck hatch and help my men aboard once they are alongside the submarine," he ordered. "They will be here in five minutes. Tell all your men to dress warmly. They will soon be topside and will be in the elements for a while."

The terrorist had no more than finished when Turgenev spotted a pair of rigid-hull inflatable boats leaving the beach and heading arrow-straight for them across the short stretch of water. As the RHIBs approached, Turgenev counted ten to fifteen men aboard each. The boats pulled up alongside the *Yaroslavl*, and its passengers swarmed aboard. They quickly disappeared down the hatch before Turgenev could get much of a look at them, but they appeared quite comfortable walking on the submarine's slick, round hull. Men of the sea. Almost certainly experienced submariners.

If his conclusion was valid, he and his crew would now have no further value to the pirates.

"Captain, I have to request that you go below," Mark stiffly ordered. "I suggest that you change into your warmest uniform and avail yourself of your heaviest coat. Tell your crew to do the same. You are all about to go ashore here."

Turgenev caught his breath. Execution he understood. But surely these terrorists were not going to put them ashore to slowly freeze or starve to death.

"You are going to abandon us in this forsaken wilderness? We will certainly suffer a horrible death here before anyone might come to rescue us."

Mark pursed his lips and stared hard at the submarine captain.

"Now, Captain Turgenev, do you assume I am such a cruel beast? We will leave you the boats. There is adequate food and reasonable shelter at our campsite on the beach. Petropavlovsk is only sixty kilometers up the coast. Now, you had best lay below and prepare. You need to be ashore and sheltered in case the weather changes suddenly."

Captain Third Rank Andrei Turgenev and his entire crew were casting off from the *Yaroslavl* when one of the newly arrived men, Igor Lodkamatros, joined Mark on the bridge.

"I see that you and the crew survived your journey and encampment," Mark observed. "Did you have any problems? Is everything as I instructed?"

"Yes, my brother," Igor answered. "We had no problems. We scuttled the fishing boat out in deep water after we moved ashore and set up camp last week. The storm yesterday was fierce, cold, and wet, but nothing compared to back home. As you instructed, the RHIBs have just enough fuel remaining to take them back to the beach. And we left one box of gematogen at the campsite."

Gematogen was a Russian nutritional supplement bar. One of its primary ingredients was cow's blood.

"Our dear *mahta* would be proud of you, Igor," Mark told him with a rare chuckle. "After all your years in submarines, you finally have one of your own to command. Did you manage to assemble a complete crew, and are they all trustworthy?"

Igor Lodkamatros answered, "Let us leave you in command, big brother. You know the mission far better than I ever could. I will be the first officer and tell you what needs to be done." He rubbed his bearded chin for a moment before sharing a concern. "Please understand that we are short a few crewmen from a normal complement. We would typically have a crew of about fifty on a submarine of this type. I could only find forty capable men that I could trust."

"Can we still do this?" Mark asked, a worried look on his face.

It was Igor's turn to chuckle. "The one place where we are really missing people is with the communications technology *michmen*. We may find it difficult communicating with Moscow, but I cannot see a need to talk with them. Other than that, we may need to double up a few places, but I am confident we can do what is necessary."

Mark nodded and looked out on the submarine's deck where Captain Turgenev's forlorn crew was gathering. He swept his hand in their direction and said, "Two rubber boats with no fuel, a box of blood candy, sixty kilometers of mountainous wilderness to trek, and an Arctic storm brewing. It will be quite a while until Captain Turgenev and his crew get back to

Petropavlovsk and tell their story. The Russians will search fruitlessly for their missing submarine and then assume that it was lost with all hands. That should give us a free pass for long enough to at least start our mission. And get to the point where we willingly let them know we are here and what our capabilities and intentions are."

Mark Lodkamatros patted the other man warmly on the shoulder and then moved toward the hatch. "Now, brother, let us get these men off to their new adventure, get ourselves submerged, and see if this crew is as good as you have assured me they are."

Igor Lodkamatros followed his older brother through the hatch, down into the submarine's interior. Minutes later, there was no trace the *Yaroslavl* had ever been there, resting in the cold waters contained between the near-vertical rock sides of the fjord.

Ψ

Ivan Dostervesky sat back in the leather easy chair and stirred his tea. The talks were going well, but he had found it impossible to train the Americans to brew a decent cup of tea. For all the amazing modern technologies onboard their ship, they could not even find a suitable samovar. And for tea, all they had was something they colorfully called a "tea bag" that he was instructed to place in a cup, drowning it with hot water until it somehow turned into drinkable tea. So far, he had found that no amount of soaking resulted in anything tasting like good Russian black tea. But at least there was plenty of sugar and lemons. And, even on a ship in the lonely North Pacific, the Americans always seemed to somehow have fresh milk available.

A large-screen television, tuned to the Armed Forces Network news channel, was broadcasting President Grigory Iosifovich Salkov as he discussed the current situation on the Kazak border with a correspondent from RT, the Russian English-language news network. Salkov was decrying the treachery of the Islamic rebels and praising the Russian military advances against those who had instigated and stubbornly persisted in the ongoing struggle which they had no hope of winning.

Admiral Jon Ward sat in the other easy chair in the well-appointed cabin. The spacious suite—spacious, at least, by US Navy ship standards—was nicely laid out for small meetings such as this one. Ward thought how very different this was from the constricted stateroom that he had occupied when he commanded the old submarine *Spadefish*. But the Navy coffee was the same. That would never change. He took a sip of it from his cup and then put it down on the little side table.

"Ivan, we have been dancing around each other for three days now," Ward said. "It's time we got down to business and talk about why you really called this little meeting."

Dostervesky smiled. "Admiral, I see that your reputation for directness is well earned. My contact told me that you lacked the subtlety that is considered so necessary for negotiations conducted in the Orient. But also stressed that you were a straightforward and honest man. That I could trust your word."

Jon Ward remained quiet. Dostervesky took a sip of tea, scowled, and then went on. "Over the last half century, small countries or people trying to create a new and legitimate country have approached your government for aid. Many expansive promises have been made. Yet, in every case, your country has abandoned them to their fates when it was expedient. That is the primary reason my source advised me to avoid the diplomats and deal with you directly, Admiral Ward. And only with you. I believe your American phrase is 'no bullshit.' The Children of the Gulag do not have the time nor the inclination to deal with bullshit."

Ward showed no emotion when he answered, "I hear all that you are saying, but what precisely are you asking us to do?"

Dostervesky slowly placed his teacup on his side table. He leaned forward and put his hands on his knees. It was obvious to Ward this answer would be the culmination of the Russian's plans for only God knew how long. But Dostervesky gave his speech with such passion and precision, it was hard to believe he had probably rehearsed it over and over.

"Admiral, we need your help in keeping the Russian government occupied while the Children establish the infrastructure of a peaceful government. One that will be supported by a majority of the world's nations. One that even Russia will have to recognize as a sovereign state, no matter how reluctant they are to do so or how determined they are to save face, in order for us to join the planet's family of nations."

Dostervesky paused for a breath. "See, our new nation will be a very long way geographically and geopolitically from Moscow. Because of the state of their current entanglements and their depleted military status and economy, there are only a few ways for President Salkov to send troops to attempt to quash our efforts. The Trans-Siberian Highway and Railway are too slow and vulnerable, and they are aware we can cause them much pain should they send troops by that means. In addition, they both end in Vladivostok, so even if he can get troops that far, they still have over two thousand kilometers of rugged wilderness to traverse before they even reach our soon-to-be declared borders. That leaves air and sea routes. The closest airfields adequate to stage from are either in Vladivostok or Petropavlovsk. Both the planes and the airfields are vulnerable, not only to our well-developed sabotage operations but to the weather this time of year. And again, even if Salkov could somehow manage to bring in troops by air, they would still need to make a long wilderness trek in what would likely be treacherous weather before they could reach us."

Ward nodded slightly. Now he knew how the US Navy fit into this bold plan. "That, of course, leaves sea transport."

"Exactly," Dostervesky said with a smile. "That is where you come in. An embargo of the entire Sea of Okhotsk would be ideal, of course. However, any protection you could offer, or at the very least if you could provide some type of advanced warning of sea attacks on our coastline, it would help tremendously in fending off those who would crush this little rebellion of ours."

Ward grimaced, then massaged the bridge of his nose. True, things had not gone well for Russia in the past few years. At least not in the eyes of most of the world's nations. Still, Dostervesky and his bunch of rebels were boldly asking him and the United States to flirt with World War III in support of a new country that may or may not ultimately be any better for its people than Mother Russia was. There was no guarantee that the new nation—if it ever came to be—would not be just another cruel dictatorship.

"Look, this is way outside of my swim lane," Ward finally said. "From what I know about you and your goals, and from what I am hearing from my other sources, we would support what you intend to do. Up to a point, that is. However, right now, the best I can promise is that I will take your message back to Washington. I certainly can't guarantee what the reaction will be in the Pentagon, the State Department, or the White House, but I will do my best to carry and deliver the reasoning behind your message."

The pair stood and shook hands.

"Now," Ward asked, "do we need to slip you back into Magadan?"

Dostervesky smiled broadly. "As much as I would enjoy another voyage on that remarkable submarine of yours, Admiral, I really need to get to Vladivostok as soon as possible. If you can arrange to drop me off in Hokkaido, I can go from there. I have much to set in motion. I can only hope your nation will support the efforts of so many brave, freedom-loving men and women who are seeking only to build the same kind of nation as your ancestors did in 1776."

"And I'm sure you understand that I can only promise what I have already."

9

Boris Paserivich was very uncomfortable with this mysterious meeting to which he had committed. Like many of his fellow Children, he had built a healthy dislike for any government that was also a prison state. The manner in which the North Koreans dealt with their own disfavored people was far too close to the methods of the old Soviet Union for Paserivich's taste.

The call from the North Korean operative had come by surprise through roundabout channels. The Children of the Gulag had decided to not yet make the official contacts with the DPRK until they could gauge the response from the United States. Then they would better know what to ask of the Koreans. But it was clear the caller carried some clout and that he was disturbingly well aware of what was afoot. He had identified himself as Tan Dan Won and he was from the North Korean Reconnaissance General Bureau. Paserivich knew the RGB as the clandestine operations arm of the North Korean General Staff. They were responsible for all manner of ventures, ranging from routine information gathering to far more direct and sinister activities, such as assassinations and sabotage.

Why Tan Dan Won would contact him was a question Paserivich could not answer, but Ivan Dostervesky left him in charge while he was off meeting with the Americans. Although his intuition was screaming to ignore the call, Paserivich agreed to meet the North Korean spy, to at least listen to what he had to say. Maybe, in the process, he could determine how the RGB knew so much already. Besides, the Children of the Gulag would likely need all the help they could get, no matter how distasteful, if they were going to succeed in freeing themselves from the jaws of Mother Russia.

Tan insisted that the meeting take place in the tiny hamlet of Ussuriysk, seventy kilometers north of Vladivostok. The location seemed innocuous enough to Paserivich. It was well away from any known threat and on reasonably neutral ground, though it would be difficult to get there quickly and quietly. They agreed to meet at a place called the Lotos Café, a couple of blocks off the main highway, in the center of what passed for a downtown area.

Tan had also insisted that Paserivich come alone, though he would be allowed to tell someone he trusted implicitly where and with whom he would be meeting. Those details were in a sealed envelope marked not to be opened unless the Children of the Gulag lieutenant had not returned within forty-eight hours after a predetermined time.

Paserivich arrived at the rendezvous a full hour ahead of time with the intent of casing the location and choosing a quick exit from potential trouble. But Tan was already seated and enjoying a cup of tea. The moment the Russian dissident entered the shop, Tan rose, waved to him, then, without a word, left a wad of rubles on the table. He signaled Paserivich to follow him out the door and then around the corner of the building, down an alley, and to a waiting vehicle. As soon as they were seated in the back of the battered and dirty Mercedes coupe, it shot down the street and out onto the highway that seemed to lead them out of town.

"Good evening. It is a pleasure to meet you," Tan finally said, in perfect Russian.

"Where are we going?" was Paserivich's response. "And what are your intentions?" This was turning into something very different from what he expected. Something bordering on being sinister.

With a smile, the North Korean spy suddenly slid an automatic pistol from his inside coat pocket. "May I assume that you know how to use this?"

he asked as he moved the slide back and handed it to Paserivich. "There is every chance you will need it before the evening is over."

The Russian accepted the pistol, placed it in his lap, and settled against the back of the seat, watching the countryside out his window as he willed his heart to slow its sudden racing. It was clear the RGB man was not going to tell him anything else for the moment. And that he seemed to be enjoying the shield of mystery he was building between them.

The town quickly gave way to deadpan-flat farmland, covered with a bitter winter's worth of sand-like snow. For a lengthy stretch, the Trans-Siberian Railway ran alongside the road. Its two tracks glistened in the low-angle, late afternoon sunshine.

Paserivich noticed when a couple of panel vans fell in behind the Mercedes. His heart rate kicked up again. Tan nodded in their direction. "Do not fret. They are with us. Sit back and relax. We have an hour's drive ahead of us yet."

There was no more conversation. The sun was dropping below the western horizon when the little convoy ultimately turned off the highway and onto a rutted dirt track following a drainage ravine dividing two fields. After another half hour of slipping and sliding along on the muddy trail, they reached a turnout that offered barely enough room for them to turn around to leave. Paserivich kept all concern from his face, but he was sure there was adequate evidence of puzzlement there. Had the North Korean intended to kill him and dispose of his body, he would not have needed to bring him this far. And why would he have given him a weapon—to go with the one stealthily concealed in its holster in the small of his back—if that was his intent? Perhaps Tan really did have something to show him. Something that would let Paserivich know that the DPRK could and would be a part of the efforts of the Children of the Gulag should they see some advantage in it for their own regime.

Tan and Paserivich climbed from the Mercedes as a dozen men piled out of the rear doors of the two panel vans. They were all dressed in winter camouflage and promptly got busy strapping on cross-country skis and checking their weapons. Tan walked around to the trunk of the car, retrieved two snow camo jackets and pants and two pairs of skis.

"Boris, my friend," he said, "I suggest that you join me in getting properly dressed for the party. I assume you know how to use the skis. You will enjoy what I am going to show you."

They started up the gully, skiing at a good pace. Paserivich noticed that several of the team were carrying RPG-7 rocket-propelled grenade launchers along with their AN-94 Nikonov assault rifles. Other squad members sported a small, strange-looking assault rifle, one with a very large bore. Tan again interpreted the Russian's expression.

"ShAK-12 Bullpup battle rifles," Tan told him. "Fires a 12.7-by-55-millimeter round that will make a hole through a concrete wall and take out anyone hiding on the other side. You Russians can come up with some really nasty firepower, you know."

"When will you tell me where we are going and why?" Paserivich finally asked.

Tan only smiled evilly and answered, "You must trust me, my new friend. This will be fun." He skied off across the open field, breathing easily, obviously in good shape. So was Paserivich. He followed along, close behind.

Fifteen minutes later, the group came to a berm that allowed an unobstructed view down onto another stretch of the Trans-Siberian Railroad. But on the other side of the tracks, a spur led into a brightly lit area that appeared to be a marshalling yard of some kind. Armed guards in Russian Army uniforms patrolled along the high fence that separated the yard from the main line of the track. Other than those guards, the place seemed quiet and mostly deserted, and the guards didn't appear to be too attentive to actually guarding anything.

Tan checked his watch and signaled his team to go to work. They spread out along the berm, perfectly ordered and separated, clearly well drilled. Tan again checked his watch.

"The fun will begin in five minutes," he mumbled to Paserivich. "Stand back here with me and watch. Oh, and by the way, you may want to keep that little pop gun I gave you handy."

As if on cue, the quiet night was abruptly ripped apart by a loud, shrill train whistle. Then a brilliant headlight swung into view from around a bend half a kilometer down the track. A gate that blocked access to the spur line swung open, and the long freight train entered like a slow-moving snake until it was all inside the fence. Then it came to a full stop in the marshalling yard.

Paserivich was startled when the first RPG arced from somewhere down the berm and across the fence before smashing with an awful blast into the front engine. A second one slammed into the following engine as automatic weapons fire began pockmarking the train cars. The ShAK-12 rounds punched massive holes in their targets.

The guards rallied and began firing blindly back at their attackers, but it was too late. The RGB men were already up and skiing away down the back side of the berm as fast as they could go. Even faster because they had deliberately left their weapons lying on the snowy ground.

Once back to their vehicles, they climbed in and sped away.

Boris Paserivich stopped at the Mercedes and glared at Tan. He was livid.

"What is the meaning of this, Tan? I met with you on your terms so we could discuss important matters. Instead, you wasted my time pulling me all the way out here so I could watch you and your soldiers punch holes in some freight train?"

Tan held up his hand while checking his watch. "In only a second or two you will..."

The rest of the answer was lost in an immense blast and blinding flash of light. Streaks of orange, red, and yellow filled the horizon, and bits of debris rained all around them.

Tan smiled. "Your Children of the Gulag just struck a mighty blow for freedom. That was a trainload of ammunition fresh from our factories, and it was on its way to the Russian Second Army Corps on the Ukraine border. This marshalling yard was stacked with many tons more of ammunition heading west. We left a little surprise in each freight car on this train with timed fuses before it left the factory."

He waved toward the blasted and burning yard behind him. More secondary explosions rocked the night. "The Russian Army is nothing if not predictable. This yard is—or rather, was—an ammunition storage and trans-shipment yard. Perfect target, but to achieve maximum destruction, we needed to make sure the train was stopped here and could not move before the fuses detonated."

They jumped into the car, and the driver hurried back toward the main road. There, he turned onto the highway and sped back toward Ussuriysk. Coming to meet them along the way was the first of the ambulances and fire trucks.

"And, Boris, we left enough evidence to tie this little attack to your cause," Tan said with undisguised glee. "Evidence that even the Russian Army can find. Then, of course, they will buy ordnance from us to replace all this, never suspecting we were actually the saboteurs who destroyed this shipment. You understand now why we are so happy to assist you and your group. We can only profit. And one day, your new nation will be a strong ally of the DPRK."

Paserivich was quiet for a moment. "I only wish you had informed us before such a drastic announcement to our enemy of our presence and intentions," he said. "I pray we are ready for the next step."

"And what is that?" Tan asked.

Boris Paserivich stared out the limo window at the cold, harsh landscape. "I have absolutely no idea."

Ψ

Captain First Rank Ivgany Yurtotov hurried down the pier toward his Improved *Severodvinsk*-class submarine, the *Yakutsk*. The entire waterfront had abruptly come alive, as if someone had kicked over an anthill. The place was in disarray, everyone hustling, scurrying, with no seeming order to the operation. Trucks rushed back and forth, delivering supplies to previously idle boats hurriedly making preparations to head out to sea. Shouts of supervisors and officers created a babel of impatient noise.

A *Kilo*-class diesel submarine backed away from pier Sierra-Two with three blasts of its horn, obviously in a big hurry, and swung around into the main channel. It headed out toward open water, leaving behind a cloud of diesel smoke in its swirling wake. Over on pier Sierra-Five, the crew of an *Oscar II*–class SSGN was busy buttoning up the boat's vertical launch tubes. Several *Kalibr* cruise missiles still lay on the pier, waiting to be loaded. But that was not going to happen now. It appeared to Yurtotov that a weapons load-out had been unexpectedly cut short in an effort to get the submarine out to sea quicker. It was very unlikely, after all, that the vessel would need cruise missiles on this mission.

Yurtotov glanced up as a pair of *Grisha*-class anti-submarine warfare corvettes got underway from the piers over in Vilyuchinsk, in the shadow of the town's volcano on the other side of Bukhta Krasheninnikova. He was amazed that those antiques could actually get underway, much less head out to sea. A blue-and-white *Rubin*-class fast patrol boat, painted with the colors of the Russian Coast Guard, escorted a much older *Pauk*-class Coast Guard corvette further out in the harbor, racing toward the open sea.

With a submarine unaccounted for and assumed missing, it was all-hands-on-deck. Anything that could float or fly was being put to use. The Pacific Fleet Headquarters, twenty-five hundred kilometers away over in Vladivostok, had ordered everything in Petropavlovsk that could maintain buoyancy to get underway and search for the missing *Yaroslavl* and her crew. Even if the only thing they could add to the search were a few more eyeballs.

Ivgany Yurtotov had already glanced at his own orders. He was to get his submarine, the *Yakutsk*, out of port and to sea as soon as physically possible. There he was to hurry to his assigned box and search an area of deep water to the east for the missing vessel.

A blast of frigid wind nearly knocked him over. His gaze swung out to the northwest. Ominously dark clouds were building up over the mountains, promising to deliver another crushing winter blow to anyone foolish enough to venture out. The normally protected harbor was already churning with whitecaps.

Just then, a pair of IL-38 "May" ASW turboprop aircraft roared directly overhead, clawing for altitude after taking off from the military side of Petropavlovsk-Kamchatsky Airport, thirty kilometers to the north. These ancient birds—first flown in the early 1960s—would climb laboriously up to a thousand meters and then head out to their own assigned search areas. A swarm of helicopters flew by, lower than the Mays. Yurtotov saw several Mil Mi-8 Hip transport helicopters and even some commercial birds flying along with several KA-27 Helix ASW aircraft. It looked like someone over at the airfield had shoved everything into the air that had a window for observers to look out.

Yurtotov shook his head, then sprinted across the brow onto the deck of the *Yakutsk*, and from there straight up to the bridge. Maybe it would be a boost to his career if he should be the first to locate the misplaced submarine. Even better if he could "rescue" the crew before anyone even realized they were likely never in any danger. That some crewmember foul-up or malfunctioning piece of navigation gear had led them astray. Certainly, there had been no confrontation with an adversary out there. Maybe a catastrophic mechanical failure, but just locating the hulk would earn Yurtotov points with those much higher up in the chain of command of the Military Maritime Fleet of the Russian Armed Forces.

The watch officer confirmed that the submarine was ready to get underway as the skipper had ordered and that he was more than ready to cast off all lines. A pair of tugs pulled the mammoth submarine away from the pier and out into the harbor, much more slowly and carefully than Yurtotov would have desired. As soon as he was faired up in the outbound channel, he cast off the tugs. By the time the boat rounded Rybachiy Point and was entering the broad reaches of Avacha Bay, all the crew were below decks and the deck hatches were secured. Yurtotov kicked up to a full bell. Seawater churned up over the bow, dashed high against the sail, and then foamed back down, flooding the main deck aft of the sail before washing into the undulating waters of the bay.

Even before the *Yakutsk* reached the open water, Yurtotov felt the pitch and roll of the stormy North Pacific. The meteorologist's report had promised rough and blustery weather with winds topping forty knots and seas running four to six meters. That forecast now appeared to have been much too conservative.

Yurtotov watched the white-painted *Grisha*s ahead of him as they headed down the channel, doing their own heaving and bucking dance in the rising seas. Once again, he thanked his lucky stars that he was on a submarine and would soon cruise well beneath the effects of this storm. The bridge was cleared and the submarine was ready to dive as soon as they were in water deep enough to safely submerge. The Mys Mayachnyy light was abeam when the submarine quickly slipped beneath the waves and disappeared into the far more tranquil deep.

10

The submarine USS *Gato* was getting quite an introduction to the wintertime North Pacific. A sea state six, with wave heights running fifteen to twenty feet, greeted the new submarine every time they ventured up to periscope depth. And since Henrietta Foster and her crew had departed Yokosuka in such a rush, Submarine Group Seven felt the need to constantly feed them a flood of information, intelligence, and instructions. That meant frequent and prolonged excursions to periscope depth and plenty of time for the crew to really earn their sea legs while they copied each of the numerous communications broadcasts.

But that also gave the XO, Eric Householder, multiple opportunities to improve the submarine's "stowed for sea" plan, taking steps to ride out all the tossing and turning they got each time they approached the surface of the rough ocean and to make sure that every piece of equipment, spare part, and can of beans was going to stay in its assigned place. By the time *Gato* arrived off the Kamchatka coast, a trip to periscope depth in heavy seas resulted in only the occasional stray, neglected coffee cup crashing to the deck.

As *Gato* entered the Avachinskiy Zaliv, the broad gulf on the southeast side of Kamchatka, Foster huddled around the navigation display with

Householder and Sharon Woolsey, the Navigator, as well as the on-watch Officer-of-the-Deck, or OOD. The electronic navigation "table," the Electronic Chart Display and Information System, or ECDIS, sat in the after corner of the control room. It provided an electronic way to visualize where they were and where they were going as opposed to the old paper charts and grease-pencil-on-Plexiglas updating. *Gato's* op area was marked off as a red box, fifty nautical miles on a side, with its northwestern boundary nuzzled up against the entrance to Petropavlovsk. The submarine's current position showed as a bright white X and was almost sixty miles due south of Petr.

Foster swept her hand over the chart. "As soon as we've planted the A-DSTP buoy in deep water, we'll do a real slow and careful ASW sweep of the entire op area. I want to be damn sure there are no surprises lurking in the bushes that might jump up and bite us in the ass."

Sharon Woolsey had a thought. "Skipper, best place to plant the A-DSTP buoy is in deep water just outside the southeast corner of the box. Best sound channels are in that direction." She pointed to a dot a couple of miles to the south and east of their op area.

Eric Householder looked at a display on the command console and then at the ECDIS. The exec had a thought he wanted to share, too.

"Boss, sonar is calculating that the range of the day for the thin-line array against our *Severodvinsk* is twenty thousand yards. It's going to take us quite a while to sweep the entire box. Why don't we make a sweep through the box and see what we find, then plant the buoy before we complete sanitizing the whole area?"

Foster smiled. She always said when she got her own command, she wanted a crew that was not only smarter than she was, but people who were not afraid to make suggestions to their skipper. She sometimes felt she had hit the jackpot with these people.

"XO, that sounds like a very good—"

She was interrupted by a series of loud pinging sounds from the active sonar intercept receiver. Almost immediately, Senior Chief Stumpf called out, "Receiving low-frequency active sonar. Three-point-seven kilohertz." Then, after only a few seconds, he went on, "Equates to a modified Bull Nose hull-mounted sonar carried on *Grisha* V corvettes." He paused for another second and then continued, "Best bearing zero-zero-seven. Signal strength plus twenty, low probability of detection."

Foster looked quickly to the ECDIS. She did not doubt a single bit of the considerable information the sonarman had just relayed. The bearing Senior Chief Stumpf had called out lined up with the mouth of Petr Harbor. No surprise that a warship might be coming out of there with its sonar warbling.

Then, before she could react, there was more.

"Skipper, picking up a second Bull Nose, bearing zero-one-five, signal strength plus twenty-five," Stumpf reported. "Looks like we have a pair of *Grishas* out frolicking today."

Foster rubbed her chin, a puzzled look on her face. Why would the Russians have a pair of those antique frigates coming out of the barn on a day with this kind of foul weather?

The active sonar intercept alarmed yet again. Okay, what now? Stumpf had the answer.

"Skipper, receiving seven-point-one-kilohertz active sonars on..." There was a short hesitation while the sonarman studied his data. "On four different bearings. These all equate to Improved Shark Gill sonars. They're carried on newer *Kilo*-class diesel submarines. Signal strengths between thirty and thirty-five. Still low probability of detection. I'm trying to pick the boats up on passive sonar, but there's way too much sea-state noise on those bearings."

Foster looked at the bearing lines to all of the active sonars on the ECDIS tactical display. They resembled a fan coming out of Petr. Somebody was making a very overt show of conducting an ASW search. Or maybe it was not a show. Maybe the Russians somehow knew *Gato* was swimming around out there, too close to their precious submarine base for their comfort.

There was more, though. Stumpf chimed in again with, "Skipper, receiving multiple twelve-point-two-kilohertz active sonars. Equates to KA-27 Helix helicopter VSG-3 dipping sonars. Receiving at least four, but it's hard to be certain. Damn things are moving around a lot."

"Damn! Did we wake up the entire Russian Navy?" Foster said, to no one in particular.

Helicopter dipping sonars were a considerable threat to any submarine. Because they could dip and reposition much faster than any submarine— even on a squally day like this—a pair of helicopters could easily play hopscotch to overcome a boat's best efforts to evade. This sudden burst of activity was starting to resemble a hairy situation. There was the possibility that *Gato* had unknowingly tripped some bottom-mounted sensor—even out here in international waters—and had announced their presence to the Russians. Even if that was the case, it was hard to imagine such detection would set off such a flurry of activity.

Foster could not be sure, but she needed to be very careful in trying to figure out what was going on. Beginning with whether or not it was *Gato* that had led the Russians to light up Stumpf's display. So far, all the sonars that they had heard were well beyond detection ranges. Curious but not immediately problematic. The ones they needed to worry about were the quiet submarine passive sonars that might be working away out there, closer to them, and on submarines that had not yet been detected by *Gato's* sensitive ears. Those were the most serious threat, and those very stealthy Russian submarines based in Petr had not been accounted for yet.

"What did you say, Skipper?" Householder asked.

"Just talking to myself," Foster answered. Her order came without hesitation. "XO, man battle stations. Let's get ready, just in case this welcome party is directed at us." She turned to Woolsey. "Officer-of-the-Deck, clear baffles to come to periscope depth. I want to do a complete ESM sweep before we call home to tell the boss about all this flash and glitter. And see if maybe they've heard any news we need to know about."

Five minutes later, *Gato's* low-profile photonics mast pierced the storm-tossed surface of the Pacific Ocean. The command console showed little more than rolling, gray, foam-topped waves in every direction. They could have been a thousand miles from any other vessel. However, the various modules on the AN/BLQ-10 Electronic Warfare Support System, off in the radio room, lit up like someone had plugged in the lights on a Christmas tree.

"Conn, ESM." It was ETC Collins, the ESM operator, calling over the 21MC announcing system. "Receiving multiple Wet Eye ASW airborne radars. Those are carried on IL-38 Mays and TU-142 Bear Foxtrots. I'm seeing at least six of them. Also, at least four EASA radars. That's carried on KA-27 Helix helicopters. I'm also receiving multiple surface search and navigation radars. Receiving multiple twenty-five-to-thirty-megahertz data links equating to Russian sonobuoy links. They must have sent out everything that floats. Nothing is a threat yet, but there is a whole lot of stuff to the north of us, and it's all coming our way."

"XO," Foster said, turning to Householder. "Get into radio and call Group Seven. Tell them the ASW greeting here is way too hot right now for us to stick around. We're going to open out and wait for things to settle down a bit before completing our mission."

Eric Householder had just stepped out of control to do her bidding when Senior Chief Stumpf called out, "Skipper, picking up an MGK-600 Irtysh-Amfora active sonar. Carried only on an Improved *Severodvinsk* submarine. Best bearing, zero-three-two. Signal strength plus thirty-eight and rising. We'll designate it as Sierra Five-Six. And she's a definite ASW threat."

Threat, indeed. It was time to beat feet. Calling home would have to wait. So would trying to determine what had set off so much anti-submarine warfare action by the Russian Navy from a base they had been told had become much quieter in the last few years.

No. First order of business was to avoid detection by the Improved *Severodvinsk* and his active sonar.

"Officer-of-the-Deck, come left to course two-one-zero," Foster quickly ordered. "Keep your stern pointed at Sierra Five-Six. That'll give the bastard the smallest target we can."

As she felt the boat swinging around to its new course, Foster glanced at the ECDIS charts. A glimmer of an idea came to mind. If the inshore sea-state noise was screwing up *Gato*'s sonar systems, it would absolutely do the same for the Russians and their listening gear. Not very far off to the west was a very rocky coastline that would definitely throw up a lot of noise in which she and her crew could bury themselves.

"Officer-of-the-Deck, make your depth two hundred feet, come to ahead full. I want you to snug up against the coast as close as you can get. We're going to hide in the noise for a bit while we figure out what's going on. Why are our Russian friends are trying to ensonify the entire Avachinskiy Zaliv

Gulf, and are we the reason they're swimming around on such an inhospitable afternoon?"

Foster looked over at her Nav. Sharon Woolsey had a look on her face and was shaking her head.

"Go ahead and tell me what you're thinking, Nav. I left my mind-reader plug back in the stateroom."

"This all has me baffled, too, Skipper. But if they wanted to confirm our presence and chase us away, they would only need the *Severodvinsk* boats and maybe the choppers and their toys. Even if they wanted to sink us, it would be the subs that would do the deed in this weather. I know we have to avoid getting found, but…"

Foster looked at her sideways. "So, tell me what you're thinking."

"It's almost as if the Russians have lost something really valuable out here, and now, they're doing all they can to try to find it."

Ψ

Vice President Harold Osterman leaned forward, arching his aching back. He always had trouble getting comfortable in a straight-backed chair like this one in the White House Oval Office. He was certain that was the very reason why Stan Smitherman insisted on having a pair of them arranged there, across the Resolute Desk from the president's much more comfortable leather office chair. The president often said that he wanted nobody sitting there briefing him in the Oval Office to get too comfortable. Across the desk from the most powerful man on the planet was no place to relax. Not even his own handpicked vice president. Especially not this vice president. Smitherman knew only too well of Osterman's own ambitious political plans.

The two politicians were still fatigued from all the previous day's inauguration activities. They had partied well into the night. This was Smitherman's second term, but it would be the first for his brand-new VP. Osterman was still transitioning from the cabinet position of Secretary of Defense in Smitherman's first term to now being his number two guy. "My Senate wrangler," the president liked to call him. But it was already common knowledge that he was making plans to be sitting on the other side of the Resolute Desk in exactly four short years, watching others squirm uncomfortably in those damned straight-backed chairs.

Now officially on the job, Smitherman and Osterman had just returned from participating in their first President's Intelligence Brief, held in the Situation Room, deep in the bowels of the White House. There they heard what the country's top intelligence organizations considered to be the top priorities in the world, what were threats, and what were opportunities. The president was always skeptical about such input. He trusted no one and was certain the high-level bureaucrats delivering the briefing were shading the information to win influence, money, or power, and likely all three. After an intense couple of hours of PowerPoint warfare, Smitherman and Osterman retreated to the Oval Office for some private discussions before venturing out for another evening of diplomatic nightlife after a live, sit-down interview with CNN. Smitherman's press secretary had compiled a list of questions the interviewer would be allowed to ask and was waiting outside to discuss them with the president. But Smitherman was in no hurry to deal with such trivial stuff. He would never have to face the fickle electorate of his country again. More important matters were now at the top of his own private agenda.

"Harold, I think we made a mistake appointing Sally Kesterman as Director of National Intelligence," the president began. Oddly, there was no trace of Smitherman's signature Texas drawl. That was reserved for public consumption. "She's a shrewd politician and too damn smart by about half. That PIB was uncomfortable in spots. I especially don't like her idea of poking around inside the Chinese government."

Osterman sat a little straighter in the chair. "Boss, you're not afraid her sniffing around might uncover our little deal with Tan Yong?"

"No, not much possibility of that," Smitherman answered, shaking his head. "We passed that money through too many offshore bank accounts before we funneled it through legitimate PACs to our campaign for anybody to follow the trail. I'm more concerned going forward. She wants to be the first female president bad enough, and she's gonna make it a lot harder for us to do any more of those kinds of little shakedowns."

Osterman rubbed his chin and stared out through the three-inch-thick bulletproof glass and into the rose garden beyond. He now knew the man spreading fertilizer at the base of the roses was Secret Service. So was the guy salting the sidewalks. But the man in the dark topcoat standing at semi-attention beside the steps was not. He was part of some top-secret agency nobody but the president and a few others knew about. Osterman had been in government service for more than twenty years, the last four as Secretary of Defense, but he was still constantly being surprised by the things he did not know.

Smitherman reached over and opened a cigar box and pulled out a pair of Habana cigars from his own private stock. He tossed one of them to the vice president and began the ritual of lighting his own.

"These are Ramon Allones Superiores Especiales. I have them custom rolled just for me. Soaked in dark rum. These suckers cost a hundred bucks apiece. The ambassador in Havana has standing orders to ship me a case of them every week. I think you'll like the taste."

Osterman deftly caught the cigar, smelled the rich tobacco. "Why don't we cut Kesterman in on part of the action?" Osterman ventured. "She wants to play big-league baseball, she needs to know the big-league rules. Or she's o-u-t." He reached for the guillotine cutter on the desk and snipped the cigar with a flourish.

"Speaking of action," Smitherman said, not so subtly changing the topic as he took the first deep draw on his cigar. "Did you catch that part about some Navy admiral meeting with those Russian revolutionaries? What the hell were they called again?"

"Oh, you mean the Children of the Gulag," Osterman shot back. He had been listening and making notes during the briefing whether his boss had or not. "Interesting name. That admiral is Jon Ward, the Director of Naval Intelligence. Real straight shooter and something of a legend in the Far East. That dust-up with the Chinese hackers last year, Ward was the guy who fixed that little problem so it didn't bite us in the ass come election time. And, although he has no idea, he also set it up for us to make a lot of money."

The veep expertly toasted the foot of his cigar and then carefully lit it, took a deep draw, and exhaled a cloud of blue smoke.

Smitherman smiled, now recalling how he knew the name.

"Yeah, Hal, that's it. And you know what? I smell a real opportunity here. Those Children want to set up their own little fiefdom in Far Eastern Russia. Our friend Grigory Iosifovich Salkov is already overextended between his problems in the Ukraine and Kazakhstan. Hell, he's about to run out of troops, I hear. If those Children go for it, he'll be real hard-pressed to try to shut 'em down and save face." He rolled his cigar between finger and thumb, his countenance almost hidden by the smoke. "I didn't get much out of all that intel blathering down there, but I did hear one thing. You realize from the Aleutians, we are twenty-five hundred air miles closer to those Children than Salkov is way the hell over there in the Kremlin?"

"Okay, so Salkov has his ass in a vise," Osterman answered, still not sure where his president was aiming. "But where's our opportunity other than sitting back and watching him take the flak?"

"Didn't you hear that other part? The part about their gold mines?" the president answered. "Somebody says 'gold,' I suddenly get mighty inter-ested. Why don't you use some of your Defense Department links to back-channel to these Children? Get in the middle maybe with this Ward guy. We'll give them covert support in exchange for gold deposited in Singapore bank accounts. For emergency disaster relief for the poor people of the world or some such if it comes up. And get hold of Tan Yong. He'll be as anxious to slip it to old Salkov as we are. Especially if he can tap some of that gold, too."

Osterman smiled. "I like it. And we can mask it all behind keeping the Russians off guard. But while I'm doing all this heavy lifting, what are you going to be doing?"

Smitherman leaned back in his leather desk chair, took another deep lungful, and blew out a perfect smoke ring that rotated upward toward the antique chandelier above the desk. He was actually grinning as he answered.

"I think that I'll soon be explaining the facts of life to Miss Sally Kester-man. She can play with us and make herself very rich and powerful." The tip of the Ramon Allones glowed cherry red as he puffed. "Or she can remain on the outside, where it can be so very, very cold and lonely."

11

Mark Lodkamatros checked his watch again. Another hour until moonset. At last, the time was approaching for them to get on with the next phase of their mission. Spending over a week quietly hiding in the depths of the storm-tossed Northern Pacific in the Russian submarine they had swiped had been a challenge for the now-former Spetsnaz officer. Even though he knew they needed to practice patience while the Russians exhausted themselves in searching for the missing *Yaroslavl*, his training and instincts favored quick action.

But now it was time. The plan was to sneak past the Kuril Island chain into the Sea of Okhotsk. The Kurils formed a continuous chain all the way from the Russian territory of the Kamchatka Peninsula down to Hokkaido. Annexed into Russia after the Second World War, the necklace of islands effectively guarded the gateway from the Pacific into the Sea of Okhotsk, a body of water the Russians considered to be their own private swimming pool. For that reason, powerful surface search radars and anti-ship missile batteries guarded the many deepwater straits between islands against surface ships. At the same time, bottom-mounted underwater sensors were used to detect submarines that might attempt to slip through.

But there was one exception. That was the Second Kuril Island Strait. At a little over a kilometer wide at its narrowest point and barely ten meters deep in that channel, the passage between Shumshu Island and Paramushir Island to the south was much too narrow and shallow for them to bother with. It was impossible for any vessel—surface or submerged—to slip through there undetected.

Igor Lodkamatros, Mark's younger brother and now second in command of the stolen *Kilo*-class submarine, looked up from the chart where he had been watching one of his hired crew plot the boat's position.

"Mark...uh, I mean Captain...we need to come to course three-three-one and come up to periscope depth. We have arrived at our transit point."

Mark Lodkamatros stepped over to consider the charts alongside his brother. Fortunately, Mark's Spetsnaz training had involved plenty of small boat navigation. He easily understood what Igor was telling him.

Igor pointed to a little dot on the chart.

"We are here. At zero-one-thirty, we need to be abeam Severo-Kurilsk Point." He tapped a point of land that jutted out from Paramushir Island. "Maximum high tide is twenty minutes later. Even so, we will need to run with the deck awash and hug the Shumshu side of the channel to avoid grounding. We then need to be abreast of Baykovo Point by zero-two-hundred. After that, the tide is falling, and we will not be able to find enough water beneath the keel for us to get through. However, from the Baykovo Point, it is straight north out into the Sea of Okhotsk."

"Does this work?" Mark asked dubiously. "The Russians did not set up and spend the money to monitor this channel for no reason."

Igor nodded agreement. "They are only protecting against a major surface incursion. For us, it is all in the timing and remaining partly submerged. That is why I recommended this way into Okhotsk. My calculations show that at maximum high tide, we will have a meter of water under us. But our window is short. We only have fifteen minutes either side of maximum high tide to get through the shallow part."

Mark nodded. His brother had been a career naval officer.

"But running surfaced, will they not detect us on radar?" Mark questioned. "Or see us if some fisherman in his house gets up for a piss in the middle of the night and looks out a window?"

"The surface search radar will conveniently be down for regularly scheduled maintenance—regular and predictable, which is good for us—

and the chances of seeing a black submarine on a dark night are very small. The only village on the passage is the Severo-Kuril'skiy Morskoy fishing port half a kilometer beyond the lighthouse."

Mark Lodkamatros nodded again and then ordered that the submarine be brought to periscope depth. A heavy overcast curtained the night sky. There was no moon. No stars. The only light that he could see was the Severo-Kurilsk navigation light flashing its warning to unwary mariners. There were no ships' lights visible, and the shoreline was dark. It seemed that the submarine and her new crew were all alone in the night.

"Mark, we need to make eleven kilometers per hour to be at the Severo-Kurilsk Point on schedule," Igor called out. "And steer three-three-two."

Mark slowly walked the scope around, but other than that lone flashing navigation light, all he saw was blackness. He was aware that he was driving the *Yaroslavl* down what amounted to a very narrow funnel. And that they would not be able to see a thing. He had to depend on his brother's skill as a navigator and a bunch of satellites several thousand kilometers overhead to tell him where he was and where he was heading.

"Come right and steer three-three-four," Igor called out. "We are getting set to the west. Ten minutes to Severo-Kurilsk Point. Time to broach up and run on the surface."

Mark felt a cold trickle of sweat run down the back of his neck. The next few minutes would be the trickiest part of this needle-threading exercise. Best case, they would slip through the narrow strait without anyone being aware of their passage. Worst case, either someone saw them cruising past and raised the alarm or they ran the *Yaroslavl* aground. Then the Russians would have a nice surprise at first light in the morning. Either way, they would end up on the receiving end of some serious firepower with no real way to defend themselves.

"Sounding ten meters under the keel," the fathometer operator called out.

"Steer three-five-five. Severo-Kurilsk Point abeam to port," Igor noted.

"Sounding eight meters."

Mark spun the periscope. The navigation light on the point of land was just past abeam to port. They were now entering the narrow, shallow part of their trip.

"Sound five meters."

"Make thirteen kilometers," Igor directed. "The current is slowing us."

"Sounding two meters."

"Navigation looking good," Igor announced. "Hope no one has dumped a load of clam shells along here."

"Sounding one meter. Loss of soundings."

Mark had been dreading that call. He knew the fathometer only registered water deeper than one meter under their keel. The device could not measure anything any shallower. The next thing he heard and felt could very well be the grating and grinding of the *Yaroslavl* going aground. But, so far, they seemed to be steaming normally. He continued to peer through the eyepiece of the scope, looking for any sign they may have stirred a response from someone.

Then, abruptly, a searchlight pierced the night sky off to port. The brilliant white arrow of light shot through the night and then slowly swept toward their position. Someone over at the seaport was searching the night. Had the *Yaroslavl* been detected? Would the next thing be a burst of gunfire from emplacements on shore? Or an incoming missile?

"Searchlight, scanning the surface directly ahead," Mark announced.

"Probably automated and timed," Igor said. "Not in our intel. We cannot dive, though."

The light continued to fan back and forth across the strait, but still out in front of them. Mark was just about to order the sub stopped to avoid the light when it inexplicably snapped off.

He wiped the sweat from his brow with his sleeve. "How fast can we go here? I want to be gone before they turn that light back on."

Igor answered, "I wouldn't recommend above fifteen kilometers. We only have ten minutes to Baykovo Point. We can hide behind it once we are past."

"Sounding one meter."

The snow squall blew in without warning. Driving, blowing snow obliterated what little Mark could see through the scope. But more importantly, it now made the submarine all but invisible in the night. He exhaled a deep sigh of relief. The harrowing passage was all but done. And they had avoided plowing a furrow in the bottom of the channel. The water should be getting deeper shortly.

Sure enough: "Sounding ten meters."

Ψ

Russian Navy Captain First Rank Ivgany Yurtotov was near the end of his patience. Two weeks of merely steaming back and forth across his allotted search area had proven to be nothing more than fruitless effort. His repeated messages back to Pacific Fleet Command—dispatches stating that his area was empty, that the missing *Yaroslavl* submarine was not hidden or sunk somewhere in these depths—were simply ignored. He commanded the finest undersea warship in the entire Pacific. It was being tasked by incompetent idiots to search the same small box over and over again, as if the missing diesel boat would somehow mysteriously appear there, churned up perhaps by the screws of his far superior submarine.

Even his *zampolit*, his political officer, onboard to keep him politically correct and to "ensure the crew's patriotic spirit" was chafing at the direction or lack thereof.

Yurtotov shook his head to clear it. It was once again time to come up to periscope depth and communicate with Vladivostok. Maybe the chess masters back there would finally decide to employ the *Yakutsk* as she was meant to be used.

The heavy, stormy seas caused even the mammoth Improved *Severodvinsk*-class submarine to pitch and heave as the boat came up to periscope depth. Yurtotov's view out the scope showed him little more than threatening skies and mountainous seas. It was necessary that he hang on to the scope as the submarine rolled heavily, first to port and then over to starboard. The captain's borscht and cabbage golubtsi dinner was not resting well in his stomach. Fortunately, the radio *michman*—the Russian Navy's equivalent of a noncommissioned officer—copied all the messages on the first attempt. That allowed them to promptly return to the calm of the deep.

When the *michman* handed him the message board, Yurtotov flipped it open and scanned the first sheet, fully expecting it to tell him to continue circling around in the middle of the gale until he and his well-trained crew were sick and dizzy. But then, the captain could not suppress a broad smile. He hurried back to the chart table. It only took him a few seconds to verify where they were and another few to see where they needed to get to.

Their new orders were to proceed at best speed to shadow an American battle group—an American battle group!—a thousand kilometers almost due south of their present position.

A minute later, the mighty *Yakutsk* was at flank speed, happily and enthusiastically heading south.

Ψ

"New contact on the thin-line!" Jim Stumpf called out. "Designate Sierra One-Two-Two or One-Two-Three. Best bearing three-one-zero or two-four-zero."

The *Gato* had been trolling for Russian submarines from the sidelines off Petropavlovsk while they watched the Russians ensonify the water like crazy. They were still at a loss to figure out what the Russians were looking for, but they were certainly putting a lot of time and effort and sonar pulses into trying to find something. Over the last couple of days, they had noted several of the surface ships had dropped out of the search, and there seemed to be fewer aircraft buzzing around. But this was the first solid contact on a Russian submarine since the Improved *Severodvinsk* had gone active and unknowingly chased them away almost two weeks before.

"What y'all got, Senior Chief?" Lieutenant Commander Steve Hanly, the on-watch Officer-of-the-Deck, asked. Sometimes his thick Mississippi drawl was near indecipherable by crewmembers from other areas of the US.

"Well, Eng," Stumpf answered as he flipped through several screens, "it certainly looks like an Improved *Severodvinsk*. I'm seeing a three-point-six-hertz line that equates to a hull flow noise. Recommend you inform the captain while we get a first leg to determine ambiguity."

Henrietta Foster was in the control room, clutching her oversized mug of coffee, almost before Hanly had replaced the phone handset. The skipper on her first submarine had suggested she just get a coffee IV and leave that massive mug at home port.

"What do we have, Eng?" Foster asked as she flipped through the sonar displays on the command console.

"Skipper, contact on the thin-line, designated Sierra One-Two-One, bearing three-zero-eight drawing aft, and Sierra One-Two-Two, bearing two-four-two drawing aft. Based on a three-point-six line classified possible Improved *Severodvinsk*. I'm coming left to zero-three-zero to determine ambiguity and to open track."

Foster nodded. "Very good, Eng. Why don't you station the fire control tracking party. We want to get in trail of this big momma as soon as we can."

The *Gato* came around to the new course, but the TB-29A thin-line array still took over fifteen minutes to stabilize in a straight line on the new heading. By the time Jim Stumpf confirmed that the array was stable, the fire control tracking party was fully manned and raring to go. The XO, Lieutenant Commander Eric Householder, watched as his team manned their "plots." In truth, the days of using paper plots to solve for target range, course, and speed were long in the past. In modern submarines, everything was solved using advanced algorithms and results displayed on computer screens. Foster called it "video game plotting."

"Regain Sierra One-Two-Two, bearing two-three-eight!" Stumpf called out.

"Drop Sierra One-Two-One, track Sierra One-Two-Two," Householder spoke into this headset. The fire control tracking team now concentrated their efforts onto the contact to the southwest, the valid one.

It took almost fifteen more minutes of gathering and integrating bits of data before Eric Householder looked over at Henrietta Foster and said, "Skipper, we have a curve. Sierra One-Two-Two is drawing right. Current bearing two-three-one. Recommend coming around to course one-three-zero. We should be able to lock in a solution while we spiral in on this guy."

Foster looked at the tactical display on the ECDIS and ordered a course change to one-three-zero. As the boat swung around to the new direction, Householder joined Foster at the ECDIS.

"XO, looks like this guy is heading pretty much due south in a hurry," Foster noted. "I need for you to get into radio. Get up on the A-DSTP buoy and tell Group Seven that we are in contact with our friend. Get us water to the south and tell them we are going to need help. Even at a flank bell, assuming we can hold contact going flank, that bastard has better than a ten-knot speed advantage on us. We'll be lucky to hold him for maybe another hour."

"Got it," Householder confirmed.

"This big chunk is up to something out here in a righteous hurry. We need to find out what."

Ψ

Admiral Jon Ward took a deep breath. It was not every day that he got summoned to the fifth floor of the E-ring over on this side of the "five-sided puzzle palace" better known as the Pentagon. But the Secretary of Defense's office had called. Admiral Jonathan Ward was expected to be there...Ward checked his watch...in exactly two minutes, regardless of elevator times and potential security checkpoint delays. Before entering the ornately paneled outer office, he checked out his uniform in the reflection from the double glass doors with the OSD emblem etched in frosted glass. All good. The smiling receptionist immediately rose to greet him and usher him directly into the secretary's private office.

Harold Osterman dropped the file he was reading, rose from behind his large walnut desk, and stepped around to greet Ward.

"Admiral, so good of you to come on such short notice," he said, offering his hand. "I know that you are a very busy man and doing important work. Which I hope you know the DOD and I appreciate."

The consummate politician, Ward thought as he took the offered hand. "Thank you, Mr. Secretary. Or I should say, Mr. Vice President. Congratulations are in order."

Osterman waved off the congrats with a grin, then steered Ward over to a settee and coffee table. From that spot, one could overlook the Potomac River five stories below. Osterman poured coffee for both of them.

"Either title will do, I guess," Osterman said with a laugh. "I probably have a couple more weeks in and out of this office until we can name an interim, and then I'll be over at the Executive Office Building, I suppose, doing all the rest of the transition stuff from there before the Senate convenes. Best I be all 'transitioned' by then. Besides, being called 'Mister Secretary' always sounded to me like I should be wearing a skirt and filing my nails at a desk in the office pool. But then, 'Mister Vice' makes it sound like I should be chasing that skirt."

Ward laughed politely as Osterman motioned for him to take the seat across the table from where he was settling into an armchair. He had assumed that the newly elected vice president would be more politically correct now that he had been officially inaugurated. Apparently not.

"Damn fine work with those Children of the Gulag characters," Osterman said as he took a big drink of his coffee and not so subtly watched Ward's reaction over the top of his mug. The admiral had no idea how much Osterman—or his boss, the president—might know about the upstart group and Ward's involvement, so he simply remained silent and waited for him to go on as he sipped his own brew. "So, what is your read on this bunch? Are they to be taken seriously? Can they really do what they say they want to do? And are they serious about wanting us to play ball for their side?"

Ward continued to sample his coffee as he gathered his thoughts. At this level in the government, and at this point in the transition to the president's second term—and his veep's first—it was impossible to discern in which direction this conversation would go. But Ward had been Director of Naval Intelligence long enough to know that anything he said—fact or intuition—could affect administration policy and, ultimately, the future of the country and the lives of men and women in the military. Positively or negatively.

"Let me answer your last question first, sir," he finally responded. "The group intends to play ball, but on their own terms. If our interests happen to coincide with theirs, then we might play together for mutual benefit. If not, I expect they will play with whoever offers what they want at a price they are willing to pay."

"Yes, yes. That makes sense," Osterman answered, maybe just a bit too enthusiastically.

"As to whether they are on the up-and-up, I sense that they are a very pragmatic group. If they really came out of the gulags, they would have to be in order to have survived not only the climate and isolation but the lack of support from the Russian government. They were, for the most part, abandoned way up there when the Soviet Union broke up. And then, the small quantity of precious metals they mined from the gulags became insignificant to the government and the oligarchs, who had already turned to petroleum, pharmaceuticals, technology—including hacking—and other very effective ways to become fabulously rich. I believe that the 'Children' are also far more sophisticated than some might suspect, considering they have grown up in the far reaches of the remote territories east of Siberia, an apparent wilderness and not what most would imagine to be a hotbed of revolution. In actuality, they have been preparing a very solid network of finances and an underground intelligence system that seems to stretch worldwide. Based on what we have learned, they are well capitalized and have access to resources to remain so. They might show up for a meeting on a dogsled or skis or a snowmobile, but they have political and financial infrastructure, we have learned, that would rival many nations that already exist. And considering all that preparation and the vulnerability of Russia at this point, odds may remain long, but these people have a good chance to pull off this plan of theirs."

Ward paused, gauging the secretary's reaction. Osterman had not touched his coffee since the admiral started talking. Ward found it hard to believe this was news to the incoming vice president, that the CIA and others had not briefed him and the president on the group and their vitality. But Ward was—so far as he knew—the only one in the US government who had personally met with the leader of the group. Maybe that gave the admiral's take on the situation more weight than what might have been delivered by some intel wonk.

"Yes, yes," Osterman said. "Please go on, Admiral."

"Sir, from what I was told by their leader, Ivan Dostervesky, and from what I have learned from other sources, they are not terrorists or simple opportunists, trying to get rich off the recent struggles of the Russian government. They sincerely are seeking sovereignty and independence for a new nation carved out of territory the Russians appear to not care much about. And they will do what it takes to achieve that aim. That includes dancing with anybody—and I mean anybody—who is willing to tango with them. It's my opinion that they will accept help from whoever offers it as long as the strings aren't too constraining. They have already made covert contact with a duke's mixture of potential partners, including North and South Korea, China, Japan, and, of course, us. Again, I believe they are thinking very strategically, far more advanced in that area than anyone might expect a bunch of miners and lumberjacks from the backwoods to be."

Osterman leaned forward, rubbing his chin, his cup of coffee now completely forgotten.

"I respect your observations, Admiral," he said. "But those sources you mention. Just how reliable are they?"

Ward again grabbed himself some thinking time by slowly sipping his own brew. He was well aware that the man across the table from him had every intention of becoming president of the United States himself in four years. Maybe sooner if the opposition party continued its incessant efforts to impeach the sitting chief executive and kick him from office.

"If I had any doubts about them or the accuracy of their input, neither would be considered as a source, nor would any of the information they brought be relayed to you and the president. I am responsible for the lives of thousands of sailors and officers all around the world, along with the safety and security of America as it pertains to the efforts of the US Navy. I would never put that at risk by not fully vetting information, regardless of its source."

"Of course, of course. I don't suppose you would want to share details of who those sources might be," Osterman asked, fishing.

"No, sir." No hesitation by Jon Ward this time.

"All very interesting. Very interesting, indeed." Osterman suddenly remembered his cup of coffee and took a drink while he thought about what he had just heard. Ward could hear the wheels whirring. Someone making the transition he was had to consider such developments from so many angles, including politically. In likelihood, mostly politically. "Admiral, I want you to continue to mine those mysterious sources of yours so we always know what is really going on. But I also want you to remain personally in touch with these...these 'Children.' Offer them our assistance in their worthy goals for forming a free and democratic nation. I speak for the president when I say we will give them what they want, right up to but not including risking open confrontation with Russia. It's an old saw but a true one. We do not want to poke a wounded bear. Of course, we must remain covert. And at least maintain plausible deniability."

"Understood, sir." Ward now looked out the window, at the winding Potomac River, waiting for the next shoe to drop. He did not have to wait long at all.

"But Admiral Ward, they must understand that in exchange for support, they will need to reimburse us for expenses and compensate us for the risks against world peace that we will be taking," the secretary declared. "I believe you reported that they are well capitalized in this secession effort of theirs. We'll arrange a back-channel conduit for payment. Nothing for you to worry about there except relaying the details to whoever manages their finances. Any questions?"

Ward shook his head. "No, sir. Pretty straightforward."

"Good," Osterman said as he rose to escort Ward out. But the admiral sensed there was yet another piece of footwear about to yield to gravity. "Oh, one last thing. Anything related to this matter is to run directly through this office. Or wherever they stick me in the interim over there on Pennsylvania Avenue while they paint and put up frilly curtains in my office. You understand, of course. I...we...don't want to risk any potential leaks about our dealings with this group, so we will for the time being necessarily limit who knows what. Right?"

Admiral Jon Ward nodded, shook hands with the new vice president, and left.

12

The ice-hardened fishing trawler *Lovets Ryby* nudged aside the brash ice as it made its way into the tiny, sheltered bay. This time of year, the fishermen had Menshikov Island all to themselves. Except for the ever-present seal herds, of course. The same animals that supplied skins that became flight jackets for Japanese aviators back in World War II. It took an especially hardy group of men to wrest their livelihoods from the Sea of Okhotsk in the winter. The bitter Arctic cold was bad enough, but the real hazards were the wind-driven storms that hurtled in from the north. The winds could drive mountainous waves out in the deep water, large enough to swamp a fishing trawler like the *Lovets Ryby*. Nearer to shore, the winds piled the ice into impenetrable ridges, easily trapping the unwary.

The *Lovets Ryby* was one of the few boats running the risks and working the edges of the pack ice this early in the season. There was a reason. They hoped to get a jump on the markets and be selling their hold full of pollack at top prices down at the Korsakov piers even as their competitors were just heading out of the harbors for the season's first catch.

The *Lovets Ryby*'s trawl nets were wrapped around the massive hydraulic reel across the ship's stern and the holds were full, but the ship would not head directly back to port. She had one more task to complete before steaming south. And this job required that they anchor in this unnamed bay on the lee shore of Menshikov Island, far away from any prying eyes, and proceed to wait for someone else.

Fedor Rybak, the captain, kept a weather eye on the barometer as he maneuvered the fishing boat into the anchorage. The barometer had been falling for the last couple of hours, and the winds had been ominously backing around to the northwest. Although his weather receiver was tuned to the Japanese Meteorological Maritime Forecast channel, he had much more reliance on his own instinctive feel for the sea. He felt a bad blow coming soon. It would surely hit well before dawn, and the sun had just dipped below the horizon for the typically long night at this latitude.

Prudence dictated using both a bow and stern anchor for this particular evolution. The bow anchor was easy. Just drop it, back down to set the flukes, then pay out the snubbing scope to hold them in place. The stern anchor took a little more work. First, they had to back down while letting out more chain on the bow anchor. When they were over the spot for the stern anchor, they dropped it and then paid out chain on the stern anchor while taking in chain on the bow anchor. It was a tricky operation but one the captain had done many times.

The *Lovets Ryby* had just finished setting their stern anchor when they sighted company approaching through the dimming light. It was a submarine, popping to the surface only a few hundred meters off the bay's mouth. The black vessel was almost invisible against the darkening evening sky, but its flashing recognition light was easy to spot.

Mark Lodkamatros waved from the sub's bridge, then shouted across the open water. "Fedor, you seadog, it is good to see you and that garbage scow of yours!"

Fedor Rybak answered right back, now close enough that shouting was no longer necessary. "Mark Lodkamatros, you have not changed. The only time you say nice things is when you want something only I can provide."

"Well, now that you mention it, our fuel tanks are getting a little low," Lodkamatros responded with a laugh. "And the groceries are becoming much too repetitive to maintain proper morale."

"Well, then bring your little submarine alongside, and we'll see what we can do," Rybak retorted, glancing up at the black sky. "But we should hurry. I do not like the looks of the weather. We have a storm brewing."

"I am disappointed in your hospitality," Lodkamatros said across the narrowing bit of open water between the vessels. "I was looking forward to some fresh fish and a little vodka in those palatial quarters that you call a cabin on your yacht."

Good-natured needling done, it took ten minutes to maneuver the *Yaroslavl* alongside the fishing trawler and double up lines. Then a ten-centimeter hose was lowered from the *Lovets Ryby* and hooked to the submarine's fueling connection. It took over an hour to fill the submarine's fuel tanks. Meanwhile, crate after crate of food was passed across and lowered into the submarine.

Even sheltered as they were on the lee side of the mountainous volcanic island, the winds were soon noticeably building. When the waves in the anchorage rolled up the submarine's hull and poured down the open hatch they were using for loading, Captain Lodkamatros understood that he had all the provisions that he could safely take onboard at this stop. Even disconnecting the fuel hose was now hazardous. Just then, a rogue wave rolled up the stern and washed a couple of crewmen into the frigid water. Had they not been wearing harnesses, they would have been swept away in the waves. And had they not been wearing special thermal suits, pulled from the icy waters immediately, and rushed below to be dried out and warmed up, they would have soon died.

"Fedor," Lodkamatros yelled across to the trawler's bridge, his words torn by the wind. "We must get underway before these winds drive us up on the beach. Rendezvous according to the plan in two weeks?"

Rybak yelled back, "*Da*, we will be there."

"A case or two of caviar would be appropriate next time," was Mark's final shot, animatedly waved off by the helpful fisherman.

The submarine promptly cast off lines and headed back out to sea, pitching and heaving as it met open water. Minutes after clearing the headland, the *Yaroslavl* again slipped beneath the waves.

It took the *Lovets Ryby* nearly an hour with the crew fighting both the Arctic storm and the freezing sea on the open deck to haul in both anchors and steer back out into the raging water. The crew braced themselves for a rough night as they headed south with the holds filled with the fish, the remainder of their hard-won cargo.

Ψ

Joe Glass charged into the Sub Group Seven Ops Center at Naval Base Yokosuka, Japan, and plopped down in the seat reserved for him at the head of the briefing table. He peered up at the large-screen monitor that covered most of the far wall. It displayed a colorful chart of the North Pacific Ocean from the Western Bering Sea all the way down to Hokkaido and over to the La Perouse Strait. The *Green Bay* Amphibious Ready Group showed up about five hundred miles due east of Hokkaido. The *Ronald Reagan* Carrier Battle Group was plotted about one hundred miles north of that. Also marked on the display were the two submarine operating areas assigned to his pair of submarines working in the area, the *George Mason* and the *Gato*.

Glass turned to the young lieutenant commander who was currently designated as the Op Center Watch Officer.

"Okay, Bill, what do we have so far?"

"Admiral, four hours ago, at seventeen-thirty Zulu, *Gato* reported positive contact on an Improved *Severodvinsk* Russian sub. That would be the *Yakutsk*, the one the Russians snuck around from the Northern Fleet. Contact was seventy-five miles east-southeast of Petr." Bill Snedley moved the big mouse pointer down to a spot off the Kamchatka coast to indicate the location. "Their best solution on the *Yakutsk* was a course of due south and a high speed, better than thirty-five knots. For coordination across the Theater ASW Command, we have designated this contact as Case Four-Six."

"Well, if she is going balls-to-the-wall like that, *Gato* sure as hell won't be able to stay with her long," Glass interjected. "Those *Virginia*s are great ships, but they sure can't keep up with a hot rod like a *Severodvinsk*."

"No, sir," Snedley agreed. "And *Gato* reported lost contact at nineteen-fifty Zulu. Their last contact still had Case Four-Six heading due south, zooming along at thirty-five knots."

Joe Glass pursed his lips. "Time for me to put on my Theater ASW Commander's hat. Any other assets reporting contact? Please tell me we have something else. And what is the intel best guess on where this guy is headed? Right now, something tells me he is highballing it straight toward the *Reagan* battle group. I would really like to have an asset out there tell me my guess is wrong."

Snedley keyed a dropdown display. Two long, narrow red cones appeared, one with its apex near Adak, up in the Aleutian Islands. The other one had its apex near the city of Kushiro, on Hokkaido. The two cones intersected well south of the Kamchatka Peninsula but right on the projected course for Case Four-Six. The intersection was shown as yet another long, narrow ellipse, but this one was yellow.

"IUSS is reporting intermittent hits on the Adak SOSUS array and also on the Hokkaido one. That gives us an uncertainty ellipse with a hundred-mile major axis and a twenty-mile minor axis." Snedley circled the mouse pointer around the yellow ellipse. IUSS was the Integrated Undersea Surveillance System, a network of all types of sonar installations that covered most of the planet's undersea territory. Just not all of them.

"He's in there somewhere with an eighty percent probability," Snedley added.

"Bill, that ellipse covers a lot of area. And I don't like that 'intermittent' word. What else do we have?" Glass asked as he scanned the screen. There did not seem to be any other friendly anti-submarine warfare assets anywhere in play.

"Boss, both of our SURTASS ships are down off the China coast," Snedley answered. "They are both tied up tracking the Chinese boats right now." The Surveillance Towed Array Sensor System was made up of ships that towed twin-line TB-29 passive arrays, very sensitive sonar arrays similar to the TB-29A arrays that the submarines trailed behind them. The SURTASS ships were necessarily very slow. Using them in theater took a lot of advanced planning and lead time. Because they were a scarce asset, they were normally deployed in answer to national-level tasking.

"Those storms up there in that area are way too rough for the skimmers steaming with the *Reagan* to be very effective with their towed arrays," Snedley continued. "Those MFTAs that the *Arleigh Burke* destroyers carry are good, but not in sea state six or seven."

"So, I guess we should only conduct ASW when the weather's nice and tranquil," Glass said sarcastically. He thought for a moment, then asked, "How about the P-8s?"

"We scrambled a P-8 out of Atsugi thirty minutes ago. It will be on station in three hours," Snedley answered. "One of the P-8s forward stationed at Adak will launch in twenty minutes, soon as it's fueled and we have a driver there. He's still three hours out, too. And we will still need a break in the weather, or neither one will be able to do anything except circle their happy asses up at thirty thousand feet trying to dodge turbulence. Boss, bottom line is all we got right now is a hope that this guy does something stupid."

Glass stood up and stared at the chart. It appeared that he had nothing but bad options.

"Hoping the other guy does something dumb is not good strategy if we plan on winning the game," Glass said, mostly to himself. Then he had another thought. "What about the *George Mason*? I know we're bringing her in for her mid-deployment maintenance period, and those boys absolutely need some liberty, but it looks like they are the only other possible players left on the bench."

Snedley nodded and punched a couple of buttons on his keyboard. "Admiral, if we move the *George Mason* over to intercept right now and move the *Reagan* group a couple of hundred miles south, it's just possible we could pull this off."

"Okay, you move the *Mason*. And get me the *Reagan* battle group commander on the horn. Let's get into position for the game-winning field goal."

Ψ

Brian Edwards could feel the excitement building in the crew. Their long but uneventful operation was finally nearing completion. The submarine USS *George Mason* had been covertly steaming around the Northern Pacific and the Sea of Okhotsk for almost three months now, performing a long list of tasks to keep up with activity by North Korea, Russia, and China—and even friendly nations—in a region most US citizens did not even know existed. One that was easily one of the more tense plots of salt water on the planet. Now, finally, Yokosuka and some well-earned rest for the crew was only a thousand miles and a couple of days' steaming south. Edwards could almost taste the fresh veggies. A cold beer would sure be good, too. And he had almost forgotten what sunlight felt like on his skin.

Edwards sat at the head of the wardroom table. They might be forty-eight hours away from some leave time, but it was also time to plan out the myriad details for the upcoming mid-deployment maintenance period at the Yokosuka Navy Ship Repair Facility. To give the maintainers as much time as possible to gather all of the parts and plans necessary to get *George Mason* right back up to tip-top condition after a long time battling the northern seas, the sub would need to "call ahead" and tell them what was broken or what merely needed to be worked on. They would not be able to simply pull up onto the rack at the express lube joint. The XO, Jackson Biddle, had gathered the key players to do a final groom on all the plans before they pulled in to port.

"Chop, you got the LOGREQ message ready to go?" Biddle asked, turning to the supply officer, Ensign Jason Wordle. "Chop" was almost always the nickname for the supply officer on a submarine, likely emanating from "pork chop," which their insignia faintly resembled. Wordle was seated at the foot of the table, the traditional place for the supply officer at these sorts of meetings. That, according to one of the captain's former skippers, was so everybody around the table would have better aim at him when he inevitably got blamed for some shortfall.

"Yes, sir!" Wordle responded, almost in a shout. "Fresh veggies will be waiting on the pier!"

As usual, the last of the fresh vegetables had disappeared from the menu two weeks into this trip. Such a luxury was now little more than a distant memory. Dishes such as three-bean salad and mushy canned asparagus had been the order of the day ever since. And they were now nearing the limit on stored food. There were disturbing rumors that they were down to the last box of ice cream mix. Such a catastrophe could lead to mutiny!

Edwards chuckled, but then turned serious. "Gentlemen, much as I want a fresh salad, too, this is, after all, a maintenance period for the boat, remember? Eng, where are you with the plans?"

"Skipper," LCDR Jeffrey Otanga, the engineer, piped up. "The CSMP is up-to-date and ready to send off. All of the message two-kilos are ready to go, too. My guys have been pulling double watches to get it all done."

The CSMP, or current ship's maintenance plan, was an up-to-date compilation of all of the maintenance that would be required to be performed on the submarine during its time in port. The 4790-2K maintenance action form—or more commonly and simply dubbed a "two-kilo"—related in detail the work and parts needed to perform each specific job to be done. Every piece of work, from replacing a fuse in the coffeemaker to major repairs on the reactor, had to have its own 4790-2K to request the fix and then to track it all the way to successful completion. It was not unusual to have several thousand 4790-2K forms for a maintenance period like the one for which *George Mason* was now aiming her bow. But even though the engineering crew had been working on the forms virtually from the day they left port, it would take less than a second for them to be sent by digital packet and receipted for down at Yokosuka.

"Okay," Edwards said, slapping both hands on the table and pushing himself upright. "Sounds like we're ready to go. XO, get the message traffic to radio. I'm going to Control to watch us come to PD."

Biddle pushed a button on his keyboard.

"All the traffic is to radio and authorized for release," he said, but his words were aimed at Edwards's back. The skipper was already headed out of the wardroom, happily but tunelessly whistling.

The crewmembers were all smiles as Edwards made his way into the control room. Two more days and they would be walking on solid ground again. The captain had been hearing quiet conversations about planned liberty trips to Tokyo. Some more adventurous members of the crew even had made plans for climbing Mount Fuji.

The trip up to periscope depth was uneventful, if a little rough in the stormy seas. They quickly determined that they had this piece of rolling ocean all to themselves. It only took a couple of seconds to send off their outgoing traffic and to download whatever incoming messages there might be. Nobody expected there to be any incoming mail of any significant importance.

They were still coming back down to their transit depth and confirming their continued course for Yokosuka when a grim-faced Jackson Biddle stepped out of the radio room and pulled Edwards aside.

"Skipper," he whispered as he handed Edwards a portable tablet. "You ain't going to like this."

Brian Edwards scanned the message, grew red in the face, and then read it again, this time in depth.

"Shit," he muttered. "Double dog shit. Okay, get the Nav and Weps up here." He turned to Jerome Billings, the on-watch Officer-of-the-Deck, and ordered, "OOD, come to course zero-seven-zero. Make your depth seven hundred feet. Come to ahead flank."

Billings frowned. That was not the bearing for Yokosuka, Japan.

Turning back to Biddle, Edwards continued, "XO, have sonar break out everything they have on a Russian Improved *Severodvinsk* submarine. Get everybody up to speed ASAP. Looks like we're gonna be trolling for a really big fish before we get to go on vacation."

13

"Well, Harold, is our Eagle Scout admiral going to play ball?" President Stan Smitherman asked as he sat back and swirled the bourbon in his glass.

Vice President Harold Osterman looked into his own drink for a minute. Smitherman knew the answer to most questions before he asked them. "Stan, by my read, Jon Ward is a straight shooter. He will play ball as long as he senses everything is on the up-and-up. The instant he feels anything going sideways, he will scream bloody murder, long and loud."

President Smitherman nodded in agreement. "Pretty much what I heard, too. Word on the street corroborates your gut feeling."

Not "word on the street" at all. The assessment of Admiral Jon Ward came from top agents in multiple government agencies and went back to even before the naval intel head actually became an Eagle Scout. They could even have found Ward's score on the test for his Morse code merit badge had they wanted it.

Smitherman took a healthy swig of his bourbon, then put the glass down on the Sheraton tea table and leaned forward. "If we are going to make this little Russian gold mine pay off, we are going to have to work around the good admiral, then. We clearly need him to open a line of communication for us to these Children. Hell, they insist on him being the link for some damn reason. But at the same time, we will need to keep him completely isolated from the payoffs."

Osterman barely tasted his highball. "That is going to take some really fancy footwork. Ward is no fool and certainly not a patsy."

Smitherman smiled. "I have just the guy to make this happen. I don't think you know Rex Wiley. He has been hanging around for a few days while I worked out the idea. He has a long history in a bunch of three-letter agencies. He's an operator over at Langley now, but on loan to the White House. His loyalty to me is unquestioned. Rock solid. If anybody can set up the payoffs and leave no trace—even no scent the admiral might pick up—it's Wiley."

There was a discreet knock on the door. Smitherman's private receptionist stuck her head into the presidential study. "Excuse me, Mr. President. You asked me to interrupt you when it's time for your call with President Salkov. White House communications has set up for you to take the call in the Oval Office."

"Thank you, Betty," Smitherman said as he rose. He slugged back the last of his bourbon and headed through the doorway into the historic room next door. "Come on, Harold. We may as well see what that crooked bastard has to say," he muttered as they walked through. "Can't stand the guy. A real cold fish. I sent the bastard a fifth of good bourbon when he got reelected for the umpteenth time three years ago. Then I saw a photo last week of him in his office. The whisky was sitting there on the shelf behind him, like some damn trophy, still full. Wouldn't surprise me if he did it just to piss me off."

Smitherman plopped down behind the Resolute Desk and waved Harold Osterman to one of the straight-backed chairs across from him. At the signal from the communications technician, Smitherman pushed the speaker button on his phone.

"Grigory, my old friend," Smitherman boomed in his best hale-and-hearty fashion. It was time for a world leader to have a discreet discussion with one of his equals, an acquaintance if not exactly an old friend. "It's been far too long since we last spoke. G20 last spring, wasn't it? In Bali. Good times."

President Grigory Iosifovich Salkov answered, "Stan, first let me offer my congratulations on your reelection and to Harold for his election. And yes, it was Bali. You took a couple thousand dollars off me at the poker table that evening, if I remember correctly."

Stan Smitherman laughed. Laughed genuinely. "Yes, and I thank you for the very nice campaign donation. But to what do we owe the honor of this call? It is quite late in Moscow, isn't it?"

Salkov turned serious. "Stan, I want to personally discuss a situation with you before our two countries get inextricably entangled once again in some affair that is not good for either of us. For our nations, that is. As you probably have heard, we had a freight train brutally attacked by terrorists in the Russian Far East. The FSB has recovered documentation and evidence that implicates a group who call themselves the *Deti Gulaga*, or 'Children of the Gulag' in English. They appear to be a group of bloodthirsty dissident terrorists who are fighting for what they see as an independent state somewhere in our Russian Far East."

Smitherman paused a moment for effect, then interjected. "Grigory, that seems to be a common problem for you lately, what with the Ukraine, Kazakhstan, and now this brouhaha in your far east. Perhaps your nation is too big to properly govern. Hell, you got, what? Eleven time zones?"

Salkov ignored Smitherman's jibe and continued. "We have reason to believe that these *Deti Gulaga* are making diplomatic contact with other governments who have influence in that area. We are sure that they had military assistance from some other government in accomplishing the attack on the train. For this reason, I am contacting all of the heads of state personally so that you and they will hear directly from me that we unequivocally will not tolerate interference in our sovereign rights in this or any other matter. We have no fear of this ragtag bunch, but when other foolish nations see this as an opportunity to take advantage of the people of Russia, we must be sure everyone understands the seriousness of the consequences. Of course, you would not tell me if this bloodthirsty splinter group had already approached the United States. But if the *Deti Gulaga* should contact you, I urge you in the strongest way, and for the sake of world peace, to steer clear of them, to stay out of this minor internal squabble."

Smitherman sat with a broad grin on his face. Salkov had just unwittingly revealed without doubt how very worried he was by this new threat to Mother Russia and how seriously he was concerned by the Children of the Gulag and their potential helpers lining up to deal misery to Salkov and his faltering nation.

Weakness. The president of the United States had just gotten a strong whiff of weakness.

"World peace," Smitherman said. "That's what we all want. Now, you about ready for another bottle of good Kentucky sippin' whisky? I know that last batch is long gone by now, and we don't want y'all to be gettin' thirsty over there."

Harold Osterman could hardly suppress a guffaw.

Ψ

Luda Egorov pulled her coat tightly around her and charged out the door. The blast of Arctic air almost blew her over as she dashed from the *Vladivostok News* building's high glass main entrance across the icy sidewalk and to the car that was waiting for her, double-parked on busy Ulitsa Aleut-skaya. The driver stood with the door open as she skated over and slid into the back seat of the Mercedes S 580 limo. Skating on sidewalks was a skill necessary for anyone living in Vladivostok, where winter daytime high temperatures rarely moved above freezing and moisture off the Sea of Japan was abundant and usually fell in frozen form.

Egorov smiled as she noted the luxury car's heaters were on full blast and doing a fine job. The rear seat heaters were an absolute luxury. Being the most influential and popular newspaper reporter in Far East Russia certainly had its benefits.

The mission from Ivan Dostervesky had come only a few hours before. It was a surprise to her. Egorov did not like last-minute surprises, especially when it came to assignments that could jeopardize her unique position of spying for the Children of the Gulag, but Dostervesky, their leader, had been his typical insistent self. She assumed this would be an important job, though. And besides, Ilya Kozlov, the governor of the Far East Federal District, was easy to manipulate, as usual. All the reporter had needed to do was call him up—his assistant passed her call directly to the governor as if it was a standing order to do so—and then mention that her editor had asked her to interview the new admiral of the Russian Far East Fleet, Sergey Morsky.

Kozlov, one of the busiest and most important men in the city, was obviously eager to oblige. Less than an hour later, Kozlov personally called her back to say that the interview was arranged. She was to meet with the admiral at the Naval Headquarters. As was usual procedure, Kozlov would be present as well, just in case there were particulars on which the admiral might not yet be prepared to comment.

In case he said something he should not, Egorov thought. That was the real reason for the governor wishing to sit in on the interview. And, of course, to be able to spend time with Ms. Egorov.

The latter became even more obvious when Governor Kozlov informed the reporter that they would ride over to Naval Headquarters together. Much more efficient in gaining entrance, he said. That confirmed two other things for Egorov. He highly valued the reporter for her propaganda capabilities. And he had interest in her beyond being just a very powerful mouthpiece. She knew she was getting older and that she was not really all that attractive—neither, by the way, was the obese politician—but her journalistic instincts also meant that she could read men quite well. The governor wanted to bed her.

The limo driver, his face mostly covered with a scarf and hat pulled low over his eyes against the wind, had opened the door for her as she slid in. By the time he had gone back around and eased in at the driver's position, she realized her driver was none other than Governor Ilya Kozlov himself. So he would also be her driver. It was just the two of them. He greeted her warmly. Too warmly. He was bragging about how much he loved the Mercedes limo and just how impressed he had been at being able to use it for this short journey, likely due to the importance of his passenger.

Egorov showed him a brilliant smile in his rearview mirror, but at the same time she clenched her jaw and gritted her teeth. Such pandering was disgusting to her, but she was accustomed to it. She got it all the time. But almost always for professional reasons.

"This is a much more prestigious ride than my usual one," he was saying. "The SsangYong Actyon that the government has allotted for my usual purposes as an official vehicle is serviceable. Most of the time, that is. But it was manufactured right here in Vladivostok, and we want local citizens to see our loyalty to the local economy, so I am stuck, you see." He paused for a moment, then hastily added, "My comments on the subject are off the record, of course."

"Of course, Governor." Another fake smile.

They turned onto the busy Pushkinskaya Ulitsa, headed toward the waterfront and the main naval base. They almost immediately ran into a construction detour. Not unusual. The flagman vigorously waved them up Ulitsa Banevura. There, a second flagman indicated they should turn down what appeared to be more an alley than a street.

If either of the people in the Mercedes had taken a look behind them, they would have seen that theirs was the only vehicle so directed. And that each of the flagmen and the construction cones disappeared as soon as the limo passed. The empty alley made a sudden blind right turn and then dead-ended. As the governor brought the Mercedes to a screeching halt before a solid brick wall, a black panel van slid to a stop behind it, effectively blocking off the only exit.

Four masked and armed men piled out of the panel van's side door and simultaneously yanked open all four of the limo's doors. Pistol and rifle muzzles were pointed directly at the occupants.

Kozlov was blubbering, pleading for his life, even as he was yanked out of the car. One of the men immediately dropped a cloth hood over his head. Luda Egorov was similarly hooded, and the two were shoved into the van and guided to bench seats at the rear. In less than thirty seconds, the panel van had backed down the alley and merged into thick, tangled Vladivostok afternoon traffic.

Ilya Kozlov, convinced he would soon die, sobbed quietly. Luda Egorov remained silent.

"Governor Kozlov, Ms. Egorov, it is very nice of you to meet with us on... uh...such short notice." The voice carried a pleasant, non-threatening tone. "You will forgive me if I do not remove your hoods at this time. I am afraid that I cannot allow you to see the faces of those of us who will be your hosts for the next few hours."

Ilya Kozlov cried and, mostly in a moan, begged, "Please do not kill us. I promise I will do anything you want. Give you what money I have. Just do not hurt us." Then, with a sudden burst of bravado, he swallowed hard and added, "And you know any harm to either of us will result in the full force of the Russian government being brought against—"

The voice interrupted. "Wait, wait! My dear governor, we have no intention of hurting you or the lady. We merely want to have a discussion with you, and I am convinced that this unfortunate means of achieving such an uninterrupted audience with the both of you is the only way we can accomplish that. We will enjoy a nice drive around the city for the next couple of hours while we talk. Then, you will be released. Released unharmed."

"Wh...wh...what could we possibly have to talk about?" Kozlov stammered, clearly not yet convinced that he would live to see the brittle sunset this day.

"I am Ivan Dostervesky," the voice answered, "and we are going to discuss the *Deti Gulaga* and our efforts to establish an independent sovereign country out of our homeland. The Russian government, and prior to them, the Soviet Union, saw fit to imprison and then abandon our parents in the wilderness of the Magadan Oblast. Now, I wish for you to carry our demands back to Moscow. And we shall also ask that Ms. Egorov publish them in the *Vladivostok News*, and do so accurately, including the reasoning behind what we are going to do."

Luda Egorov finally spoke up. "Mr. Dostervesky, if you expect me to accurately report your demands, I will need to remove this hood so that I may take notes."

Dostervesky chuckled. "We anticipated the needs of a journalist. And a bureaucrat, too. We are already recording this conversation, and we will provide each of you a digital media copy when you are released. So, you will not need to take notes or rely solely on your memories in such a stressful situation. Nor will you see our faces. For your technical people, there is no point in attempting to trace the origin of the flash drives, either. Their purchase cannot be traced. Nor can the computers on which they were formatted, nor the devices that are being used to make the recordings. Now, let us begin."

After almost exactly two hours of discussion and seemingly endless left and right turns, periods of running at top speed and others locked in traffic, and sometimes sitting still for five or ten minutes in quiet spots away from the noise of the city, the pair of prisoners felt the van come to a halt once again. But this time, they heard the panel doors slide open and felt the intrusion of cold, damp wind.

As they were helped down out of the van onto solid ground, someone handed each of them a small object. "This is the flash drive, the recording of our conversation that we promised," Dostervesky explained. "Now, to be perfectly clear, I expect to see our demands published in your newspaper within one week, Ms. Egorov. And Governor, I expect you not only to relay the information to the Russian government but to make certain everyone understands why meeting our demands is not only the best option for them but also that they comprehend what will happen if they choose not to. You have one week to relay back to us by the means we have enumerated what the government's reaction is. Otherwise, or if they refuse, we will commence with the activities that we discussed. Understand that we are not bluffing. It is entirely in your hands to prevent the needless loss of life and destruction of property that we promise will come if these demands are not fully met."

With that, the door suddenly slammed shut, and the van raced away amid screeching tires and blue smoke. Ilya Kozlov yanked off his hood, turned wide-eyed to Egorov, and began speaking breathlessly. "I apologize that knowing me got you involved in this thing, my dear Luda. Dealing with terrorists is one chore that I am required to perform. Not you. They should not be dragging an innocent reporter into this sort of evil, and I fear it is all my fault. They surely have a spy, and he knew of this excursion this afternoon."

Luda Egorov worked to suppress a smile as she pulled off her own hood. She quickly determined that they had been deposited only a couple of blocks from her office.

"Ilya, it is certainly not your fault. It is the world we live in."

"But I should never have come to collect you without guards. Or without having an armed security detail following us. Not in these treacherous times. I can only apologize."

"Had you done so, there might well have been gunplay, and who knows how many of us would have been hurt in the crossfire." She squinted as her eyes adjusted to the bright afternoon light. "Now, if you care for my opinion on this whole Children of the Gulag scenario, I suggest you contact Moscow and relay their demands exactly as they made them. Let them decide how to proceed. Meanwhile, I will draft up a story about our little adventure." Then, she added, "I also hope you will apologize to Admiral Morsky for our having to miss the interview. Perhaps we can reschedule in the next day or so."

The governor looked puzzled. "The admiral? Oh. Oh, yes. Next day or so." Then, as an afterthought and with a near smile, he told her, "But I am sure he will understand the reason for the most unfortunate postponement. And you and I can reschedule."

Governor Kozlov was on the phone with government security officials the instant he returned to his office.

Luda Egorov got a diet soda from her office fridge, sat at her computer, and pulled up the story about the kidnapping that she had already written the day before. She wanted to check once more for typos.

14

Russian Air Force *Starshiy Leytenant* Maly Yastreb finally had found the time to review the mission plan as he led his flight of two low-altitude jet attack aircraft across the Sea of Okhotsk and up into the mountains at the north end of the ice-covered sea. The details had only arrived moments before they were to depart. The briefing took place in the cramped transport on the ride out to the flight line. Biggest issue: the mission was right at the edge of their combat radius. The addition of drop tanks gave them some margin on fuel, but that came at the expense of being able to carry more ordnance. There really was not any other option, but everyone—including Yastreb—felt they would have more than enough firepower to do the job they had just been assigned.

The hastily drafted orders had come down from the Eastern Military District Command of the General Staff of the Russian Armed Forces. The GRU, the Russian central military intelligence organization, had gleaned bits of intelligence information about a supposed terrorist training camp that was well hidden in the snow-covered mountainous wastelands way up in the Magadan Oblast. The data seemed to support the likelihood that this was where the self-styled guerilla group that attacked the ammunition train out of Vladivostok had trained for that cowardly attack. There was also the possibility that this might be an outpost—maybe even the headquarters—

of the upstart group, the *Deti Gulaga*, that everyone was suddenly whispering about.

Satellite imagery had located the training camp hidden in a mountain valley far from any civilization. An area fit for only wolves and Amur tigers. The camp appeared large enough to house a hundred troops or more, and they could see a couple of vehicles that looked suspiciously like anti-aircraft missile launchers. All that made it well worth the fuel, ordnance, and effort required to take them out, even if they in no way could be a serious threat to Mother Russia. Not what was likely from a group of unsophisticated rubes plotting fantasies of secession and country-building from way up there in the wilderness.

There was also the word that a group of a dozen well-armed military police had gone in on snowmobiles to investigate the camp. They were almost certainly lost in one of the region's sudden blizzards, but there remained the slightest of possibilities that the would-be terrorists had somehow intercepted and defeated them. Plausible but highly unlikely. Still, that was another reason to justify the air strike.

Besides, whoever they were, they had rocket launchers. And those launchers were to be Yastreb's target today. They had to be taken out before the airborne troops on the choppers coming in behind them could swoop in and excise the tiny rebellious cancer before it metastasized and grew and eventually required a more robust and potentially costly surgery.

The place was inaccessible to anything but a helicopter insertion of ground troops. The only helicopter with both the range and the lift needed for this mission was the mammoth but venerable Mi-26 Halo—the world's second largest rotary-wing airship—so they were also a part of the day's assault force. With all of the fighting going on far to the west, in and around the border of European Russia, there were only four Mi-26s in all of the Far East region. All four of them were being utilized on this mission. And they carried a hundred well-trained and heavily armed troops. Nobody wanted to have to come back up here again in the wintertime to finish the job.

Yastreb and his wingman were in the two SU-25 Frogfoot ground attack aircraft that were escorting the Halos. They barely cleared the heavily wooded ridgeline as they popped up and over it, then quickly dropped down again into a narrow mountain valley. The roaring wind swirling down the pass from the North Pole threatened to smash the low-flying aircraft against rock-lined canyon walls, requiring the full attention of the single-seat jets' pilots.

Yastreb glanced to his left just to confirm that his wingman was still back there. He barely caught a flash of the brown-camouflage-painted beast, still airborne, when his radar intercept alarm abruptly emitted a high-pitched screech. An anti-aircraft missile fire control radar had activated and was actively tracking their planes. The pilot quickly glanced at his display. It was a Pongae-6 Flap Lid radar. That just happened to be their target for this mission.

Convenient, he thought. Providing him with a well-defined aim point. There certainly would not be a plethora of such technology up here in this remote, frozen land.

He hit the weapons release for the two Kh-31 anti-radiation missiles that were slung beneath his wings as he ordered his wingman to go ahead and simultaneously launch his own weapons. Four flaming smoky trails marked their paths as the missiles raced down the mountain valley toward their obligingly advertised target. Easy work!

Yastreb had just started his pull-up when he observed the missiles slam brutally into their quarry. His radar intercept alarm emitter immediately went silent. Mission accomplished.

The pilot smiled as he keyed his microphone and cleared the Mi-26 troop transport helicopters to come on over the ridge and drop down into the valley. It was time for the troops to mop up anything or anybody that might have survived. Meanwhile, he and the other SU-25 would bank around and make a gun pass before heading home. He could see the helos just cresting the ridgeline and dropping into the valley—zeroing in on all the smoke and fire he and his wingman had set loose—as he lined his own gunsights up on what looked to be a command trailer, set far enough away from all the damage so it had not been destroyed. Yet.

He did not even see the first Stinger missile that slammed hard into his starboard engine exhaust. It was followed a millisecond later by two more hits. But he certainly felt the mighty jolt. Then he was too busy futilely trying to save his doomed aircraft to see that his wingman had been hit as well by a pair of Stingers and promptly slammed head-on into the rocky canyon wall.

The Mi-26 helicopters had no defense against the hail of Stingers that rained down on them from up on the tops of the nearby mountains. In less than a minute, all four were little more than hunks of burning metal, funeral pyres for the troops and crews that they had carried.

Through his binoculars, Boris Paserivich looked down from his perch high on the ridge and allowed himself a broad smile. Their trap had worked perfectly, exactly as designed. For the expense of an old surplus radar simulator and a few large but empty tents, the Children of the Gulag had just cost the Russians another major defeat.

And they had also once again demonstrated to the Russian Federation that they would not be dealing with a pitiful, impotent clan of poorly prepared backwoods peasants and former slave laborers.

They would soon know just how one of the world's major military powers would respond to such a threat. Or if Russia might now be more willing to consider the demands of this surprisingly adept upstart group.

Ψ

Captain First Rank Ivgany Yurtotov ordered the *Severodvinsk*-class nuclear submarine *Yakutsk* slowed to normal search speed. The much faster run down from Petropavlovsk was over. According to the latest satellite intelligence, the American battle group should be about a hundred kilometers due south. It was time for the sub to become the stealthy hunter she was designed to be.

Yurtotov checked his sonar displays. Although his intel plots showed the Americans to be well within range of his sonar systems, the screens only revealed a jumble of sea noise. If the US Navy vessels were out there, they were effectively being hidden by the winter storms that routinely blasted through this area. He had no choice but to go up to periscope depth and see if the *Yakutsk*'s RIM HAT ESM system was up to the task of spotting the American ships. Yurtotov was well aware that if the *Ronald Reagan* battle group was really up there, the massive aircraft carrier would have her radars rotating and radiating. He knew from experience that the American carriers never turned off all their radars. He had watched too many times when they said they were practicing "EMCON" and operating blindly only to pick up one or two of their radar systems still emitting plenty of radio frequency energy.

As it slipped up to periscope depth, the massive Russian submarine began to pitch and roll, but not nearly as badly as when they were farther north. Yurtotov estimated that the seas were three to four meters high and coming from the northeast. Much better, but still rough enough to send coffee cups and any loose equipment skidding across the control room.

The ESM mast had only broken the surface when the operator announced that he had detected an American SPS-48 air search radar. The best bearing was one-nine-zero. The American aircraft carrier was still out there, and it was not very far away at all.

With the slightest of smiles on his face, Captain First Rank Ivgany Yurtotov ordered his submarine back down into the curtaining depths and set a course of one-nine-zero.

Ψ

Captain Third Rank Andrei Turgenev frowned as he considered the huddled, shivering remnants of his crew that had been marooned from the captured submarine *Yaroslavl* for a long, miserable month. It seemed, though, like years since the terrorists had abandoned them in the wilds of the Bukhta Russkaya Bay on the Kamchatka Peninsula, leaving them many miles from any civilization when the pirates steamed away over the horizon with the purloined submarine. What meager food the terrorists had left them had long since been consumed. They had been forced to subsist on lichen grubbed from beneath the deep snow. They had also discovered a colony of edible mollusks in the tidal pools. Senior Lieutenant Matvey Preobrazhensky had proven to be quite a good survivalist. He snagged several giant Kamchatka crabs that helped to keep the hunger pangs at bay for a few days and a small horde of cedar nuts thankfully undiscovered by the scavenging jays.

Captain Turgenev knew he now must come to a decision. They had stayed in the crude camp for a month. No one had come searching for them, and it was readily evident nobody would. After all this time, he knew that his commanders likely assumed that the *Yaroslavl* was lost somewhere out in the deep and the crewmen were all dead. They had surely given up hope and were no longer searching. Such a notion caused great distress among those crewmembers who had families.

But they had bigger issues to cause them concern. Most of the crew was suffering from malnutrition. Frostbite was prevalent. They had already buried ten crewmembers as deeply as they could manage in the frozen earth. Turgenev estimated that if they were stuck here another month, none would be left alive. The time had come for them to do something.

The winter storms were far too severe and the seas too rough to try paddling the RHIBs back to Petropavlovsk, even if they remained close to the shoreline. They would not make it out of the Bukhta Russkaya Bay without capsizing, let alone cross forty miles of turbulent ocean. Hiking up the coastline was out of the question. It would take weeks to traverse the long series of mountainous cliffs that dropped precipitously down to the water's edge. The only choice was the same as it had always been, for someone to hike out up and over the mountains to get help. Some of the crew had suggested such a trek the first time the weather improved, but Turgenev had stubbornly refused to try that plan.

Turgenev knew of a rough dirt road that meandered down the peninsula's central spine, servicing a series of mines, oil well heads, and logging camps. If they could only reach the road, they would have a reasonable chance to find help. But it would be at least thirty kilometers of rigorous and challenging hiking up and over a mountain pass and then along the shoulder of Mount Mutnovsky, an active volcano shrouded in smoke at its twenty-five-hundred-meter peak. Then the hikers would need to locate the road and hope that it was not closed by the winter snows.

Finally, though, even if it was a long shot, Turgenev decided it was their last and only hope.

It would be suicide for most of the crew to even attempt this strenuous trek. Better for them to wait in the relative safety of the camp while a few of the healthier men attempted the journey. Turgenev pulled Preobrazhensky aside and informed him that the senior lieutenant would be the one to lead the four-man team up and out of the valley. Turgenev felt that as captain, it was his duty to remain behind and oversee the care of the rest of the crew. Preobrazhensky was to find the road and then follow it until they found an occupied camp or encountered a vehicle. Hopefully, whoever was inhabiting the camp would be able to send rescuers for the crew or communicate with someone who could.

Speed was important. Every day lost meant fewer survivors would remain to be rescued. The men spent several days fashioning crude snow-shoes from pliable spruce boughs and hiking poles from the scrub birch that littered the valley up from the beach while they waited out another winter storm. Then it was time to head out.

The sky was still dark, with the barest cold glimmer out to the east, when the four hikers left the camp. Once away from the beach, though, a full moon reflecting off the snow lighted their path to the west, almost like a beacon. The first kilometer was reasonably easy as they followed the course of a frozen stream. Then, as they progressed upward toward the volcano's south shoulder, the snow that covered the ground they were required to traverse became progressively deeper. Preobrazhensky was sure that the accumulation was at least five meters deep. Had they not worn their crude snowshoes, the valley would have been impassable. As it was, the going was hard enough. The next two kilometers required four hours of exhausting hiking.

Then the track got discouragingly steep. The senior lieutenant recognized that they were climbing out of the valley's watershed and would eventually enter a pass between two towering peaks, the Mutnovsky volcano on their right and some unnamed mass of sheer rock walls on their left. The sun was at its peak in the southern sky but still hidden by the mountain in that direction when Preobrazhensky called for a brief rest at the crest of the pass. The group plopped down and broke out their meager rations. They each slowly, tiredly chewed some leathery mollusk flesh and a few cedar nuts. Then it was time to head down the other side of the pass. They quickly learned that snowshoeing downhill was no easier than doing so uphill.

As the group rounded a shoulder, they spotted steam rising out of the snow in the distance. Hiking toward the mist, they smelled the heavy rotten-egg aroma of sulfur just before they came upon a small pond of open water. Bubbles continuously rose from the steaming cauldron before bursting in the much colder air. The small hot spring did offer some warmth for the team, for the first time since they left their nice, cozy submarine weeks before. But they knew they could not rest there for long. The road was still kilometers to the west. The sun was falling below the southwestern horizon. And the weather could spiral downward at any time and with little warning.

Stopping for the night was not really an option. They had no winter camping equipment. Even digging a snow cave was not a good choice. The crew back on the beach was depending on them. There was no time to rest. The full moon illuminated their trek across the alluvial fan spreading across the mountain valley, and there was always the possibility—even the likelihood—that some wild carnivore could be trailing them, looking for supper. With no weapons, the submariners would have unwillingly supplied the predators what they sought.

Preobrazhensky was the first to spy a bright light in the distance. This orb was moving! A vehicle! The road could not be more than a kilometer ahead. The group broke into a slow, disorderly run as they charged forward across the valley as best they could.

By the time they tumbled onto the narrow, rutted, snow-packed roadway, the truck had long since disappeared. But its heavy dual-wheeled tracks were easy to see. They followed it south, hoping a mining camp would suddenly pop up just beyond the next bend in the road. Each turn, though, only revealed more open road surrounded by heavy forest or rock outcroppings.

Finally, just before the sun was beginning to rise again—and their spirits were falling precipitously—they stumbled into a fenced enclosure right there at the roadside. The sign said, "Trevozhnoye Zarevo." One of Russia's largest mining companies. There would be people here and, hopefully, some means of communication with the rest of the world.

It took some minutes for the miners to take in and believe the submariners' story. Crossing those mountains in the dead of winter was just impossible, even with modern equipment and adequate supplies. These men had done it with essentially no food and with only primitive equipment. And submariners? Their vessel taken by terrorists? Then being stranded on the seashore for a month? The entire episode was bizarre.

A telephone call back to the naval base at Petropavlovsk was met with similar disbelief by the duty officer who answered the ring. But then he realized these were some of the men who had triggered the massive search operation emanating from his base. That was what finally got helicopters in the air, moving to rescue the crew—or what remained of them—at Bukhta Russkaya Bay and to pick up the four frostbitten trekkers at the mine.

At last, the Russian Navy knew what had happened to the *Yaroslavl* and who was responsible for the submarine's disappearance. But they were no closer to finding out where the boat was or what the intentions were of those who had seized and now held her.

Nor what they could possibly do to put a quiet but final end to the whole unfortunate situation.

Ψ

"Jim, you hearing anything from your Chinese girlfriend lately?"

Had anyone else been eavesdropping on the phone conversation—had anyone even been able to do such a thing—it might have sounded like a perfectly innocent dad-to-son question. But the query and the potential answer carried great weight on several key and dangerous fronts.

Admiral Jon Ward, Director of Naval Intelligence for the US Navy, was speaking with his son, Commander Jim Ward, US Navy SEAL team leader. The two men were half a world apart with the Director of Naval Intelligence sitting in his Pentagon office while his SEAL son, fresh off his assignment driving a mini sub and delivering a mysterious passenger to where his dad had been waiting, was now wrapping up an exercise with the Marine Force Recon battalion on Okinawa. Their secure phone connection was intermittently interrupted with crackles and pops of static, but that did not concern either man. That was just the subtle noise of switching algorithms, changing encryption schemes, and constant alteration of signal paths to assure no one else could hear the father-son chat.

"We don't get to talk or see each other nearly as much as I would like," the younger Ward admitted. "What with these odd jobs I've been doing for you and the regular missions the Navy expects me to do, I've been pretty busy and on the road a lot lately. And she and I are still trying to figure out how to negotiate the minefields we both have to navigate in our respective jobs. But we love each other, Dad. She's an amazing woman. You and Mom never had those issues, I'm sure. Most folks don't, I understand."

"No, our biggest problems were what to pack and what to throw away every time we got moved by the Navy. And getting word to her while I was at sea about when I'd last changed the oil in the car."

Li Min Zhou was Jim Ward's love interest. She just happened to be a Taiwanese spy, one with tentacles that reached into the highest levels of the convoluted infrastructure of the Chinese Communist Party. The SEAL and the spy had worked together several times already, preventing untold destruction and military success for China, but also resulting in a mutual attraction and subsequent hot-and-heavy romantic relationship. No surprise that the secrets and clearances of their separate jobs resulted in their walking a precarious tightrope and some very cryptic pillow talk when they did get to spend rare time together.

To further complicate things, Li Min only trusted a few people. Jim Ward and his father were two of them. Being so cautious about people with whom she would work had been, in her opinion, the only way she did what she did and still remained undetected. And alive. It made things complicated for the Wards and the US government. Both men had tried to convince her there were other intelligence operatives and SEAL teams besides the Wards who could be trusted. She rejected that argument. Jim was the only SEAL in the US Navy whose father happened to be the head of Naval Intelligence. Never mind that the SEAL was very talented at what he did and his father was uniquely capable of moving mountains to get things done. Such a thing made the two of them invaluable allies in her determination to bring down Communist Party control of China. And she just happened to be madly in love with the young SEAL commander.

So, they would have to do it her way or not at all, she stubbornly insisted. And, as the admiral often said, "It is what it is, and that's all that it is."

So far, it had worked out positively for Taiwan, the US, and world peace.

"Understand I really wasn't prying into your personal life, Jimbo," the elder Ward said with a chuckle. "I was actually asking if she might have casually mentioned if she had heard anything from the Chinese about our new and dear friends up in the frosty northern territory. You know she won't tolerate me ringing her up for a chat on the subject."

"Never stopped you from interrogating any of my dates before, all the way back to junior high. I still can't believe you asked Penny McCutcheon what her GPA was. And she was still in junior high!" They shared a quick laugh. It was true. "Actually, no. Nothing really substantial, Dad. She heard that they might have talked with the North Koreans and just about everyone else on the Pacific Rim and beyond. Looks like they aren't playing favorites in their choice of playmates. They're reaching out to everyone in the region. She heard that they had even spoken with Ukraine and dissident groups in the various 'Stans about mutual benefit, whatever that means. I suspect the Children will find plenty of takers if they can convince everybody they are legit and have a chance to pull this off. Russia has few friends lately, as you well know.

"There might be more than one game going on. Li Min thinks our inscrutable Chinese friends may be trying to play a plot within a plot. You know them. They don't play chess. They play 3-D chess. There are some subtle indications that they might be aiding and abetting the North Koreans to arm the Children on the down-low while they are ostensibly standing beside their Russian allies against the big, bad world. All while the DPRK is selling ordnance to Russia. It's an upside-down world, Dad."

Jon Ward chuckled. "That certainly sounds like something that back-stabbing bastard Tan Yong would try. And it certainly correlates with intel we are getting from the South Korean National Intelligence Service. It looks like the North Koreans actually engineered that ammo train ambush outside Vlad. They blew up an entire trainload of ammo that they had just sold the Russians. Quite a fireworks show, I understand. The Children got the blame or benefit of the attack, the North Koreans get to sell another trainload of bullets to the Russians, and the Chinese get to console their Russian allies while paying to have them kicked in the ass. Winners all around, except, of course, the Russians. Complex, subtle, and absolutely impossible to prove. Or draw a conclusion about how all this might end."

There was a pause then. Crackles. Pops. Jim knew his dad was about to ask him to do something. The longer the pause, the more dangerous and cloak-and-dagger that "something" typically turned out to be.

"Listen, Jim, could you ask Li Min to see what else she can find out without arousing any undue interest?" Jon Ward asked. "Tell her to keep it really low-key. We don't want even a hint that we might be snooping, and we certainly don't want her sticking her neck out for this."

Another long pause. Long enough to convince Jim there was more he was about to be asked to do. He was going to get another one of those "Dad and country" missions that required Admiral Ward to go over the heads of everyone in Jim's command structure so he could put his son to work doing something scary and exceedingly clandestine.

"Go ahead, Dad. You still outrank me, so just tell me what you need," Jim finally said.

"Yeah, but if I get you hurt, I have to answer to my top commander, 'Admiral Mom.' And she knows where I live." The two had a quiet laugh, though the joke had long since grown threadbare. "Okay, here's what I need. I have a simple little task for you and that band of pirates you call a SEAL team. I want you to covertly slip into the Magadan area and take a look at what these Children of the Gulag appear to need to be a viable military force. At the same time, try to gauge what their actual capabilities are."

"So, your 'simple task' is that you want me to once again piss off everyone above me in my chain of command, slip into Russia in the dead of winter, and spy on this bunch of miners and lumberjacks who may have already killed a considerable number of Russian troops and sailors in some very brutal ways?"

"That's pretty much it," the admiral admitted. "Except you'll be there at the invitation of your old buddy, Ivan Dostervesky. He shares the blame. He specifically asked for you and your team. You must have made an impression on him when you two were snorkeling all over the Sea of O. Before we back these yahoos and risk pissing off Moscow and the rest of the allegedly 'neutral' world—including most of Congress, the State Department, the Pentagon, and probably CNN—we need to be sure it's worth the effort and peril."

"Sure," Jim Ward shot back. "As previously mentioned, you outrank me, Dad."

15

"Boss, you know I get seasick real easy," Joe Dumkowski complained weakly. "And the stink from all those fish only makes it worse."

As he spoke, the burly SEAL was hunched over the bridge rail of the fishing trawler *Lovets Ryby*. And he was trying very hard to keep his last meal in its proper place as the little ship was tossed about on a frighteningly rough sea.

Jim Ward did his best to suppress a chuckle, though he did feel bad that one of his men was in such distress. The hardened SEAL—a warrior who had faced down death scores of times and in many different and scary ways—now had a face that was almost as green as his heavy foul-weather jacket. Before Ward could come up with a smart rejoinder, Fedor Rybak, the grizzled skipper of the *Lovets Ryby*, spoke up.

"Youngster, if you need to puke, puke over the side, and downwind. I do not need my ship decorated with the remnants of your lunch." Then he gruffly added, "And that isn't the stink of fish. That is the smell of money. There is almost ten million rubles' worth of fine pollack in our holds right now." The captain paused to scan the cloudy horizon. "As soon as we complete this rendezvous and get you all off my vessel, we will be heading back into Korsakov to sell this catch and go home."

Jim Ward, Joe Dumkowski, and Jason Hall, the third member of the small SEAL team, had been guests aboard the *Lovets Ryby* for over a week now. They joined the fishing trawler during a clandestine, nighttime, small-boat transfer that took place twenty miles north of Rebun Island, the north-ernmost Japanese island in the Sea of Japan, just at the western end of the La Perouse Strait.

This entire round-about trip had been cobbled together so that Commander Jim Ward and his team could slip covertly into Russia's Magadan Oblast, where the home of the Children of the Gulag was located. When his dad had tasked them with observing the Children's military capabilities and needs, Jim quickly recognized that his biggest problem was how to slip into the most remote and undeveloped oblast in all of Russia without the country's security apparatus going on full alert. Since nothing typically happened there, anything out of the ordinary would surely set off alarms.

The transportation system in and out of Magadan's Arctic wilderness was very primitive. The few modes of access were closely monitored by Russian security. American SEALs would certainly not be able to buy tickets and fly in on one of the two daily commercial flights into Magadan Sokol International Airport without being detected. The only other access to the outside world was a two-thousand-mile motor trip over the Road of Bones from the town of Yakutsk in central Siberia. Not something to be contemplated in the middle of a Siberian winter, even if Russian security would not recognize immediately that they had unwelcome tourists in their midst.

There was another disappointing development. Ward's search of the inventory of sneaky devices available for use in special operations had come up empty.

That was when the SEAL commander decided the simplest answer was to allow the Children to provide him and his guys access. Ivan Dostervesky —or at least one of his aides—was only too happy to do so.

The young SEAL did not have the slightest idea how this plan would work, but Dostervesky convinced him to trust the Children. The first step had been relatively obvious. A fishing boat was probably the least conspic-uous means for crossing the Sea of Okhotsk without arousing unwanted Russian security interests. But that would only go so far. Jim Ward was well aware that the northern end of the sea—and particularly Magadan—was still ice-bound and would remain so for a couple more months. Once again, Dostervesky told Ward he would need to trust him. A way would be found. He just could not disclose details to the SEAL yet.

Fortunately, the *Lovets Ryby* was conveniently unloading her first catch of pollack at Korsakov, at the south end of Sakhalin Island. It would be only a short jaunt south and west to pick up the SEALs and then head north, back to ply the fishing grounds.

Jim Ward and his team had found themselves playing fishermen in the Sea of Okhotsk. It was tough, hard work, and Captain Rybak was serious about making them earn their keep on his vessel. The fishing grounds off the north side of Sakhalin Island proved to be unusually productive as, time after time, they lowered the mammoth trawl nets into the ice-cold water and then hauled them back up an hour later so laden with fish, they strained the strength of the machinery and the deck crew. In their week aboard, the SEALs had learned enough about trawling to progress from mostly being in the way of the experienced fishermen to actually becoming useful on deck. With the small crew on the *Lovets Ryby* on this run, the strong backs of the unexpected passengers were needed and welcomed.

Jim Ward was standing on the deck, awaiting the next haul, when something moved just at the edge of his vision. It was a UAV—an unmanned aerial vehicle or drone—that had darted out of the clouds and promptly hovered a few hundred meters off the fishing vessel's starboard beam. The green-and-blue Russian Coast Guard symbol was easily visible on the miniature helicopter's side. After a moment, the UAV began slowly orbiting the *Lovets Ryby* while the turret-mounted cameras on the device maintained unblinking eyes on the ship.

Ward had taken a couple of steps back into the shadows. Thankfully, Dumkowski was feeling well enough by now to be assisting some of the deck crew with lines in preparation for the next haul. A seasick fisherman might raise suspicion.

Fedor Rybak simply ignored the airborne visitor, seemingly unconcerned about the spy bird's presence as he directed the crew to keep hauling in the money-fish.

"This is normal," he quietly told Ward. "Those *bespilotnyy vertolet* are the eyes for a Coast Guard border patrol cutter. We will see the warship, the *Dozornyy*, in a few minutes. It is typically on patrol duty around these waters. You and your men just need to keep your heads down and stay busy. I will do all the talking."

Ward nodded that he understood. Then, right on cue, a blue-and-white cutter emerged from a snowstorm no more than two kilometers to the fishing boat's port side. The smart-looking patrol vessel pulled up a hundred meters from the *Lovets Ryby* and then easily kept station with the slow-moving fisher as men on the cutter retrieved the UAV. A warmly bundled officer stepped out of the patrol boat's bridge house, put a hailer to his lips, and called across the short distance between them. Ward was fluent enough in Russian to understand that this could be a very serious development. For him and his SEALs as well as for Rybak and his boat.

"On the fishing boat. This is the *Beregovaya okhrana Pogranichnoy sluzhby Dozornyy*. Stand by for boarding to inspect your papers and the immigration status of your crewmembers."

Rybak inexplicably grinned as he grabbed his own loud-hailer. "Captain Teploye-Palto. It is good to see you again. I have some really good vodka in my cabin if you want to join the boarding party and come over for a warming drink."

The Russian laughed as he answered. "Captain Rybak, I did not recognize that rust-stained garbage scow of yours. You really should be more diligent about maintaining her."

Fedor Rybak retorted, "We earn no money in drydock! The *Lovets Ryby* must earn her keep with hard work in poor weather. Not like that state-owned yacht that you drive. Now are you going to join me in a drink?"

"That will necessarily have to wait until we both get back home to Korsakov. I do not wish to splatter my uniform with fish guts." Captain Teploye-Palto waved a goodbye across the way and then stepped back into the bridge house, out of the bits of sleet borne on a brisk, biting wind. The *Dozornyy* promptly turned away, showing her stern, and headed south.

Rybak let out a long sigh of relief. "That was close, *Komandir* Ward. Perhaps closer than you realize. Do not let his banter fool you. If Captain Teploye-Palto had actually come onboard, he and his men would have smelled you out in an instant." The captain wiped his lips with the sleeve of his heavy coat. "Our holds are full enough. We will now head north to send you and your men on to wherever it is that you need to be."

Ψ

Ostrov Kusova slowly grew from a shadowy blur on the distant horizon until the island ultimately loomed high over the *Lovets Ryby*. Fedor Rybak deftly guided his fishing boat into one of the narrow canyons that had been carved by wind and sea into the high rock cliffs that made up the south side of the small uninhabited wedge of land, the southernmost of the Shantar Islands. There was barely room for Rybak to steer between the sheer rock walls. The fjord cut into the island only a few hundred meters, but it still provided a cramped anchorage, sheltered from the wind and the sea surge. But more importantly, it also effectively shielded them in all directions from any prying eyes.

As Rybak was directing his crew in anchoring the *Lovets Ryby*, they were joined by another vessel that somehow knew which crevice in the rock to enter to rendezvous with the fishing boat. It was the *Kilo*-class submarine *Yaroslavl*.

Jim Ward stared from the fishing boat's deck in amazement as the diesel submarine steamed very slowly into the small harbor. Men standing on the sub's bridge waved, and the crew and captain of the *Lovets Ryby* returned the greeting warmly. Okay, where in hell had the Children of the Gulag acquired themselves a freaking submarine? And a front-line, modern Russian one to boot? You simply did not pick one of those out and order it from Amazon!

Ward was impressed. It was becoming obvious that Ivan Dostervesky and the Children of the Gulag had more reach and capability than the US —and probably the rest of the world that even knew about the secessionists —would have imagined.

The submarine moored snugly alongside the fishing boat in what little space was available to them. Refueling and stocking provisions was a well-practiced choreography for the two crews by now. Well hidden in the fjord or not, they made quick work of it. The three SEALs barely had time to bid Captain Rybak farewell and move their gear aboard the submarine. Then the *Yaroslavl* cast off, carefully turned about, and headed back out to the open sea. Meanwhile, the *Lovets Ryby* raised anchor and then slowly followed the submarine back down the short, narrow channel. They left no sign that a clandestine rendezvous had occurred in this narrow crevasse in an obscure island in a remote corner of the world.

Still, to further reduce the chance of observation, after clearing the mouth of the fjord, the *Yaroslavl* immediately dove and carefully matched the contour of the sloping bottom out to deeper water. Then, Mark Lodka-matros, the submarine's rebel captain, and his brother, Igor, joined the SEALs in the submarine's compact wardroom. There had been no opportunity for introductions or a welcome in the frenzy of the transfer of materials in the anchorage.

The big man genially held out his hand and said in heavily accented English, "*Komandir* Ward, welcome aboard the *Deti Gulaga* submarine *Yaroslavl*. Let me introduce myself and my brother. I am Mark Lodkamatros, and this is Igor."

Igor, a younger, slightly smaller version of his brother, nodded and almost smiled.

"Ivan Dostervesky told us that we were to extend every courtesy to you while you were aboard and to demonstrate what this submarine can do while we ferry you to Magadan and your meeting with our leader," Mark Lodkamatros went on. "I presume that you will have some questions."

Jim Ward nodded vigorously. "You bet I do! We can start with the obvious. Where did you get this boat, and how have you managed to keep it hidden? From your fellow Russians and the rest of the world, folks who tend to keep tabs on any and all submersible warships?" Ward was almost shouting by the end of his questions. Lodkamatros smiled. The young SEAL commander was duly impressed, and that was good.

Then, as Lodkamatros answered, the pieces of this elaborate jigsaw puzzle finally began to fall into place for the SEALs. Stealing the boat right out from under the Russians in Petr, a very secure naval facility, and then sneaking it into the Sea of O was a tale of daring worthy of some farfetched military thriller novel. The Russian Navy deploying all its assets out of the Kamchatka base in a futile search for their lost submarine and, in the process, raising an alarm with the American submarines observing the frenzy now all made sense. But Lodkamatros made it abundantly clear that this story could not yet be told. Not until after the Children had sprung their submerged surprise on the Russians and they had successfully carved out the territory to form their own nation.

Mark Lodkamatros slapped his knees, signaling he was finished for now, and rose. "Now, we shall get you settled in for some much-needed rest. And on the way, Igor will give you a tour of the *Yaroslavl*. You may not find it as spacious as the American nuclear submarines with which you are familiar, but I believe you will find it to be quite sophisticated. Then it will be time for *uzhin*—that is what you call 'supper' in English, I understand—a meal which I am confident you will enjoy. In fact, in honor of your presence, we will have a special treat tonight, a classic Russian dish, *mintay graten*." The Russian noticed curious looks on the faces of the SEAL team members. "Oh, that is fresh pollack au gratin, a specialty of our cook."

Jim Ward struggled to keep a straight face as he noticed Joe Dumkowski was already beginning to turn green.

Ψ

The *George Mason* moved through the Western Pacific waters, now some eight hundred miles east-southeast of Hokkaido, Japan. The *Ronald Reagan* battle group was twenty-five miles to the submarine's southeast. Brian Edwards breathed a sigh of relief. It had taken a couple of days of hard charging across the storm-tossed Pacific to arrive at this point. Case Four-Six, the Improved *Severodvinsk* Russian submarine, was supposed to still be fifty miles to the north based on the best estimates by the wizards back at Sub Group Seven.

"Mr. Wilson, bring the boat to periscope depth," Brian Edwards ordered. "Let's see if those P-8 drivers are done with their surf-and-turf lunches. They might even be ready to earn their keep by hunting submarines."

P-8 Poseidon aircraft had been flying out of Adak in the Aleutian Islands, attempting to coordinate ASW searches with the *George Mason*, but so far the sea state had been too high for them to deploy their sonobuoys. The only cuing that Edwards and his crew had received was intermittent hits from the bottom-mounted SOUSUS arrays. They provided some localizing information, but they still left an awfully big chunk of ocean to search. And with a contact as quiet as Case Four-Six, they were searching for a very elusive needle in an exceedingly large, wet, and storm-tossed haystack.

The low-profile photonics mast had barely popped up above the sea surface when the Link-16 receiver began obediently downloading data. Chief Jason Schmidt, the Weapons Department Leading Petty Officer, called out, "Link-16 track for Case Four-Six is active. Looks like one of the P-8s has him on a passive sonobuoy string. Best bearing zero-six-eight, range ten miles."

Edwards could not suppress a pleased grin. He nodded and ordered, "Roger. Acknowledge receipt of the track and tell them we are going sinker to close."

He stepped back to the ECDIS chart table. Jackson Biddle, the XO, was already standing there looking intently at the tactical display.

"What's the play, Skipper?" Biddle asked. He pointed down at the display. "Looks like if we scooch a little over to the east, we'll be in a direct line between our Russian friend and the battle group."

"That's my plan, XO," Edwards confirmed. "Let's mosey over there and see if we can slip in trail on this big, ugly character." He rubbed his chin as he thought. "But here's the thing, XO. I'm wondering why we don't have him on the thin-line yet if he's at twenty thousand yards. Foster and *Gato* reported contact at an estimated thirty thousand yards on a three-point-six-hertz tonal."

Almost on cue, Josh Hannon called out, "Passive narrow-band contact on the thin-line, best bearings zero-six-eight and one-one-two. Received frequency, three-point-seven hertz."

Edwards looked at the tactical plot. No real reason to resolve bearing ambiguity here. The P-8 contact had already done that for him. He knew precisely in which direction the Russian submarine was. "Officer-of-the-Deck, let's get a leg on this course, then come around to course one-two-zero. We're going to sneak around behind our friend real quiet like and see what the hell he thinks he's doing."

Ψ

Captain Louise Gadliano stepped onto the bridge of the USS *Diane Feinstein*, one of the modern trend to name US Navy destroyers for a politician rather than a naval hero. Gadliano gazed out proudly on her brand-spanking-new Flight III *Arleigh Burke*–class warship. It was just a little over a year before that her previous command, the LCS ship *Canberra*, had been shot out from under her down in the Dangerous Grounds of the South China Sea by a Chinese battle group in their attempt to defend waters they brazenly claimed as their own but were in fact international. That incident had never shown up on any TV network's nightly newscast or in any of the few remaining daily newspapers. Even she and her crew had to report, if asked, that the ship had suffered a catastrophic mechanical failure. But now, here she was, in command of the Navy's newest and most powerful surface warship. And she was heading out on another very similar mission. One that put her, her crew, and her beautiful new ship in harm's way.

Gadliano watched carefully as she crossed the bridge space. The watch-standers certainly knew that their captain was on the bridge. The quarter-master-of-the-watch had loudly announced, "Captain on the bridge," the very second her foot hit the deck. But then everyone kept on about his or her duties in their normal professional manner. Only the OOD, Lieutenant Commander Sam Starson, had acknowledged her presence, and that was the way it was supposed to work. Starson greeted the skipper and walked with her as she moved over to the elevated seat on the port side of the bridge, the spot reserved for the captain.

"Skipper, steering course zero-three-one at ahead standard on both shafts and four turbines. Ship control is in normal mode. All sensors are operational. We hold no surface contacts within thirty miles and no warship contacts. And I'll say it again. This baby is one sweet ride."

Sam Starson was the *Feinstein*'s senior watch officer as well as the ops officer. Gadliano was still doing plenty of observation of her wardroom and the rest of her brand-new crew. That was to get a sense of who she could depend on, who she couldn't, and which ones were worth the effort to bring around to her standards. Starson fell into the first group. He would make a good XO soon, and it was only a matter of time before the young Ohio State University Navy ROTC grad had his own command.

On the other hand, her current XO was not on the skipper's good list. Commander Susan Biddleson was the only daughter—only child—of Vice Admiral Thomas Biddleson. She was well aware that it was her birthright to rise to high command in the modern version of the US Navy—now that females were able to do so—and she had proven over and over that she was willing to cut every corner necessary to get there as quickly as she could. But that was not a problem Gadliano could solve way out here and on this particular tightwire of a mission. She would have to live with Biddleson, at least for the time being.

"Agreed, Sam, but we better not put a dent in her, or Daddy might not let us take her out again," Gadliano told Starson, then quickly shifted gears. "Have you seen the OPORD we just got from Seventh Fleet?"

"Not yet, Skipper," Starson answered. "Combat said that we had new tasking come in a few minutes ago, but I haven't had time to read it yet. Sounded like we had a few hours before we initiated the orders."

Gadliano stared out through the glass at the gunmetal skies for a few seconds as she formed her thoughts. "We do have a little time, but this op is going to take some detailed planning. And there isn't much time for that. The *CliffsNotes* version is that someone very senior back in the Pentagon wants to get the Russians' attention out here in West Pac to remind them who the big dog is. They tasked INDOPACOM, and then INDOPACOM tasked Seventh Fleet. Seventh Fleet looked around for someone not doing anything useful, and they immediately took notice of us."

"Skipper, what are *CliffsNotes*?" Starson interrupted, a quizzical look on his face.

"Never mind. Before your time. Just suffice it to say that we are the bottom ugly face on this totem pole. And that shit tends to roll downhill. The turd we have been given is to run our battle ensign up the mast like we're thumbing our noses at the Russian Federation and steam proudly and unafraid into the middle of the Sea of O. Someone back in DC wants to tell the Russians that the Sea of Okhotsk is not their private lake and we will damn well play in it if we want to. Now, when you get off watch, read through the OPORD carefully and break out the FONOPS instructions. Get the department heads together for a meeting this evening so we can plan this out. Oh, and let the XO know."

Gadliano grabbed her binoculars and eased back in her seat as she scanned the horizon. Nothing out there but smoky-gray skies and slate seas.

"Hey, what do I have to do to get a cup of coffee around here?" she asked, complaining mockingly.

Ψ

The Russian messenger pulled back the curtain on Jim Ward's rack and shook him awake. With a mixture of gestures, rudimentary English, and Ward's very limited Russian, they finally came to the understanding that Ward's presence was requested in the submarine's control room.

Wiping sleep from his eyes, Ward stumbled down the narrow passageway and into the darkened compartment. Only a very faint red light illuminated the crowded space. Since the control room had obviously been rigged for black, and because he could feel the slight rolling of the sub, Ward knew that they were at periscope depth in a fairly calm sea. He could faintly discern Mark Lodkamatros hugging the periscope, peering through its eyepiece.

Igor Lodkamatros shoved a cup into Ward's hands. "Here, my friend. It appears that you need this," the Russian whispered. "I know you Americans are addicted to coffee."

Ward took a sip. It was obviously instant coffee and tasted like cardboard, but it was hot and probably had caffeine in it. Perfect. "Thank you very much."

"Mark wants you to watch this," Igor said, again whispering. "We are one thousand meters off the port quarter of the *Dozornyy*. I believe you are familiar with that particular vessel."

As Ward nodded in agreement, Mark Lodkamatros called out, "Final observation on the *Dozornyy*. Range one-one hundred meters, bearing zero-seven-six, angle on the bow port one-two-two."

Ward was impressed. The Russian sounded like a real submariner. Or was doing a damn good impression of one.

The fire control system operator called out, "Observation checks with solution."

The captain ordered, "Practice fire tube one at the *Dozornyy*." He pulled away from the eyepiece and waved for Ward to join him at the 'scope.

The SEAL peered through the periscope optics. Dawn was just breaking on the eastern horizon, filling the sky with reds and oranges. The blue-and-white Russian Coast Guard ship nearly filled the device's field of view. The cross hairs were centered just aft of the Russian Coast Guard warship's bridge. At this range, it would be nearly impossible for a torpedo to miss the hapless ship as it steamed on, innocently oblivious to the undersea killer lurking a mere thousand meters away.

"We have 'killed'"—Mark Lodkamatros made air quotes with his fingers —"the *Dozornyy* a half dozen times over the last couple of weeks. Including during the time while they were stopping you a couple of days ago on the fishing vessel. Unfortunately, that little yacht is not worthy of one of the few torpedoes we have onboard. Finding torpedo reloads would be one very important thing that your country could do to help us in our struggle for freedom, *Komandir*."

Jim Ward nodded. He had heard his father discuss the very limited capacity of a submarine torpedo room and all the difficult logistics in reloading the submarine in any kind of shooting war. He also could easily imagine the tremendous tactical advantage the *Yaroslavl* had while it roamed free and undetected in the confines of the Sea of Okhotsk. They would immediately lose that advantage if they were required to leave the area to reload. Ward was not sure how the problem could be solved, though. That was something for his father and the heavyweights back in the Pentagon to figure out, but he could certainly relay the request and allow them to noodle out a solution.

Mark Lodkamatros ordered the submarine down to normal cruising depth and steered young Ward back to the navigation table in the after corner of the control room. He had a large-scale chart of the Sea of Okhotsk and the surrounding landmasses called up on the electronic display.

"*Komandir* Ward, you are probably trying to deduce why we went to so much effort to capture a submarine," Lodkamatros said as they both looked at the chart. "Yes, it is useful for defending our homeland from the few

Russian Navy warships that can mount a threat way out here, but we could do that and certainly more effectively with a few batteries of land-based missiles. The only shipping that is really worthy of our efforts are the lique-fied natural gas tankers that come out of Prigorodnoye." He pointed to a small harbor on the southeast side of Sakhalin Island just a few kilometers east of Korsakov. "Tankers departing there average over one hundred thousand tons. Sinking one of those would make a really big boom and put a serious dent in Comrade Salkov's already dwindling treasury. And maybe you can deduce why we have Fedor Rybak and the *Lovets Ryby* operating out of Korsakov. It is a very convenient way to keep tabs on what is happening there."

Ward nodded in understanding. The Sakhalin II LNG terminal was one of the world's largest and the pride of Gazprom, the Russian-government-owned energy giant. Sinking an LNG tanker coming out of there would close the port until the threat was located and neutralized.

Ward rubbed his chin in thought for a few seconds. Then he asked, "Captain, I think I understand your strategy here, but why don't you strike the terminal itself? A couple of those *Kalibr* missiles that your brother showed us would blow the place into the next generation."

Lodkamatros chuckled. "That would be a real sight and would give me utmost pleasure, but we have a problem. Those land-attack missiles get all their targeting data from a shore target facility just before they are launched, much like your Tomahawk missiles once required. The Russians still maintain a very centralized control on them. We do not believe that we can convince their targeteers to send us, out of the kindness of their hearts, the parameters necessary to hit Sakhalin II. But that is something else that you can help us with. Send us the software so that we can make effective use of our *Kalibr* missiles, and we will have a major impetus to get our former government to the negotiating table with minimal loss of life."

Ward nodded, mentally adding the request to the list of things to discuss with his father.

Igor Lodkamatros broke in. "Excuse me, *Komandir*, but breakfast is ready in the wardroom. Your team is...I believe their exact words were, 'chowing down.' And, 'If the boss don't get down here soon, we may eat it all.' I believe you might want to go now and get some breakfast while any of it remains. My brother and I will be down in a few minutes, as soon as we wrap up here, so we may continue our discussion."

As Ward left the control room and they were certain he was out of earshot, Igor turned to Mark and asked, "Do you believe he is persuaded?"

Mark smiled and answered, "To use a fishing analogy, he has bought our requests so far hook, line, and sinker. He will obtain for us the technology to launch our missiles."

"Brother, do you think the American SEAL even suspects you may have told him the truth, but not all the truth?" Igor asked.

The elder Lodkamatros looked hard at his sibling. "No one can know all the truth at this critical time. The attitude of the world toward us and our cause would change immediately if they learned that two of the missiles in our possession are thermo-nuclear."

Ψ

Henrietta Foster was growing more and more bored. That is, if the captain of a US nuclear submarine could be bored when she and her boat were cruising, submerged and hidden, twelve miles off the largest Russian submarine base in the Pacific. But since that Improved *Severodvinsk* sub had blasted out of the base at Petropavlovsk, heading south at flank speed, everything seemed to have eerily quieted down. Now there was nothing for *Gato* to do but march back and forth at the gate, waiting for someone... anyone...to come out to play. So far, no one of any significance had done so.

Eric Householder stepped out of radio and moved over to the command console where Foster was scrolling through the sonar displays in a vain effort to conjure up a contact...any contact.

"Skipper, shift the display over to comms," he said as he stepped up to stand next to her. "There's a message that I think you're going to want to see."

"Okay, XO," Foster responded hopefully, even as her fingers danced across the drop-down menus on the screen. The latest message traffic flickered up on the display. She quickly scrolled through them, mostly routine Navy bureaucratic admin stuff, nothing really worth reading. Unless she needed to know that the annual diversity and inclusivity training reports were to be submitted electronically using NAVPERS Form 5467K. Or that Rear Admiral (lower half) so-and-so was being transferred from Naval Station Mayport, Florida, to Naval Station Norfolk. But then she came to a message that Householder was only too happy to point out to her. She rapidly scanned through it. Then she went back and read it more carefully.

The more she read, the more excited she became. Sub Group Seven finally had a mission for the USS *Gato*, and it promised to be a lot more interesting than watching the snow pile up on the Kamchatka Peninsula.

"XO, get the Nav up here," Foster ordered. "She needs to get our new transit course laid down. We don't have all day." She stepped back to the ECDIS table and looked at the chart display. After a couple of quick eyeball measurements, she ordered, "Officer-of-the-Deck, come to course one-nine-zero. Make your depth six hundred feet, ahead flank." Turning to Householder, she added, "That will get us moving in the right direction until the Nav can smooth in a good track. Get the department heads in the wardroom in an hour so we can plan this out. I'll be in my stateroom reading up on FONOPS."

Precisely an hour later, Henrietta Foster stepped into the *Gato*'s wardroom. She filled her signature oversized thermos mug of coffee from the coffeemaker on the counter and sat down at the head of the table. The XO, department heads, COB, and department senior chiefs already sat around the burgundy Naugahyde-covered table, all behind their own cups of coffee. She flicked on the large monitor that was hung at the foot of the table. Sub Group Seven's message popped up on the screen.

"Well, team," Foster began as they all read the naval message, "you can see that the boss finally wants us to go do something useful. We're going into the Sea of O for some interesting ops. It seems that some bigwig back in the five-sided puzzle palace wants to restart FONOPS against the Russians."

Steve Hanly, the boat's engineer, piped up, "Ma'am, ain't FONOPS one o' them thar skimmer-type hickies?" As usual, Hanly's Mississippi drawl and vocabulary was such that most people needed a translator. Fortunately, Foster spoke fluent Mississippian.

"Good point, Eng," she answered. "As usual, you are correct. FONOPS—freedom of navigation operations—are to show the other side that you don't recognize their claim to whatever territory they are professing to own. Hard to do that when you're submerged. Seventh Fleet is vectoring an *Arleigh Burke* around to actually do the FONOPS in plain view of the Russians. We're the hidden escort to keep an eye on things and protect the destroyer if the Russians decide to get frisky."

Foster flipped up a chart of the Kuril Islands, the strand of volcanic rocks that were lined up from Kamchatka to Hokkaido, Japan, forming the southeastern boundary of the Sea of Okhotsk. A sinuous red line angled down from the northeast to the southwest, marking a distance of twelve miles to seaward of the islands all the way down the length of the chain. The line then skirted across to the north of Hokkaido and over to the southern tip of Sakhalin Island.

"As you may remember, the Russians claim the Sea of O as an historic inland sea. That means that they are claiming the whole shebang as their very own sovereign waters. No warships, no overflight without their permission. And of course, no submarines. We reject the claim, out of hand. So do the Japanese, by the way, but they've not been able to win that argument either. We—or at least the destroyer, with us underneath—are going to steam through there to make our point and see what they have to say about it."

Everyone nodded. They also understood such a thing could be considered a provocation at best, an act of war at worst. Someone, though, must have a good reason to push the Russians' buttons.

Flipping off the monitor, Foster looked carefully at the faces of each member of her team.

"Remember, FONOPS are supposed to be peaceful. We aren't trying to start a shooting war here. But when you poke a bear, it's possible things could get rough. I want each of you to brief your people on what we are doing and what to expect. Eng, I need this ship to be so quiet that fish bump into her. Weps, check out all the weapons systems to assure they are in peak operational order. COB, have the DC gear inventoried and checked. Nav, make sure nav systems are groomed and that radio and ESM are groomed, too. Any questions?"

There were none. As everyone rose, grabbed their mugs and cups, and went off to do their skipper's bidding, she noticed not a one of them had taken so much as a sip of his or her coffee.

That confirmed for Commander Henrietta Foster that her key team members fully understood the sensitivity and inherent danger of what they were about to undertake.

16

The president of the Russian Federation, Grigory Iosifovich Salkov, tiredly removed his eyeglasses and laid them on the ornately inlaid Louis XVI table. He leaned back in his chair and massaged his temples. Perhaps, in this way, he could coax the headache to loosen its grip on his cranium. Truth be told, though, listening to this intel briefing was the cause, and the throbbing would not subside until it was thankfully concluded. Or got decidedly more encouraging in its content.

Salkov glanced around the large gold- and gilt-decorated hall. Seated at a table to his left were his Minister of Defense, Anatoly Shatitsnevcom, with several of his aides gathered around. To Salkov's right, Chief of the General Staff, General Nikolai Marastopov, sat and quietly conversed with a couple of his junior officers. The chairs that lined the room's mirrored walls were filled with various senior officers or high-powered bureaucrats. To a man, they were intently watching the president, awaiting his reaction to the presentation so far.

"President Salkov, should I continue?" the uniformed briefer asked as he flashed up the next slide onto the big screen at the far end of the room.

"*Da*, please go on with your most discouraging report." Salkov waved his hand in a rolling movement. "But could someone, please, fetch me an aspirin? And at least a grain or two of good news for a change."

An aide scurried out of the room, quietly shutting the heavy doors as the briefer impatiently—or nervously—danced his mouse pointer across the screen.

"The Ukrainian situation remains at a stalemate. The Twenty-Second Army Corps is being reinforced by units of the Three-Zero-Fifth Artillery Brigade in the Donetsk region and the One-Twenty-Seventh Motor Rifle Division at the border in the Tetkino region. Both divisions are being redeployed from the Fifth Combined Arms Army. And the Eleventh Air Force is reinforcing the available air assets with two hundred ground attack aircraft."

President Salkov grunted, blinked hard, and asked, "Isn't the Fifth supposed to be positioned in the Far East, mostly along our borders with China and North Korea? And is not the Eleventh Air Force headquartered out of Vladivostok?"

"You are correct on both counts, Grigory Iosifovich," the briefer respectfully replied. "In light of these ongoing challenges, these are the units that the Main Staff have determined can best be utilized. Neither China nor North Korea pose us any significant threat at the moment. Plus, we trust they will not learn of the movement of these units from our shared borders should they wish to exploit such a vulnerability."

Salkov rubbed his temples even more vigorously. In his head, he translated the briefer's double-speak into plain Russian. What the man was really saying, but trying very hard not to say, was that these ongoing battles were eating up the Russian Armed Forces. These newly transferred units were pretty much all they currently had available.

"Where are those damned aspirin?" was the president's only response.

The briefer quickly changed screens. A map of Central Russia and Kazakhstan came up. Several red-flame symbols dotted the map.

"The group calling themselves *Islamskiy Boytsy* have increased both the number and effectiveness of their attacks around the Kazak border. They continue to use guerilla hit-and-run tactics, but several of the recent assaults have been battalion-sized." The briefer pointed to the explosion icons. "We have been attempting to engage them with both air power and mobile armored units." The screen shifted to pictures of crashed aircraft and burning tanks. "We suspect forces in Kazakhstan are supplying these rebels with anti-armor and anti-air weapons. And though I regret reporting such, we have reason to believe we have serious intelligence leaks in the region. It seems they anticipate with one-hundred-percent accuracy our attacks."

"Let me guess," Salkov snarled as he slapped the table, "the Main Staff is redeploying more divisions and aircraft to the steppes, too!" Glaring at General Marastopov, he asked, "Just where are we supposed to get the rubles to pay for all this equipment and all these soldiers that you insist on squandering at our borders? How are we supposed to defend Mother Russia at this rate?"

Salkov scooted back his chair and rose to leave.

"Excuse me, Grigory Iosifovich," Minister of Defense Shatitsnevcom interjected. "We have not yet briefed the situation with the *Deti Gulaga*."

"I trust that it is only more bad news," Salkov growled. He delayed his departure from the meeting only long enough to say, "You military geniuses have stripped the Far East of just about everything that shoots or drops bombs. Figure out how to destroy these *Deti*. Otherwise, we may well be forced to live with them like the infestation of vermin that they are."

Ψ

The wintry white land was flat and barren for miles in all directions. The only way to discern the demarcation between the snow-covered land and the frozen surface of the sea was the high ridge of ice that was piled up along the shoreline. The Ulya River delta and its surrounding marshland were devoid of any signs of human habitation. Even the ruins of the old Ulya Gulag were little more than mounds of snow a few meters back from the shore.

Just a faint wisp of smoke rose from the largest mound. It was barely visible in the feeble evening light. Someone had built a small, carefully concealed fire to keep their hands warm and stave off frostbite in this icy-cold land.

As the wan yellow sun edged below the western horizon, the ice a couple of hundred meters out to sea suddenly heaved up into a small mound and then broke open. The black fin seemingly belonging to some primordial undersea creature rose another meter free of the icy sea surface. Then men emerged onto the sail of the submarine *Yaroslavl* as three snow-mobiles roared at top speed from within the Ulya Gulag ruins and raced across the ice on a well-practiced route to where the vessel had emerged. It was clear the *Yaroslavl's* arrival had been anticipated.

The three SEALs, Jim Ward, Jason Hall, and Joe Dumkowski, climbed down from the submarine and hurried over to where the snowmobiles waited for them. As Ward was stowing his gear on one of the vehicles, Mark Lodkamatros yelled down from the bridge of the sub. "Good hunting and good luck, my young friends." He promptly disappeared back down the hatch.

As the men were mounting their rides, the *Yaroslavl* disappeared back below the ice. The snowmobiles raced back toward the shore. Meanwhile, the brisk Arctic wind quickly scoured the sea ice of their tracks. The piled-up heap where the sub had broken to the surface was now only another ice mound among the thousands of others randomly strewn all around.

The SEALs were shepherded into the ruins of what was the largest building that remained of the Ulya Gulag. The two-story cement block structure also appeared to be the only building left in the compound that still had any of its roof intact. Three more snowmobiles and several sleds were parked under an overhanging canopy that looked as if it might collapse under the weight of the snow at any moment. They saw that one of the first-floor rooms had been turned into a reasonably snug camp, though, and that it appeared to be protected from the worst ravages of the wind as well as from prying eyes peering down from overhead.

The SEALs entered the warm room and started to remove their Arctic gear. One of the men who had met them on the ice barked out in heavily accented English, "There is not time to get comfortable! We have many kilometers to travel tonight. Ivan Dostervesky is waiting for us. For you."

"Just a minute," Ward interjected, refusing to be rushed without more information. "Just who are you, and where are we going? And what's the reason for the sudden rush now? We just spent the last couple of weeks cooling our heels on a nice, relaxing ocean cruise. Total waste of time."

"I am Daniil Semenov, and I apologize for what appears to be lost time," the Russian answered with a courteous nod. "I am the chief scout for the *Deti*

Gulaga, the Children of the Gulag. We have many facets to our operation, and sometimes things defy prediction. However, tonight we are going up the coast to a village called Novoe Uste." He pulled out a detailed topographic map and pointed out to Ward the coast route they would be following. "It's a tiny settlement at the mouth of the Okhata River, about ninety kilometers north of here. The coast road—if you can call it a road—chews up and swallows logging trucks in the summer but is actually quite easy passage for a snowmobile in the winter. Our journey should only take a couple of hours. We will spend the day there. Tomorrow night, we will head up the Okhata River to our base at Arka."

Ward shook his head. "Why are we only going a couple of hours tonight?" Ward asked. "This mission is important. And I have to think that time is important in getting you the help you are requesting."

Semenov swept his hand up the map to indicate what looked to be a steep, forested river valley. "It is only another ninety kilometers from Novoe Uste to Arka, but even with the river frozen over, the route is much more difficult because of the terrain. If we are lucky, we can do it in a night. If not, we will be required to camp out along the route. There is too much chance of being detected during the day. Our enemies, who are now aware of our existence as well as our intentions, have satellites perfectly capable of tracking us during the day. Out here, any movement raises their interest. And their ire. Arka is too important to our plans to allow them to locate it. For that reason, we only travel to and from there at night."

It all made sense to Jim Ward. He, his team, and the rest of the group soon mounted their snowmobiles and shot off down the snow-covered road at what seemed to the SEALs to be a dangerous pace. But they could only hang on and trust the drivers while observing the scenery. Judging by the trees and shrubs growing right up to the edge of the narrow track and the lack of bridges across the marshes, rivers, and streams they crossed, Ward quickly determined that this road was only passable in winter, when everything was frozen.

True to Semenov's word, they pulled into Novoe Uste almost exactly two hours later. It was only a very small village with a couple of what might loosely be called streets and maybe two dozen rustic log homes. Judging by the looks of the place and the small harbor, Ward guessed that the inhabitants scratched out a meager existence from fishing and maybe some up-country mining. And had likely done so for generations. If Novoe Uste had ever been in any way prosperous, it would have been in the village's distant past.

Semenov led them into a log barn at the edge of town where they could stay out of sight for the short sub-arctic winter day, less than six hours of daylight. After devouring a meal, refueling the snowmobiles, and restocking supplies, the group bunked down for the day.

The sun was low on the western horizon when Semenov gathered the group to head up the frozen-over Okhata River. As he had warned, the going immediately became tough. The river—which was actually more a maze of small channels winding through a plethora of sandbars and wooded islets—presented a trail that could best be described as a rugged jumble of broken chunks of ice. The going was slow and treacherous. They had barely left the village behind when the first mishap occurred. One of the snowmobiles flipped over on a chunk of unstable ice and landed on its side. Fortunately, both the driver and the passenger, Jason Hall, were able to jump free, but uprighting the unwieldy machine took them the better part of an hour and required considerable effort.

That became the story for the remainder of the night. High walls of muddled-up ice chunks, frozen into rock-hard obstacles, or stretches of boulder-strewn open marshland with odd stumps and tree trunks suddenly jutting up precariously in their path. By midnight, Ward estimated that even after six hours of hard riding, they had made maybe twenty kilometers of progress. If Semenov's estimate of distance to their destination was accurate, they still had eighty kilometers of slow-go snowmobiling ahead of them.

Semenov apparently had the same thought. At their next rest stop, he pulled out his topo map and searched for an easier route. Off to the east, maybe ten kilometers from the river, the map showed a logging/mining road that roughly paralleled the waterway for fifty kilometers before sharply turning east.

"We will go cross-country over to that road," Semenov explained, pointing out the features on the map to Ward. "Once we are on it, we should be able to make up a lot of time, and the topo shows nothing but frozen marsh between here and the road."

"We're in your neighborhood, my friend," Jim Ward told him. "Let's just hope whoever did the survey for that map was not writing fiction."

Semenov nodded seriously. It was a real possibility, of course. But he mounted his snowmobile and led them away, up out of the riverbed before shooting across a low marsh pretending to be an ice rink. Sure enough, they soon reached the indicated road. It appeared to be a seasonal track for summer use, and that meant it had never been cleared of the winter's considerable snow accumulation. It was a smooth and easy run for the snowmobiles. They were soon climbing out of the river delta and up into the foothills. High mountains loomed ominously to their east. And even more ominously directly ahead of them.

"Those are the Suntar-Khayata Mountains," Semenov explained. He swept his arm around and then pointed off to the west. "They make a wide arc all across this area. They will soon protect our new homeland from our Russian neighbors over in Siberia. There are only two passes through to Siberia, either down the Ulya River several hundred kilometers to the west or the Okhotsk Perevoska, which is located above Arka. That one is a very narrow and difficult passage, impossible to traverse in winter and nearly so in the summer. Nobody in his right mind would use it." He smiled and winked. "A US Navy SEAL would understand perfectly that this is precisely why we plan to use that particular pass to mount raids from Arka."

As the road pitched upward, they soon found themselves riding along the side of a steep slope, looking down on a broad, empty valley below. The steep, rocky terrain was open, devoid of any vegetation poking through the snow. Ward now had the uneasy feeling of vulnerability, of being stuck out in the open with no cover to seek in any direction should they need to. They only had the choice of two directions: up and forward or back and down.

Of further concern, daylight was approaching. Coming more slowly than at lower latitudes, but they could soon be in danger of being easily seen, especially from overhead.

That was when he heard the worst possible sound. The roar of some kind of jet aircraft hurrying up the valley from behind them. An especially loud roar indicating there was more than a lone plane heading their way.

Ward spun around to see and had the barest instant to recognize a camouflage-painted attack jet with a large red star painted on its tail. An SU-25 Frogfoot, with a heavy load of ordnance suspended beneath its swept-back wings. Before the SEAL could turn back around, a second one flashed by, and then a third. The third jet passed almost directly above them, and a fourth was coming from farther back.

Ward heard a loud whooshing noise. At first, he thought one of the Russian planes was shooting at them. But then he saw the brilliant trail of flame rocketing up from behind him, arrowing straight for that third Frogfoot. Someone on a snowmobile behind him had shot a MANPAD anti-air missile at the new arrivals. The arrow headed straight toward the plane's jet exhaust, where it did exactly what it was designed to do. It knocked the Frogfoot from the early-morning sky in a ball of smoke and flame. The plane spun into the valley far below.

The SEAL commander cringed. No way to know if the Russian jets had seen them before the missile launch or not. Whether they would have attacked, even if they had spotted the snowmobilers. No doubt now. The MANPAD shot had made certain they were now in a battle with the aircraft with no foxhole or bunker in which to hide. Ward could only hope they had enough firepower with them to stave off the three remaining aircraft before they could blast them right off the mountainside. And they probably had enough firepower to knock most of the mountain out from under them.

The fourth jet jinked hard to the left and swung around in a broad banking circle. The other two that remained made steep climbing turns to also come back around and see who had dared to throw that deadly dart at their buddy. They surely meant to avenge their brother.

Semenov jammed his snowmobile into the uphill side of the roadway and jumped off. He yelled at everyone to take cover, even though there was none. All they could do was try to hide as well as they could in banks of snow. Several more MANPADs suddenly appeared from the tow sleds along with automatic rifles. They might be caught in the open, but Ward was glad to see that they were not defenseless.

Semenov tossed an AK to Ward. The SEAL deftly caught the rifle, then checked it was loaded and ready before diving to the ground. He was not sure how much good it would do against the armor of the SU-25s, but it was better than throwing rocks, his alternative defense.

The trailing jet came in low, making a gun pass. His thirty-millimeter nose cannon winked wickedly. The mountain road was being torn up with geysers of rock and snow walking up the way toward the snowmobiles. Two of the vehicles exploded and burst into flames as the jet roared past overhead and stopped firing.

But just then, two more missiles zoomed up and began following the escaping jet like dogs chasing a car. The pilot tried to duck and dive to avoid the determined missiles. At the same time, he ejected a steady stream of diversionary flares. One of the chasing missiles was flummoxed by the flares and proceeded to dive directly into the side of a bluff directly below Ward and the others. But the second missile buried itself in the Frogfoot's wing-root. The formidable warplane immediately morphed into a smoky ball of fire that inertia carried all the way until it slammed into the mountainside a couple of miles to the north.

The remaining two SU-25s, now aware they faced a formidable foe down there, came around in a coordinated attack, one from ahead and the other from behind. Then they both fired off their complete load of fourteen three-point-one-inch S-80FP rockets in a devastating ripple launch before ultimately closing in for what they likely assumed would be a mop-up gun attack. The hillside exploded in flames, shrapnel, and rock debris as the two waves of missiles converged on the snowmobile convoy. Then the hail of cannon fire only added to the destruction as the planes completed their pass and flew away to line up and make yet another deadly pass.

Ward saw one of the men ripped nearly in half by a thirty-millimeter cannon shell. Several of the others were left lying in bloody lumps where the rockets had picked them up, ripped them apart, and tossed them back into the snow. The snowmobiles were now nothing more than ugly masses of metal, smoke, and flame.

Ward grabbed a MANPAD from where one of the dead fighters had dropped the weapon. It seemed to be unscathed. Only one way to find out.

He centered the aiming reticule on one of the fast-departing jets and half depressed the firing button. The missile immediately emitted a low tone, and Ward saw a green light in the reticule. The device was locked on to its designated target. He jammed down on the firing button. The missile leaped out of the tube, rapidly came to speed, and arrowed straight into the fast-fleeing jet. That bird joined its other two wing mates as burning pyres amid the rock and scrabble on the snow-covered mountainside.

The last SU-25, likely convinced there must be a more daunting force down there than he could see, beat a hasty retreat to the west.

After all the battle noise, the winter quiet—little more than the slight crackle of flames from the wasted vehicles—was disorienting. The wind fanned the flames from the snowmobiles to disturb the otherwise utter silence. Then there came the moans of a badly injured man.

Ward quickly found Hall and Dumkowski trying to render first aid to one of the Russians, but the man had already passed. The three SEALs searched through the wreckage, finding only two of the Russians still alive, both severely wounded.

Semenov was dead. He had been ripped through by several pieces of shrapnel and had apparently bled out in seconds.

"Now what, boss?" Dumkowski asked.

"Well, let's patch these two up as best we can," Ward answered. "We'll put them in a sled and see if we can find the Arka base that Semenov was talking about."

"Roger," both SEALs responded.

"And let's do it quick before the Russians come back and try to turn this mountain into a gravel pile."

17

Tan Yong, president of the People's Republic of China, sat back in his big chair, deep in thought, his fingers templed beneath his chin, and listened to the tinny voice on the telephone speaker and then the translation. The personal phone call from Grigory Iosifovich Salkov, the president of Russia, had come as a bit of a surprise. The Russian ruler was not particularly gregarious by nature and certainly was not a close friend. Tan Yong could sense that Salkov was stretching his charisma to the limit as he tried to ease the conversation through the small-talk phase and into the meat of the call, all while establishing a sense of *hemu*, harmony and concord. But the normally taciturn Russian leader was failing miserably.

The Chinese president allowed Salkov to suffer for a bit, mostly twisting in the wind, before he finally broke in. "My dear friend, we are *mengyou*. I think your Russian word is *soyuzniki*. But I am afraid the subtleties of our Mandarin word are easily lost in the translation. We are confederates, allies, and accomplices on the world stage. We share our goals and our triumphs. If you need the assistance of our nation in some matter of importance, you have but to ask. Our resources are yours. If you require a phantom penalty called in the final minute of a match, you need only make the request and it will happen."

Tan Yong could hear the subtle change in tone as much of the tension eased out of Salkov's voice. "My good friend, I will be quite frank. My government finds itself in a difficult situation. As you well know, the Ukrainian situation and the ruthless attacks by terrorist forces on our Kazak border are stretching our resources dramatically. And now, the *Deti Gulaga* sense our distraction and are playing opportunists out in the remote reaches of Far East Russia."

"My friend, do you need supplies, ammunition, armor, aircraft? As I have already assured you, you have but to ask." Nothing the Russian president had said so far came as a surprise to Tan. His Ministry of State Security had already briefed the Chinese leader that Salkov would express need for all of these assets as well as logistical means to transport them to multiple fronts. And, in many cases, they would also require the expert warriors to properly deploy and utilize these modern weapons. The Russian leader had offered Tan an excellent opportunity to firmly establish that he was the senior partner in this little alliance and Grigory Iosifovich Salkov was very much the junior partner.

Salkov confirmed that he needed everything on Tan Yong's list and he needed it now. However, in addition, he would prefer intervention—preferably covert—to stop the *Deti Gulaga* in their tracks, quickly and finally, with minimal fuss and furor, before the Russian people or most of the world's governments were even aware of their existence. Though they were little more than a boil on the backside of the Russian Federation, the small group was creating yet another diversion at a very sensitive time.

"Grigory Iosifovich, but of course. I understand your situation perfectly. And my solution is as simple as asking my Ministry of Defense to speak with yours. They know and trust each other already. Between them, we should have trains moving in a week." Tan Yong paused for a bit before adding, "Of course, manufacturing all these weapons and transporting them to where they will be utilized will require considerable resources and energy on our part. It would be most helpful if you could increase coal and gas exports to our nation and a few of our strategic friends and do so at a most favorable rate."

Tan stifled a laugh at the rapidity with which Salkov agreed to his request. From there, the exchange began to wind down, then ended with the usual half-hearted pleasantries. The conversation was barely disconnected when Tan Yong placed a call to Nian Huhu De, Special Ambassador Plenipotentiary for the People's Republic of China to the Democratic People's Republic of North Korea. When Nian came on the line, Tan Yong dispensed with all pleasantries. "Ambassador Nian, contact your DPRK counterparts and especially the Foreign Minister, Gan Tong Ja. We want the Children of the Gulag supplied with every military assistance they have requested. Assure Minister Ja that we will pay well for the supplies and that a bank account in his name and sole control is opened in Singapore. But make sure it is subtle. There must be no way for our Russian friends to track the Korean assistance back to us."

Ambassador Nian did not hesitate in his reply. "I am having lunch with the Foreign Minister in a few hours. I will speak with him there. By the second course, he will understand the importance of your request. And before dessert, he will be fully aware of the importance of not allowing anyone to know of our involvement in this matter."

Ψ

Jim Ward and his small band of SEALs carefully assayed their situation. On the plus side, the six sleds contained all the supplies they would need for a week or more in the sub-arctic wilderness, and especially now that there were fewer of them. The Russian rebels, ever mindful of the dangers of being stranded in the remote snow and ice, had even packed in cross-country skis, just in case they could not make use of the snowmobiles. On the minus side, though, the SEAL team members were now stranded foreigners in a hostile land, many miles away from the nearest aid. And they had two critically wounded Russians that needed immediate medical attention. Leaving them behind was not an option. Adding to the difficulty factor, there were only the three of them to ski out of their predicament, towing sleds with the wounded men and their supplies while dodging any more attacks, air or ground.

This mission was now officially in danger of going seriously sideways.

It took a couple of hours to give what emergency first aid they could to the wounded men, to pack them as comfortably and as warmly as they could, and then to stow in the remaining space on two of the sleds the food and supplies that they felt they might need. Joe Dumkowski fashioned a couple of jury-rigged harnesses to those two sleds using some line and web strapping. It was crude, but it would work. Then they busily covered over the other sleds and wrecked snowmobiles with snow, effectively hiding evidence of them having been there, at least from the sky above. A ground party would not be so easily fooled.

By the time they were finally ready to venture out, the sun was nearly as high in the sky as it would get in the middle of a winter day this far north. Though Ward recognized Semenov's concern with traveling by day, he figured that they needed to put as much distance as they could between themselves and the attack site. And do so as quickly as they could manage. Even way out here, the Russians would not lose three warplanes without sending some serious retribution back to the scene.

The real question now was which way to go. Backtracking to Novoe Uste was one option. Maybe the most attractive one at the moment. Ward calculated that they would have sixty or so kilometers of tough skiing back to the rude settlement, followed by some tough explaining to do to the locals, who may or may not be loyal Children. But at least they knew the way back there and could be assured someone was there to help the wounded men.

On the other hand, poring over Semenov's topo map, it looked like they had about sixty kilometers to travel in order to reach the area where Arka was supposed to be, but the terrain along the way was completely unknown. Ward did not even know exactly where the rebel base was located. It did not have its own dot on the map. He only had a general idea that it was to the north of their present position and near the Okhata River. Going north at least gave them some chance of carrying through on the mission.

Commander Jim Ward and his two men had orders. They were bound to do all they could to complete the mission as assigned. That ultimately meant the team would continue heading north up the snow-covered road in search of Arka and time with Dostervesky to gauge the strengths and weaknesses of the Children of the Gulag and their potential for success.

The SEALs rotated chores, with one of them breaking trail while the other two each pulled a sled. This worked for the first couple of kilometers on relatively level terrain. But then the road steeply pitched uphill once more. It took all three of them to pull each sled up the steep incline, frequently stopping to rest and then backtracking to bring up the second sled. It was grueling work, and their progress seemed to be best measured in feet and inches, not kilometers or miles. Every time they rounded a shoulder of rock and ice and thought the trail might be starting its descent, the road pitched upward yet again. The river valley was even farther below them, but still they climbed. They avoided speculation on how easy the progress would have been had the Russians not killed their snowmobiles and part of their team.

The sun was well below the horizon, leaving them navigating by starlight, when the track finally leveled out a little. The three SEALs stopped and rested for a bit. There was no time to cook, and, of course, they could not start a fire and generate telltale smoke. Even so, the cold food tasted like a gourmet meal. The two wounded Russians were still unconscious, and there did not seem to be any change to their conditions.

"Okay, I'm never going skiing again, no matter what the wife says," Dumkowski proclaimed, knocking his boots together to shake off the packed snow from their treads.

"You said the same thing about scuba diving after that deal we did in the Bahamas," Jason Hall reminded the big SEAL.

"And skydiving while we were on the Bali mission," Jim Ward added.

"Then it's settled," Dumkowski said, settling back even deeper into a snow bank. "I ain't never doin' nothin' no more!"

After an hour, Ward suddenly stood. It was time to move on. But as they stepped out of the limited cover of the rock cliff above them, all three noticed that the wind had picked up out of the north and the sky had darkened ominously. An Arctic storm was brewing. Being caught out in the open was a sure way to die and become supper for bears. The three grabbed the sleds and made a mad dash for the tree line, three hundred meters lower down the slope and a kilometer away.

By the time they reached the shelter of the fir and spruce, the wind was already howling at better than fifty knots and the temperature had dropped dangerously low. The wind-driven snow made it impossible to see anything at all beyond the spot where they landed. The men had luckily found a spot between two boulders. Tipping the sleds on their sides and covering them with a couple of tarps formed an effective snow cave, bolstered by the rapidly accumulating frozen precipitation piling up against their shelter. At any rate, it protected everyone from the wind and blowing snow.

There was nothing they could do until the storm blew out. They had no way of knowing whether that would be in a few hours or several days. Best to take advantage of the situation by getting some replenishing rest. That was exactly what they did.

Dawn broke quietly on a snow-covered pristine wilderness. The storm had waned just before sunrise. Ward, awakened by the silence, emerged from their snow cave to a bright orange-and-pink sky. Thankfully, the wind and driving snow had moved off someplace to the east. It was time to press on.

By the time the three had repacked their sleds and made their wounded passengers safe and secure, the sky had lightened to a brilliant cerulean blue. Slipping and sliding down the mountain slope was not as physically taxing as lugging their sleds upward, and the fresh snow seemed more powdery and slippery, but it was every bit as trying on the nerves as the uphill sojourn had been. After an anxious hour of constantly holding back on the heavily laden sleds to keep them from getting away from them and gingerly steering them around the bends in the ever-descending track, they finally found themselves back on the valley floor. Looking back, it was hard to believe they had navigated that mountainous terrain, sheltered from a fierce storm, and dodged the murderous rockets of Russian Frogfoot aircraft.

New quandary: the rough road they had been following through the mountains now forked. And, of course, there were no road signs. One fork ran off to the east. The other headed to the northwest. The topo map showed both routes, but the northwest one dead-ended at the edge of the Okhata River, only a couple of kilometers away. And to make matters less promising, the map showed a steep precipice at the road's end.

"You two make camp in those trees over there," Ward directed. "Best as I can make out from what Semenov told us, Arka should be over in that direction somewhere, and not that far." He pointed up the northwest road fork. "I'll head that way and see if I can find them. Or maybe they'll find me first. Either way, I should be back before nightfall. If I'm not back by the time your supplies get low, though, head downriver to the sea and use your comms to call for a taxi out of this damned icebox."

"We don't leave anybody behind, Commander," Hall said. "You know that."

"If I'm not back by then, I'm bear shit. Okay? And SEALs are not obligated to retrieve bear shit. You have your orders."

With that, Jim Ward skied off down the lonely, narrow, forested track at a fast clip. About the time he neared where he expected the river to be, he began to get an odd feeling. Well-honed intuition told him that he was not alone out there in the midst of nowhere. His senses screamed that someone —or something—was out there in the dark shadows of the forest watching him, shadowing him. But try as he might without slowing his pace, he could not see anything out of the ordinary. There was nothing else to do but keep heading toward where he believed Arka was and remain very alert for some other evidence besides his gut that he was being stalked.

He could only hope that evidence would not be a bullet to the head.

The track suddenly ended at a bluff high above the boulder-strewn, frozen-over Okhata River, just as the topographic map predicted. Ward was intently scouting for a path that might lead him down the treacherous slope when he was startled by a sound behind him. The sound of a human voice, calling out from the darkness behind some brush.

"*Komandir* Ward, could that possibly be you, my friend?" Despite the racing pulse in his ears, Ward recognized the raspy voice of Ivan Dostervesky, the leader of the Children of the Gulag. Then the man stepped from the shadows, a broad, welcoming smile on his face. "I trust you and your team had a pleasant hike through only a small portion of our beautiful new nation."

"I will be happy to supply a detailed brief, Mr. Dostervesky, including my own observations on how we might have arranged this meeting in a far safer and more effective way without compromising the location," Ward said, but without even a hint of a smile. "But now we have two of your men in urgent need of medical attention and two of mine—and their leader— who are cold, hungry, and royally pissed off."

At least their ski trek was now complete.

Ψ

Lieutenant Jimmy Wilson picked up the phone on the second ring. "Office of the Director of Naval Intelligence. Lieutenant Wilson speaking. This is not a secure line."

The female voice on the other end of the call was soft, alluringly sexy, and held just a trace of an Asian accent. Wilson recognized it immediately. But he also knew better than to flirt with her. Or even be polite.

"Hello, Lieutenant. I need to speak with the admiral," was all she said. As usual. This was the normal way for Li Min Zhou to conduct a call. No introduction and no names. Nor did she ever ask for anyone else in the naval intelligence director's realm. Only Admiral Jon Ward himself.

"I'll connect you with Admiral Ward. This may take a few seconds. He's traveling, so I will need to forward this call to his mobile."

In fact, Jon Ward was in a C-37B, the military's version of the Gulfstream 550, on his way from Andrews Air Force Base near Washington, DC, to Hickam Field, Hawaii, when his sat phone buzzed. When he answered with simply, "Ward," the voice on the other end of the call quickly told him what to do. "Admiral, let's go secure."

Ward, of course, recognized Li Min Zhou. The stunningly beautiful Chinese spy—and nowadays his SEAL team commander son's girlfriend—would keep her time on an open phone line to an absolute minimum. Considering her work, it was far too dangerous to do otherwise. Ward also knew that Li never called just for small talk, even if there was a remote possibility that she could be his daughter-in-law one day. If she called, whatever she wanted to relay was important. World-order important.

Without a word, Ward pressed a button on the side of his satellite phone. A red LED blinked twice and then morphed to solid green. He listened as the phone chirped and buzzed a couple of times as his device and hers synced up.

"I hold you secure," he told her.

"I hold you the same," Li responded. "Admiral, you asked for me to call you if I heard anything regarding the Children of the Gulag. My sources in Beijing tell me that Tan Yong and Grigory Iosifovich Salkov have just completed a very interesting discussion. Salkov was pleading for all manner of assistance with the Ukraine situation and on the Kazak border, as well as with the Children. He is even requesting troops and technicians to operate the Chinese equipment that might be provided."

"Very interesting," Ward acknowledged. "I am not aware of a request like that being made before, and it sounds as if Salkov is at the point of desperation to have done so now."

"I agree. But that is not the best part," Li went on. "Immediately after he ended his call with Salkov, Tan Yong rang up the Chinese Embassy in Pyongyang. He is working to double-cross his Russian friends and will do so by using the North Koreans to do his dirty work. And to top it off, he is bribing the DPRK Foreign Minister with a fat Singapore bank account."

"Next you'll tell me you have the account number and password," Ward said, only half joking.

"As a matter of fact, I do," she answered with no humor whatsoever.

18

Louise Gadliano knocked on her XO's stateroom door, waited for acknowledgment. Hearing nothing, she opened the door and stepped inside.

Susan Biddleson reclined on her bunk, shoes off, and was busy talking with someone on her cell phone. She held up a hand to signal Gadliano to wait a minute.

"Love you, too, Daddy," she was saying, completing the call. "Best to Mother. Talk to you soon." She pressed a button, dropped the phone on the bedside table, and sat up to stare without expression at her captain.

"Please tell me you weren't discussing our operations," Gadliano told her as she stepped further into the stateroom. "That's an unsecure line, as you well know. There's no telling who might be listening." Biddleson started to say something. Gadliano anticipated the response. She had heard it before. Many times. "And yes, I know your father is a flag officer. And I do not give a royal rat's ass."

Biddleson snorted. "Captain, you know as well as I do that this is a bull-shit assignment. It'll accomplish nothing except pissing off the Russians and putting us in danger for no good purpose. I did what any good exec would do. I took advantage of the tools at hand. I asked Dad to get this mission quashed."

Gadliano could not believe her ears. This was a new low, even for Biddleson. A potentially deadly new low.

"Goddammit, XO!" Gadliano roared back. "You went over my head and circumvented the chain of command. And without permission. I'm now well past the end of my string on your high-handed and potentially dangerous approach to everything."

Biddleson leaned back against the bulkhead and smiled at her skipper's outburst. "Don't worry, Louise. I'm about to be out of your hair, at least temporarily. I'm flying down to Yokosuka to be our liaison with Seventh Fleet for the balance of this operation." She glanced at her wristwatch. "They should be rolling out the chopper right about now."

As if on cue, the 1MC announcing system suddenly blared, "Now, rig ship for flight ops. All personnel stand clear of all weather decks. Helicopter unit, man your aircraft. Now, flight ops."

Gadliano's jaw dropped. Not only was Biddleson totally disregarding the destroyer and its mission and had now set in motion a flight ops maneuver aboard the vessel Gadliano commanded without the captain's knowledge, but she was actually bailing out on ship and crew just when the going might get dangerous and require everyone to be available and in top form.

Gadliano could only stand there, mouth open, stunned at such impertinence.

"Louise, you are getting your beloved mission after all," Biddleson said, virtually crowing. "Daddy did his best to make it go away, for you, and for his baby girl. But he soon found out the orders came directly from the Oval Office. President Smitherman himself has a cob up his butt over something, and he was the one who ordered this. Something about wanting to teach the Russians a lesson in raw power." The XO stood, grabbed her flight bag and jacket from the deck, and stood very near her commanding officer, waiting for her to move so she could exit the stateroom. "Now, if you'll excuse me, Captain, I have a flight to catch. I'll be sure to send you a postcard."

Ψ

Admiral Sergey Morsky sat up straight in the bed and reached over to the nightstand for a cigarette. The sex had been remarkably good. However, it had not relaxed him enough to allow him to go to sleep. Maybe a smoke and a glass of vodka.

"What's the matter, Sergey?" Luda Egorov asked as she sat up next to the admiral. The sheets fell away and lay crumpled at her waist. She knew Morsky loved to look at her breasts. "Something must be troubling you, my dear. You should be sleeping like a kitten now. You were certainly roaring like a lion a moment ago."

A smile flitted across his face as she leaned in closer to him, but it was quickly replaced with a dour frown. He poured himself a generous slug of vodka into a glass and took a deep swallow without bothering to ask Luda if she might want one, too.

"Those *bespononleznyye zhaby* in Moscow!" he growled. "They understand nothing and want everything. It is not enough that they take all my armor and troops to grind up and abandon on the steppes. And all my modern fighter aircraft and my very best pilots. Even my mediocre ones! The airframes that they leave me with are so old that they were first flown in Afghanistan by the *dedushki* of my current pilots."

Luda Egorov listened carefully, making sympathetic cooing sounds to accompany Morsky's angry rant. This kind of pillow talk provided golden information for the *Dedi Gulaga*. This part of being a spy was not so bad for a woman of her age and with her average looks. The admiral had proven to be an adept lover. He often bought her expensive gifts and took her to dinner in the nicer restaurants of Vladivostok. But even better, he became a fount of information once he got talking, which he usually did after their lovemaking.

"They leave me nothing with which to do my job!" Morsky rambled on. He was building up a real head of steam. "And then they dare complain to me that I am not doing enough to crush these rebels, these *Dedi Gulaga*. Do they not understand that we are talking about a trackless, snow-covered, windblown wilderness bigger than all Russia west of the Urals? How am I supposed to police that with no troops, no armor, and only a very few ancient planes? Oh, and not to mention the vast Pacific Ocean."

Luda leaned in even closer. "You must be calm, Sergey. You will devise a way to knock down those amateurs."

"But you do not understand. Those *Deti Gulaga* are smart. They are setting traps for our young pilots. Still babes, fresh from their *materi*." Egorov could not believe it, but she could see tears in the hardened admiral's eyes. "No combat experience and barely enough flying time to know how to get those old crates in the air. And the rebels lure them into attacking some camp in the middle of nowhere. Surround the place with hundreds of MANPADs. They shoot those missiles as if they have the world's stockpile of the weapons at their disposal. Where are they getting so many of them? It must be either the Chinese or the North Koreans, which is, of course, the Chinese. Those murderous bastards would not sell Russia a roll of toilet tissue unless they had China's permission." He slammed his fist down on the nightstand, sloshing some of the vodka from his glass. "And as a final insult, that snake Salkov calls President Tan Yong and begs the Chinese to help him quash the *Dedi*. That *kitayets* can and will maneuver rings around that corrupt old bureaucrat Salkov. I swear, Luda, we will all soon be eating our *pelmeni* with chopsticks."

"Easy, Sergey," Egorov said, now whispering seductively. "You'll work yourself into a heart attack, my dear." She slowly, deliberately, reached beneath the sheets. "Now, I believe I know just the thing that might help calm you."

Ψ

Henrietta Foster brought the *Gato* to periscope depth to take a casual look around. It was almost showtime for the FONOPS operation. The *Gato* was where she needed to be, exactly seventy-five miles east of the southernmost point of Sakhalin Island. They were standing by ten thousand yards off the *Feinstein*'s expected track. So far, there had been no contact with the destroyer. Had the op been canceled and someone forgot to tell the submarine? It would not be the first time for a foul-up like that, Foster well knew.

FONOPS stood for "freedom of navigation operations," in which the US would, by God, fly, sail, and operate wherever international law allowed them to, regardless which bullheaded regime claimed the waters to belong to them. It was a way to not allow countries to simply annex whatever body of water they wanted as their own. Such ops had resulted in mostly bluster and threats and even a few shots fired. And, on occasion, battles had taken place, ships had been sunk, and warriors had lost their lives. Most of the world knew nothing of the deadly actions. Typically, both countries involved had reasons to keep these flare-ups a secret.

The *Gato's* low-profile photonics mast broke the surface to reveal a dull gray, pitching sea with a canopy of rain-streaked cloudy sky. For the umpteenth time in her naval career, Henrietta Foster thanked her lucky stars that she was down here, inside a warm, dry submarine, not standing up there on the frigid, wind-swept wing of a destroyer.

"Captain, ESM is picking up a SPY-6V(3) to the southwest," Eric Householder whispered in her ear. The SPY-6 was the multipurpose radar carried on ships like the *Feinstein*. "I'm guessing our friend is running a little late."

"Sonar have anything on her?"

"Not yet. But I'm not surprised. Those Flight III *Burkes* have a reputation for being very quiet. We have her track on Link 16. Showing a hundred miles to the west, just coming out of the La Perouse Strait."

Foster did a 360-degree scan of the horizon. Nothing out there but cold, dark seawater.

"Sonar have any other contacts?"

"Just a bunch of shipping way to the north. Nothing heading our way."

Good. Damn good. It was her job to remain hidden. *Feinstein* would have responsibility for raising the ruckus.

Foster decided to stay at periscope depth for a bit while the destroyer caught up. Might as well ventilate the ship while they waited, she decided. A little fresh air would be welcome.

The low-pressure blower had just started pulling outside air into the sub when Senior Chief Stumpf called out, "Contact on the *Feinstein*. We have her on the hull array. Bearing two-seven-zero, range one hundred thousand yards."

Foster asked, "You sure it's the *Feinstein*, Chief?" The hurt look in Jim Stumpf's eyes caused her to immediately regret she had even asked the question. If the Senior Chief said it was the *Feinstein*, then it was the *Fein-*

stein. If he said it was Taylor Swift, waterskiing behind a motorboat and playing guitar, she could be damn sure that was what it was.

"New contact on the link," Rick Sanson, the Officer-of-the-Deck, called out. A red diamond had appeared at the north end of Sakhalin Island. It was moving rapidly to the south. "Link is evaluating it as an *Udaloy*. Making better than thirty knots and heading our way."

A Russian destroyer was coming out, and it probably was not there to welcome and shuttle them to a resort hotel.

ETC Collins, the ESM operator, reported, "Picking up an MR-320 M Topaz surface search radar to the north. Best bearing three-five-two. That confirms it. That's our *Udaloy*, all right."

"Gettin' crowded out here all the sudden," Foster said, mostly under her breath.

She did a little quick mental math. With the *Udaloy* charging south at thirty knots and in this present sea state, the best the two US ships heading north could do would be about twenty knots. That meant they would probably meet just north of the Mys Terpeniya light on Sakhalin Island.

"XO, signal *Feinstein* and tell her we are going deep and heading north. We will rendezvous five miles north of the Mys Terpeniya light in seven hours."

With that message sent and receipted, the *Gato* angled down into the deep and surged forward. Even at a flank bell, the *Udaloy* would enjoy a better than five-knot speed advantage on the Block-VI *Virginia*-class submarine, but Foster could make up for that by planning well ahead and getting into position before the other guy even showed up on the block.

Almost exactly seven hours later, the *Gato* slid up to periscope depth. They found the *Feinstein* there, too, hull down on the southern horizon. The *Udaloy* was not yet in sight, but the Link 16 track had it one hundred and thirty miles further north, still steaming south—in their direction—at better than thirty knots.

"Let's tell *Feinstein* that we want to head north at a leisurely pace. Twelve knots will allow us to stay at PD while doing an ASW search and generally keeping track of the situation."

The *Feinstein* steamed up until it was abreast the *Gato* and ten thousand yards to port. The pair headed north in tandem, as if bracketed together.

"Conn, ESM, picking up MR-760 MA Fregat air search radar from the *Udaloy*. And their surface search radar has to be painting the *Feinstein* by now. We'll know things are serious if we pick up their Garpun BAL surface-ship missile targeting radar. That would verify they were ready to shoot if they're going to."

"Conn, Sonar, she just lit off her Zvezda M-2 hull-mounted active sonar. They are really beating up the water for some reason." Senior Chief Stumpf was clearly perplexed why the Russians would turn on their active.

"Any chance he has us?" Foster asked.

"No, none. Not at that speed," Stumpf answered. "And she just kicked it in the ass. That bucket is doing better than thirty-five knots now. Big dog going for a juicy bone."

Foster gazed out at the sea. She estimated that the sea state was somewhere about five or six. With things that rough and moving as fast as they were now, the Russian sailors on the destroyer were certainly getting knocked around.

Then the *Udaloy* appeared on the northern horizon. The Russian battle ensign was flying from the destroyer's main mast. The bow rhythmically rose high in the air and then plunged back down with a crash so that the whole front of the vessel disappeared under the waves, only to pitch up again with seawater cascading off her decks.

The *Udaloy* steamed straight at the *Feinstein* as if by aim. Suddenly the channel 16 bridge-to-bridge radio speaker blared, "American warship, this is Russian Federation warship *Admiral Panteleyev*. You are steaming in recognized Russian sovereign waters. This is an act of war. You will lower your flag and depart Russian waters immediately."

The two ships were three thousand yards apart and heading on a collision course. Below the surface, Henrietta Foster eavesdropped with a strong sense of déjà vu. It had not been that long since she had heard a similar command, but that had been in the South China Sea, and the person delivering the ultimatum had carried a Chinese accent.

"*Admiral Panteleyev*, this is the American warship *Diane Feinstein*." Foster recognized that voice. Commander Louise Gadliano. A classmate at Annapolis. A friend. But one who had picked the surface navy as opposed to the correct choice, submarines, just because female officers in the Silent

Service were a rare thing at the time. "The United States does not recognize your claim. These are international waters under the Law of the Sea. We are engaged in a transit through international waters. Your interference is unwarranted and illegal."

You go, girl! Foster thought. Gadliano sounded firm and assured in her reply.

The two ships were by now down to less than a thousand yards and closing fast. And they seemed bound on playing a dangerous game of maritime chicken.

At the last possible moment, both ships threw their rudders over hard to starboard. They scraped down the sides of each other, tearing away some rigging and a lifeboat or two, but apparently neither inflicted serious damage on the other. Then the two vessels opened out to a thousand yards, eyeing each other while taking stock of the damage, as Henrietta Foster observed from below.

"Skipper, picking up a submarine!" Stumpf abruptly yelled. "Best bearing north. Best range, eight thousand yards. He's opening his outer doors! Torpedo in the water!"

The sonarman's blow-by-blow account grew frantic by the end. Foster grabbed the secure radio and yelled, "*Feinstein*, torpedo in the water from the north. Take evasive action. We are counter firing."

But then there was another voice on the circuit. A voice that Foster did not recognize as it boomed authoritatively out of the speakers, "*Gato, Feinstein*, you both are weapons tight. I say again, weapons tight. Do not engage."

Foster pounded the desk in rage. She had the sneaky bastard of an ambushing submarine clearly in her sights and a torpedo ready to unleash. *Feinstein* may not be able to evade, but *Gato* was ready to deliver appropriate retribution. Now the voice of God was telling her to stand down.

"Best torpedo bearing zero-zero-six, drawing left," Stumpf called out. "Best bearing zero-zero-three."

The torpedo was definitely heading in the general direction of the *Feinstein*. Foster watched as the US destroyer heeled around and headed south at flank speed to try to dodge certain carnage. All the time, she was dropping countermeasures into the water, trying to confuse the onrushing death-fish. And constantly changing course a few degrees. None of it appeared to faze the torpedo.

Meanwhile, the *Udaloy* charged off to the west, as if its captain believed it to be he who was under attack. The skipper was screaming invectives into the radio mic about the treacherous Americans who had opened fire on his ship right there in Russian waters.

"Skipper, the torpedo looks like it has acquired the *Udaloy*," Stumpf yelled. "It is in re-attack on it now. You don't think it was the target all along, do—"

Then the sonar screens were blanked out by a tremendous explosion. Foster looked in time to see the *Admiral Panteleyev* breaking in half. The bow and stern of the Russian destroyer rose high out of the water, and then both halves of the warship slipped below the surface amid smoke, swirling water, and a hail of debris falling from the sky. Where a few seconds ago a proud warship had floated, there was now only oil and flotsam.

Foster realized she had not breathed in a full minute. She looked around the control room. Shock seemed to be the general expression on each crewmember's face. Shock, and then it was replaced with a quizzical expression. What should they do next?

Foster realized only she could and would answer that question. And at the moment, she had no idea. But she could not admit that either. She was the skipper.

The secure phone crackled, interrupting her quandary. "*Gato*, this is *Feinstein*. We are moving in to pick up survivors. Suggest you chase down that submarine and determine whose side he's on."

Before Foster could confirm, the secure phone crackled again. Again, it was the deeply mysterious voice.

"*Gato*, verify that you did not fire any weapons."

Foster's frustration was growing by the second. How did whoever it was even know that she was the *Gato*? What the hell was happening out there?

"No, dammit. We did not fire any weapons. We're going deep, and we intend to find the bastard who did."

19

Commander Louise Gadliano stood on the bridge of her destroyer with her mouth agape. One second, she was playing dodge-'em cars with an angry Russian destroyer. The next, she was trying to outrun a torpedo coming her way out of left field. And then the Russian warship blew up and sank right before her eyes.

Then, as she stood there watching the results of it all, the training kicked in.

"Sam, get us over close to the sinking," she ordered Sam Starson, the Officer-of-the-Deck. "And get both our birds in the air. I want to use the Fire Scout to find survivors. And employ the 60R to pick them up. We'll use the small boat teams to rescue more as soon as we're close enough."

"Aye, Skipper," Starson answered as the ship heeled over and picked up speed, hurrying toward the sinking some five miles away. "But we only have one small boat. We lost the port side boat when we swapped paint with the Russian."

Gadliano nodded acknowledgment as she punched the button beside her chair so she could talk with Combat. The Tactical Action Officer answered immediately. Gadliano ordered, "TAO, get me Seventh Fleet on the secure phone." She muttered under her breath, "Maybe my XO could be useful for something after all."

The red UHF secure phone buzzed almost immediately. She grabbed it and hit the push-to-talk button.

"Seventh Fleet, this is Gadliano on *Feinstein*." She released the button.

"Captain, this is Biddleson," the speaker squawked. "What can we do to help? Sat images are coming in now of the sinking. Looks like a bodacious screw-up out there by somebody."

Gadliano reconsidered her idea that having Biddleson in Yokosuka was a benefit. Her XO was already working to hang blame for this sinking, and Gadliano assumed she and her destroyer were the most probable targets.

"Look, XO, let's play the blame game later, when this is all done." Without even trying, her voice came across as ice-cold. "Right now, we don't know if there will be more shots fired, this time at us. But there are a lot of Russian sailors in the water praying for someone to come save them." Gadliano stopped to take a breath and to calm herself down. "We are moving in to rescue survivors of the *Admiral Panteleyev*. I need liaison with the Russian Pacific Fleet to fly injured directly to a hospital somewhere on Sakhalin. We'll handle what we can onboard, but there will be casualties we're not equipped to deal with. And I'd prefer the Russians are aware we're in there to help. Gadliano, out."

The captain did not wait for acknowledgment from Biddleson. She had lost track of shipboard operations during her verbal joust with her exec. She was surprised when the Fire Scout roared past the bridge, flying away down the port side. Quickly followed by the MH-60R Seahawk, zooming away parallel to the destroyer's starboard side. In what seemed like seconds, the two birds started an orbit of the sinking site, the Fire Scout down low and the Seahawk higher up.

She felt the ship slow as she watched the Seahawk go into a hover and lower its winch and collar. Then a rescue swimmer dropped out of the bird and put the collar around a survivor. While the first person was being lifted, the swimmer kicked over to a second victim. In a matter of five minutes, they had plucked six sailors from the water and were heading back to the *Feinstein* to drop them off. Gadliano marveled at the bravery and expertise of the Seahawk crew, but there was an issue. Helicopter rescue was too slow when there were hundreds to be lifted from the sea. It was taking too much time, and the men in the frigid water did not have much of that particular commodity left.

Gadliano watched as the starboard-side nine-meter RHIB was lowered. The additional boat would help, but like the helo, its capacity was limited. Officially, it was rated at six passengers and a crew of two, but Gadliano knew that her team could skirt the "official" capacity. Or at least by as much as was reasonably safe. But she knew there had to be a better, quicker way to get those people out of the water. Then it hit her.

"Sam, pop all the starboard-side life rafts. Have the RHIB tow them out. That'll at least get people out of the water and wind until we can get them aboard over here."

The MK8 inflatable life rafts that *Feinstein* carried were stowed in metal canisters hung on each side of the ship. They were designed to be automatically launched if submerged in seawater or to be manually launched if need be. The round, inflatable raft was covered with an orange tent to shelter the occupants. Each would accommodate twenty-five people.

Gadliano watched as the RHIB labored to tow a line of eight empty life rafts out into one of the areas where the survivors were waving for help, calling out pitifully for rescue.

The red phone buzzed. Gadliano grabbed it and thumbed the push-to-talk button.

"Gadliano."

"Captain, this is Susan Biddleson. Our liaison has just spoken with the Russian Fleet. They are incensed that we attacked and sank one of their ships. They're threatening all kinds of action, including sinking your ship."

"XO," Gadliano growled. "I'm going to say this one more time, and it had better sink into that thick coattail-riding skull of yours. We didn't sink anybody. We have not fired a shot. We have no idea who launched that torpedo, other than it was not the *Gato*. They haven't fired so much as a BB. If anyone attacks *Feinstein*, they do so at their own risk. Now, where are we supposed to fly the survivors we're pulling out of the drink?"

"Roger," Biddleson answered, seemingly uncowed by Gadliano's words. "The Russians say the nearest hospital is Tsentral'naya Rayonnaya Bol'nitsa. It's in the town of Poronaysk. Coordinates are four-nine-point-two-zero north, one-four-three-point-zero-seven east. They have allocated frequency three-five-seven-point-three-one megahertz for comms."

The line went dead. Gadliano looked out onto the water surrounding her warship. The *Feinstein* was sitting there at "all-stop," bouncing easily on the swells. Sam Starson had expertly brought the ship broadside to windward of the site where the Russian ship went down. The twenty-knot wind was shoving the ship down among the survivors, giving them a calm lee to be pulled directly onboard.

"Sam, call down to CIC and bring our sensors up to full alert. You heard what the XO said about the Russian reaction. And start the 60R shuttling the worst of the injured to this hospital."

She braved the biting wind and stepped out onto the bridge wing to watch the rescue. The fully loaded RHIB was now towing the first of the life rafts back. It was loaded to overflowing with survivors. There were even twenty or thirty of them clinging desperately to the outside of the raft.

Gadliano stood on the wing shivering as much from the tension as from the cold. She pulled her jacket close around her. She was wondering how frigid the water might be. She looked on as the RHIB pulled the life raft past her, heading on back toward the boat deck. Just then, one of the people clinging to the raft lost his grip, slipped into the water, and began to float away. No one seemed to notice as the guy's head slipped under the surface, bobbed up once, and then disappeared, going under again. There was no one close enough to go to his rescue. And it was obvious the man could not swim. Or was not able enough to do so by now.

Without even thinking about it, Louise Gadliano threw off her coat, kicked off her shoes, and jumped over the side. It was almost sixty feet to the water. Training again. She knew enough to jump feet first. A standard dive might break her back. The water still slammed into her like a brick wall. It was numbing and impossibly cold. She bobbed back to the surface, but the cold made it difficult to breathe. There was already an iron band tightening around her head and getting tighter.

She took a quick bearing on the ship and swam a couple of strokes before diving under. She found the guy she was looking for about fifteen feet down and slowly sinking. Gadliano grabbed him by the hair and kicked toward the surface with all her might, towing the Russian behind.

She could see the late afternoon sunshine glistening off the water over-head, but she did not seem to be getting any closer. A final set of desperate kicks was all she had left.

She broke the surface and into the glorious sunshine, gasping for air as she dragged the inert sailor up. She looked back at her ship. The decks were lined with sailors, and every one of them wanted to help. A couple of them jumped in and swam over to aid her. When they got alongside the destroyer, she found that she could no longer use her hands to climb the rope ladder that dangled over the side. They were just too cold and numb to grasp anything. One of her sailors, a big, burly boatswain, grabbed her and threw her over his shoulder as he climbed the ladder. Blankets and hot coffee awaited her on the main deck. The Russian that she rescued was still alive as he was carried off to sick bay.

Gadliano shrugged off her corpsman and his entreaties for her to go to sick bay herself. She fought her way through the crowd of congratulatory sailors and made her way to the bridge.

Sam Starson met her as she stepped onto the bridge. "Damn it, Skipper, the next time you want to hold swim call, let me know first, all right?"

That was when she noticed someone wrapped in several blankets, standing by her chair. The guy was shivering uncontrollably. He was sloshing coffee from his cup onto the deck.

She nodded toward the stranger and asked Starson, "Who's that?"

"Captain First Rank Yevgenny Matros," he answered. "He is the skipper of the *Admiral Panteleyev*. Or, at least, he was until a half hour ago. He speaks very good English."

Gadliano worked to control her own shuddering as she stepped over to the Russian captain and extended her hand. "Captain Matros, I am Commander Louise Gadliano, the commanding officer of this vessel. I am very sorry about the loss of your ship."

Matros ignored the extended hand and enveloped Gadliano in an enormous, sincere bear hug. "Captain, I insisted on coming to your bridge to thank you for saving my crew. But I arrived just in time to see you jump into the water and proceed to save my cook from the drowning. Krepostnoy is the finest cook in all of Russian Navy. Now, I must help with rescuing my *ekipazh*, my crew."

"Captain, let's get you warmed up, a hot shower, and into some dry clothes first. You can use our XO's stateroom. No one home there now." Gadliano looked down at her own sopping-wet uniform and the puddle of seawater in which she was standing. "And I hope you will understand if I do the same, sir."

"A very good idea, Captain," the Russian told her through chattering teeth. "And perhaps then we can both try to understand what happened out there today."

"Yes. Yes, maybe we can."

Ψ

The first batch of heavily laden snowmobiles roared out of the Arka camp well before dawn. They quickly disappeared from sight up the Okhotsk Perevoska, but the snarl of their engines echoed in the stillness long after they had disappeared. The second group followed them up the frozen river just as the sun reached its zenith, but the orb could not even be seen because of the deep layer of clouds blanketing the area and threatening more snow. By the time the third contingent was ready to leave, huge snowflakes, the size of a man's hand, had begun to drift down. It was difficult to see anything more than a few yards away.

Ivan Dostervesky had already explained to Jim Ward and his team—who were along to observe—that the attack plan itself would be simple. It was the logistics that would make it very complicated. Fifty of his fighters would attack the remote communications site at Krest Khaldzhay—which they expected to be very thinly protected—destroying or stealing everything they could lay their hands on. The Russians, being traditionally paranoid and overtly security conscious, had all of their in-country tactical and strategic communications running over hardened landlines. No data or voice messaging of any value went out over the air or through satellites. This facility was a key relay point for the ICBM stations and early warning radars that were located in a broad ring much farther to the north.

"The station should be an easy target," Dostervesky proclaimed proudly. "Its destruction should serve notice to President Grigory Iosifovich Salkov that the *Deti Gulaga* are a force to be reckoned with. And they will have lost an invaluable channel. It will be weeks before it can be restored, especially at this time of year."

The problem, the rebel leader admitted, was getting them and their ordnance there. The communications site lay along the Aldan River, hundreds of kilometers from anything even resembling civilization. That meant a trek of over six hundred kilometers for the raid team, up the treacherous Dzhugdzhur Mountains, over the Okhotsk Prokhodit Pass, and then down onto the broad, flat Yakutsk Plateau. A six-hundred-kilometer mountain trek in the Arctic winter promised many life-threatening challenges.

Dostervesky laid a topo map out across the snowmobile's hood, clearly anxious to show the SEAL team members that he and his raiders knew what they were doing and were perfectly capable of completing a successful assault.

"We divide the attack force into three teams. The first team will set up a supply cache here on the Urak River." He tapped a point where a small tributary dumped into the larger river, leaving them a relatively flat area in which to work in the otherwise steep and lengthy canyon. "It's a good one-day trek upriver. The second team will leapfrog to a second cache on the west side of the Okhotsk Prokhodit Pass even as the first team comes back down the trail to reload and bring up more supplies."

Ward stared hard at the topo map. Even drawn out on paper, it looked complicated. He had learned long ago that complicated was not a good thing for any military operation. Too many spinning plates in the air meant too many chances for something to go way haywire. The SEAL scratched his head and stared some more. However, try as he might, he could not think of any better plan than the one the Children had concocted.

Dostervesky went on. "The third team is made up of the attack element. They supply at the second cache and then head down the Maya River. They will set up a cache in the foothills just before the Maya spills out on the level ground. From there, it is only about one hundred fifty kilometers to the target across flat, open land. Easy striking distance. Meanwhile, the second team heads back for resupply while the first team is working its way upriver to restock the second cache. That will assure that all the caches are fully stocked and manned to support the return to camp, even if the weather turns nasty or we have to hide from the damnable Russians for a bit."

You're a Russian, Ivan, Ward thought. But he remained silent. Apparently, the Children already thought of themselves as citizens of a new and different nation. Considering where Ward and his two men were and what they were about to do, that was a good thing.

"You're going to want to hit the base sometime after midnight," Ward suggested. "Are you going to be able to sneak up on it from as far away as that final supply dump is?"

Dostervesky laughed. "*Komandir* Ward, this is some of the most desolate country on the planet. Right now, it is frozen solid, but come spring, it will be nothing more than a massive bog and virtually impassable. In winter we could easily roar across there at two hundred kilometers per hour, followed by a full brass band, jugglers, and a parade of elephants and no one would be likely to see us. We will, of course, be a little more discreet than that, but the whole approach will only take two to three hours, and the chance of our being observed is virtually nil. You will see shortly."

Dostervesky folded the topo map and tucked it into a pocket. He quickly mounted the lead machine, pulled his googles down over his eyes, and roared off down the track. Ward simply shook his head and jumped onto the second machine. He followed a few meters back, leaving just enough distance to avoid all the icy flotsam Dostervesky's snowmobile was kicking up.

The trek up the river reminded Ward more of their slow, difficult trip from the coast than of some wild charge across the mostly level steppes. The river was bordered on either side by high rock cliffs, canyons right out of the Rockies back in the USA. Ward had spent plenty of time in Colorado and Wyoming on winter warfare training exercises and had always planned to go back and try recreational, non-pressure skiing instead.

Although the river was frozen solid, it was not exactly a glass-smooth superhighway either. Plenty of boulders, fallen trees, and ice dams kept the speed down and the ride way more interesting than it should have been. Halfway up this leg of the transit, they met the first team heading downriver for resupply. Jim Ward would admit that he was plenty tired when they finally arrived at the first cache six hours later and took time to rest.

Dostervesky ordered the team to refuel the machines and for everyone to get a hot meal. They would take an hour for recuperation before heading out again. The portion of the trip that took them up and over the Okhotsk Prokhodit Pass would be even more challenging than the first leg.

"You know what there ain't none of out here?" Joe Dumkowski quietly asked as they ate.

"Palm trees and bikinis," Jason Hall promptly responded. "Sand, seashells, margaritas..."

"People. No people far as the eye can see," Dumkowski said, answering his own question. "I still can't figure what these Gulag Kids want this place for. Not a Dairy Queen anywhere."

Jim Ward grinned, then, quietly enough that none of the assault party members could hear, said, "Under all this snow, boys, there's probably minerals and ore we've never heard of or could pronounce if we had. That stuff will be more valuable than gold or silver directly. Remember, too, that New York and Massachusetts were mostly trees and rocks and dirt when Washington and his guys chased the Redcoats off it and ran Old Glory up the flagpole."

Not long after getting underway again, and as expected, they met the second team on their way back down the trail, returning to camp. That was just as Dostervesky's team was about to depart the river trail and begin the climb over the pass. At that point, there was not enough room on the trail for two snowmobiles to slip past each other, so they rested for a few minutes while the second team went by. The noise of their machines was quickly swallowed up by the near perfect silence of the wilderness. Then Dostervesky, Ward, and the assault team resumed the climb.

The trail pitched up steeply as they left the river valley and climbed up to the pass through the higher mountains. The ten-thousand-foot-tall Pik Mus-Khaya, the highest peak in the Suntar-Khayata Range, loomed high over Ward's right shoulder. There was no sign of any other human being as far as he could see. Not even a jet contrail across the sky. This place might be devoid of Homo sapiens, but he was sure there were plenty of predators —likely hungry predators—out there eyeing the moveable buffet plunging noisily past them.

The trail finally leveled out as they reached the summit of the pass and then started back down and made the turn to the west. A mile down the trail, in a hidden wide spot, they found the second cache. Dostervesky again called a halt. After fueling and restocking the snowmobiles and eating a hot meal, he ordered everyone to get a few hours' rest. It was almost daybreak, and the upcoming night would be very busy.

Ward watched as Ivan Dostervesky roamed around the camp, talking with each group of his men, making sure they were ready for the upcoming action, that they had their assignments down pat. The SEAL commander also observed the reactions of the men to their leader, before, during, and after their interaction. Ward had already been impressed with the man's stamina and planning capabilities. The head man of the Children of the Gulag appeared to be a natural combat leader.

It was late afternoon when Dostervesky rousted Ward from a deep sleep. The camp was already buzzing with activity as they prepared to head down out of the mountains for the final run on their objective. The trail out of the mountains was reasonably smooth and wide. It offered easy going after the climb up to the pass. They made good time and arrived at the final cache location at dusk. Or as close to dusk as Ward could determine. There was no sun. Dark storm clouds were building and appeared to be moving down from the north. There would probably be snow before morning, if not sooner.

At their last stop, Dostervesky ordered everyone to offload anything that they would not need in the upcoming strike and possible running gun battle. Camping gear, extra food, and spare parts all went into the cache and were hidden beneath the piles of snow already on the ground. The strike element needed to be fast and agile, not weighted down with unneeded gear. A half dozen men and three snowmobiles stayed back at the cache site as the strike element roared out of the mountains and down onto the broad, flat plain.

Dostervesky had explained that they would be following two rivers, first the Maya and then the Aldan. Ward took his word for it. All he knew was that they were racing across this flat land at breakneck speed. Even in darkness and ahead of a blowing snowstorm, such an open run with the unmuffled snowmobile engines screamed of a lack of caution and the loss of the element of surprise, their biggest advantage should there be a well-armed and properly trained defense force waiting for them.

Suddenly, the SEAL was having some doubts about Mr. Dostervesky and his military acumen.

The only way they knew that they had arrived at the Krest Khaldzhay was when they saw several runs of barbed wire strung just above the snow. Beyond that, the cluster of cinder block buildings were empty. Lights blinked inside double-thickness windows; there was a distant hum of an electrical generator. There was nobody there. The relay station was unmanned.

After thinking about it for a moment, it all made sense to Ward. This place was, by definition, in the middle of nowhere. As good as US intel was, there was nothing on this remote waystation. Likely only the Russian military—and very few there—knew of its existence or importance. But the Children knew.

So why station a few troops here to protect something that was so far off the beaten track? Something so secretive? Especially when the Russian Federation needed troops for far more crucial duty elsewhere?

Dostervesky was about to order his men to destroy the place when Jon Ward had a brain flash.

"Wait! Ivan, don't blow this place! I think we may have a potential gold mine here."

The Russian looked at Ward questioningly.

"But *Komandir*, we have an opportunity to cut off the head of this snake ahead of our move for freedom!" Dostervesky responded.

"Ivan, think about it. All of the high-level comms between the Kremlin and Far Eastern Russia passes through these little shacks here. We put a tap on this line and we'll be able to listen in on everything Salkov and his top guys are saying. I'll guarantee you my dad—and probably ninety percent of the intelligence weenies in the world—would give their left nut to listen to this stuff and make notes. It's your party, of course, but I suggest we clean this place up like we were never here and head on back to camp. Start restocking your caches. Then get a crew together to bring some people and gear out here. My dad can get the recording and re-transmission equipment and the technicians to install, maintain, and run it in a way the Russians will never suspect anything's wrong. You just need to get them out here and then have somebody watching for regular refuel and maintenance crews coming in, of course."

Ivan Dostervesky was smiling already. "But would it work?"

"There has been proof of concept," the SEAL said. "A submarine, the *Halibut*, tapped into a comms cable between Vladivostok and Petropavlovsk at four hundred feet down in the Sea of Okhotsk way back in '71. The *Parche*, another boat, then ran with the tap for another ten years. They never got caught." Dostervesky looked at Ward with a blank expression. "There's been a book about all this sort of thing."

"Not many bookstores way up here," the Russian said. "Or time for reading. I must have missed it."

"Real Cold War stuff, believe me," Ward said. "This will be much easier and, if this station is as crucial to Moscow and Vladivostok as you say it is, it could be even more productive than that little underwater eavesdropping mission was."

Dostervesky nodded, and the smile slowly returned to his ruddy face. He sensed that he had something that the West might well be willing to pay for. And pay handsomely. In not only money but in both military and diplomatic assistance.

The heavens had opened up, and snow had begun to cascade down blindingly as the dissident leader signaled for his men to mount up and head home. No need to cover their tracks. God was doing a wonderful job of that for them.

They had more than accomplished their mission. They had discovered that the station was unmanned and unprotected, ripe for the scheme the SEAL commander had come up with, and they had done it without firing a single bullet.

Ψ

Senior Chief Sonarman Jim Stumpf diligently searched the ice-cold waters of the Sea of Okhotsk for any hint of his quarry. Somewhere out there a mystery submarine lurked. And it was a boat that had sunk the Russian destroyer, *Admiral Panteleyev*, without warning and right there in what she had been claiming was her home waters. But, so far, nothing of the rogue boat was showing up on the *Gato*'s sonar displays. The large-aperture conformal bow array was revealing a sizable pod of orcas happily feeding at the ice edge well to the north. On the large vertical flank arrays, Stumpf could watch—and listen to—a gaggle of fishing boats somewhere over the horizon to the east, trying to make a living in a very difficult way. But there was no sign of an errant and potentially deadly submarine.

"Senior Chief, you seeing anything?" Dale Miller, the Officer-of-the-Deck, asked. He was standing back at the command console, looking at the same displays that Jim Stumpf was perusing.

Stumpf shook his head. "Nada, Mr. Miller. We sure could use a towed array to help sort out that trash to the east, though. You think you could ask the skipper if we can deploy the TB-34?"

The TB-34, or fat-line towed array, was a line of hydrophones that the sub snaked along behind it using a tow cable. The array, a sausage of hydrophones and environmental sensors, was stowed in a long tube running up the submarine's side when housed. Because it was both much shorter and much fatter than the TB-29 thin-line array, the TB-34 was easier to use in restricted waters, like the Sea of Okhotsk. However, it was also less sensitive at very low frequencies. Searching at very low frequencies was essential when looking for a nuclear submarine, but this target was a diesel boat. That made the TB-34 the sensor of choice.

"Senior Chief," Miller answered, "get your people on station to deploy the fat-line. I'll go get the skipper's permission."

"Permission for what?" Henrietta Foster had just stepped into the control room and was already leafing through the sonar displays.

"Skipper, request permission to deploy the TB-34 to full scope," Lieutenant Miller said. "We're well clear of Sakhalin Island, and water depth is greater than three hundred fathoms."

Foster took a deep draw from her oversized coffee mug, then nodded. "Deploy the TB-34. Let's see if we can find our elusive friend on that. The hull sensors don't seem to be doing diddly."

A seawater pump literally flushed the TB-34 fat-line array out of its long stow tube and sent it out into the sea along the submarine's port stern plane. This made certain that it stayed well behind the boat's jet pump propulsor, so there would be little danger in the "sausage" getting chopped up by the propulsor. That is, unless the submarine backed down with the array deployed. It had happened before, a great embarrassment to the skipper and expense to the taxpayer.

The TB-34 had barely stabilized and started integrating when Jim Stumpf called out, "New contact on the TB-34. Designate Sierra Four-Seven, bearing zero-eight-nine, and Sierra Four-Eight, bearing three-three-one. Eleven-point-two-hertz tonal. Equates to a Russian *Kilo*-class submarine propulsion tonal."

Bingo!

Foster smiled. "Well, that didn't take long. Let's resolve ambiguity and see if we can figure out what this guy is up to. And just in case he objects to our looking up his skirts, let's man battle stations and make tubes one and two ready in all respects."

The *Gato* hummed with activity as the crew prepared the sub for potential battle. It was well-rehearsed choreography. The damage control party laid out their gear on the mess decks, ready to charge to the scene of any casualty they might suffer. The weapons-handling party mustered down in the torpedo room to be in place and ready to reload the torpedo tubes if they were to be shot. Back in the engine room, the nukes put the engineering plant in the safest, quietest lineup. All the while, the fire control team was trying to resolve as best they could what the target was doing. It took less than two minutes to bring *Gato* to fully battle-ready.

"Captain, we have a tracking solution on Sierra Four-Eight," Eric Householder announced. "Course two-two-zero, speed four, range one-five thousand yards. Looks like he's heading back toward the Sakhalin coast."

Foster studied the tactical display on the ECDIS table. The track showed that the mystery submarine had scooted to the north after torpedoing the Russian destroyer. Now it was trying to sneak back down south, almost certainly using the Sakhalin coast as cover. Just what was this guy up to?

"Officer-of-the-Deck," Foster ordered. "Let's move over behind our friend and see what he's going to do next. Position yourself on his port quarter. I want you to stay out at ten to twelve thousand yards range while we try to figure this out."

Householder stepped over and studied the tactical plot. "You figure he might be trying to sneak back into the area and take out the *Feinstein* this time?"

"No." Foster shook her head. "If he was going to do that, he would have shot them both when he had the chance, not knowing we were there and ready to make him pay. No, I suspect something has caught his interest down around the southern end of the island. I just can't imagine what it might be."

"Well, maybe he will eventually show us."

"I hope so." Foster nodded. "And before it's too late if it's something dastardly."

20

After leaving the Krest Khaldzhay comms relay site undisturbed, Ivan Dostervesky gathered the strike force at the third campsite for a quick debrief. Their wristwatches said that it should be dawn by now, but snow clouds obliterated any chance of seeing the sky or a low-on-the-horizon winter sun. At least a foot more of the white stuff had fallen since they had departed the comms relay site, and there were no signs of any letup. Leaving now for a run up to and over the Okhotsk Prokhodit Pass in the teeth of a winter storm did not seem very prudent.

Their tents and snow caves did a good job of keeping them out of the wind and cold. They had more than enough supplies to last them a couple of weeks, if necessary. However, Dostervesky's fighters were already chafing at the possibility of days of enforced, boring idleness. Especially after the anticlimactic nature of the planned raid on the comms hub. Jim Ward's two SEAL team members were getting itchy, too.

Ward and Dostervesky sat in a rude tent shelter stretched between their snowmobiles and discussed some possibilities. Dostervesky pulled his topo map out of his jacket pocket and unfolded it. He pointed to a location just on the east side of the Lena River, across from the regional capital of Yakutsk. It was obvious this was the closest thing to a city for a thousand miles in any direction. But he was actually indicating an airfield twenty kilometers to the east of the isolated little burgh.

"This is, believe it or not, a major base for the Russian Far East Air Force. It would be an easy plum to pick, and we do still need some kind of very obvious and destructive attack to fit our plan."

Ward looked at the map, his face showing his doubts. "Ivan, it's six hundred kilometers from here to there across the plateau. It will take us two days to get there if everything goes well, and then two days to get back here after the attack if we don't get our asses shot off or captured in the process. And even then, that would be in clear weather, not in the middle of this damnable snowstorm. Is there even a target there that would be worth the effort and especially the risk?"

Dostervesky smiled and winked. "*Komandir* Ward, our Russian friends have an entire squadron of IL-78 aerial refueling planes stationed there to service all the aircraft they are shuttling to the west nowadays to meet their needs there. A few of those will make a fire the heat from which Comrade Salkov will feel all the way to Moscow. Rumor has it that they have the first couple of the brand-new A-100 *Prem'yer* AWACs planes stationed there, too, because two of their primary spy satellites over this region have recently become unreliable."

"You're determined to get me and my guys in the middle of a running gun battle with troops of the Russian Federation, aren't you, Ivan?"

Dostervesky smiled again. "You came all the way out here, and you and your men have traipsed over some of the most deserted and rugged real estate on the planet, all so you could determine for your father just how well prepared we are to stage an insurrection against one of the world's strongest military powers, should violence become necessary. We would not want all your time and energy to have been wasted, now would we, *Komandir*?"

The team rested for a full day as they continued to hone their new plan. The snow continued mostly unabated all through that day and into the early hours of the next night. By the time they were ready to saddle up the convoy of snowmobiles and head out, an additional four feet had accumulated on the flats, with considerably more piling up in drifts behind anything that would slow the wind and allow the huge flakes to settle down. They headed out in single file, taking turns breaking trail through the deep powder. Other than the mining camp of Chymnaii on the Anga River and the tiny farming village at Sylanskiy Nasleg, which required that they do a zigzag maneuver around them to avoid detection, the route was straight, the land tabletop flat and impressively barren. The place even seemed too desolate for wildlife. They saw nothing else alive way out there.

The snow finally petered out halfway through the second day of travel. The clouds scudded away, leaving a brilliant blue sky. Or at least it was visible for the short hour before the sun dipped below the horizon. Just as the last rays flickered out on the western horizon, they crested a small ridge that overlooked a long, flat-floored valley. One covered with an impressive array of small buildings and a pair of very long, crisscrossing runways. There, stretched out before them, was the sprawling Yakutsk Air Base. But nowhere in sight was there a fence to mark the perimeter. No guard towers or bunkers. It was as if the Russians assumed no one wishing them ill will would ever make the trek way out here by land to do them harm. No doubt their defenses were directed skyward.

There was activity along the two runways. The team watched through their binoculars with some amusement as the airmen unfortunate enough to find themselves stationed in this bleak, icy outpost were struggling to clear the runways and taxiways of the massive piles of accumulated snow. Bulldozers, huge snowblowers, and heavy trucks equipped with snowplows were all busy. Several teams were also laboring furiously to dig some large airplanes out from under the deluge of snow. These workers were not so well equipped, having to rely on shovels and grunt labor to attempt to get the job done before the aircraft might be needed.

Dostervesky pointed off to the north, along the frozen river, at a cluster of very large domes rising out of the snow. "Those are the fuel storage bunkers. They should be near full, considering the amount of westbound aircraft traffic lately. I suspect they will burn very nicely if someone lights their wick."

The attack plan was simple and quick. Ward and his two SEALs—who had agreed to help if needed—would slip into the tank farm and plant charges on as many fuel tanks and feeder pipes as they could. Meanwhile, Dostervesky and his strike force would slip in closer to the flight line. They needed to be no farther away than five hundred meters for their RPG-29 *Vampir*'s to be within reliable range. Accuracy would not be much of a problem since the aircraft they hoped to kill presented very large targets. Dostervesky's teams would open fire with the rockets when the first storage tank exploded. They would exhaust their supply of thermobaric warheads and then skedaddle over the ridge before the few troops stationed down there could realize what was happening. They would all meet up ten miles back down the trail and head toward home.

Dostervesky was convinced the Russians would not pursue such shadowy attackers, even if they had the men and equipment to do so. Everyone who lived through the attack would likely be engaged in fighting fires. And the wind that had kicked up would effectively cover the tracks of the snowmobiles within minutes. Once back to the main base of the Children, Dostervesky would issue a communication to Salkov, taking credit for the attack and threatening to tell the world just how vulnerable the Russian Federation was if they did not begin serious talks concerning an amicable secession.

All this presumed, of course, that the attack was devastating enough to back up the power of the message, that they got away with their lives, and that the Russians never discovered that three members of the assault party were US Navy SEALs.

Jim Ward, Joe Dumkowski, and Jason Hall filled their backpacks with Semtex, detonators, and timers. Then they scurried off from the ridgetop, headed in the direction of the tank farm.

"Boss, how come we're missing the real fun?" Joe Dumkowski complained as they slithered on their bellies in frozen mud through a very convenient drainage culvert. That was how they were able to work their way beneath a chain link fence, the only thing they could see that was protecting the fuel farm, without risking being spotted. "They get to play with rockets, and all we do is tape Semtex to a bunch of tanks. We got firecrackers. They got cherry bombs."

"Damn, Joe!" Jason Hall grumbled. "You'd complain either way. You're just mighty fond of bitchin'."

"Will you two quit jawing and get to work?" Ward growled as they emerged from the culvert. "Keep your eyes out for trip wires or cameras, though I haven't seen anything yet. These guys are mighty lax. We got a dozen charges to place and timers to set. I'd kinda like to be out of here when they go off. Wouldn't want to singe my lovely eyebrows."

It took the SEALs a few minutes to sort out the maze of piping and valves serving the tank farm. The Cyrillic letters were meaningless to them, of course, but they eventually figured out the best placement if they were to put the field permanently out of action. With the timers all set, they crawled through the culvert and hustled back over the ridge. They had just gotten back to where they had hidden their snowmobiles when the first charge detonated, like low, rumbling thunder that quickly amped up to a massive shock wave. That was rapidly followed by a string of powerful explosions. Looking back, they saw a broad column of black smoke and brilliant fire climbing high, illuminating the velvet night sky and the barren, snow-blanketed land for miles around.

Ward's jaw dropped as he watched the fireball grow into a giant mushroom cloud. He had seen plenty of awful explosions before. Lots that he had initiated himself. But never anything this massively impressive.

Then they saw rocket trails arching across the sky from just beyond the perimeter of the base, followed by still more huge and impressive blasts as the rockets' warheads tore through the thin aluminum skins of the parked aircraft and detonated. Looking down from the ridge, Ward counted at least two dozen burning pyres that had once been high-flying—and very expensive—reconnaissance aircraft and warbirds That accounted for at least a squadron of the Il-78s and probably the A-100s as well.

If this did not get Salkov's attention, nothing would.

The three SEALs then jumped on their machines and soon joined the stream of snowmobiles roaring off to the rendezvous site to the east.

Mission accomplished.

Ψ

President Stan Smitherman looked across the Resolute Desk at the group huddled across from him. With this bunch, he did not even bother to try to hide the uncorked whisky bottle or the act of refilling his coffee cup with the brew several times during their brief meeting.

Vice President Harold Osterman sat next to Sally Kesterman, the Director of National Intelligence. General William "Winking Willie" Willoughby, the Chairman of the Joint Chiefs of Staff, rounded out the trio. As usual, Smitherman had not gathered the group to seek their professional advice. On this cold Washington, DC, morning, the president of the United States was very much in directive mode.

"Gentlemen and lady," he began, with a deferential nod toward Kesterman. "I will not have the Russkies sending one of their rust buckets out and threatening us every damn time we decide to steam in international waters anywhere in their vicinity. And I will not have them trying to blame us if that piece of junk of theirs blows up and sinks," he ranted. "They have to be taught a lesson. The damn CNN poll this morning on our foreign policy strength is down three points. We cannot have that! Military action plays well in the press and the polls. That's what we need right now, dammit!" He turned sharply toward Willoughby. "General, send the *Reagan* battle group into that Sea of Oak...Ock...whatever the hell it is. I want them right smack dab in the middle, and I want them conducting flight ops there that'll rattle windowpanes all over Vladivostok."

General Willoughby stared hard at his commander in chief. The infamous tic in his left eye was going a mile a minute. He began to stammer out a protest when Harold Osterman held up a hand.

"Just a second, Stan," the vice president said. "You need to think long and hard about escalation right now. The Russians just lost a ship. They are claiming...and we tend to agree...that it was torpedoed by a submarine. We know it wasn't one of ours. We think the Russians know it was not one of ours. But neither one of us knows whose it is or why they decided to shoot. And why they chose to shoot at the Russian ship when we had one in the area, too. If we send the *Reagan* charging in, then we not only have to worry about the Russian reaction but also about whoever it is that has that other unknown submarine operating in the area. What are they going to do? Shoot at us next time? Try to get us and the Russians shooting at each other? Suggest we hold off on kicking Salkov in the nuts for a little bit, Mr. President."

The brittle look Smitherman shot the vice president said it all. His most trusted sidekick had just betrayed the president in front of some very powerful people. In President Smitherman's world, that particular sin was unforgivable. He set his coffee cup down so hard a bit of Kentucky's best sloshed out on the historic desk.

"Okay, then, Harold, what do you have in mind?" he asked icily.

Osterman quickly recognized that he had crossed a line that he had not intended to. He immediately fell back on one of his prime political skills. Backpedaling. "Mr. President," he said respectfully. "What I mean to say is that I just don't think that this is worth the risk of starting a shooting war over. At least not yet. Especially when there is a mystery player in there that we don't know anything about. We'll have ample opportunity for force should things escalate without us pushing the action. And so far, voters don't even know anything is going on out there."

The president still frowned, though, as he dabbed at the spilled whisky on the desktop with his fingertips and then licked them clean.

Sally Kesterman spoke up next. "Actually, we probably know—or can infer—quite a lot about that unknown submarine. There are only a few nations that have subs that can or would be operating in those waters. We know with total certainty it isn't one of ours, the South Koreans, or the Japanese. As always, we are keeping tabs on all the Chinese subs as well as the North Koreans, so we are confident that it isn't one of theirs, either. There is no reason the Russians would sink their own ship. If they had done so solely to blame it on us, they would be crowing about it in the United Nations and on the seven o'clock news already. So, I'm confident we can discount them."

Smitherman leaned back in his chair and scowled. "Sally, you just ran through all the countries with boats anywhere nearby. You suggesting that this damn submarine is from outer space and driven by aliens or something?"

Sally Kesterman shook her head and smiled. "Nothing quite so exotic, Mr. President. There is, however, one sub that is still not accounted for, the one the Russians lost earlier this winter. They are claiming that it sank with all hands, probably a mechanical failure of some kind. I'm suggesting that it's still out there in the Sea of Okhotsk, and someone actually swiped it."

"Someone?" The president's arched eyebrow confirmed he really wanted to know.

"Our friends, the Children of the Gulag."

"Very interesting idea," Stan Smitherman mused. "But, so what? I still want the *Reagan* in there with flag flying."

General Willoughby jumped in. "Why don't we put out a news release that the *Reagan* battle group is going into the Sea of O to stabilize the situation and to protect the *Feinstein* while she conducts rescue operations?" Both the veep and the head of the country's intelligence efforts sat there blank-faced. The general's idea was most likely a seed of an idea, thrown out for more discussion.

But President Smitherman was finished with the whole thing. He stood, shoved the cork into the top of the whisky bottle, dropped it into a desk drawer, and started for the door. "Fine," he growled, popping a couple of Tic Tacs. "Just make it happen. I got a hundred Girl Scouts freezing their hind ends off in the Rose Garden waiting for me to come help them sell cookies."

The meeting was clearly over.

Ψ

Brian Edwards watched his team at work. Trailing Case Four-Six had been taxing in the extreme, but they had tenaciously held contact on the elusive Russian submarine. So far, the Improved *Severodvinsk* had sniffed around the edges of the *Reagan* battle group, but it had not made any move to penetrate the group, nor had it conducted any exercise that Edwards could call as being hostile.

Edwards was keeping his own sub, the *George Mason*, deep in Case Four-Six's baffles. That had them pretty close to the edge of detectability. So far, the US boat had been holding solid contact at between eight and ten thousand yards on the flank array. There did not seem to be any indication that Case Four-Six had a clue that *George Mason* was anywhere in the same ocean, let alone trailing them a few thousand yards away.

"Skipper, possible contact zig," Jerome Billings abruptly called out. The young lieutenant, junior-grade, had been analyzing the sonar inputs to the fire control system. "Downshift in received frequency. Analyzing."

Edwards stepped over to Billings's screen and looked over his shoulder.

The stack of dots was definitely trailing off. Case Four-Six had either slowed or turned away. Something had lowered his speed in the line of sight.

Just then, Bill Wilson called out, "Dropping bearing rate. Contact has zigged."

Edwards did some quick mental math. This guy had now both lowered his speed in the line of sight and across the line of sight. He had definitely slowed and turned. Did he pick up something from *George Mason* that raised his suspicion that he was being shadowed? Was he trying to sniff out a possible sonar contact?

"All stop," Edwards ordered. "Our friend has zigged. We'll just sit here, nice and quiet like, and see what he's up to. Everybody on your toes." Not much changed. The control room was still a quiet hum of activity as everyone tried to suss out what might be happening eight thousand yards —more than four miles—out in front of them.

"Skipper, I'm picking up some real quiet hull creaking," Josh Hannon, the Sonar Supervisor, called out. "Sounds like he's going shallow."

Edwards checked his watch. Four-Six had developed the habit of going to periscope depth, likely communicating back home, about every twelve hours. This latest maneuver was off schedule. It had only been five hours since the last time. Something must be up.

Edwards turned to Jeff Otanga, the Officer-of-the-Deck. "Eng, if our friend is up calling home, it might be a good time for us to see if we have any mail, too. Come to periscope depth, copy the traffic, and get back down."

The trip to periscope depth and back down was uneventful. Ten minutes later, the *George Mason* was once again at patrol depth. But the sub they had been tailing remained near the surface. Evidently, Case Four-Six wanted to ventilate for a bit. Sonar could hear the other submarine's blower sucking air into the boat. The guy did not seem to be in much of a hurry, nor was he especially concerned about being detected. Edwards was sure that the circling P-8 Poseidon aircraft high above was probably easily painting the Russian target's periscope and snorkel mast with its AN/APY-10 radar in the periscope detection mode.

Edwards smiled as he had a flashback to the days when he was a young junior officer. Submariners used to laugh at "Airedales"—slang for naval aviators—who told stories of detecting submarine periscopes. They had raised their scopes with impunity, daring an ASW aircraft to try to detect them. It was a much different environment now. A submariner who stuck up a pole when an ASW aircraft was in the area was pretty much guaranteed to get nailed by the better-equipped plane.

Jackson Biddle, the XO, stepped out of radio and walked over to the command console where Brian Edwards still stood, pondering the situation. "Skipper, got a change to our tasking," Biddle told him. "You might want to punch it up on the console."

Edwards flipped through a couple of drop-down menus and uploaded the message traffic to his screen. Sure enough, right at the head of the list was the new tasking. He quickly read through it and turned to Biddle.

"Better get the Nav up here to update our areas and expected track. Looks like the *Reagan* is going into the Sea of O. If our friend decides to follow them through the Kurils, we're to stay in trail and run interference. You see that part about not letting him within weapons firing range of *Reagan*?"

The XO grunted and nodded. Edwards ran his hands through his thinning hair. A perplexed look claimed his face.

Okay. Just how the hell were they supposed to accomplish that?

21

Ivan Dostervesky, Jim Ward, and the rest of the attack party finally struggled back into their base camp at Arka, dog tired and bedraggled. The treacherous Okhotsk Prokhodit Pass and the trail leading through it had been made even more dangerous and difficult by the heavy snowstorm that seemed to have decided to hover over that area for the rest of winter. The outbound trip through there had taken three days. Coming the return direction had consumed a week and a half. Ward lost count of the number of snowmobile accidents, snow slides, and other obstacles they had encountered in the process. After launching two military attacks in which none of the group had even come close to being wounded, many in the team now had broken bones, concussions, and various cuts and bruises from the trek. Several of their sleds had been converted to makeshift ambulances just to move the injured men back to base camp.

But, finally, they had arrived at Arka. And Jim Ward had urgent business.

"Ivan, I need to get in contact with my dad right now," Ward told Dostervesky before the SEAL had even started to remove his layers of clothing. "If we're going to tap those comms lines, he will need to get the gear and techies in here to make it happen, and the sooner the better, considering all the moving pieces involved. I also need to report on how and what you guys are doing out here, let them decide how much help they want to give you, and, if they're willing, let them know precisely what you need. How far will I need to go to find a secure and reliable comms circuit I can use?"

Dostervesky smiled, reached into a box resting on the floor, pulled out a mobile phone, and tossed it to Ward.

"*Komandir*, be a good boy. Call your father. Let him know you are okay. We have good INMARSAT connectivity here, and their encryption is pretty good. We do business all over the planet that way. I only request that you head down trail a couple of miles before you make your call. We have no indication that the Russians are intercepting our calls, but there is still no reason at this crucial time to become careless."

Ward was amazed. He assumed that the Children had worked out some convoluted method of communications that would probably involve a week or more of traipsing across the sub-arctic wilderness before being able to safely and secretly pass a hidden message out to the Free World. But here was Ivan Dostervesky simply handing him a typical cell phone to use to call home. Too easy.

And, indeed, the call proved to be a piece of cake. Lieutenant Jimmy Wilson, Jon Ward's flag aide, answered on the second ring and immediately passed him on through to his father, the head of Naval Intelligence. He might just as well have been calling to get his dad's thoughts on Sunday's Commanders-Giants NFL game.

"Jim, my boy! Glad to hear from you by now! Where the hell you calling from?" Jon Ward's voice boomed.

"Hey, old man! Look, I'm on an INMARSAT line. It's encrypted, they assure me, but I probably shouldn't discuss where I am," the younger Ward answered.

"Just a minute," Jon Ward said. "I'm sending you an app for a one-time encryption. Double the pleasure, double the fun. That way we can talk freely."

"You have an encryption app ready to go?" Jim Ward asked. "And you know how to activate it?"

It was not something he figured his father would even know about, although he was the head of Naval Intelligence. After all, the man still sometimes had trouble adding an emoji to a text message.

"Jim, you think you're the first spy to call in on a cell phone?" Jon Ward chuckled. "Just load the app and follow the instructions on your screen. It's preset to ask your mother's birthday—all numbers, no dashes, four-digit year—for a password."

"Uh-oh," Jim said. "Did I forget about her birthday again?"

"Yes, but your girlfriend remembered. She sent your mother her favorite orchid, a beautiful little paphiopedilum. And I hate to tell you, but your mother is making noises about disowning you and adopting her."

The app blinked on the phone, and the younger Ward entered the date. It took a few seconds, but then a screen popped up proclaiming that they were now talking securely. Even more securely than before.

Jim took a few minutes to explain all he and his two-man team had been involved with. There was a gasp or two from his dad when Jim offered details of the attack on the air base. The admiral, of all people, knew how critical a loss of those assets was to the Russians. And the ramifications if the Russians found out some US Navy operatives were even in the vicinity, let alone setting charges. Next, the SEAL downloaded all the information he had so arrangements could be made to get the gear and techies on the way to tap the Russian Federation comms line. It was no surprise to Jim Ward that his dad was even more excited than his son over the possibilities that little wiretap presented. And that they could do it with minimal risk.

Then the admiral asked the question that had him most baffled. "Jim, do you think the Children may have gotten their hands on a submarine somewhere? Someone used a sub to sink a Russian destroyer off Sakhalin Island last week. No one is claiming credit, the Russians are keeping it hush-hush, and apparently neither they nor we can figure who might have done it, unless it ties back to Dostervesky and his plot somehow."

"Yeah, sure. They got a *Kilo*-class named the *Yaroslavl*," the younger Ward answered nonchalantly.

"Jim, how the hell can you be so damn sure about all that?"

There was a chuckle on the other end of the line. "Well, we rode it for almost a week up to a little place named Ulya a couple of weeks ago. A good deal of that trip was under the ice, and then we've been busy busting our humps snowmobiling all over Asiatic Russia, so I haven't had a chance to fill you in yet. The skipper is a guy named Mark Lodkamatros. They claim they stole the boat from the Russians over in Petr. I'm not surprised you haven't seen it on the news channels yet, but I figured all that spook power you got at your beck and call would have heard something about it."

"Things fall through the cracks sometimes," Jim Ward mumbled, still considering the upshot of this confirmation.

"A pirated Russian *Kilo* is a pretty big thing to be falling through the cracks, don't you think?" Jim prodded.

"But what you're telling me fits," Jon Ward said, ignoring his son's jibe. "You got any idea what they plan to use the boat for? Other than sinking Russian destroyers and shuttling around some of our SEALs?"

"Well, Lodkamatros and his brother, Igor, were showing a lot of interest in those LNG plants on the south end of Sakhalin. They have a couple of *Kalibr* cruise missiles they would like to lob in there just to show Salkov and the Russian military—and us, too—that they are serious and capable. But one thing they need from us is help with the targeting. I only promised them that I'd ask you about that. And of course, they could always torpedo one of those LNG tankers. That would make a boom that would rattle hotel windows in Waikiki."

The line went silent for a bit. Long enough that Jim Ward thought they might have been disconnected or his pop's encryption app may have failed.

"Dad, you still there?" he finally asked.

"Yes, just thinking. And worrying. Mostly worrying. That place is about to get damn crowded. President Smitherman just ordered the *Reagan* battle group into the Sea of O to hassle Salkov. The Russians have a sub tattle-tailing it, and, of course, we have one trailing the Russian boat closer than a barnacle on its backside. We already have the *Feinstein* in there doing FONOPS, thumbing their noses at the Russians and almost getting herself rammed and shot in the process, and another one of our boats is underneath her, providing cover."

"You're right, Dad. Like the 405 in LA at rush hour. You could have a fender-bender."

"Already have. Already have. But that's what scares me. If somebody so much as sneezes at the wrong time, the place could go up like a tinder box."

"What do you want me to do, Dad?"

"For now, just keep your head down and stay as close to Dostervesky as you can. Let me know if you catch wind that something interesting may be about to happen. And son?"

"Yes, sir?"

"Be careful over there."

Ψ

Captain Louise Gadliano watched as the MH-60R helicopter lifted off the deck of her destroyer and headed west, toward Sakhalin Island and the hospital in Poronaysk. The chopper was making the last of multiple trips, shuttling the survivors from the Russian ship *Admiral Panteleyev* to the beach. Those passengers included Captain Yevgenny Matros, the unfortunate ship's commanding officer. Gadliano hated to see him go. She knew that she would miss Captain Matros. He had proven to be a godsend interacting with both the Russian civilians at the hospital and with the Russian Navy over in Vladivostok in what could easily have been an even messier situation.

As the chopper disappeared in the sea mist and snow, she smiled and shook her head. Now that the rescue mission was almost done, it was time to be off to their next adventure. She could not have known that escapade would be partly revealed to her ten seconds later.

"Captain?" It was LCDR Sam Starson who interrupted her thoughts. "We have two new messages that you will want to see."

He handed her a tablet with the first communication already on the screen. She gave it a quick read and then went back through it more carefully. She stepped back and took a long look at the electronic chart display. After punching in the coordinates contained in the message and reading the cursor display, she immediately ordered, "Officer-of-the-Deck, steer course zero-three-five, come to ahead full. We have ten hours to rendezvous with the *Reagan* battle group at four-eight-point-six-zero north, one-four-eight-point-six-six east."

Starson asked, "What about our helo?"

"Tell the TAO to contact them and give them a new vector for their return flight," Gadliano answered. The tactical action officer on the ship oversaw and acted on information about potential threats to the vessel. He controlled the sensors, weapons, and communications systems. "We'll still be well within their flight envelope for a while yet. Even if we are hauling ass."

The *Arleigh Burke*–class destroyer was already wheeling around sharply and then steadied up on the new course. That caused the ship to crash through the oncoming waves, sending torrents of green water cascading over the main deck. Spray and sea spume spattered on the bridge windshield as the ship charged to the northeast.

Now that they were underway on the newly assigned course, Gadliano scrolled down to the second message that Sam Starson had told her about. No surprise there. Her XO, the still-absent Commander Susan Biddleson, would be delayed in returning to the *Feinstein* for at least another week. Though the language in the dispatch was cryptic, it appeared that the Pentagon had extended Commander Biddleson's TAD orders with Seventh Fleet while they conducted an investigation of the FONOPS mission and the mysterious attack on the Russian warship.

Gadliano was well aware of what was going on. Biddleson and her vice-admiral daddy were already at work, finagling the back-office Pentagon politics to ensure that Gadliano took the fall for anything that might result negatively from what happened while Biddleson came away as the hero. Though she was disgusted with such obvious backstabbing-for-gain, Gadliano also knew that she was still in command of the *Feinstein* and anything the ship did was her ultimate responsibility. Plenty of people depended on her to do her best, including almost three hundred sailors and officers that made up her crew. She was confident she had done everything properly and that the rest of her crew would stand by her. But now, more than ever, she needed to be wary of the political rocks and shoals that lay ahead.

Besides, there were more finite and immediate threats to consider right now. Once they were clear of Sakhalin Island and out in deeper water, *Feinstein* needed to resume being a frontline US warship. It was time for them to use all their sensors to try to make sure no one got the drop on them.

"Officer-of-the-Deck, I want a full sensor search done for surface and airborne threats. Nothing closes the *Feinstein* within twenty-five miles without them being challenged and me being informed," Gadliano ordered. "And stream the MFTA array. I'd like to go fishing."

The MFTA, or TB-37 Multi-Function Towed Array, was very much like the TB-34 array on the *Gato*. It was a fat-line system that the *Feinstein* could tow behind the ship with the primary goal of detecting very quiet submarines. The MFTA sonar array could detect minute sound signatures over a wide frequency range. As with any sonar array, the biggest problem was created by the speed of the vessel that was tugging it along through the sea. Flow noise across the hydrophones as the array sped through the water greatly degraded the sonar's ability to detect any noise from a vessel specifically designed to be extremely quiet and stealthy. Like a submarine.

"Mr. Starson, when the MFTA is deployed, I want you to steam at a full bell for an hour, then slow to ten knots and do an ASW search for twenty minutes, maybe catch a chaser by surprise. Then rinse and repeat. Got it?"

Sam Starson smiled and nodded. "Got it, Skipper. Oh, and suggest we energize 'Prairie Masker' and really screw up that submarine's day."

Prairie Masker was a surface-ship system that essentially hid the vessel's propulsion and screw noise behind a screen of air bubbles. Any submarine listening on passive sonar would hear what sounded like a rain squall where the ship hid.

"Real good idea. And when the MH-60R gets back, have it loaded out for an ASW mission and at a ready fifteen on deck. We know there's a sub out there that already has a taste for blood. We just don't know if it's a multinational preference or not." Gadliano stepped toward the after bridge hatch. "I'll be down in Combat if you need me. Warn the TAO that I'm on my way."

Ψ

As he listened to the incessant yammering on the other end of the telephone line, Admiral Sergey Morsky gazed forlornly out the window of his office overlooking his domain, the Vladivostok's Bukhta Uliss Bay and the sprawling navy base that encircled it. The base was now as much a hive of activity as it had been since the more glorious days of the Cold War, when

Admiral Morsky had first been billeted there as a raw junior lieutenant, serving mostly as a clerk for the commander. But, by following the political route, he had quickly progressed, growing with his country's sea forces as first the Soviet Union and then the Russian Federation became one of the planet's largest and most feared naval powers. Now, here he was, overseeing the Russian Pacific Fleet.

Such as it was. As he listened to the phone and while he watched through patches of frost on the big window, all the Russian Navy's Pacific Fleet surface ships that were stationed there—all eight of them—were busy making preparation to sortie at the same time. With the current austere level of financing for ship maintenance, getting all of his ships underway was a major evolution. Morsky knew that, in all honesty, two or three of the vessels would never be able to cast off lines, even if he did need every ship he could muster to be up in the Sea of Okhotsk.

It would have been easy to now dream of once again being a commanding officer and steaming one of his beloved ships out into the Sea of Japan. Dream of not being forced to sit here with his ear firmly stuck to the telephone, listening to Anatoly Shatitsnevcom, the Minister of Defense, rant about the ineptitude and incompetence of his fleet. The bureaucrat's nasal voice and high volume were giving Morsky a splitting headache.

The only good thing was that Shatitsnevcom was over seven thousand kilometers away in his Kremlin office. Otherwise, the admiral might well have throttled him already.

"Admiral Morsky, our BARS-M ocean surveillance satellite shows the American *Ronald Reagan* battle group entering the Sea of Okhotsk through the Kuril Islands even as we speak," Minister Shatitsnevcom growled. "It is essential that you stage a show of force and push the Americans back into the Pacific, by threat or by action. Now, more than ever, we must protect our sacred sovereign seas and not allow the US or any other nation the opportunity to reject our claims."

"Minister, I must ask, then, what precisely would you have me do?" Morsky finally responded, realizing he was, by asking the question, challenging the Kremlin official. "With the loss of the *Admiral Panteleyev*—and we still do not know to whom—I have only four destroyers and five corvettes that are fit to go to sea. It is over two thousand kilometers from

Vladivostok to intercept the Americans. That is, at best and subject to weather, two full days of steaming at a flank bell just to get there. And once my ships are there, what do you propose I do? Invite the American admiral over for a drink, a cigar, and a chat?"

Now that he had broken protocol, Morsky was working up a real head of steam. He recognized that being completely honest with a very senior government official in this manner would probably bring about an abrupt end to the long career he had crafted for himself. If not a lengthy stint in Lubyanka Prison. But it was too late for him to stop himself now. It had to be said. "Your naval staff have already stripped me of all my attack aircraft. And now, after the recent assault on the air force's base, you do not have the air-refueling tankers to make it possible to send them back to Vladivostok. And as if that is not enough, I have blind satellites your technicians cannot repair, and I am totally unable to get an AWACS plane up to monitor the Americans, the Chinese, the North Koreans...and, of course, this new faction that seems bent on thumbing their noses at the mighty Russian Federation."

There was only the sound of angry breathing on the other end of the telephone line. Minister Shatitsnevcom was momentarily speechless, aghast at the effrontery from this strutting military popinjay. Where did this admiral come off, questioning the priorities of his military and its government? Did he not realize that he would just have to accomplish his tasks with the resources with which he was provided, regardless the challenges?

After all, that was the Russian way. And it was not to be challenged.

"Admiral Morsky," Minister Shatitsnevcom finally answered, very coldly. "Please be aware that I will personally discuss your reluctance for proper action with President Salkov." Then the man's words became heavy with sarcasm. "I am certain that you will receive appropriate sympathy from the president. He will appreciate your input, Admiral, and especially since they directly challenge his own decisions regarding allocations of strategic assets. Yes, I am certain President Salkov will take your complaints to heart and respond appropriately."

The telephone line went stone-cold dead.

Ψ

Captain First Rank Ivgany Yurtotov guided his Improved *Severodvinsk*-class nuclear cruise missile submarine up to periscope depth. They had been easily tracking the US Navy's *Ronald Reagan* battle group on sonar as the American warships steamed unerringly for the Bussol Strait, a deep passage through the Kuril Island chain between Broutona to the south and Simushir Island to the north. No surprise about the route if the group truly intended to brazenly enter the Sea of Okhotsk. The channel was more than thirty miles wide there and a favored passage for American whaling ships way back in the mid-nineteenth century and for US submarines coming from and going to the Sea of Japan late in World War II.

Yurtotov's orders were still only to shadow the Americans, but the waters around the Kurils and the Sea of Okhotsk beyond were sovereign Russian waters. If the Americans dared enter there, what was he to do? The intruders would be committing an act of war. However, if he actually unleashed his weapons on an American aircraft carrier and supporting vessels, he could at best be putting his submarine at grave risk against a very capable adversary. And at worst, he could be the one to ignite World War III. He needed guidance from his superiors, and he needed it to come soon.

Yurtotov pondered his problem as the submarine's periscope broke the surface. He made a careful visual search, but it was far too gray and foggy to see anything at all beyond a few thousand meters. He ordered the RIM HAT ESM mast raised to take a look at the electronic spectrum. The Americans might be able to hide visually in the vapor and haze, but they would never be able to conceal themselves from his ESM system.

Almost immediately, the *michman* operating the ESM reported that he had contact on an American SPS-48 radar system in use. That would likely be on the American aircraft carrier. He also had detected two different SPY-6 search radars on two different *Arleigh Burke* destroyers. The bearings agreed with where sonar had been tracking the Americans and confirmed they were coming, fast and determined. They were now in the Bussol Strait and plowing toward the northwest.

Yurtotov made a decision. Unless he was otherwise notified, he would run northeast around Simushir Island and then through the Diana Strait into the Sea of Okhotsk. That shortcut should get him out in front of the Americans and give him time to report back to Pacific Fleet Headquarters on what the interlopers were doing. Then, when he communicated those details, he would also request orders. Specific orders.

As he commanded the submarine to dive and assume the new course, Yurtotov felt marginally better about the impending situation. If it was ultimately his duty to fire the first shot of World War III, it would be on direct orders from headquarters.

Then, whether he emerged dead or alive, he would forever be a hero of his nation.

22

Brian Edwards and his submarine, the *George Mason,* followed Case Four-Six, the big Russian sub, as it abruptly turned north, away from the *Reagan* battle group. Meanwhile, the approaching group of American ships continued steaming to the northwest, heading into the Bussol Strait through the Kuril Islands. Edwards stood back and watched his team work as he tried to figure out what the Russian captain was trying to do. It really did not make good sense for him to be hauling off well to the north when his target was transiting through a barrier of islands on a course that would take them right into the Sea of Okhotsk.

"Skipper, solution is tracking," Jackson Biddle announced. "He has steadied up on course zero-one-five, speed now twenty-two."

Edwards nodded. At least that made sense. A speed of twenty-two knots was just about forty kilometers per hour, a nice round number for the Russians. Sonar had good, solid track on Case Four-Six on this course and speed, but if the Russian sped up much more, the *George Mason* would not be able to keep up. The Improved *Severodvinsk* was just a lot faster.

Edwards studied the tactical display on the ECDIS. Case Four-Six was quite clearly making a run for the Diana Strait. Narrower than the Bussol Strait, but just as deep, the Diana Strait gave the submarine a chance to do an end-around on the battle group if it raced all out to get ahead of the

Reagan while taking advantage of its noise being shielded from the oncoming American ships by the islands.

Biddle noticed the look on Edwards's face as he tried to make a decision about what to do with this new development. He left the fire control team and stepped over to where Edwards stood staring hard at the tactical display.

"Skipper, why don't we come to flank and get out ahead of this guy while we can. Stay close inshore on Simushir Island and skirt right around the corner into the strait." Biddle traced out his plan on the ECDIS with a finger. "Right now, we have a three- or four-knot speed advantage on him. That'll give us a head start if he kicks it in the butt like we think he's going to do shortly."

Edwards smiled. There had been a time when Edwards resented crewmembers jumping in to make such unsolicited suggestions. And especially when others might hear. But he had soon learned from both experience and other skippers under whom he had served—now-Admiral Joe Glass, for one—that his people were smart, well trained, and often could offer a valuable perspective on dicey situations. Biddle was exceptionally good at it.

"It just might work. Cozying up to the island will hide our noise in the surf and will also make for a shorter trip. But on the other hand, if he stays on this course and doesn't go through the strait, we'll almost certainly lose him."

It was Biddle's turn to smile. "If he stays on this course and doesn't dodge into the strait, he is on a course to take him home. That means he wouldn't be tracking the battle group anymore. And it also means he isn't a problem anymore. Mission accomplished. However, if he turns into the strait, we have the drop on him. Again, mission...well...partly accomplished."

"Sounds like a plan, XO." Edwards turned to Jeff Otanga. "Officer-of-the-Deck. Come to ahead flank, make your depth eight hundred feet. I want you to put us close to Simushir Island. Stay three miles off the coast. Change course to three-one-zero when Broughton Cape passes astern. If we lose our friend, I want you to set up an ASW barrier search across the strait, five miles the other side of the island."

Otanga acknowledged the commands as the *George Mason* surged ahead.

Ψ

Admiral Sergey Morsky was still trying to figure out the answer to his quandary. How to appease the Kremlin. And, in the process, maybe find a way to stay alive. Then the message came in. He hastily read the flimsy piece of paper emblazoned with *Samyy Sekretryy* in large red letters. Then he uncharacteristically allowed a smile to claim his face.

There, in the "most secret" document, was the answer to his problem. Morsky was not that familiar with the submarine commander, Captain First Rank Ivgany Yurtotov, or his submarine, the *Yakutsk*. They had only very recently showed up at the Far East Fleet and without any forewarning from Morsky's superiors. He had made a note to call Yurtotov in and learn more, but the lost submarine and then the appearance on the horizon of the American battle group had taken its toll on his schedule.

It took him a couple of minutes to find the dossier on the newcomers, but after a quick read, his smile broadened still more. A submarine armed with TE-2 electric anti-ship torpedoes, which could easily sink a carrier. And also armed with the 3M54K *Kalibr* supersonic cruise missile, a weapon that was specifically designed to be an effective aircraft carrier killer.

The fact that this Captain Yurtotov obviously lacked the *yaichki* to act on his own, that he had resorted to calling back for specific guidance from his superiors, gave Morsky considerable pause. Even in the Russian Navy, a submarine commander was expected to exhibit some independent thought and initiative.

Then the admiral thought for a few seconds. It really did not matter. He would relay the Kremlin's instructions verbatim to the commanding officer, this Yurtotov. Then, should the *Yakutsk* be successful—that is, either sink the American carrier or chase it and its escorts off—or even if he failed and lost his vessel in the process, then both the sub captain and Admiral Morsky would be heroes and fixtures in Russian Federation history textbooks forever. If the meek, hesitant CO managed to light off World War III in the process, it would be at the Kremlin's specific direction.

Morsky was only following orders, and he held the proof right there in his hands.

The message to Yurtotov and the *Yakutsk* took only a few minutes to draft and send out to the ship. Morsky was careful to precisely copy the orders from Minister of Defense Anatoly Shatitsnevcom and to send a copy of the message to both him and Chief of the General Staff General Nikolai Marastopov.

Now, let the chips fall where they may.

Ψ

The setting was ideal for Tan Yong to find the opportunity to clear his head and stimulate his thinking. The small glass sunroom that he had ordered built onto the terrace off his office clashed significantly with the Ming-dynasty building itself. However, it allowed him to enjoy warmth and sunshine while being surrounded by beautiful orchids, even in the middle of a Beijing winter when temperatures often fell below freezing. And setting up the Yuan-dynasty rosewood weiqi table had been, he told himself, a bit of personal genius. The color and scent from the flowers calmed him while the challenge of the more than 2,500-year-old game served to awaken new ideas.

With the chill and rain outside not a concern, Tan Yong sat and watched his opponent carefully. In his mind's eye, Tan could already see all the possible moves and countermoves until the game's ultimate completion. But Nian Huhu De, his adversary in this particular game, was able to do the same. The mental challenge, the subtle twists and turns of strategy, were what fascinated and attracted the Chinese president to the game. Weiqi— or "Go," as it was known in the West—had only two rules. Even so, the nineteen-line-by-nineteen-line board allowed for an almost infinite number of possible combinations for the opposing stones.

Tan had been tutored in the finer points of the game by a nine *dan* master. He had quickly moved to the point where he played at a seven *dan* level himself. But Nian Huhu De, who bore the title Special Ambassador Plenipotentiary for the People's Republic of China, was the nine *dan* master who had mentored the president. Nian had taught Tan that a master must see at least forty moves ahead. Tan had long since concluded that Nian worked at twice that level.

The ambassador deftly lifted a white jade stone from his bowl and gently placed it at an intersection of lines on the ancient rosewood table. Then he sat back, apparently to contemplate his strategy as he pulled a cloth from his suit coat pocket and wiped his spectacles. Only then did Tan realize that Nian's move had brought them to the endgame and that his options were severely limited. The time had come for him to resign with his honor still intact.

Tan looked over at Nian. The elder statesman was quietly smiling as he continued to polish the lenses. "A challenging game," Nian murmured. "With practice and study, you could soon rise to nine *dan*. Your mind works already at the long-term strategic level to confound your opponent."

Tan was sure that his ambassador was, as usual, being self-effacing and diplomatic. He smiled and replied, "Nian, at the weiqi table, I will continue to call you *zhangwo*. Now, I must confess that my strategic thoughts go elsewhere. Let us discuss the current situation to the north for a bit."

Nian Huhu De eased back in his chair and listened attentively. His seven *dan* student had just transformed back into the president of China. And Nian was no longer the weiqi master. He was once more the president's special ambassador and advisor. And humble servant.

"Those Children of the Gulag are showing themselves to be quite resourceful," Tan began. "So far, they have certainly been more than Salkov and his Far East military have the capability or capacity to handle, especially over such wide territory. With the little aid that we have slipped them through our friends at the DPRK and with whatever the US has given them or done for them, they have a real possibility of being successful in this bold insurrection of theirs. The question is, how do we use this to our advantage?"

Nian put his glasses back on, stroked his chin for a moment, and then answered, "We must think like a nine *dan* weiqi master and work many steps into the future of the game. If our long-term objective is to restore the Middle Kingdom, how do we employ this situation to aid us in accomplishing that? The Americans are a distant problem and are so far only muddying the waters in this affair. Salkov is the key, the 'loose cannon,' as the Americans are wont to say. He must be convinced that his only course is to negotiate a peace with these Children and that such a course will only strengthen him militarily and empower him politically if he plays it correctly."

He paused to take a sip of tea and added another stone to the grid on the game table. "But Salkov, being Russian, will never negotiate in good faith," Nian continued. "Instead, he will take whatever opportunity he can to attempt to crush these Children of the Gulag, even after he has shaken hands with them and promised the moon and stars." Nian looked hard at the weiqi board then up at his president. "Especially after shaking hands with them."

"So, do we chase the Americans away before they set Salkov on some needless and counterproductive conflagration?" Tan questioned. "And then guarantee the Children the security of our protective umbrella while they build their little country up there amid the snow and conifers?"

"Exactly," Nian agreed, nodding. "And, as usual, we slowly draw them into our orbit until we eventually subsume the Children and their considerable slice of former Russian territory—and whatever riches might rest beneath its topsoil—into the Middle Kingdom. We know there is oil and coal there. We hear there may be other resources in this new nation that will be even more valuable on the world market in the future. We already control the market on some of those substances, and the Children could cause us some difficulties with any competition. It will be to our advantage to add to our inventory at some point. And we can do so without firing a shot or sortieing an army."

Tan nodded. "This could work. First, a message to the Americans. We certainly have the leverage to ensure President Smitherman will do our bidding. Then, we will need a serious discussion with President Salkov about the realities of life in the world of realpolitik."

"And that, my president, will assure we are well ahead of our opponents in this particular game of weiqi," the ambassador told him, looking up at the president, a sly smile on his face. "The endgame will then be near, but none of them will even be aware they have already lost."

Ψ

Ivgany Yurtotov glanced up at the bright-red numbers on the digital clock. It had been six hours since he had sent the message back to Vladivostok requesting guidance and clarification on what was to be expected of him in regard to the incursion of the American warships into the Sea of Okhotsk. He had continued his stalking of the trespassing battle group, having transited north through the narrow Diana Strait before steering around to the west. That made him practically invisible behind Simushir Island as he waited to once again draw a bead on the American aircraft carrier. If that battle group had, as he expected, brazenly steamed through the much wider Bussol Strait and then out into the Sea of Okhotsk, his submarine, the *Yakutsk*, should be very near to a perfect position to intercept them and call their bluff. Or make them regret having dared to test the Russian Federation and its sovereignty.

Now it was finally time to see if the High Command back in Moscow had instructions for him. He ordered the *Yakutsk* to periscope depth. Staring through the 'scope's eyepiece, Yurtotov spun it in a complete circle, looking for any ships that could possibly be a threat to them. Happily, the horizon was clear. There was only the boring but non-threatening dingy cloud cover and the constantly pitching colorless waves. When he had sufficiently determined that he had this portion of the sea entirely to himself, Yurtotov ordered an ESM search and for the message traffic to be downloaded. He could only hope there would be the guidance he sought.

Almost immediately the *michman* operating the RIM HAT ESM system once again reported that he had reacquired contact on the American carrier's radars, bearing two-zero-five, and on several SPY-6 search radars on practically the same bearing. They were precisely where they were expected to be and still steaming the same course as before.

Admiral Morsky's message from Vladivostok arrived only a few seconds later. Yurtotov read it twice, then clutched the slip of paper hard as he peered at the electronic charts. In some ways, his instructions had become even more vague. The problem was no longer academic. It had just become deadly serious.

His new orders were to stop the Americans from violating Russian sovereignty. The Rodina must be protected, the text of the message proclaimed. But how was he and his submarine to accomplish this?

Morsky's orders did not answer this question at all. Nor did they offer any assistance in determining and then executing such a course.

There were sixteen *Kalibr* anti-ship cruise missiles in the *Yakutsk's* vertical launch tubes. The other sixteen tubes had land-attack missiles. The latter would be useless for this operation. The supersonic anti-ship cruise missiles were deadly accurate from a range of more than six hundred kilometers. But Yurtotov's problem was targeting data. To be accurate and effective, the missiles needed to know where they were supposed to fly and what they were supposed to attack when they got there. And they would require that information before they were ever launched.

Yurtotov did not have any sensor data with targeting information on the Americans, and he did not know where he could get it. Such crucial targeting information would normally be supplied by some airborne asset, either by an ancient TU-142 Bear-F maritime reconnaissance aircraft or a newer Beriev A-100 *Prem'yer* early warning plane. However, there currently was none of either asset available in his part of the world. As a backup, he would have normally been able to launch based on satellite tracking data, but that appeared to be unavailable, too. The requisite birds reportedly had been suffering technical glitches for the past few weeks.

If he used his electric torpedoes, he would need to get in a position close enough so he could actually see the Americans. The torpedoes just did not have either the range or accuracy to blindly shoot them from over the horizon and hope that they would track down the American ships. That meant he would have to get within twenty kilometers of the American carrier, well inside the envelope of their sonar systems.

His only remaining option was to launch the *Kalibr* missiles, his best anti-ship weapon, pretty much shotgun style, and doing so based solely on the bearings to the American carrier's radars. The deadly missiles would simply be instructed to fly down the bearing lines and then destroy whatever they found there at the source of the radio frequency energy. None of the fancy final attack tactics, no supersonic sprints, no pop-up and vertical dive, no coordinated attacks from all axes. Just barrel in and blow up.

Yurtotov reviewed the message one more time. Admiral Morsky was pretty clear about one point. The mission was to get the Americans out of Russian sovereign waters. The submarine captain decided there were two ways to accomplish that job. He could sink the American ships. Or he could frighten them badly enough that they would leave the Sea of Okhotsk on their own.

That indicated to the submarine skipper that a missile attack might be his best choice. Even if he was not successful in hitting the Americans, it would fill the sky with enough potential explosive power that it would chase them back through the channel and out into the Pacific Ocean. And, if that was not enough, he could then use his torpedoes.

Yurtotov calculated that the *Yakutsk* was close enough to the Americans that each missile would only have a two-minute flight. The entire attack would be completed in less than five minutes. But the time to launch it for most effectiveness was quickly approaching as the arrogant US Navy vessels drew close.

It took a couple of minutes for Yurtotov to bring his crew to battle stations, spin up the anti-ship missiles, and open the two massive hatches covering the vertical launch tubes. Then, when Yurtotov gave the launch order, each of the sixteen missiles roared sequentially out of their launch tubes, flung up into the sky by a powerful rocket booster. They leapt high into the brutally cold air, the rocket motor burned out and fell away as designed, and then the missile transitioned to horizontal flight.

The sixteenth missile had barely cleared the launch tube when Yurtotov ordered the hatches shut and for the *Yakutsk* to go deep. He then turned the submarine's bow toward the carrier and sped up to flank.

He assumed he would soon need to evaluate the results of his attack, and he wanted to have as good a view of the carnage as possible. Yurtotov was not able to see that missiles six and ten had not transitioned to horizontal flight. Instead, they fell harmlessly back into the sea. Missile number five ignored its preprogrammed instructions and roared off to the north instead, destined to give some seals and seagulls somewhere a very bad day.

However, thirteen anti-ship missiles did exactly what they were designed to do. They sped off toward the *Reagan* battle group with decidedly ill intentions.

Ψ

"Captain, loud transients from Case Four-Six," Josh Hannon called out, sheer alarm rising in his voice. "Sounds like outer doors opening. No! Belay that. Missile hatches." Then, after a slight pause, he added the chilling report, "Launch transients. Son of a bitch is launching missiles!"

The sprint around Simushir Island that Jackson Biddle suggested worked out just as planned. They had ducked through Diana Strait, snuggled up against Broughton Cape, before slowing from their flank bell run. Almost as if choreographed, Case Four-Six had reappeared about ten thousand yards out in front of them. Brian Edwards maneuvered the *George Mason* so that they followed the Russian submarine deep in that sub's port baffles. It was almost as if the Russian had been privy to Biddle's plan, too.

Then the bastard started shooting.

"Snapshot, tube one on Case Four-Six! Tube two will be the backup weapon," Edwards called out. They were poised to fire the torpedo in tube two on the skipper's command. Fire it at a Russian warship. One thing was obvious. Whoever the Russian was shooting at, it was not the *George Mason*. And so far, there was no reason to suspect that the Russian sub even knew the American boat was there, shadowing them.

With a ripple shot of sixteen birds, the target could only be the *Reagan* battle group. Nothing else would warrant that kind of firepower. It was too late to stop the launch. Even if they had had the time to consider the guy's intentions, they would not have fired just because he had opened his missile tube doors. But it was certainly not too late to take out the launcher. First, though, he needed to warn the *Reagan*!

"Officer-of-the-Deck, broach the ship, maximum up angle," Edwards ordered Jeff Otanga. "Radio, line up for emergency voice comms to the carrier!" he called out.

There would only be a few seconds, maybe a minute, to warn the carrier before the missiles arrived, but that minute might be enough time to do some good.

The *George Mason* immediately adopted a sharp up angle, sending untethered items skating across tabletops and decks and crashing against the after bulkhead. The sub flew up to the surface with a forty-degree angle. Even as it nosed high out of the water, splashed down hard, and settled out on the surface, Edwards was already raising the low-profile photonics mast. He grabbed the red radio handset and thumbed the push-to-talk button hard.

"Romeo Alpha, this is *George Mason!*" he yelled into the handset. "Inbound vampires, best bearing to you zero-six-zero. Estimate sixteen birds. TOA, one minute."

The harried voice on the other end responded, "*Mason,* roger. Now tracking. You guys get the bastard! Out."

Edwards left the handset dangling from its spiral cord and lowered the photonics mast. He took a quick glance around the tense control room. All eyes were on him, awaiting his next order.

"You heard the man. Let's get the bastard!"

Jackson Biddle was studying the fire control solution on Case Four-Six. He shook his head.

"Skipper, he kicked it in the butt right after he shot. Sonar's tracking him at forty knots. He's already out of weapon range."

Ψ

Louise Gadliano had just stepped into the USS *Diane Feinstein*'s darkened combat information center and grabbed herself a cup of coffee. That was when every alarm bell in the world seemed to begin chiming all at once and at painful volume.

The TAO yelled out, "Vampires! Vampires! Inbound missiles! Looks like at least a dozen, tracking, bearing zero-seven-six!"

Gadliano did not hesitate. "Designate and launch Sea Sparrows. Put CIWS on full auto. Launch Super RBOC and NULKAs. Jam them with the SLQ-32." The Sea Sparrow was an anti-missile defensive system. The Phalanx close-in weapons system was a gun-based anti-missile protector. Super RBOC and NULKAs filled the air with distracting chaff and a simulated target to attract incoming missiles away from the ship. The destroyer skipper was using every toy she had to confuse and possibly take out the deadly weapons headed toward the aircraft carrier she was bound to help protect.

As her crew scurried around her, taking all the actions to defend the *Feinstein,* the *Ronald Reagan,* and the rest of the battle group, Gadliano had a quick bout of déjà vu. It had only been a little over a year before when she suffered a very similar Chinese missile attack, but her ship had been the only one under assault. That one ended up with her LCS ship being blasted out from under her. At least she had firsthand experience on her side this time.

Within seconds of giving her commands, she felt the sharp shove of the first Evolved Sea Sparrow missile as it blasted off from its vertical launch tube on the destroyer's deck. That shock was followed by three more as the quad pack was emptied into the sky. Three more quad packs sent a total of sixteen advanced anti-aircraft missiles out to challenge the incoming vampires.

Gadliano slid into her command chair and watched the big-screen monitor in front of her. On the display, the incoming vampires were inverted Vs with an *M* inside, painted red, all thirteen tracks coming right at them. The outgoing green tracks showed the Sea Sparrows racing off to intercept. It looked like a very fast-paced but extremely deadly video game. Or a plate of very colorful spaghetti.

The inbound tracks were closing at better than Mach 2 even as the outbound Sea Sparrows arrowed off at better than Mach 4. With a combined closing speed of over forty-two hundred miles an hour, it was less than fifteen seconds before the missiles collided. Or at least most of them did.

Ten of the red vampire tracks disappeared from the screen as Sea Sparrows knocked them out of the sky. But three red tracks remained.

Three inbound anti-ship missiles had somehow managed to leak through the team of Sea Sparrows. The range was down to ten miles. There were only seconds left. The NULKA decoy made a more inviting target than anything else to the first of the remaining incoming missiles.

Scratch another vampire.

The second elusive weapon got hopelessly confused by the chaff cloud from the Mark 36 Super RBOC. It followed the cloud of metal confetti right into the sea, where it promptly and harmlessly blew itself up.

But the final missile was still coming arrow straight. And it was headed directly at Gadliano and the *Feinstein*.

"Jesus. Not again," she whispered. Gadliano could hear the chainsaw-like sound from the CIWS twenty-millimeter Gatling gun. It fired fifty armor-piercing tungsten rounds a second at the lone incoming missile, hoping to hit something, anything vital.

The range was down to less than a thousand yards. The CCTV painted a hopeful picture of the stream of outbound bullets as they intersected with the incoming Mach 2 missile.

Then, there was only red haze at that point on the screen.

The missile had been shredded into a million pieces. But that also meant that two tons of flying junk was still hurtling at her ship at better than sixteen hundred miles an hour. The worst of it smashed into the helo deck. Most of it skidded right on across and fell into the sea. But the biggest hunk of junk, what remained of the heavy turbo-jet engine, plunged through the after stack and down into the engineering spaces below.

The unburned jet fuel and hot metal ignited fires in the compartments. The *Feinstein*'s damage control team was immediately at work, activating firefighting equipment and battling the fires as the ship slowed but continued to move forward, now only on one engine.

Even before Gadliano had time to react to the damage reports ringing out on the speakers above her, Sonar called out, "Positive contact on the Multi-Function Towed Array. Range twenty thousand yards. This guy's hauling ass."

A red V with a dot appeared on the screen off to the north. The TAO was busy informing the ASW Warfare Commander, "Romeo Sierra," back on the *Reagan* about what had happened and what they were seeing of their attacker.

Gadliano still had revenge on her mind. She ordered the track of the fleeing submarine be sent to the AEGIS fire control system to task two RUM-139 ASROC anti-submarine missiles that were patiently waiting in the *Feinstein*'s Mark 41 vertical launcher system. Only seconds after Romeo Sierra ordered an attack, the two birds roared out of their tubes. They raced out to the horizon where each missile dropped a Mark-54 torpedo into the water. Their jobs done, they plunged into the water and sank to the bottom of the Sea of O.

The two aerial torpedoes had dropped a mile astern of the fleeing *Yakutsk*. Their Otto-fueled engines pushed the torpedoes at better than forty-five knots—normally more than fast enough to catch the Russian boat —unerringly reeling in the vessel. Its massive size painted a target that the torpedoes' sonar processors could not miss.

But there was a problem. The *Yakutsk* was running at forty knots. The Mark-54 torpedoes had the speed to catch her, but they simply did not have enough fuel to close the range before their tanks ran dry. And that was exactly what happened. Both fish ran out of fuel only five hundred yards astern of the Russian. They sank to the bottom, where they exploded harmlessly.

Only then did anyone onboard the *Yakutsk* have any indication of just how narrowly they had outraced certain death.

23

"Get me that asshole Salkov on the red phone right damn now!" President Stan Smitherman shouted out to his faithful receptionist, seated at the main entrance to the Oval Office. "I'll have that Russian bastard's balls!" he ranted, then slammed his fist onto the desktop with considerable force. Vice President Harold Osterman, the only other person in the room at the moment, did not even flinch. He was quite familiar with his president's histrionics.

Smitherman suddenly stood and tossed the *Reagan* battle group after-action report right back to Vice President Harold Osterman, who had delivered it to him personally as soon as the Joint Chiefs had perused their copies.

"Dammit to hell, I'll teach that lowlife that he can't push me around like he did my predecessors. The people voted for and elected a strong president, and that is exactly what I intend to..."

Surprisingly, Russian Federation President Grigory Iosifovich Salkov came on the phone after less than two minutes. It was a new record, even for the red phone.

"Stan, my dear friend. How may I be of service to you?" he asked, his English pristine but the tone in his voice betraying a certain wariness.

"You can stop shooting at my ships, you SOB," Smitherson growled. "Get your trigger-happy submariners under control!"

"Stan, let's at least attempt to remain civil," the Russian president said smoothly. "You and I are quite aware that your battle group was intruding well inside Russian territorial waters. My legal experts assure me that such incursion is an act of war. My men were only protecting the Rodina, as is their duty. And you must know we could have destroyed the entire battle group, had we so wished, and would have been perfectly justified in doing so."

Smitherman swirled the bourbon around in his glass, contemplating the hypnotic amber liquid for a half minute before answering. This time, he was surprisingly calm. Shockingly calm.

"You're just real lucky that your crap missiles only managed to scorch a little paint on one of our destroyers. Otherwise, you'd have a shooting war on your hands. One you can't afford with all your problems in the Ukraine and Kazakhstan and right there in Moscow in that corrupt government of yours. If I was you, Grigory—and I'm real glad I ain't—I'd quit picking fights that I can't possibly win. The next time you attack one of our ships, we start flying air strikes. Most of the world will cheer us on, and the rest of 'em will be quietly rooting for us. I'll take out your entire Pacific Fleet before breakfast, and from what I hear, it would not be much of a loss. Capiche?"

Message delivered, Smitherman took a generous slug of the bourbon, smacked his lips, and then grinned as he listened to Salkov spit and sputter on the other end of the phone line for a half minute. The president of the United States then very gently placed the phone back into its cradle and proceeded to light up a huge, hand-rolled Cuban cigar.

Ψ

Henrietta Foster sat back and did what most good submarine skippers did on occasion. She proudly watched her team going about their jobs the way they had been taught, the way she had drilled them, the way they were supposed to do them. She and her boat had been tracking this unidentified diesel boat, designated target Sierra Eight-Two, for more than a week now.

Yes, the *Gato* team was well honed and worked smoothly together. And they had Sierra Eight-Two's routine down so accurately that Eric Householder, *Gato*'s XO, bragged that he could write its POD, the target's "plan of the day." The diesel boat was very quiet, too, but whoever was driving it either did not know they should periodically clear their baffles or they did not even care if someone might be tracking them. They just continued to steam a straight course, and then, every evening at precisely eighteen hundred, Sierra Eight-Two came to periscope depth, snorkeled for an hour, probably communicated with home base, and then went deep again.

Foster's worry now was that her crew might get complacent, become bored and inattentive, and miss some important change in Sierra Eight-Two. That could cause them to lose contact or, worse, get counter-detected. And since Sierra Eight-Two had already shown a willingness to shoot at somebody—albeit another Russian vessel—counter-detection could be a dangerous development.

Gato's OOD, Lieutenant Dale Miller, looked at his watch. He must have been reading Foster's mind. "Skipper, it's that time again. Eight-Two is scheduled to come to PD in five minutes. We don't want to get careless now. I'm going to open out another thousand yards to give him some room."

Foster looked at the tactical display on the ECDIS chart table. An extra thousand yards would put them a little over ten thousand yards out on Eight-Two's port quarter. Cape Crillon, the southernmost projection of Sakhalin Island, was just over five miles to the north. *Gato* had plenty of room in that direction to maneuver, if necessary. And the surf noise from the high, rocky promontory would help mask them while Eight-Two would be out in the open waters of the La Perouse Strait. Eight-Two had been traversing a racetrack across the mouth of Aniva Bay between Cape Aniva and Cape Crillon. It almost seemed as if the diesel submarine was guarding Sakhalin Island's broad, half-moon-shaped southern bay. But from what? This had been a hotspot in World War II but not so much now.

"Okay, open out to ten thousand yards," Foster agreed. "He should be turning in an hour, right after he snorkels, if he stays true to form. Keep on your toes, though." She stood and stretched. "Hey, it's time for dinner. Grilled pork chops night. I'll be in the wardroom. Call me if anything comes up."

She was heading out the back of the control room—already tasting Cookie's wonderful pork chops with seasoned gravy—when she heard, "New sonar contact on the conformal array. Designate Sierra Nine-Nine. Best bearing, zero-three-two. Classified merchant. Based on sound, he may be a deep draft."

Foster nodded, more to herself than anybody else, and headed on to the wardroom. Large, deep-draft ships coming out of the liquefied natural gas facility near Korsakov, up at the north end of Aniva Bay, were a regular thing in this part of the Sea of Okhotsk. Probably just another load of LNG on the way down to the Chinese so they could make more plastic toys and junk for the American market.

She continued on to the wardroom, hoping Cookie had also whipped up a pineapple upside-down cake, too.

Ψ

President Grigory Iosifovich Salkov poured himself a glass of Zyr vodka, chilled to the point that it was almost frozen, just the way he liked it. He knew it was stereotypical. The Russian leader constantly sipping vodka. But it was stereotypical because it was valid. He loved it. And it was the only way he could truly find peace anymore.

On this night, peace was his primary objective. The staff was well aware that the evening was to be devoted entirely to the president's relaxation. First, the vodka. Then a fine dinner, alone. And finally, one of his mistresses, the blond and buxom Varvara, nestled beside him in his huge bed to keep him occupied until he finally found restful sleep. Tomorrow, he would return to the meat grinder that was the life of one of the most powerful men on planet Earth, but at least he would be rejuvenated, ready to face the challenges. It had always worked before.

As he enjoyed the first anesthetic effects of the cold vodka, Salkov gazed out the wall of glass toward the beautiful Black Sea. The late-day sun still scattered sparkling jewels of light on the waters as they danced away, far below the windows of his hilltop dacha. It was good, invigorating, to get away from Moscow's frozen, slushy winter and enjoy a little warm subtropical sunshine. Vesyoloye, wedged in between Sochi and the Georgia border, was the perfect spot. It offered consistently great weather and yet was isolated enough so he could fully relax, but with all the access he needed to effectively oversee the government from there.

He involuntarily jumped when his personal cell phone suddenly buzzed raucously at his elbow. He had left specific instruction to his staff that unless the world was ending in a fiery apocalypse, unless Hitler himself had risen from the grave and was once again intent on a winter invasion, he was not to be bothered. He had already had the evening's requisite conversation with his wife. It could not be her. She was likely quite busy with her "personal trainer" by now, anyway.

So, by deduction, this incessantly growling device could not be good news. For a moment, he considered not even answering. Then he knew he must.

He grabbed the offending device and spat out, "*Kto gavarit?*"

"Good evening, President Salkov. My name is Ivan Dostervesky." The voice was deep, almost gravelly, but wavering enough to indicate it was obviously arriving from some distant point. "You do not know me. Yet. Your FSB does not have much of a dossier on me as of now, but I expect, as a result of this conversation and actions that have and soon will occur, that fact is about to change."

Salkov had bothered to write down the caller's name on the pad on the table next to his lounge chair. No, he did not know anyone of this name. He was on the verge of hanging up the telephone. Then this Dostervesky person mentioned the Federal Security Service. The infamous Russian Federal'naya Sluzhba Bezopasnosti was responsible for internal security, and they were quite good at it. The agency maintained an extensive dossier on even the most innocuous dissident. Citizens who had done little more than complain about a pothole to a local party official or griped to a neighbor about the cost of bread soon had their own file folders and computer server space at FSB headquarters in Lubyanka Square in Moscow. For someone to call the president himself and brag that the FSB did not know about him was highly unusual and quite dangerous for the caller. Such a claim also had Salkov more than a little bit curious. He decided to remain on the call a few seconds longer.

"*Da?*"

"Grigory, it is finally time that we talked. Talked frankly and man-to-man. I believe I have something to offer that will dramatically and positively change how you and the Russian Federation are perceived in the eyes of the world's nations." By using the president's first name, this caller was not very subtly telling Salkov that they were equals in this conversation. At the same time, employing his old intelligence skills, Salkov analyzed the man's speech patterns. He was detecting a slight Far East Russian accent. But the man was speaking very good Russian. Almost certainly a native speaker, but not from anywhere west of the Ural Mountains. "My people, the *Deti Gulaga*, are descendants from the prisoners that your government abandoned to die in the gulags upon the collapse of the Soviet Union. As you can tell, however, we did not die out."

Salkov pushed a button on a small box on the table. It would automatically begin recording the conversation on the cell phone while also setting in motion a very sophisticated trace of the call. He and his top security people would know where this Dostervesky was calling from by the time the conversation was completed. Know within a few meters. And that was another reason for the president to remain on the line.

"*Da?*"

"Over the years, we have slowly built our little forgotten corner of the Rodina into our own homeland. Your FSB and other agencies never saw what we were doing, even as we began working with governments and financial players around the world to prepare for our eventual goal. Now, Mr. President, we are ready to make that goal a reality. I am calling you to inform you that we...the *Deti Gulaga*...wish to separate ourselves and our homeland from Russia and join the ranks of independent, sovereign nations of the world. I will be happy to provide you with the precise geographic coordinates that will define our borders. We are, if nothing else, students of history. And history has shown us that such a secession practically never happens peacefully. That is certainly true the times people have attempted to leave Russia. So, we have already provided a few demonstrations of our ability to make things very uncomfortable for you and the Russian Federation. And believe me when I tell you these are mere examples of what we are capable of, militarily, politically, or economically. You can ask your air force how things are going with aerial refueling in the eastern region of the country. Or how many AWAC missions have been flown in the same region in the past two weeks, or how effective your key satellites have been since the beginning of the month. Or you can call up your Far East naval commanders and ask about their missing submarine or sunken destroyer. Or I will be pleased to send to you some of the account numbers and passwords of the supposedly secret banking accounts that belong to you and many other top officials in your government, Mr. President. Again, confirming what I am telling you will only provide you a taste of the actions that we are not only capable of taking but we are perfectly willing to do so if you do not willingly provide us what we seek."

Salkov threw his vodka glass against the wall. It shattered with a loud bang. How dare this...this terrorist...call him on his personal telephone while he is relaxing in his private dacha, and then proceed to threaten him in this manner!

"*Unspokoit'sya*, Grigory. It sounds as if you may have reacted angrily to my offer. You must remember your heart. The atrial fibrillation. You have not been taking your blood thinning medication as directed, and you could easily suffer another stroke should you become agitated. You know your doctor has repeatedly warned you about forgetting your medication and allowing yourself to become too excited." Dostervesky spoke coolly, calmly, maddeningly matter-of-factly. "That minor stroke last June. We do not want you suffering something much worse this time, now do we?"

Salkov gasped. How could this man know about his heart condition? The minor stroke the past summer. Not even his closest team knew of these things. He had to keep such a sign of weakness or vulnerability away from those who might most benefit from such knowledge.

The Russian president sat back in the chair and closed his eyes, trying to calm himself. "So, continue." He must at least listen to all that this man had to say before he could contrive a defense.

Dostervesky obligingly went on. "We both know that you are dangerously overextended on your European borders, and with your current problems with the Kazak rebels, you cannot afford another fight on yet another front. Not with oil prices where they are and little else to export to raise more cash. Even your oligarchs are reluctant to loan you money. Your economy is in shambles, and every government on earth is questioning the ability of your once impregnable military. All we ask is that you peacefully grant us our independence, and we will all be friends. Helpful neighbors to your east that you do not have to fear. But most beautifully, you would be able to paint such a grant as Russia righting a social injustice foisted on you by the corrupt government of the Soviet era. Think of your legacy. You would certainly win the Nobel Peace Prize and be hailed as a benevolent visionary."

Grigory Salkov sat there, phone at his cheek, the irregular heartbeat loud and ominous in his ears.

"Never," he quietly answered. "Not in a thousand years. A million years. What we will do is we will hunt you down and crush you like the flea that you are..." He looked at the name on the pad that he had written down. "... Ivan Dostervesky."

"Your initial response to our proposal does not surprise me at all, Mr. President. Now, I urge you to pay particular attention to your intelligence reports tonight. Consider them carefully before Varvara arrives. You would not want her exceptional oral skills to distract you from what you will see there. We will talk again tomorrow. And Grigory, there is no point in continuing to attempt to trace this or my next call. It is being bounced off more satellites than you even knew existed. In the end, your security people will discover it is originating from the lovely Varvara's bedside phone in her private chamber at the far side of your dacha. You might also have them ask her how she enjoyed her *okroshka* and stroganoff tonight, though she did complain to Chef Babanin that the beef was a bit tough for her preference. At any rate, until tomorrow, *do svidaniya*."

The line went dead.

Ψ

Mark Lodkamatros had his eye pressed hard onto the *Yaroslavl's* attack periscope eyepiece. For the most part, the rebel was staring out into a pitch-black night sky. But there was one small white light just barely visible on the horizon, between them and the shore of Sakhalin Island.

"There he is, Igor," he said quietly. "But how can we be sure this is our guy?"

"Mark, as usual, we rely on our best sources," Igor Lodkamatros answered. "Luda Egorov assured us that the *Nikolay Yevgenov* was the only ship leaving Korsakov today and that it carried a maximum load, headed for the Jiangsu LNG port." The younger Lodkamatros studied a computer display for a moment. "Besides, he is up on AIS and tracking right where you are looking. Unless you see a second identical ship right next to him, that is our target."

Mark Lodkamatros continued to stare at the oncoming vessel. The white light had now resolved into two lights, one right above the other. The *Nikolay Yevgenov* was coming right at them. The mast head and range lights were in a perfect vertical line. He thought maybe he could see a red and a green light lower down on either side but was not quite sure.

"Igor, let's get a sonar range on this guy," Mark suggested. "We must not allow him to pass us by or we will never be able to catch him."

"We'll have to go active," Igor answered. "But that will not be a problem. Unlike a military warship, he will not hear anything. It will take a minute to line up the sonar system to go active."

Mark nodded, his eye still fixed on the onrushing tanker. He could now clearly see the red and green lights. He guessed that the *Nikolay Yevgenov* was at five kilometers. If that was accurate, they would need to be shooting soon for their best chance of success.

Mark heard the first 3.5 kilohertz ping from the MGK-400EM Shark Gill sonar. A few seconds later, Igor called out, "Range to the *Nikolay Yevgenov*, four thousand meters." He paused for an instant as he pushed some buttons. "Solution set in fire control. Mark, it is time for us to shoot."

Mark Lodkamatros nodded. "Shoot the torpedo in tube one," he quietly ordered. "Another shot for the Children of the Gulag and our future nation."

Igor pushed the button that caused the torpedo to be flushed out of the submarine. The torpedo's electric motor started right up, driving its two counter-rotating propellors so that it quickly raced away from the sub, speeding up to better than forty-five knots. All the while, the steering vanes nosed the weapon around toward the *Nikolay Yevgenov*.

But the torpedo sped right on past the tanker, completely ignoring the massive steel ship.

"It should have hit the target by now, right?" Mark asked, concerned.

"Wait," was all his brother told him.

As the weapon crossed the big tanker's frothy wake, it began to make a hard turn, right back toward the target. Sensors in the torpedo's guidance system recognized the churning waters and aimed the fish right in toward the source of all that disturbance, the ship's screw.

Three hundred kilograms of high explosive detonated right beneath the LNG tanker, effectively breaking the ship's back while simultaneously venting a cloud of burning hot gas upward into the midst of all the other destruction it had just unleashed. That included the ruptured LNG tanks. They began leaking the LNG—a liquid at −260 degrees—out into the hot gas. It immediately flashed into vaporized natural gas and exploded in an otherworldly, blinding white flare.

Igor could see the flickering illumination on his brother's cheeks and forehead as Mark ducked away from the 'scope eyepiece. Then they could feel their submarine being shoved away by the awful force of the explosion.

The *Nikolay Yevgenov* had just ceased to exist.

Ψ

Henrietta Foster had just picked out the very best-looking pork chop from the platter and was transferring it over to her plate when the 1MC blared, "Torpedo in the water! Snapshot, tube one!"

Eyes wide, she shoved her chair back, jumped up, and rushed down the passageway toward control. Eric Householder was hot on her heels.

She could feel the deck angling sharply downward and the *Gato* rapidly accelerating while she ran, trying to keep her balance.

As she charged into the control room, she was met by Dale Miller, the OOD. "Skipper, Eight-Two went active on Shark Gill and then shot a torpedo. We're at flank, coming to course south and at a depth of a thousand feet. Tube one is ready in all respects."

"And the torpedo they shot?"

"We lost it in our baffles during the turn."

Senior Chief Jim Stumpf called out, "Skipper, the torpedo just passed through our baffles, drawing left. It ain't after us." That was good news. The active torpedo had run right through *Gato*'s blind spot, obviously on its way to some other target. But who or what?

The sonar operator had barely gotten the words out of his mouth when the *Gato* was suddenly catapulted sideways by an impossibly massive explosion. The big sub heeled over and pitched down sharply, as if shoved hard by a massive hand. Crew and gear flew across the space. Foster was knocked off her feet and slammed hard into the ECDIS table, first hitting her shoulder and then her head.

The room went foggy, then black.

In a daze, she saw someone standing there, seemingly unaffected by all the turmoil swirling madly all around them. Henrietta Foster quickly realized it was her long-departed dad, Master Chief John Henry Foster. He stood there in full dress uniform, just the way she remembered him from the time he put it on for the last time for a Veterans Day parade. He was smiling, talking to her. "Get up now, girl. It's time to fight, not lay around on the deck waiting for somebody else to get this done."

She clawed her way back to consciousness. Dad was right. When she opened her eyes, she realized that Eric Householder was cradling her head and holding a blood-soaked chem wipe. All around her was a scene of destruction and disarray. The emergency lights were on, but the normal LED ones were out. Some of her people were slowly climbing back to their feet, but several were still on the deck, some not moving. There were moans and groans, but otherwise it was unusually quiet in the space. She looked around. All the computer screens that she could see were dark.

How in hell could they get the bastard that had shot them if her boat was without power?

Foster tried to stand. The XO forcefully restrained her.

"Take it easy, Skipper. You had a real hard knock on the head. The corpsman is on his way, and you shouldn't move until he checks you out. We'll take care of fixing this."

She tried to shove Householder aside. "XO, tell the corpsman to work on the injured people. I'm fine." Then, as she again tried to stand, she gasped and lay back. A searing, breath-taking pain had shot through her shoulder. "Uh, okay, so maybe I'm not fine. But I still don't need the doc."

"We got this, Hen. You need Doc to take a look at you."

Foster looked up at the XO. "Mutiny, huh? Look, Eric, sit me up and then get the boat back. We're swimming around down here deaf, dumb, and defenseless. We need power, sensors, and weapons back before that SOB decides to take another shot and finish the job." She used her good arm to press a chem wipe to her bleeding forehead. "Get busy and quit coddling me. I'll behave."

As the XO nodded and stood, the 1MC blared, "Commencing a fast-recovery start-up." The submarine's nuclear reactor had scrammed—automatically conducted an emergency shutdown—as a result of the explosion. Now the engineers were bringing it back up. Unless there were major issues with the ship's propulsion or electrical systems, that meant they would have full power back in a few minutes. As if to confirm the promise, the LED lighting in control suddenly flickered on.

Then the voice on the 1MC reported, "The reactor is at the point of adding heat." The reactor was providing enough fission to resume heating the water in the steam generators. They could draw a limited amount of steam, enough to restart the most vital electrical systems up and down the length of the boat.

Indeed, some of the computer screens flickered to life. A few of the watchstanders—at least those who were ambulatory—began the start-up sequences for the computers. They had drilled this exact scenario scores of times. Now they could do it almost automatically.

The speaker in control scratched again as the Engineering Officer of the Watch, in charge in an engineering space, thumbed the push-to-talk button. "The reactor is in a full-power lineup. Answering bells on the main engines."

More good news. They had propulsion back. They could move. Move fast if need be. And the reactor was supplying full power.

Foster felt and heard the fans come online. Between her headache, her throbbing shoulder, and worries about whether or not all systems would respond, she had not even realized how quiet and stifling hot the control room had become. She used her good arm to pull herself upright until she stood, unsteadily but bracing herself against the ECDIS table. The world still swirled dizzyingly around her. The solid table, the one that caught her mid-fall, still made a good support to keep her from collapsing back to the deck.

Doc Halliday, the *Gato's* corpsman, was there, just finishing bandaging up Jesus Cortez, who had been the on-watch pilot before he got slammed into the ship control panel. Doc then moved over to look at Foster. When she started to protest, the corpsman shushed her. "Skipper, this is the one time I outrank you. You know I'm not gonna let that opportunity pass." He guided her to a seat. "You be still while I bandage up that cut on your forehead. And you say your shoulder's not right? I'd say dislocated."

"All right, Doc," the CO answered grudgingly. "But how's the crew?"

Halliday cleaned the gash on Foster's forehead with an antiseptic wipe and started to wrap a bandage around her head. "I don't think you need stitches, Skipper. As for the crew, there are lots of cuts and bruises. A couple of broken arms. Mercifully, nothing worse. At least, not yet," he reported as he prodded her shoulder joint. She grimaced and jumped. "We'll have to keep watch for concussions with a few people, like the COB." He nodded his head toward Cortez and then looked Foster in the eye. "And you. You took a pretty good lick there. I reckon I'm going to be busy stitching people up for the next day or so. You get things under control here, and I'll sedate you and shove this arm back into its shoulder socket. You're right-handed, right? Good. It'll be a few weeks before—"

"Skipper, update." It was Dale Miller, the OOD, sporting his own bandage on an arm and the beginning of an epic black eye. "XO and Eng are back looking at the number two air-conditioning plant. We may have a refrigerant leak, and it's for sure out of commission. XO reports that besides the air-conditioning plant, the drain pump was knocked off its mounts. Trim and drain systems have been cross connected so we can still use the trim pump. The TB-34 is gone. Those are the only casualties besides a lot of broken dishes in the crew's mess and the wardroom. We're at four hundred feet, ahead one-third, course south."

"That's it, then?" she asked.

"We're able to answer all bells."

"Thanks, Dale." Foster tried to smile as she answered. "Where's the bastard who shot us?"

Miller hesitated a long second before answering. "Well, Senior Chief

Stumpf has the conformal and hull arrays back online, but he's reporting that the area is so ensonified by the blast that it will be a while before we can hear anything at all." The sensitive sonar gear would effectively be deaf until the acoustic echoes of the massive blasts had died away.

Foster pulled herself erect and shuffled carefully over to where Jim Stumpf worked on his sonar system.

"What happened, Senior Chief?" Foster asked him.

"Well, Skipper," Jim Stumpf said, his drawl more pronounced than usual. "You remember Sierra Nine-Nine, that deep draft we picked up just when you were heading off for dinner?"

Foster nodded. The guy coming down out of the Aniva Bay. It looked like he was heading for the La Perouse Strait and the Sea of Japan. Just another big merch.

"Well, I think Sierra Eight-Two shot at him, not us. His cargo must have been very, very explosive. I'm guessing one of those LNG tankers. It blew up with one hell of a bang."

"I may have noticed," Foster said, closing her eyes.

"Well, I'm guessing that it'll be an hour or more before we can hear anything. Eight-Two will probably be long gone by then."

She opened her eyes again and tried to ignore the hammering pain in her head and dislocated shoulder.

"Okay, but let me know the instant you're hearing stuff again," she said. "We need more than ever to try to find that guy and figure out what the hell he's up to before the Russians find out we're here and go blaming us."

Then she was off in search of Tylenol and a fifty-five-gallon drum of black coffee.

24

Tiaowen Kuzi's limousine, a Chinese-made Hongqi H-9, did not look that much different from scores of other stretch limos flashing about in the rainstorm as it turned off 15th Street Northwest and onto Pennsylvania Avenue. Once they pulled in at 1600, the Chinese ambassador paid little attention to the conversation as his security detail spoke with the Uniformed Division Secret Service agents who manned the gate at the entrance to the White House. He was busy reviewing his notes from Tan Yong concerning this visit and exactly how he was to present the Chinese president's message to the president of the United States.

The limo was quickly cleared through the gate and turned onto the sweeping drive that led to the building's majestic North Portico. Tiaowen could not help but compare this building to Zhongnanhai, the former Imperial Garden compound where Tan Yong met with his official guests. In the opinion of the Chinese ambassador, the White House came up sadly lacking in both history and grandeur.

The H-9 stopped at the foot of the stairs up to the North Portico. A Marine in dress uniform opened the limo door, holding an umbrella to shield the ambassador from the typical Washington winter rain squall. He escorted Tiaowen up the steps to the covered portico where Vice President Harold Osterman stood, remaining protected from the precipitation.

"Mr. Vice President, so good to see you," Tiaowen gushed. "And it is so kind of President Smitherman to meet with me on such short notice."

Osterman took the proffered hand and shook it vigorously. "But of course, Mr. Ambassador. Our doors are always open to you. In these troubling times, we nations who lead the world must openly communicate with each other."

He ushered Tiaowen Kuzi toward the tall glass doors, which were promptly swung open by a pair of Marine guards, and then guided the ambassador to the West Wing and, finally, the Oval Office.

Stan Smitherman rose from behind his desk, smiled broadly, and hastened to the door, hand already out, as the Chinese ambassador entered. As they shook hands, Tiaowen pointedly dispensed with the usual pleasantries.

"Mr. President, I bear a confidential message from President Tan. His instructions to me were quite explicit. I am to personally deliver the message to you and you only. I am not privy to the message's contents, but he made it clear to me that it was a most delicate situation and would require your immediate personal and private attention."

The smile was frozen on the president's face as Tiaowen removed a flash drive from his pocket and handed it to Smitherman. "My president said that no formal answer is required, but that you should read the message and heed it accordingly."

Tiaowen Kuzi bowed, turned, and promptly exited the office as both men stood there and watched him go.

"Jesus," Smitherman finally said. "That was damn peculiar."

"He said this was private, Stan," Osterman noted. "You want me to step out?"

"What? Naw. You're my 'mate,' right? 'Sides, I may need your thoughts on whatever the hell this is all about." He studied the little device in his hand for a moment, as if he could somehow intuit its contents that way. "Well, I guess we better find out what that sleaze wants this time. No tariff relief, I'm telling you, so he might as well quit his begging on that one." The president glanced at the closed office door, where the ambassador had just departed. "Considering the way he chose to deliver it, I'm bettin' it ain't good."

Smitherman fumbled with the drive but finally got it inserted into the slot on his seldom-used laptop computer. The screen came to life and informed him there was only one file on the device.

"What do I do? Click on it twice real quick?" he asked. When he did, a video sprang up on the screen. It was the Chinese president's image, poorly lit, fumbling with a webcam he held in his hands and apparently alone in a mostly dark room. Then Tan spoke in near-perfect English. He never used English in public.

"Stan...Mr. President...since you are viewing this, I am assuming that Tiaowen delivered my message as instructed and that you are treating this as private and very confidential communications. It is confidential for your sake. I really do not care if it shows up on CNN, in the *New York Times*, or what other propaganda machines you have there. But I do not believe you will want that to happen."

Smitherman and Osterman looked sharply at each other. "What the hell?" the president asked quietly. Osterman reached over and clicked on the "pause" button.

"You sure you don't want me to leave, boss?" he asked. Smitherman shook his head, and the vice president restarted the video.

The image shifted abruptly to a grainy satellite shot of the Sea of Okhotsk and quickly zoomed in on what appeared to be the *Ronald Reagan* battle group. A subtitle, in both Mandarin and English, appeared on the screen confirming the fact just in case Smitherman was not sure what he was seeing.

The Chinese president's voice played on as the out-of-focus image of his face returned to the screen. "Stan, I could be subtle in my messaging to you, but I fear the possibility that it might be lost on you. It is crucial that you understand just what I am telling you. It is really quite simple. Simple enough even for you to understand. Your ships are causing President Salkov a great deal of angst. Normally, I would view angst between your two nations as a good thing for myself and the people of China, but not at this point in time. Quite the contrary. I cannot have our Russian friend backed into a corner where he might do something irrational. And even you, Stan, must surely understand that such drastic action on his part is possible. Because of his many problems, the man has become quite unstable. Now, here is what you will do. I want your ships to steam out of the Sea of Okhotsk and return to their home ports. And I want your promise to honor the Russian claims here in Asia. At least for now and the foreseeable future. You may do that publicly or do it privately through diplomatic channels. I do not care which. But you will do it at your first opportunity."

The scene shifted once more, this time to a video recording of Smitherman and Tan Yong sitting together at a desk. Smitherman well remembered that day. It was the meeting where Tan had first surreptitiously agreed to begin funneling money—a lot of money—into Smitherman's presidential campaign coffers, all laundered through a maze of political action committees and supposedly privately owned American businesses. The audio of the meeting was not playing, but Smitherman remembered his promise. In return for the millions in campaign funds, were Smitherman elected, he would assist Tan in whatever ways he required. Within reason, of course. But essentially, the then-candidate for the nomination of his party to become president had agreed to be the Chinese president's vassal, operating from the White House, should he win.

"Stan, I know that you would not want this video, or the several others that we have available, to show up on Fox News or *Meet the Press*. Please do not view this as a threat. I am only asking that you provide the service which we purchased from you already. But if we do not receive that service, there is a real possibility that the videos will find their way to people you would not want to have access to them."

With that, the video abruptly ended. For once, President Stan Smitherman was speechless.

Ψ

Mark Lodkamatros sat quietly behind a steaming cup of tea in the tiny closet that was almost mockingly named "Captain's Stateroom" on the *Kilo*-class submarine *Yaroslavl*. He was thinking out the strategy for their next move, but it all depended heavily on what some of the other dancers in this complicated ballet decided to do. Now that they had sunk the LNG tanker at the mouth of Aniva Bay, they had quickly skirted around Cape Crillon, the southwest tip of Sakhalin Island, and then pulled out into the Sea of Japan.

He had to figure out an array of potential options for what they would do next. Of course, primary was to keep from being caught by the Russians. Secondarily, they needed to inflict even more pain on the Federation to convince them to free his people and cede a broad swath of territory to the new nation. Assuming they had not done enough already and Mother Russia was on the verge of being uncharacteristically magnanimous.

But right now, there was a more practical problem to ponder. That was fuel. Plain old diesel fuel. They would need to refill their tanks pretty soon if they intended to do more damage with *Yaroslavl*. Or continue to use her for observation. Fedor Rybak and his fishing boat, the *Lovets Ryby*, were now many miles to the north and on the other side of Sakhalin Island. Too far away to be useful.

Igor Lodkamatros stepped into the tiny stateroom without knocking and plopped down on a stool opposite Mark.

"Brother, you look troubled," Igor said as he poured himself his own cup of tea.

"Yes, we are running low on fuel. Not enough to be termed a serious problem yet, but it soon will be. And that restricts the options we have going forward. Our next rendezvous was supposed to be up north again, but running back through the La Perouse Strait would be taking too great a risk. I am thinking of going instead up the west side of Sakhalin, through the Nevelskogo Strait." He used his index finger to trace out his plan on the chart spread across his tiny desk. "What do you think of such a plan?"

"It is good, deep water all the way, but it becomes very narrow in the straits." Igor measured the distance between the Russian mainland and the island. "It is only eight kilometers wide. We would certainly be threading a needle. Why do we not just ask Dostervesky to arrange for refueling down here, somewhere easy to reach? He has the resources, I suspect. We could safely use the back side of Moneron Island. It is uninhabited and very, very lonely."

Mark shook his head. "I do not want to risk a message for something as simple as a little fuel. Too much risk of being detected for not enough return."

"Yes, but the fact remains, we will need to fill our tanks if we intend to do too much more swimming around out here." Igor took a sip of his tea, then smiled and handed Mark a manual he had pulled from a jacket pocket. "But maybe this is important enough to call home."

Mark looked at the red notebook for a long moment. "What is it?"

"My brother, it is the complete instructions for accurately and effectively launching our *Kalibr* cruise missiles. It even tells us how to select targets." His voice rose in excitement as he spoke. "And Mark, you know what this means."

"Yes, brother," Mark responded, his own face brightening. "Yes, I do. It means that the Children of the Gulag are now a nuclear power!"

Ψ

Captain First Rank Ivgany Yurtotov studied the sonar display in front of him. He had gazed at displays just like this for so many years that he could almost hear what the waterfall display picture portrayed. Like listening to an orchestra and picking out each set of instruments, the brass, the woodwinds, the strings, the percussion. The heavy, low-frequency beat of the contact at bearing two-one-two was the aircraft carrier *Ronald Reagan* steaming northward, blatantly gouging even deeper into the Rodina's home waters. The higher frequency churning to the right was one of her escort destroyers. The 3.5 kilohertz pinging farther off to the right was another of the carrier's escorts using their SQS-53 active sonar system to search out the oceans, likely trying to locate Yurtotov's own submarine. He could picture a swarm of ASW helicopters flitting around, trying to find the elusive *Yakutsk* and intercept him before he could deal the final death blow to these invaders.

Yurtotov maneuvered his submarine carefully around the American battle group. It would not do to be detected and attacked now, just when he was ready to unleash a killing blow in defense of the pride and sovereignty of the Rodina. Because of the extra caution, it took a couple of hours to get his submarine in the right position. The task was made more difficult by the battle group changing course randomly—a usual complication in these sorts of puzzles—but the Americans always seemed to be heading to the north-northwest, daring to penetrate deeper and deeper into the Sea of Okhotsk.

Finally, Yurtotov was where he wanted to be to most effectively strike his righteous blow. The American aircraft carrier was fifteen kilometers away and heading just slightly to the left of directly toward where the *Yakutsk* lay in wait.

The fire control solution showed that the carrier would steam within three kilometers of the *Yakutsk* at its closest point. That would never happen. Yurtotov knew that the carrier would be sunk well before it got that close to his submarine.

The Russian captain slowed his massive Improved *Severodvinsk*-class submarine and slid up to periscope depth. It was time to get a final visual picture to confirm what his electronic systems were telling him. Then he would launch a pair of TE-2 electric anti-ship torpedoes, followed a few seconds later by two more of the deadly metal fish. The two hundred and fifty kilograms of high explosives in each of the first two weapons would fatally wound the American nuclear-powered aircraft carrier. The second two would seal its doom and certainly assure the big warship ended up forever on the bottom of the icy sea. All four torpedoes waited, poised, ready to launch on his command and go racing toward their unsuspecting target.

The periscope broke the surface. Yurtotov was immediately staring at the American carrier. But he was not seeing what he expected to see. The ship should have been steaming directly at him. Instead, what he was seeing was the vessel's broad stern.

"She has changed...," he began, whispering.

"Captain," the sonar operator called out, "the American carrier has changed course. It is now steaming south."

Yurtotov bit his tongue to keep from yelling out in frustration. Just when he was in a perfect position to sink it, the American carrier had turned south, apparently headed toward the Bussol Strait and out of the Sea of Okhotsk toward the open Pacific Ocean.

"Captain, should we give pursuit and try to get into attack position again?" his executive officer asked.

Yurtotov watched as a dense patch of sleet and snow blanketed the

Ronald Reagan, making her and her escorts virtually invisible ghosts. His orders were explicit. He was only to attack if the Americans continued to proceed northward. There was no command to pursue if the group appeared to be vacating the area.

"No. We have successfully completed our mission," Yurtotov told him, loud enough for everyone in the submarine's control room to hear his positive assessment of the operation.

The *zampolit*, his political officer chimed in, "We have chased the foolish Americans away from the territorial waters of Mother Russia. It is a glorious day for the *Yakutsk*, for the Navy, and for the Rodina!"

Ψ

"Possible contact zig, Case Four-Six," Josh Hannon called out. "Looks like our sub buddy has slowed."

Brian Edwards was hunched over the ECDIS tactical display, watching the Russian submarine maneuver while the *Ronald Reagan* battle group steamed directly toward it. As expected—and feared—the Russian skipper had positioned himself in the perfect place to make a torpedo attack on the American battle group. Accordingly, Brian Edwards had positioned the *George Mason* in a spot from which he could try to stop him.

Jackson Biddle checked the fire control solution on Four-Six. Sure enough, neither the incoming bearing nor frequency were tracking where the system predicted. "Confirmed target zig," he announced. "Set anchor range at one-six thousand yards. Resume tracking." Biddle stepped over to the ECDIS display to speak with his captain. "Skipper, Four-Six slowed. He's probably going to PD."

Edwards nodded. "That's my guess, too. And I bet you he's making a final visual observation before he shoots. That's what we'd do if we were about to sink the *Reagan*."

"You're gonna shoot first, right?" Biddle asked.

"Can't," Edwards answered with a frustrated grunt. "Damn *Rules of Engagement* says we can't shoot unless shot at. Even if we know damn well we're about to get shot at. Or they're about to shoot somebody we know and love. That's what you get when you put lawyers in charge of war. But nothing says we can't go ahead and cock the gun." He raised his voice so everyone in control could now hear him. "Firing point procedures, Case Four-Six. Tube one will be the primary tube. Tube two is the backup."

Aston Jennings, the Weapons Officer, ordered tubes one and two flooded with seawater and that the outer doors be opened. When the electrical checks were completed, he called out, "Weapon ready!"

Jim Shupert, the battle stations OOD, checked that all the ship parameters were correct and reported, "Ship ready!"

Jackson Biddle checked that the firing solution was tracking and confirmed, "Solution ready!"

All that was left was for Brian Edwards to order, "Shoot!"

Then the Mark-48 ADCAP heavyweight torpedo in tube one would race out and search down the Russian sub. There was almost no way it would fail in sending the target sub to the bottom.

But then the entire process came to a sudden halt.

"Possible contact zig, Case Four-Six," Josh Hannon suddenly called out. "Sounds like he has gone deep and turned away. He's speeding up. No launch transients."

Tensions immediately eased in the control room. But each man was also disappointed, even if he likely would never say so out loud.

Four-Six, the target they had been so judiciously tracking for so long, was not shooting after all. The crew had been ready, though. And at least they were not going to war in the next few seconds.

"Secure from firing point procedure. Resume tracking Case Four-Six," Edwards ordered. "Good job, everybody. We were ready, locked, and loaded. I doubt we had anything to do with him backing down. But we were by-god ready."

Now it was time to uncock the gun and get back to trying to figure out just what the hell this guy was doing out here.

25

The ancient Ilyushin Il-18 turboprop aircraft was getting bounced all over the sky by the typical turbulence in this rugged part of the world. Jim Ward did his best to hold on to his seat while keeping his lunch down. It did not make him any more comfortable knowing that this airplane was older than his father. Or that it had clearly seen its share of rough flights over all those years. If he had found any other choice of transportation out of Magadan, he would gladly have taken it. But this was the only option unless he wanted to fly right into the home of Russia's huge submarine base at Petr for a leisurely layover.

Ward jerked involuntarily when he felt and heard the flaps grinding downward and then the landing gears drop out of the fuselage from beneath him. He risked a glance out the tiny window to see the plane banking sharply around what he assumed was his first stop, Khabarovsk Novy Airport, still in Russia but only thirty kilometers from the Chinese border. The flat, snow-covered land was dotted with houses and smoking chimneys. The city of Khabarovsk looked to be a major town, spreading out off into the distance along the iced-over Amur River to the west.

The plane creaked and groaned but ultimately settled in for a surprisingly smooth landing on the snow-blown runway. But Ward did not relax until the aircraft screeched to a full stop half a football field's length from the terminal. The Il-18 was too old to accommodate an air bridge, so the few passengers were sent down a rickety set of steps and dumped out on the tarmac, left to claim their bags that were being roughly lined up alongside the plane, then to fight the wind while making for the door to what appeared to be a new and modern terminal.

Ward stepped inside and tried to find some convenient source of heat to warm himself. Something or someone poked him in the back. Gun barrel or knife? Either way, he had no chance to do anything but stop and stand up straight until he could assess the threat.

"Sailor boy wantee good time? Chinee girl make plenty warm."

The accent was a horrible and offensive parody. Still, Ward immediately recognized the voice.

"Li Min, if you ever...," he fussed as he turned and grabbed the beautiful Chinese lady who had sneaked up behind him and gotten the drop on him. But Li Min Zhou silenced him with an embrace and a long, hard kiss. Finally, when she turned him loose, he asked, "What the devil are you doing here of all the possible places on Earth?"

"I could ask you the same question, but you probably couldn't tell me," she answered and flashed the smile he loved so much. "As for me, your father asked me to meet you." She glanced around, making certain no one could hear them, then kissed him again. Acting leery would be a sure tip-off to anyone monitoring the numerous cameras all around them that this was more than a girlfriend-boyfriend rendezvous. "He asked me to—in his words—'escort you out of Indian country.' So come on. We have a flight to catch." As they walked, she handed Ward a satellite phone. "But first, your father wants to speak with you. And yes, this device is all kinds of encrypted."

The couple settled back in a secluded part of the waiting area where Jim Ward could have some privacy. He punched in the numbers for Jon Ward's secure phone before checking his watch. It was already ringing when he realized that it was two in the morning back in Washington.

Even so, Jon Ward answered on the second ring.

"Jim, my boy. Good to hear your voice. I see that Li Min has caught up with you, as she usually does."

"No hiding from that one, no," Jim confirmed.

"Look, I just want you to know what great work that was in getting that tap on the landline. It's giving us a gold mine of info, and I don't know if they will ever realize what's going on unless they have reason to look at every wire in the place. The Indians are very talkative when they're convinced that they are still on a secure landline." Then, the admiral's patented pregnant pause that signaled a change of subject. "Can you get a message to Dostervesky?"

"I can try," the younger Ward answered. "Not exactly the easiest guy in the world to chat with."

"Well, he needs to know that the Russians have figured out that his stolen submarine is one of the primary causes of all that pain they've been experiencing lately. They are mounting a full-court press to take it out, and they're willing to risk war to do so. They already have one nuke boat in the area, and Vlad is sortieing everything they have that can even spell ASW. Whoever the Children of the Gulag have on that boat needs to know to keep their heads down."

"And let me guess," Jim said. "We probably have a rowboat or two in the area as well. That lake is probably real crowded about now."

"We'll make sure our folks know what's going on," the admiral replied. "Or at least what we know and what we think is going on."

Jim Ward looked around, making sure again that no one was nearby. Li pretended to be reading a paperback book. "Pop, Dostervesky and his people will not back down. They don't mind shooting, and they've got bullets and people who know how to throw them. And they don't mind dying. And they don't really care who's in the crossfire as long as the outcome serves their purpose."

The elder Ward grunted an acknowledgment, then changed subjects again. "Li Min tells me that she is bringing you out through China. Then I've got you cleared to head home for some leave time. Your mother's starting to worry that you don't like her cooking anymore."

Jim Ward chuckled. "Tell Mom to fix my favorite pork chops with applesauce and I'll be there with bells on. And I'll even bring Li Min if I can convince her to take a few days off from single-handedly saving the world from communism."

With the call completed, Jim Ward was in a quandary. Ivan Doster-vesky had not given him any line of communication whatsoever. How was he going to get his dad's message back to that forgotten corner of the world? Hopping on a flight, backtracking, was not an option. There was not time with all that pending action in the Sea of O about to take place. And besides, there was a very real probability that he would be caught this time. A Navy SEAL commander and the son of the Navy's head spook caught with a cadre of wild-eyed Russian dissidents would be one big mess.

Li Min, ever the practical spy, had the solution. "Jim, the Chinese are playing a rather elaborate double game on this whole thing. They are busy telling Salkov that they are loyal allies while very quietly helping the Children. I know someone in Beijing who can reliably get word to Dostervesky that we need to communicate with him. We can talk to him as soon as we are in China."

"Is there anything you cannot do, ma'am?" Jim said with a grin.

"Well, there are several things I'd like to do to you right now," she told him, smiling slyly. "But such a public display might shut down Khabarovsk Novy Airport and a good portion of Far East Russia."

Ψ

Ivgany Yurtotov continued to shadow the American carrier and its battle group even as the surface ships beat what certainly appeared to be a hasty retreat back into the Pacific. He wanted to be sure it was not a feint. Besides, it was easy to follow them from a distance. The Americans made no effort to hide their presence, evidently taking no shame in being chased out of the Rodina by a lone submarine and its brave crew. Now, though, it was time to find out what his superiors wanted the *Yakutsk* to accomplish next to follow up this very successful mission.

Satisfied the shamed Americans were leaving Russian waters, he finally turned to the west, heading back into the Sea of Okhotsk before slowing and bringing his submarine to periscope depth and receiving traffic. Minutes later, Ivgany Yurtotov had his new orders and the *Yakutsk* was at flank speed, heading, as commanded, toward the south end of Sakhalin

Island and Cape Crillon. He read his orders again before he conferred with his executive officer and his *zampolit*.

They would all need to be on the same page. A submarine of unknown origin had boldly sunk a Russian merchant ship in the La Perouse Strait. Criminally done so, without any reason or warning to the vessel's crew. Admiral Morsky was now ordering the *Yakutsk* to find and sink that rogue submarine and not to bother to report back until that objective had been accomplished.

Yurtotov sat in his stateroom, sipping tea, waiting for his two top officers to arrive for the crucial meeting. He smiled. Two opportunities for him and his crew to strike solid blows in defense of the Rodina! Two chances in the same week to ultimately demonstrate his will, his capabilities, his loyalty.

Though he would hate leaving his beloved submarines behind, Yurtotov was sure now that much higher command responsibility would soon be his. His goal since entering Kuznetsov Naval Academy so many years before would finally be realized. The years of sacrifice, of serving under incompetent and disloyal commanders, of being denied the opportunity to excel in defense of Mother Russia by weak-willed functionaries who had bribed their way into high political positions.

Yes, Captain First Rank Ivgany Yurtotov was finally about to receive his just due.

Ψ

Commander Brian Edwards watched as Case Four-Six took off again. The Russian submarine was running pretty much arrow straight and apparently directly toward the La Perouse Strait.

"The guy probably thinks he single-handedly chased the *Reagan* group out of their little swimming pool," Edwards said, mostly to himself. "But considering the hurry he's in, they have him on the way to do something they think is pretty important."

But Edwards knew one thing for sure. He and the *George Mason* had no chance of keeping up with the Improved *Severodvinsk*-class submarine. Not when it was going balls-to-the-wall at better than forty knots. He could not even reach thirty.

But he could sure call home, tell them about this sudden race to the west by the Russian boat, and ask for help.

Ψ

Henrietta Foster got as comfortable as she could manage and reviewed the damage reports from the close-by destruction of the tanker. Given that *Gato* had been within a few meters of being directly below the hellish blast, they had gotten off surprisingly well. It was certainly a testament to the quality of the vessels that had been constructed by Electric Boat and Huntington Ingalls, though neither partnering defense contractor would ever be able to use the incident in their PR efforts.

She still saw nothing materially that required immediate attention or that would seriously limit their operations. The loss of the TB-34 was the only problem that constrained their ability, and even that had workarounds. As long as they did not work in shallow waters, the TB-29 thinline array would be fine. It was an even better ASW sensor. She would order it deployed tonight.

In the meantime, and unless otherwise ordered, they would stay at periscope depth and slowly proceed south into the Sea of Japan. Seventh Fleet was bound to have more questions, and it was a good idea to be ready to answer as quickly as possible.

She could not help but wince in pain as she reached over to pick up the stack of Doc Halliday's injury reports. Even with her shoulder in a sling and mostly immobilized, and after taking copious amounts of ibuprofen, it still hurt every time she forgot about the injury and dared to move. Doc reported that he had stitched up seventeen people with various degrees of lacerations. Three of the crew had concussions, but only the COB, Jesus Cortez, had a serious enough bump on the head to be restricted to his bunk.

All in all, *Gato* was still in the fight.

"Skipper," Eric Householder said as he stuck his head in the door. "Just received a Link 16 contact report from *George Mason*."

"Go ahead, XO, make my day."

"Well, he was tracking an Improved *Severodvinsk* designated as Case

Four-Six that was sniffing around the *Reagan* group when the guy floor-boarded it and took off eastward. It's heading this way at a flank bell. Using a little mental math, he'll be in our vicinity in only about ten hours if he keeps pedaling that hard."

"Well, let's get ready to welcome Four-Six to the neighborhood, XO," Foster said with a smile. It would be good for the crew to have an actual mission, not just get nearly blown to hell while on the sidelines. She started working out how to best intercept this speeding sub.

The chiming of Foster's phone interrupted her calculating. She grabbed it. "Captain."

"Captain, Radio. Just received a change to our op ord. It's up on your server."

"Got it. Thanks. New op ord, XO."

She punched up her message board on the computer there in her stateroom. The operations order change was the first message to pop up on the screen. Without bothering to ask permission, Householder read over her shoulder as she scanned down the message. She would be sharing its contents with him soon enough, he knew.

"Wow!" Householder whistled. "This shindig is about to get really interesting."

Foster nodded, shifted in her seat, and then groaned as the pain shot through her shoulder and down her back. "So, the sub that shot the tanker is from some kind of Russian revolutionary bunch called 'Children of the Gulag' whose goal is to be a burr under the saddle of Mother Russia for some nefarious reason. 'Children of the Gulag.' Good title for a military thriller novel, don't you think? And this guy, Case Four-Six, is being sent over here at flank to attack the Children. All we got to do is stop our friend Four-Six from doing so when he gets here. Yeah. Interesting is right."

"Like I said."

She scrolled further down, biting her lip as she read. "Eric, you see the *Rules of Engagement* here? They tell us to protect this mysterious, murderous diesel boat, and then they turn right around and tie our hands." She pointed to a paragraph that said they were to be "weapons tight." Use of force was authorized for self-defense only.

Foster stood and started to walk out of her stateroom, paused, leaned against the bulkhead, and then sat back down hard.

"Eric, I'm still just a bit woozy. Head us out to set up a barrier search across the La Perouse Strait and deploy the 29." She looked hard at her second-in-command. "And if you say anything to Doc about me being woozy, I'll see you get prosecuted for gross insubordination."

26

Mark Lodkamatros steered the *Yaroslavl* out into the Sea of Japan. They needed to snorkel to recharge the batteries while he waited for Dostervesky to arrange a refueling for his boat. And they needed to be especially careful how and where they did it. The Russian Navy would likely have every asset they could muster looking for whoever sank the LNG carrier. Out, well away from shore and well away from shipping lanes, was the best place to be when he needed to run the diesel engines. The diesels were loud and easy for anyone with any ASW capability to find. Best to do the job off in a lonely corner somewhere. West of Moneron Island appeared to be a very good spot. No one was likely to be looking for him there, and there would not be much shipping up through the Tatar Strait this time of year.

"Igor, make sure the sonar watch is extra alert," he told his brother. "The Russians are bound to be *obozlenny*."

"Angry" was not an adequate word, though. The Russian leaders—and especially the military—would be apoplectic, risking having the world learn that they could not even protect commercial shipping in waters they so vigorously claimed as their own private pond. And if other nations got wind that the perpetrator of the deadly assault on the tanker was one of the Russian Navy's own submarines, hijacked right beneath their noses from a pier at their largest super-secure sub base in the region, the political and military ramifications would be massive.

But that, of course, was the point. Mark and Igor had given their leader a tremendously valuable bargaining chip in his demand for secession.

All they and the *Yaroslavl* had to do was keep themselves from being blown to smithereens in the seething fallout that was sure to follow.

Ψ

"Sonar contact, bearing three-four-six, designate Sierra One-Six on the hull array," the sonar operator, ST-2 Tom Watson, called out. "Diesel just lit off. Snorkeling submarine, equates to a *Kilo*-class."

Eric Householder punched up the hull array sonar display on the command console on the *Gato*. There it was, making plenty of noise. A *Kilo* for sure and located pretty much where he was expected to be, so it was reasonable to assume that Sierra One-Six was the dude *Gato* had been ordered to protect but told to not use their weapons in the process.

"Maybe we can fire some of my kid's Nerf bullets at the Russian boat," Householder had told his skipper. "I probably got some in my sea bag." Henrietta Foster had not been amused.

The display showed a range of forty thousand yards to the snorkeling diesel boat. The XO stepped back to the ECDIS table and looked at Sierra One-Six's position. He was about fourteen miles south and west of some chunk of volcanic rock named Moneron Island. Not at all close to anybody or anything else other than the island.

Well, if he was here to protect this particular boat, it would probably be best to set up a barrier a little closer to where he was recharging his batteries. Where they were, there was too much chance of someone slipping around the very obstacle the guy was hiding behind.

Householder turned to Sharon Woolsey, the OOD. "I want you to set up an east-west barrier search from twelve miles off Cape Crillon out to fifty miles. Set your search speed at a standard bell. Make sure everybody is on their toes. We expect the Russian nuke in about an hour, and if we can hear the diesel boat, then you can bet the Russian can, too. I'll be in talking to the skipper."

"Well then, you need to turn around, XO." It was Foster, standing there behind him, grinning.

"Skipper, you're supposed to be in your stateroom resting," Householder admonished her.

"What? And miss out on all the fun? Not a chance!" she retorted. "I'll just sit here at the command console for a bit and watch the finest submarine crew in the Navy do their thing." She plopped down on a bench.

"Skipper, picking up a three-hertz tonal on the TB-29. Designate Sierra One-Seven. Best bearing one-two-two," Jim Stumpf called out. The party crasher was getting close, and he was early. "Equates to an Improved *Severodvinsk*. Looks like our guy."

Foster looked at the contact and nodded. Yes, by their calculations, he was a little early, but it sure looked like Case Four-Six. She ordered, "Redesignate Sierra One-Seven as Case Four-Six. Man battle stations, torpedo."

There was very little difference in the activity or demeanor of the crew as they began to bring *Gato* up to a state of full readiness. In thirty seconds, all stations had reported. Eric Householder turned to Foster and updated her.

"*Gato* is manned for battle stations." They were ready to fight.

At least, everybody but the submarine's skipper was fully ready.

"XO, I'm going to sit here and watch, okay? You fight the ship," Foster quietly told Householder. "Just be sure you keep *Gato* between Sierra One-Six and Case Four-Six. He's going to hear that boat snorkeling and go right for it. Our job is to shield whoever and whatever that diesel is. We'll stand in the nuke's way."

"Skipper, how are we going to stop him if we can't shoot?" Householder asked, again quietly enough so no one could hear.

Foster shifted, trying to find a position that did not hurt like hell. She spoke louder this time. Everyone in control needed to hear what she was saying.

"XO, line up to go active. When it looks like he's getting into a shooting position, we'll paint him with active sonar and convince him that launching any kind of weapon would be really, really dumb."

"Skipper, possible contact zig, Case Four-Six," Stumpf, the sonar operator, said, interrupting. "Downshift in received frequency. A drop-down in bearing rate. He has definitely slowed."

Foster nodded. "Sounds about right. He's through the Strait and is slowing so he can begin to search. It won't take him long at all to hear the diesel and turn northwest to go after him."

"Bearing rate now zero," Stumpf reported. "Looks like he's turned toward us. We're getting hits on the hull array. Bearing one-four-seven. Wave curvature range two-two thousand yards."

The hull sonar array was able to determine contact range by measuring the curvature of the arriving sonar energy at the hydrophones and then using the curvature to calculate the range of whatever was sending the pulses.

Eric Householder looked at the fire control solution. "Looks like he's on a course of three-four-six. He's already aiming right at the diesel. He's got him in his sights. Speed looks to be not quite thirteen knots."

Foster smiled. "XO, if you plug in twenty-five kilometers per hour, I'm betting you would have a dead-nuts solution."

A few seconds later, Householder reported, "We have a shooting solution on Case Four-Six." Then muttered so only Foster could hear him. "But dammit, we can't shoot."

"Officer-of-the-Deck, come around to course north," Foster ordered. "Keep us between One-Six and Four-Six. And make sure you keep contact on the hull array."

"Skipper, I calculate that it's twenty thousand yards between Four-Six and the diesel," the XO said. "If he's really intending to shoot, it's gonna be real soon. He can't afford to have One-Six secure snorkeling. He'll lose contact. The diesel boat will disappear."

Foster looked at the ECDIS tactical display. "I agree. Paint him with an active, full-power pencil beam. Let him know we are out here watching him and that we mean business." She lowered her voice. "Even if we don't."

The conformal bow sonar array transmitted more than two hundred and forty decibels in a highly concentrated two-degree-wide pencil beam. That was enough acoustic energy to instantly kill any fish unfortunate enough to be in its path and within a few feet from the *Gato*. The outgoing energy pulse was so intense that it could be plainly heard onboard the *Gato*.

Thirty seconds later, Jim Stumpf chimed in with, "Positive active return, range one-six thousand yards." Householder was about to acknowledge the report when Stumpf suddenly added new information, his voice rising noticeably. "Launch transients, Case Four-Six!" Then, after a very short pause, he yelled, "Torpedo in the water. Bearing one-four-six. Second torpedo in the water. Same bearing."

So, the son of a bitch was shooting! Whether it was at *Gato* or at the boat she was shielding did not matter.

"Ahead flank!" Sharon Woolsey, the OOD, ordered. "Make your depth one thousand feet." Everyone aboard could feel it as *Gato* leaped ahead and angled sharply down.

"Snapshot, tube one, Case Four-Six!" Foster ordered. She had completely forgotten she had wanted her XO to handle things if they got busy. But so had Householder. They fell into their usual, well-practiced roles. And the skipper now had also completely forgotten the throbbing ache in her bad shoulder.

Both were more than aware now that they could ignore the restrictions in their ROE orders. They had just been shot at. They could do what was necessary to defend themselves, even if it might already be too late.

"Solution ready," Eric Householder immediately reported.

Sharon Woolsey quickly followed with, "Ship ready!"

Rick Sanson's fingers danced across his panel, then he yelled, "Weapon ready!"

"Shoot on generated bearings!" Foster ordered. Sanson punched the button.

Down in the torpedo room, the high-speed water turbine flushed the Mark-48 CBASS torpedo out of tube one. Its Otto-fuel-driven engine started up and sent the powerful weapon off and on its way.

"Incoming weapons bearing one-four-four and one-four-five!" Jim Stumpf called out. Serious problem. Very serious problem.

"Launch two evasion devices and come around to course west," Foster directed. She immediately heard two distinct bangs as the evasion devices were shot out of the boat's two dihedrals, the stabilizing "wings" low down on the sub's stern. The devices would hang there, creating a wall of noise that they hoped would distract the onrushing torpedoes.

"Own-ship weapon running normally, in pre-enable high speed," Rick Sanson reported. They were not the only ones literally under the gun now. So was the newly arrived Russian.

"Sonar holds own-ship weapon in high speed," Jim Stumpf stated.

"Make tube two ready as the standby weapon. Make the CRAWs in both dihedrals ready," Foster ordered. The CRAW, or Compact Rapid Attack Weapon, was essentially a six-inch-diameter miniature torpedo. It was designed not necessarily to use to try to sink a sizable target but to be employed as a short-range, very lightweight torpedo. But even more likely as a highly agile anti-torpedo torpedo, essentially a bullet to stop an incoming bullet.

"Incoming weapons bearing one-four-four and one-four-five!" Jim Stumpf called out, his voice now back to normal. He might just as well have been tracking a pod of whales. But his next words confirmed the deadly torpedoes were both coming straight at the *Gato*. "Zero bearing drift."

"Skipper, these are SET-80s. Max speed, sixty-five knots. We aren't going to outrun them," Stumpf said. His voice was still very matter-of-fact.

"Own-ship weapon in active search," Rick Sanson reported. The torpedo that *Gato* had just launched in retaliation was looking for Case Four-Six. And that boat so far had shown no signs that he was aware that he had return fire coming his way.

Foster glanced at her watch. "Launch two more evasion devices and come to course north." She turned to Senior Chief Stumpf and told him, "Yes, I know. We're just gonna have to use the evasion devices to outsmart their dumb asses."

"Incoming weapons bearing one-four-four and one-four-five!" the sonarman called out. "Still zero bearing drift."

Still boring through the sea directly at *Gato*.

"Both incoming weapons have blown past the first evasion devices."

Foster muttered, "Shit!" She did some quick mental calculations. "XO, we have about two minutes yet. Those incoming weapons have to be about five thousand yards out right now. Shoot two more evasion devices. Wait ten seconds and shoot two more. Then launch both CRAWs."

At her last words, the *Gato* was rocked by an explosion. Stumpf looked up. "The left-most incoming went for an evasion device. Right-most is range gating." One fish had taken the bait and was no longer a factor. But the remaining incoming torpedo had caught the scent of its prey and was homing in on *Gato*.

"Detect," Rick Sanson yelled. They might be fighting for their lives, avoiding the other incoming torpedo, but their own weapon had found the enemy and was about to take him out. "Detect! Acquisition!"

Foster heard the double jolt as both CRAWs were shot out of their storage tubes. Those, she knew, were *Gato*'s last hope.

"Incoming weapon bearing one-four-one. Range gating. Hold both outgoing CRAWs running normally."

Now it was a race. Would the two miniature anti-torpedo torpedoes reach the incoming Russian weapon before it got to the submarine and did its lethal job? Or would they, in the process, generate a blast close enough to *Gato* that it could still be damaging or even fatal?

"Loss of wire on own-ship weapon," Sanson reported. That was quickly followed by a distant explosion overridden immediately by a much closer one. The nearby one thoroughly shook *Gato* and threw many of the crew toppling to the deck yet again. The lights blinked, and Foster could hear alarms going off up and down her ship.

But there was one thing she did not see. A massive wall of inrushing, ice-cold seawater. That meant the CRAWs had done their job. They had taken out the lone remaining Russian torpedo.

"No longer hold any weapons running," Jim Stumpf hollered, a smile of relief painted across his face. "And...yes...breaking-up noises on the bearing to Case Four-Six."

Henrietta Foster gave Eric Householder an enthusiastic high-five, ignoring the pain. They had sunk the aggressive Russian nuke boat. They had done their jobs and done it under the strict ROE parameters they had been given.

"Listen good for the diesel boat," she called out. "We don't want him to get antsy and think the wrong boat got sunk over here."

"Good job, guys," Householder added. "Still at battle stations, torpedo. Stay alert." He glanced over at his skipper. Henrietta Foster now had a big frown on her face. "You're not still woozy are you, Skipper? Not after all that?"

She looked his way and grinned. "No, I just realized something. We shot a Russian submarine. You got any idea just how much damned paperwork that's gonna create for you and me?"

27

President Grigory Iosifovich Salkov had been expecting the call. Ivan Dostervesky seemed to be a man who kept his promises—and his threats as well. He had certainly kept both the promises and threats from his earlier call. Based on the events of the past few months, and especially those most recent ones, the ring of the telephone was inevitable.

President Salkov had already been busy with the distressing day that Dostervesky and these *Deti Gulaga* had caused him so far. The morning started with the newspaper clippings from some Far East Russian rag called the *Vladivostok News*. The front page was entirely dedicated to a mysterious explosion of a liquefied natural gas tanker leaving Sakhalin Island. The hack reporter, someone named Egorov, went out of her way to sensationalize the whole event, even implying the explosion was the result of some sort of deliberate attack, not the freakish accident it had been portrayed to have been by the governmental authorities.

That was followed by an irate call from the American Secretary of State loudly protesting what she called "an unwarranted and unprovoked attack" on some American ship in the Sea of Japan. She was quite specific and loudly adamant that the attack had happened in international waters and that a Russian submarine had fired on an American one, forcing the American to "make a defensive response." She did not elaborate on what that defensive response or its result might have been.

This all, of course, was a complete surprise to the Russian president. No one had yet informed him of the incident—a fact he could never share with Madam Secretary—and the American official's irate call temporarily knocked him off-kilter. Weakened by such subterfuge by his underlings, he could only deny, deny, deny. But also promise to investigate to see what might have really happened out there.

His ears were still ringing from the secretary's shrill voice when he was again disturbed by the annoying peal of the telephone. This time it was his own defense minister, Anatoly Shatitsnevcom, calling to tell him that the Far East Fleet Command was again reporting a lost submarine. This time, though, it was one of their brand-new nuclear boats, the *Yakutsk*. Apparently, it had missed several communications cycles and had not yet responded to messages to report. It had last been confirmed to be on station in the Sea of Japan. This was after it had been shadowing an incursion by an American battle group farther north, in the Sea of Okhotsk.

Altogether, it had not been the calming morning that he expected. And that he so desperately needed.

Then his personal cell phone buzzed. The call he had been expecting? He grabbed it and growled his usual, "*Da!*"

"Grigory, you really must work on your phone etiquette," Ivan Doster-vesky quipped. "I trust that you are having an interesting morning. How are things with the great Russian Federation and all of your close *sosedi*? Your neighbors? As the Americans like to say, is everything good in the neighborhood?"

"You know damn well how interesting my morning has been," Salkov angrily answered. "My phone etiquette has not been a problem. Your *Deti Gulaga* have been."

"Dear Grigory," Dostervesky replied, his voice heavy with false concern. "I am very sorry if we have caused you any consternation. But it would be quite simple to turn the *Deti Gulaga* from a painful cancer in your Far East into a shining example of Russian benevolence and a faithful ally. All you need do is agree to grant our demands for a free and independent home-land. The geographic area is of no great value to you, either economically or strategically. And, if properly presented, such a move could dramatically change the world's opinion of you and your nation."

"You know I will never even consider giving up even a spoonful of Russian soil," Salkov shot back. "Never! And especially to insolent terrorists like your group."

"Let's be pragmatic, then," Dostervesky went on, ignoring Salkov's rebuke. "We can continue to be a very painful toothache for as long as it takes for you to see reason. And we can continue to further expose how unprotected your once-mighty nation has become. Since you are already so overcommitted west of the Urals, you are really powerless to stop the pain. The pain we are well prepared to not only continue but intensify. The Americans are working quietly to help our cause, of course. The Chinese are much more subtle, playing a two-sided game to slip aid to the *Deti* surreptitiously while convincing you that they remain your strong and loyal friends. On some level, you must already know that they have long-term plans to add the *Deti Gulaga* as a satellite to the Middle Kingdom and regain what they see as their rightful dominance in Northeast Asia."

"Your words sound like the plot of a very bad movie," Salkov said, but his voice had grown weaker. "Would China give back Hong Kong? Would the Americans surrender California as a newly independent nation?"

"Well, the Americans might," Dostervesky said with a laugh. "But the point is, they have much to gain by helping us achieve our noble goal. And they will, ensuring you will not be able to prevent us from eventually becoming our own sovereign nation."

"No. There is no further purpose for this call. I will hang up now."

"You do not want to do that, Mr. President." Dostervesky shifted gears. "I apologize for digressing. Let us talk serious business. You have seen some examples of our reach and power already. You have certainly by now found just how far-reaching our economic efforts are and how well capitalized they are. I had hoped those would have been enough to make you more amenable to doing the right thing. I had also hoped to avoid sounding as if I am threatening you and the Russian Federation further. But you now leave me little choice."

He paused for dramatic effect. It worked. Salkov was shaking his head side to side, dreading what might be coming next from this maddeningly self-assured bastard.

"As you are now aware, we have captured one of your submarines right from beneath your noses, and we were able to easily do so at one of your most secure bases in the Far East. We have now used it conventionally twice to demonstrate our capabilities and willingness. As you also likely know— assuming this is not another fact your military is hiding from you—that the *Yaroslavl* has onboard two nuclear cruise missiles. We are in possession of all launch codes and targeting information that we need. That puts all of the Russian Far East at risk. It would be most unfortunate to see Vladivostok or Petropavlovsk—or maybe both—disappear in a nuclear flash."

Grigory Salkov's chin was now on his chest, his eyes closed, as he weighed his options in light of this new information. On the short term, there really was no decision to be made. His only valid option was to give in. Maybe, on the long term, he would then be able to maneuver and ultimately win. He could not allow this ragtag bunch to give the world any reason to believe the Federation was weak, vulnerable. No matter how true that might be. Afghanistan had done that once, and his country still felt the ramifications of that debacle. Even now, Ukraine and the Kazak rebels were thumbing their noses at the mighty Russian military.

History, as it so often did, would show him the way to the future. Maybe he could work to set up something similar to the Chechen Republic. Or, at worst, Georgia. Yes, his propaganda machine could make an allowed secession to occupants of such useless wasteland sound like a positive for Russia. Show his nation was willing to make retribution for the past sins of the corrupt Soviet-era fools. That would be the best possible spin and polish on the deal, to make Russia the magnanimous grantor and its president the beneficent world leader, strong enough to willingly allow the formation of a new nation to be carved away from its territory.

Perhaps the Nobel Peace Prize could, indeed, be his!

He raised his head, opened his eyes, and smiled. As with any deal into which he entered, he would immediately begin maneuvering to find a way to eventually quash not only the deal itself but also those who had been so naïve as to threaten him in order to get their way with this travesty.

"Grigory, are you still there?" Dostervesky finally asked.

"Yes. Yes, I am still here."

"Then do you have a response to my proposal?"

Five very long seconds passed.

"President Dostervesky, I welcome you to the world of independent leadership," President Salkov answered with what was quite obvious forced joviality. "May the free state of *Deti Gulaga* find peace and prosperity as the planet's newest nation and a true ally of the Russian Federation."

EPILOGUE

Jim Ward's phone rang. He almost let it go to voice mail. He was resting peacefully on the patio at his parents' house in Virginia Beach, sipping a cold drink and deciding if the water in Lake Christopher was warm enough for a swim just yet. It was Li Min Zhou, stretched out on a chaise lounge nearby, who gave him that withering look that shamed him into taking the call after all.

"Who knows?" she said. "Could be important."

All her incoming calls were important. Jim assumed all his were telemarketers.

"Jim Ward."

"*Komandir* Ward, my good friend." The SEAL immediately recognized the upbeat voice of Ivan Dostervesky. "I wanted to once again thank you and your father for all the help with our recent efforts. And I want to personally invite you to Magadan to be a guest of honor at our independence celebration!"

Ward took a deep breath. "So, it's official. It actually happened? Russia has agreed to secession and independence?"

"*Da*, but *neokhotno*," Dostervesky answered. "With great hesitation. I think your American saying applies. Salkov promised, but he had his fingers crossed behind his back. Our independence will continue to hinge on balancing the Russians against the Chinese, and carefully mixing in you Americans. It will be delicate and difficult and require great patience on our part, but we are a long-suffering and pragmatic people. Formal announcements and all the spin will begin within the month, and we will make it very difficult for Salkov to back away just now. Then we must keep a wary eye on our neighbor. One thing is for sure, though. Spring has finally arrived after our long winter in the gulags. We gleefully celebrate and then go back to working hard to continue to achieve our goals."

Ward smiled. "Well, I would be honored to attend the celebration, providing my bosses don't have me off in some other part of the world. And, of course, that I don't have to sneak in or out of the country."

Ivan Dostervesky laughed. "We will even fly you to Magadan and put you in our best hotel. This place is beautiful in the summer, once the snow melts. I might even suggest that you use the trip as a honeymoon. You and your bride will love it, and we owe her our considerable gratitude as well."

How in hell did Dostervesky even know he and Li were engaged? Or about her role in the past few months' maneuverings?

"I will have to ask her first, of course."

"So, the mighty SEAL warrior is already...how do you say it...henpecked?"

"Diplomatic. I prefer to call it 'being diplomatic.'"

"Which is precisely what I should be doing at this moment, my friend." Dostervesky sighed. "I have a constitution to draft and get ratified, treaties to sign, an election to plan. Beginning a country like Nash Dom is hard work, even if we have had decades to prepare for such a happy occurrence."

"Yes, I suspect the really hard part may have just begun for you, Ivan. Good luck with all that."

"Thank you." A pause, then, "Oh, and *Komandir*, one more favor, please?"

Uh-oh, Ward thought. What else could this dude want?

"Yes?"

"Save me a seat at the wedding, won't you? I am most happy when good things...the right things that are meant to be...defy the odds and become a reality."

SOUTHERN CROSS

A hostile takeover.
Political and economic chaos.
South America is imploding and a pair of US Navy submarines and a SEAL team may be the only ones to stop it...

As the winds of change sweep through South America, chaos and uncertainty reign. A radical political takeover looms, threatening to plunge the entire Western Hemisphere into turmoil. And the unrest doesn't stop there. Seeing the destabilization, China moves to exert its influence economically and politically—further threatening peace and freedom in the region.

But hope is not lost—a team of elite Navy SEALs and two submarines race to determine and then confront the threat. With the fate of the region hanging in the balance, they embark on a dangerous—and likely impossible—mission.

In a volatile political landscape where China seeks to expand its influence, the SEALs and submariners navigate high stakes showdowns and make split-second decisions that will determine the future of not only the hemisphere but the world order.

Get your copy today at
severnriverbooks.com/series/the-hunter-killer

ABOUT GEORGE WALLACE

Commander George Wallace retired to the civilian business world in 1995, after twenty-two years of service on nuclear submarines. He served on two of Admiral Rickover's famous "Forty One for Freedom", the USS John Adams SSBN 620 and the USS Woodrow Wilson SSBN 624, during which time he made nine one-hundred-day deterrent patrols through the height of the Cold War.

Commander Wallace served as Executive Officer on the Sturgeon class nuclear attack submarine USS Spadefish, SSN 668. Spadefish and all her sisters were decommissioned during the downsizings that occurred in the 1990's. The passing of that great ship served as the inspiration for "Final Bearing."

Commander Wallace commanded the Los Angeles class nuclear attack submarine USS Houston, SSN 713 from February 1990 to August 1992. During this tour of duty that he worked extensively with the SEAL community developing SEAL/submarine tactics. Under Commander Wallace, the Houston was awarded the CIA Meritorious Unit Citation.

Commander Wallace lives with his wife, Penny, in Alexandria, Virginia.

Sign up for Wallace and Keith's newsletter at
severnriverbooks.com/series/the-hunter-killer

ABOUT DON KEITH

Don Keith is a native Alabamian and attended the University of Alabama in Tuscaloosa where he received his degree in broadcast and film with a double major in literature. He has won numerous awards from the Associated Press and United Press International for news writing and reporting. He is also the only person to be named *Billboard Magazine* "Radio Personality of the Year" in two formats, country and contemporary. Keith was a broadcast personality for over twenty years and also owned his own consultancy, co-owned a Mobile, Alabama, radio station, and hosted and produced several nationally syndicated radio shows.

His first novel, "The Forever Season." was published in fall 1995 to commercial and critical success. It won the Alabama Library Association's "Fiction of the Year" award in 1997. His second novel, "Wizard of the Wind," was based on Keith's years in radio. Keith next released a series of young adult/men's adventure novels co-written with Kent Wright set in stock car racing, titled "The Rolling Thunder Stock Car Racing Series." Keith has most recently published several non-fiction historical works about World War II submarine history and co-authored "The Ice Diaries" with Captain William Anderson, the second skipper of USS *Nautilus*, the world's first nuclear submarine. Captain Anderson took the submarine on her historic trip across the top of the world and through the North Pole in August 1958. Mr. Keith lives with his wife, Charlene, in Indian Springs Village, Alabama.

Sign up for Wallace and Keith's newsletter at
severnriverbooks.com/series/the-hunter-killer

Printed in the United States
by Baker & Taylor Publisher Services